THE QUIET WAR is Peter Widdows' second novel and follows on from his debut novel, *Incorporated Evil.*

Born in Manchester, UK, Widdows has spent most of his adult life to date living in other countries, including: the USA, Australia, New Zealand and Germany. A former soldier, he spent a long period as a CEO for a multinational food company, before returning to the UK to pursue his writing career.

He now lives in Cheshire, UK, with his Australian partner, Louise, and their Bernese Mountain Dog, Lily.

Other Books by this Author

INCOPORATED EVIL

A BUSINESS WITH ONE GOAL ... ABSOLUTE POWER

Charles Barker-Willet is the world's richest man and the brilliant Founder & CEO of BW Corp. When failing business journalist, Sean McManus, is sent on a routine assignment to write a piece about BW Corp, he decides to take a closer look into Barker-Willet's affairs, in the hope that he might find something to revive his flagging career.

Within days, McManus's world is turned upside down and his career ambitions are replaced by the simple will to survive. His investigation takes him around the globe and puts his life in ever increasing jeopardy as he battles insurmountable odds to expose the heinous truth.

THE QUIET WAR

PETER WIDDOWS

Matador
9 Priory Business Park
Kibworth Beauchamp
Leicestershire LE8 0RX, UK
Tel: (+44) 116 279 2299
Fax: (+44) 116 279 2277
Email: books@troubador.co.uk
Web: www.troubador.co.uk/matador

ISBN 978-1784622-749

British Library Cataloguing in Publication Data.
A catalogue record for this book is available from the British Library.

Printed and bound by CPI Group (UK) Ltd, Croydon, CR0 4YY
Typeset in 11pt Minion Pro by Troubador Publishing Ltd, Leicester, UK

Matador is an imprint of Troubador Publishing Ltd

MIX
Paper from responsible sources
FSC® C013604

Projected onto a wall of the European Parliament building in Brussels; the following quote greets visitors:

> ...national sovereignty is the root cause of the most crying evils of our time and the steady march of humanity back to tragic disaster and barbarism... The only final remedy for this supreme and catastrophic evil of our time is a federal union of the peoples...

Lord Lothian (Philip Kerr), *The Ending of Armageddon,* 1939.

Such a blatant display of anti-sovereignty propaganda may surprise most people. But this out-dated and out of context quote says everything the EU wants you to believe: that a single European state, in which once powerful nations like France, Germany and the UK are reduced to nothing more than provinces, is the *only* way to a peaceful and prosperous future.

Prologue

Today. A warehouse near Krupka, Czech Republic.

'Now is our time,' the speaker shouted venomously into the microphone, energizing the select group gathered before him. On the inner rows, the *Kravattennazis* ('Tie Nazis') were dressed smartly in business suits, their neat hair combed carefully into place. On the outer rows, the *Stiefeinnazis* ('Boot Nazis') were clad in shortened jeans, with calf-high Doc Martens and sweatshirts, their freshly shaved heads shining in the bright lights.

'The people grow tired of the weak politicians driving our great nations ever closer to financial ruin and racial obscurity. And in their torment, who do they turn to? Us… real leaders… leaders with the guts to put right the Jew-led wrongs of the past 100 years.' The speaker paused to let the loud cheers die down before continuing.

'It's a terrible injustice that our great Führer didn't live to witness the events that are about to unfold; to see his inspired vision take shape and watch us take our rightful place as the leaders of Europe. Not the fractured Europe created by the traitors of Versailles, but a united Europe, working together to bring the Aryan dream into reality.'

As the speaker stepped away from the podium, the lights were dimmed and a long vertical flag was unfurled in the darkness at the back of the stage.

Suddenly, a single spotlight penetrated the blackness and highlighted the bright blue flag, with a ring of gold stars in the middle. Inside the ring of stars, a white circle adorned with a black swastika shimmered in the bright light. Following some gasps of appreciation, the room erupted with repeated shouts of *'Sieg heil'*, as the impassioned group raised the Nazi salute.

If the European Union becomes a single federal state, it will be the world's largest economic and military superpower, and its leader will be the most powerful person the world has ever seen.

PART ONE

Chapter One

Monday, 7th September. London, England.

Sean scratched at the scar on his neck. The doctor had told him not to and it irritated Liz, but he just couldn't resist any longer.

'It'll never heal properly if you keep doing that,' Liz said, temporarily removing her concentration from a bowl of popping Rice Krispies.

'I know, but it's just so… well… grr,' Sean replied, clenching his fist.

'That's descriptive for somebody who's supposed to be an award-winning journalist.' Liz smirked.

'Was.'

'What?'

'I *was* an award-winning journalist. *Now* I'm a washed out invalid with nothing to do but watch TV and pick my toenails.'

'Oh, come on. You're only thirty-five and the doctor said you were ready to go back. If you want to, that is,' Liz said, after swallowing a mouthful of food.

'What's that supposed to mean? You know I want to get back to work.'

'Then take my grandpa's offer. It's the best you'll get.'

Liz's grandfather had offered to support them while they established themselves as a freelance reporting team: Sean the reporter; and Liz the researcher; just as they had been at the *Financial Daily* before the collapse of its owner, BW Corporation, had sent it into bankruptcy and they'd lost their jobs. It was a generous offer, made with good intentions, but it felt too much like charity, and Sean was just too proud to take it.

Pride aside, the thought of returning to a dreary business desk, in a nondescript office, writing boring pieces about dull corporate types, was almost unfathomable after the BW affair. He'd tasted success briefly and he wanted more. But there was more to consider than just blind ambition. *Could he actually do it again? Or had the BW piece just been a fluke?*

Although he was well-educated, apparently good-looking, and secretly hard-working, Sean always felt inadequate when he compared himself to Liz. Everything just came so easily to her; she was stunningly beautiful, highly intelligent and a part of one of the richest families in Korea. More than that, she was so at ease with herself: happy with who she was and content not to let peer or societal pressure change her. Because of this, she projected an aura of calmness and confidence, which had entranced Sean ever since they met.

Casting his mind back to the events that led him to the best scoop of his life, he thought about how he and Liz had exposed the nefarious dealings of BW Corp. *Had it just been luck?*

The piece he'd written on BW had earned him widespread critical acclaim and an Ernie award for outstanding journalism, but it had also left him with a bullet in the neck, another in the chest and two stab wounds. Following two weeks in a coma and six months in recovery, he'd finally been declared 'fit' last Friday. Unfortunately, during his enforced six-month hiatus, the noise around his piece had died down, and he was almost back where he'd left off, viewed as a relatively competent business journalist, who'd maybe got lucky once, but failed capitalise on it.

'I can get another job with a newspaper,' Sean answered.

'Okay. Take one of the offers you've already got then,' Liz said, clipping her words.

Her tone didn't surprise Sean; he deserved it and he knew that she was growing tired of the same circular debate. 'They're all crap. I want to do some *real* journalism, but nobody employs investigative journalists anymore,' he said.

'Hmmm… what to do.' Liz rolled her eyes.

Even when she was angry Liz was still beautiful, but Sean resisted the urge to laugh. 'I'm sorry. I know you think I'm being stubborn and that I could have the job of my dreams if I just accepted your granddad's offer, but it just seems, well… cheeky. We've only been together for six months; it hardly gives me the right to start raiding your family's fortunes.'

'Sean, we're not setting up a competitor to Apple. It's just a few grand to keep us going until we can sell some stories. We've been living off him since you were shot. What's a few more months?' Liz's face conveyed her exasperation at the seemingly illogical situation.

'That's different. I wasn't capable of working… and I was living off *you. You* were living off him.'

'Semantics.'

'Principles!'

'Whatever.' Liz returned to her breakfast, breathing in heavily. When she'd finished, she looked up. 'Okay then, Mr Principles, how about this? I borrow the money from Grandpa, then I own the company and you work for me?' Liz opened her eyes wide, exposing the bright white area around her dark brown irises.

Sensing that he should object, Sean tensed, but then found little he could object to and slumped back into his seat.

'That is, of course, unless you don't want to work for me? I am two years younger than you, after all,' Liz added, a slight grin breaking out on her face.

'So, you'll be my boss?' he said, lowering his head slightly at the question.

'Yes, and don't even think about pulling any of the stunts you did at the *Daily*. There'll be no sloping off for a cheeky pint at three o'clock; no pieces that could've been written by an illiterate student… and… '

'And?'

'You have to massage my feet every afternoon.' Liz was now grinning broadly.

Every instinct told him to say no; that it was just thinly veiled charity. But why? It was a reasonable way out of the obstinate corner he'd painted himself into. Plus, he would get to do the type of work he wanted to. Rubbing his hands together in deep thought, Sean tried to dissect the reasons for his stubborn resistance.

Ten minutes passed, during which time Liz washed the pots and returned to the table with a steaming coffee. Searching his mind for truthful responses, Sean had only come up with one reason to reject Liz's proposal: his fear of failure; the fear that if he let her down, he'd somehow lose her.

'Okay, but let's do it properly. We'll set up a company; you'll own all of the shares; and in due course, I'll buy half back from you… at a price based on the market value at the time,' he suggested.

'Done. I'll call Grandpa. He'll be delighted. He's been looking for an opportunity to repay you for saving my uncle's life.' Her paper-white teeth showed through her long smile.

The comment made Sean flinch. 'You know he owes me nothing. Bill wouldn't have been in that situation if I hadn't put him there in the first place.'

'Yes, I know that and so does Grandpa, as does everybody else that you've told over the last six months.' Liz rolled her eyes again. 'But you *did* save his life *and* risked your own in the process. Please, just accept it: you did something very brave; something you should be proud of, not apologise for.'

Seeing the warmth in Liz's smile, Sean decided not to push the point. Secretly, he knew that he hadn't been brave. He'd been on autopilot, acting instinctively, and given time to think about it, he may have acted very differently.

'When should we start then?' Sean asked, purposefully changing the subject.

'I could do with a foot massage now, but if you mean work, how about next Monday? It's Praew's first day at school, so we'll have a clear day.'

The mention of Praew brought a glint into Liz's eyes, which made Sean tingle. The fact that Praew was starting school in London and wasn't required to sit with children years her junior, was completely down to Liz's efforts. For six months she'd spent ten hours every day home-schooling the thirteen-year-old Thai girl that they'd rescued during the BW investigation. 'Is she ready?' he asked.

'Yes, I think so. She'll be a bit behind in most subjects, but she's smart. She'll catch up.'

'Amazing after what she's been through.' Sean shook his head.

'She's not out of the woods yet. The bloody Home Office are

still being difficult about her staying here. To adopt her, we need her parents' consent and you know we can't get that.'

Sean's mind wandered back briefly to the dingy street just north of Bangkok, where he'd taken the thirteen-year-old Thai girl away from her booze- and drug-addled family: a father and brother intent on selling her back into prostitution. Then he thought about the squalid London brothel they'd first rescued her from, naked, scared and half-dead. 'We need to find a way. It's ridiculous to think that the government would rather return her to a life filled with people traffickers and child molesters, than let her stay here with a caring family… just because she isn't British.'

'I know, but they've only given us until the end of the school year to come up with a solution. Clive's given me the name of a good human rights lawyer, so I hope she can help.'

'I'm not letting her go back to that life, even if we have to go on the run again,' Sean said, shaking his head.

'I know.' Liz reached out and took Sean's hand and caressed it gently.

'I owe her, Liz, she saved my life.'

'And mine,' Liz said, moving closer to him.

In 2004, the EU drafted its own constitution. It was designed to supersede all previous treaties and lay the path for the federalization of the union. The wording was agreed and signed off by all member state governments. However, because it was a *constitution*, not a *treaty*, certain member states were legally bound to hold a referendum of the people before final ratification.

Following resounding 'no' votes in France and the Netherlands, the constitution was dropped.

On 1st December, 2009, the Treaty of Lisbon was passed into EU law. As it was a *treaty*, not a *constitution*, most member governments did not see the need to subject it to a referendum, even though all were aware that it had the same purpose and content as the previously presented constitution, and all that had really changed was the name.

The Labour Government of Gordon Brown ratified the Treaty of Lisbon on 16th July, 2008. He chose not to consult the British people, despite the fact that he had promised a referendum on the proposed constitution with the same purpose.

Chapter Two

Monday, 14th September. London, England.

The formalities of registering a company had been easily taken care of, but waving Praew into the gate at her new school was proving far more challenging. She looked adorable in her purple blazer and grey skirt, with a straw boater topping off the image, and she'd entered the school genuinely excited to be there. But it didn't stop Sean from worrying about how she'd cope. *I hope she doesn't get bullied; kids can be so cruel.* They'd chosen the school because it had a large number of international students and they thought that Praew's race and accent were less likely to make her a target for bullies there.

After returning home, the two new business partners sat opposite each other at the designer dining table, in the luxurious Fulham flat that they now shared. It belonged to Liz, as did pretty much everything else in their relationship, the one enduring feature of Sean's life being that he was still penniless, despite penning a globally acclaimed news piece. Thankfully, it didn't seem to matter to Liz. She welcomed him without question, sharing everything equally. *Does she regret that now?* Sean thought. *She could do so much better than me.*

'What do we do now? How does it work?' Liz asked, showing her eagerness to get started.

'There are two ways to go about it: one, we approach editors with an idea and try to get an advance against the sale of the later piece; or two, we write a piece and then try to sell it.' Sean shrugged.

'Which is the best?'

'We'd make more money out of the latter, assuming we could find decent stories that is. A finished piece is worth much more than a concept, plus we could market it to multiple outlets and still own it. But it means financing everything ourselves until we get a finished piece. The other way, we get cash up front, but we have a set price and probably have to work to a set deadline. Whoever pays for it owns the story too.'

'The choice seems obvious to me,' Liz responded.

'As long as you're willing to fund the gap; expenses can be quite high on these things, as you know from the BW affair.'

'Good, then that's settled. We're on our own. Where do we start?'

'Strangely, I think the best thing we can do is study the news — TV, papers, Internet, newswires, everything — until we find something that we think is worth a closer look. Why don't we just get stuck in and at lunchtime prepare a short list of ideas?'

'Great, just in time for my foot massage!' Liz said, flicking her long black hair behind her ears.

Their new venture started with a burst of activity, Sean went out to buy newspapers, Liz watched news channels on TV and they both trawled the Internet. By 12 p.m., they'd both scribbled a short list.

'You go first,' Liz said.

'Okay. I've got Lyle Walsh, the Baptist priest from Cornwall who's trying to get one of those American-style TV churches going here. I think it's just a scam.'

Liz frowned. 'Isn't all religion? You know, give me your money and do as I say, or my imaginary friend in the sky won't invite you to his parties when you're dead?'

'True, but I think this is less well disguised. He's a former postman who now drives a Bentley.'

'And the Catholic Church is one of the wealthiest institutions in the world, never mind the Mormons, the Church of England and every other fear-mongering collection of weirdoes that foist their idiotic ideas on us daily.'

The comment made Sean laugh. He knew Liz was very anti-religious and that she never missed an opportunity to have a rant about it. 'I'm guessing you don't want to follow this up then?'

'Only because highlighting the misgivings of the fringes of religion somehow lends credibility to the more mainstream versions. In my view, they're all as wacky as each other. The others have just been around longer.'

'Okay, who've you got?' Sean conceded reluctantly.

'I've got Vladimir Koryalov, a Russian oligarch living in London. There's a rumour he's a frontman for the Russian President, laundering corrupt money for him.'

'Right, I'll get my body armour out then and start looking out for people with poison-tipped umbrellas,' Sean smirked.

'Hmm, you're right. If it's true, it could be a bit on the dangerous side. How about Nick Allsop? He's on my list too.'

'Really, why?'

'I just thought that we know so little about him, but he seems to be gaining popularity at a rate of knots, maybe even enough to break the duopoly of British politics.'

Sean pulled a face, pushing his lips forward. 'He's just a rabble-rousing cretin — here today, gone tomorrow — isn't he?'

'There are rumours that he has some secret racist agenda, that he's been fiddling his expenses as an MEP for years, and of course, that he's sleeping with a fellow MEP from Germany.'

It was obvious that Liz was serious and that she was ready to defend her choice. Personally, Sean didn't think that writing about an idiot like Allsop would be very challenging, but maybe it was a good place to start. They could use it to create a decent system of working together. 'Okay. Settled. I'll call his constituency office and set up an interview,' he said.

'Will you get one?'

'You said it yourself: I'm an award-winning journalist, and he's a politician, and most would agree to an interview with a plastic spoon if they thought they'd get some publicity out of it.'

As predicted, Allsop consented to an interview. Although it surprised Sean how quickly he wanted to do it. It was arranged for two days' time, in the small Cheshire village in which Allsop lived.

'I'd better get cracking with the background research,' Liz said.

'I don't think you'll find anything that interesting,' Sean responded. 'Every newspaper in the country will have been looking into the obvious areas to try to get a scoop. Plus, the other parties have probably had their goons crawling all over him, looking for something they can use to discredit him.'

'So what do you suggest; just an interview? He's not going to tell you anything incriminating.'

'That depends on the questioning, but I think you're probably right. Maybe we need to follow him and find out what he really gets up to when he's out of the spotlight?'

'Really? I'm not sure how I feel about that. Is it legal?' Liz scrunched her nose.

'As long as we don't enter any private places, or tap his phones, we should be okay.'

'Hmmm, okay, but we can't do it ourselves. Should we get Clive to do it?'

Clive Miller was an ex-Detective Superintendent from Scotland Yard, turned private security consultant. During the BW investigation, he'd proven invaluable at keeping Sean, Liz and Praew alive, as well as clarifying their thinking using his vast experience. In fact, Sean thought that he was probably the most intuitively intelligent person he'd ever met, despite the fact that he didn't have a single academic qualification to his name. Unfortunately, Clive had also sustained life-threatening injuries in the battle against the Findlow family, but had now recovered to a point where he could work. The only lasting damage was that he'd lost his right hand and now had a prosthetic limb.

'Can we afford Clive? He's expensive?' Sean questioned.

'I think so. Anyway, what's the alternative? Somebody we don't know? We can trust Clive. He's worth the investment.'

Unsure that any investment was worthwhile in what he considered would be a dull repetition of previous stories on the eccentric politician, Sean went along with it. 'You're the boss,' he said smiling.

'And don't you forget it,' Liz grinned, waving her feet in the air.

Clive's offices on Dover St. in Mayfair looked exactly the same as they had previously; tastefully decorated and neatly laid out. He still had the same efficient secretary, who ushered them into the small waiting area and, as before, he appeared on the dot of the pre-arranged time.

'I see you've got rid of that blond mess you used to call a hairstyle,' Clive said, shaking Sean's hand firmly with his left hand. 'About time!' He wrinkled his eyes, as a broad smile broke onto his face.

In reality Sean had never called it a 'hairstyle'; he'd just not cut or brushed it that often. When he first met Clive, he'd been the living stereotype of a disgruntled hack: untidy hair; bad clothes; and an unhealthy level of cynicism. His injuries, and probably more influentially, Liz, had changed that. He was now dressing better, in dark jeans and a tailored shirt today; had shorter hair, although still blond, and he overtly portrayed quite an optimistic demeanour, although his journalistic scepticism was still alive and well. Clive, on the other hand, hadn't changed at all. He still dressed like a city banker in expensively tailored suits; his bald head still sported designer glasses; and his facial features still seemed to somehow project the sharpness of his intellect.

Once the meeting started, Sean explained the new business arrangement he and Liz had entered into, and then he told Clive who they were targeting as their first subject. Clive's eyebrows twitched at the mention of Allsop.

'You think that's a mistake?' Sean said, picking up on the expression.

Stroking his chin before responding, Clive said, 'Journalistically no, but be careful. Back when I was on the force, we looked into rumours that he was associated with some pretty nasty neo-Nazi groups.'

Lifting her eyebrows, Liz looked directly at Sean, saying *I told you there was more to this,* without actually saying it. 'Really? I wonder why that hasn't come out?' she said.

'It was just when he was starting out as an MEP and we couldn't prove anything, so we let it go.' Clive responded.

'Couldn't prove anything?' Sean commented upon the non-committal remark.

'Well, he certainly met with members of neo-Nazi organisations, but we never saw him actively involved: demonstrating, or worse.'

'Worse?' Sean asked.

'Yes, we're not talking about your run-of-the-mill skinheads here. These organisations are secretive and serious. Some are in the UK, but the others emanate out of Eastern Europe: Germany, Russia and the Ukraine mostly. They're thought to have been responsible for a number of political assassinations and race murders.'

'So why did you stop looking at him?' Liz asked.

'He got wind that he was being tailed and he has some powerful friends. On the surface we had to back off, but… '

'But?' Sean asked.

'We passed our findings over to the security services, MI5 and 6. From there I don't know, but given his current position, I'd guess they got nowhere as well.'

'Can you follow him for us now?' Liz asked.

Clive didn't respond for a few seconds, clearly grappling with something. When he started to speak, it was deliberate and his words were carefully chosen. 'Yes, but only in public places, and even then, only from a distance. We think he had very active undercover security cover in the past. They'd follow him looking for others doing the same, and they were well trained; probably former Stasi or KGB.'

'Do you think we're biting off more than we can chew?' Liz asked.

'I think you've both proved that you're capable of chewing quite a lot. Taking on the Findlows and the BW Corp was no easy feat, but don't assume that this will be any easier. The people in these organisations are ruthless and if they think you're watching them, they'll kill you without thinking twice.'

'What do you think, Sean?' Liz asked.

'I don't know. It all sounds a bit far-fetched to me, but I guess the only way we'll find out is to investigate it. If it is true, are you sure you're ready to do something that may be dangerous again, so soon after the BW experience?'

Liz shifted uncomfortably in her seat. 'I don't think I'll ever be ready for that again, but why don't we take a quick look, and if it gets too dangerous, we can beat a retreat?'

'Okay,' Sean agreed. In his mind he wanted to get it over with as soon as possible and get on with investigating the Cornwall priest, still convinced that this work would prove brief and unfruitful.

'I'll get Terry's team onto it. We'll tail him for a week and then regroup. Okay?' Clive said.

'Thanks, Clive. It's great to see you again,' Liz said, standing to leave.

'Be careful,' Clive replied, before ushering them out of the door.

On the 6th June, 1975, the British people voted in a referendum to stay in the European Economic Community (EEC): the free trade alliance which the Conservative government, led by Ted Heath, had joined some two years earlier, without consulting the people.

Since that time, the British people have never again been consulted on membership, despite the UK's ratification of the Treaties of Maastricht, Nice, Lisbon, etcetera, which have resulted cumulatively in the EEC – that the UK joined in 1973 – morphing from a benign free trade alliance into the current European Union (EU): a political superstate, where British interests and laws are subserviènt to those of the Union.

Chapter Three

Wednesday, 16th September. Mobberley, England.

The small country pub chosen by Allsop for the interview sat beside a large medieval church in the quaint village of Mobberley, in North Cheshire. Inside, Allsop had sectioned off an area for privacy, and judging by his familiarity with the staff, he was a regular. This was a tactic Sean had seen from many of his interviewees: their press relations staff would arrange to get him onto 'their turf' and create some kind of perceived home advantage. It never worked, and Sean was always dying to tell them that an interview wasn't like a football match. But he let it go.

Following Clive's warnings, Sean wondered whether any of the bulky security detail that greeted him were members of some secret neo-Nazi society. They certainly looked menacing, dressed from head to toe in black suits, which did nothing to disguise the rippling muscles beneath the shiny fabric. Something still told him that it was highly unlikely though.

Allsop kept Sean waiting for a few minutes, while he made a point of chatting with the portly landlord. When he finally came over to the table carrying a freshly pulled pint of bitter, he extended his arm and smiled broadly.

'Nick Allsop,' he said as their hands met. He looked exactly as Sean had seen him on the news: middle-aged; grey hair, neatly parted; and dressed like the country gentleman he almost certainly wasn't.

As Sean started to introduce himself, he was quickly stopped and told that he needed no introduction, that he'd followed his BW story intently. Then he congratulated Sean on a great piece of journalism and upon the important results it had created. 'You actually stopped a war. Well done you,' Allsop said, before taking a huge gulp of beer.

The thinly veiled attempt at flattery didn't distract Sean from his mission and he started with his first question. 'What made you want to become an MEP, given your anti-European stance, that is?' It was an easy question, designed to get the ball rolling and put Allsop at ease. Sean knew that he'd been asked the same question often, and he knew what to expect from the response.

'I thought it was better to fight what I saw as a growing European federalism from the inside, where I hoped that I'd at least be heard.'

'And did that work?' Sean asked immediately.

'No. I think the people in Britain are starting to listen now, but that's taken me ten years, and as for being heard in the European Parliament, that'll never happen. They aren't interested in my views, or the views of anybody from the UK for that matter.'

'Why do you think that is? Do you think they're offended by your comments?'

Allsop pulled the type of cheeky smirk that a schoolboy caught telling a dirty joke would. 'Look, some of my comments have been a little edgy, I know. But when you only get sixty seconds to speak, you have to make your point memorable. And when I first started, I tried to be diplomatic and they ignored me just as much then as they do now. The truth is, they don't want to listen to anybody that sees Europe differently than they do.'

'And how do they see Europe?'

'As a single federal state, similar to the US.'

The straightforwardness of Allsop's answers surprised Sean. He'd been conditioned to politicians doing anything not to answer a question, but Allsop seemed different somehow.

'And you?' Sean asked.

'As a group of sovereign nations, cooperating on important issues.'

'That's quite a gap. How do you think the British public sees Europe?' Sean asked.

'Frankly, I think most people still think of it as the EEC, with free trade being its primary goal.' Allsop shook his head, making an inverted curve with his mouth.

'Why do you think that is?' Sean prodded.

'Because it morphed by stealth and they've never been told what the real agenda is, nor have they been consulted on their agreement to participate in it.'

'What makes you think that a federal state is their goal, versus your goal of cooperating nations?'

Allsop chuckled. 'Cooperating nations only need a forum to discuss common issues. A meeting four times a year between heads of state and ministers would do it. We already have that relationship with other countries, such as the US. It's not as if it's an alien concept.'

'I guess,' Sean said, already beginning to think that his pre-held view of Allsop as the court jester may be somewhat ill-conceived.

'So, what do you think the defining attributes of a federal nation are?' Allsop suddenly turned questioner.

Sean thought briefly; it was best not to answer questions an interviewee posed, but he'd let it go for now. 'A separate government; currency; system of law.' Even as he was speaking, Sean realised that he'd walked straight into Allsop's trap.

Now grinning broadly, Allsop continued. 'So, using your definition, the EU is already a federal state. It has a government, the European Parliament, of which I'm sadly a member. It has its own currency, the euro, and a central bank to manage it. It has its own laws, backed up by the European Court of Justice.' He clapped his hands together to emphasise the point.

'How about an army or a police force? I think they could also be classified as defining characteristics of a federal state?' Sean said, quickly trying to regain lost ground.

'What makes you think the EU doesn't have an army?'

The question made Sean feel uncomfortable. He'd prepared for the interview assuming that Allsop would be an extremist buffoon. He'd done a little research on the structure of the EU, but in reality, his knowledge was little better than that of the average man on the street. 'Do they? Have an army I mean?' he asked.

'Would you consider 66,000 soldiers, ready to go at the drop of a hat an army?' Allsop grinned again, knowing that he had Sean on the back foot.

'What?' Sean said, genuinely surprised at the comment. *Is this just bull? Is he playing me?* Although it was a possibility, Sean's instincts told him that he wasn't; that at least Allsop believed it to be true. 'Why haven't you been shouting this from the rooftops? I really don't think anybody but the political elite would know about that,' Sean questioned.

'Would you like to read the full transcripts of my last 100 interviews? I rarely talk about anything else?'

'Then why hasn't it been reported?'

'It gets through to some political rags, but the mainstream media and the political heavyweights like to portray me as a racist idiot, and most of my arguments don't suit that image, so they don't get published.'

'Are you a racist?' Sean asked, taking the opportunity Allsop had opened for him and trying to get back on the front foot.

When Allsop just laughed, he realised that it hadn't worked. 'That old chestnut! I'd hoped *you'd* be a little more imaginative. If you mean do I dislike people for the colour of their skin or the land of their birth, then no, I don't.'

'Then why are you so often branded one?'

'Because it's a very easy way to discredit me. The EU debate in this country is purposely steered towards immigration, so that they can label any dissenting voices as racists. It's a simple thing to say and a hard thing to deny, as it fundamentally questions a person's character. Meanwhile, the real debate that we should be having is about sovereignty and the fact that it's been given away without even telling the British people that it's happened.'

It was a reasoned response, which took Sean by surprise. Allsop had always come across on the TV as a bit loutish and ill-considered. Now he was speaking intelligently and freely, without hesitation. 'What do you mean by that?'

'I mean exactly that. We have a group of faceless grey men in Brussels, creating laws that we don't want, but we have to follow. Isn't that a surrendering of sovereignty? Isn't sovereignty precisely that: the right to set our own laws and govern ourselves?'

'I guess so, yes,' Sean reluctantly conceded another point and was starting to lose any hope that he could ever get the interview back under control. *I underestimated my opponent; a mistake I won't make again.*

'Did anybody knock on your door and ask you, as a British citizen, whether you were okay with being governed by a group of unelected officials, who hold a completely different ideology from you?' Allsop continued.

'No,' Sean shrugged, 'but politicians make decisions all the time without consulting the electorate.'

'Never ones that important. In fact, there's never been a decision so important for the British people: whether to give up being British and accept that we're European; or to back out gracefully, now, before it's too late.'

'You mean the referendum that you're pushing?'

'Precisely.'

'But the government have promised that it'll happen in a few years' time, haven't they?'

'False promises designed to delay. This government doesn't think the people are fit to decide whether the UK should stay in the EU.'

'Really? Why do you say that?' Sean asked.

'Because if they did, they'd have the referendum now. Why wait?'

'Isn't this all a bit paranoid?' Sean asked.

Allsop paused for the first time in the conversation. 'Perhaps I have good reason to be paranoid.'

'Go on,' Sean encouraged.

'Off the record?'

'Okay,' Sean agreed, even though they both knew that there was no such thing.

'Since I became an MEP I've been under constant surveillance. First it was the police, then MI6. The reason I do interviews like this in pubs is because they can't bug every pub in Britain, and my guys can make sure they don't come in. But they'll be out there, waiting for me to leave.'

In normal circumstances this would have been confirmation to Sean that his subject was indeed suffering from acute paranoia, but Clive had said that the police files had been passed to the security services. He decided to take a chance and go against the agreement he had with Liz not to mention the neo-Nazi links. 'Isn't that because you're suspected of involvement with neo-Nazis?' he asked, holding his stare, looking for the tell-tale signs of a lie: a twitch, or looking down.

Allsop did neither. He held Sean's stare and didn't flinch, but his jovial demeanour was gone. 'Where did you hear that?'

'Just a rumour,' Sean said, lifting his shoulders.

'No, it isn't. I know all the rumours about me. I pay a lot of money to very good people to find them out. Where did you hear it?'

Suddenly, Sean was regretting the question, and he instinctively started to scan the room for quick exits, but there was no way past Allsop's bodyguards. 'I just picked it up when I was doing research for this interview,' Sean bluffed.

'Detective Superintendent Clive Miller. I know he worked with you on the BW investigation. He was in charge of the police detail following me before they switched to the spooks. I guess he's a likely candidate?' Allsop didn't break his stare.

A painful pang hit Sean's stomach, something he hadn't felt since his encounter with Brigadier Findlow. 'It wasn't actually. I've not seen Clive since I was in hospital.'

The tension was palpable as Allsop scanned Sean's face, obviously weighing him up, before he finally looked away to order another pint of beer. 'Look, you can tell Mr Miller and whoever your readership will be, that I'm not, never have been, and never will be a Nazi.'

'Why should they believe you?' Sean countered.

Taking a long slurp of his drink, Allsop eyed Sean up and down again. 'Can I trust you?' he asked.

'To do what?' Sean replied.

'To do your job and write a completely unbiased story, based on the facts as you see them?'

'Yes,' Sean answered honestly.

'Then meet me in Strasbourg next week and I'll give you the scoop of a lifetime.'

Sean hesitated. Seconds earlier, Allsop had looked like he was about to kill him. Was he just luring him out of the country after he'd mentioned the Nazi ties? Studying his face, there was no way to tell; he'd just have to go along with it. 'Okay,' he said cautiously.

'Good.'

They quickly agreed a place and time, shook hands, and Sean left the small pub, as Allsop ordered yet another beer.

Outside, Sean looked around for the people Allsop had said would definitely be there, but he couldn't see anybody.

Following the two-hour train journey to Euston from Wilmslow, Sean made his way down to Lincoln's Inn, where Liz had been meeting with the QC recommended by Clive.

'How did it go?' he asked quietly, noting that Liz seemed upset.

'Not great, but there's a chance. She thinks that the easiest way through is for Praew to gain the right to study in the UK until she's eighteen. Then, as an adult, she can apply for a residence visa.'

'That sounds promising. So adoption is definitely out?'

'Yes, and there are some conditions with the education visa and our suitability as carers.'

'What conditions?'

'Praew will need to maintain a high grade standard at school to remain eligible, and we're going to have to meet a suitability test as carers for her.'

'That's a lot of pressure for her, given she's only just gone to school,' Sean commented.

'Yes, but the lawyer was more concerned about us, and the fact that we've only been together for six months. There's a requirement for a *stable relationship* between the carers.' Liz squeezed Sean's hand tightly.

'What does that mean?'

'It's subjective, and down to the view of a Home Office assessor.'

'What if we fail the test?'

'Praew will be taken into care briefly, then deported back to Thailand to her family.'

'Is there any alternative?' Sean queried.

Breaking her stare, Liz looked into the distance before turning back to face him. 'She said that it would be more certain if I were alone, because there's no relationship to test, only personal suitability, which I would more than qualify for.'

The comment hit Sean hard and his paranoia immediately went into overdrive. *Is this just a way of getting rid of me?*

Moving quietly in front of Sean, Liz took his other hand. She stared into his eyes. 'Don't worry. We'll work it out. We don't have to do anything yet. We've got until the end of the school year.'

A sense of foreboding still growing inside him, Sean lent forward and kissed Liz gently on the lips. 'I love you,' he said quietly. He meant it with every bone in his body, but he knew that if it came down to a decision between Praew being returned to Thailand, or their splitting up, he'd have no choice.

Despite the common belief that the EU does not have a military capability, it is a significant military power:

- The European Battle Groups (EUBG) come under the direct control of the EU and command 60,000 military personnel, which need to be mobilization-ready with just 5 days' notice.
- EUROCORPS directly employs 6,000 soldiers.
- The European Gendamarie Force is a 3,000-strong militarised police force, directly accountable to the EU.

These forces were established to undertake the Petersburg Tasks, which are essentially peacekeeping and natural disaster response. However, in more recent times, the list of 'allowable tasks' has expanded. Most notably, it includes peace-*making*, a far more active military stance than peace-*keeping*.

Chapter Four

Wednesday, 23rd September. Strasbourg, France.

'Are you sure you want to go through with this?' Liz asked, as the breakfast waitress poured a coffee for Sean.

'She's right, Sean. I would've preferred that you met him in his office. It'd be a lot safer,' Clive added.

'He thinks it's bugged,' Sean said.

'I'd like to say that he's mad, but given what Terry saw, he's probably right. He's got two groups of people following him, not just one. One group look like MI6, but it's hard to tell. I'm not sure who the others are, but they seem to be watching the MI6 guys, so they may well be his own people. Either way, he's attracting some pretty serious attention.'

'Do you think he's a Nazi?' Sean asked Clive.

'Yes, I do,' Clive answered quickly.

'Then what do you suppose he wants me here for?'

'I don't know, but I'm fairly sure you're the first journalist to ask him about his Nazi ties. Our previous operation was very hush-hush.'

'It can't have been that hush-hush; he knew you were watching him,' Liz commented.

'As I said, he's got some pretty serious protection,' Clive defended himself.

'Do you think I'm in danger?' Sean asked.

'I've no idea. It's certainly a possibility. We've checked out the bar that he wants to meet in and it seems pretty kosher. It's been there forever and hasn't changed hands recently. Just stay in the public areas and if in doubt, run.'

Sean breathed in deeply. Allsop didn't seem dangerous, but then neither had David Findlow at first. He instinctively touched his injuries: it was a nervous reaction, they were fully healed and he was as fit as he'd ever been. *Am I really ready for this again?* 'Will Terry's men be watching?' he asked.

'No. Too many others and not enough space.' Clive shook his head.

'What's he been up to since he got to Strasbourg on Monday?' Sean asked, changing the subject.

'He's been attending the Parliament during the day and at night, he seems to spend his time in the company of Anna Faustein, the German MEP.'

'Maybe there's something in the affair rumour then?' Sean said.

'That's not what we're here for. Let's leave sex scandals to the tabloids,' Liz countered.

'We may need to sell this to a tabloid. If we want to make money, that is,' Sean said.

'I'd rather not make money that way,' she replied.

The urge to say that it was easy for her to make those judgements when she was sheltered by one of the richest families in Korea came to Sean, but he bit his lip. Since their discussion in Lincoln's Inn, they hadn't talked about the situation with Praew again, but he had a nagging feeling that Liz was becoming increasingly distant; maybe trying to prepare herself for the inevitable decision that had to be made.

'Anybody else hanging around?' Sean asked.

'We couldn't get close enough, given all his current tails, so who knows. The hotel he's staying in is full of EU types and lobbyists. He could've met with any one of them and we wouldn't know.'

'Okay, I guess the only way to find out what he wants is to meet him,' Sean ended the debate.

Le Petit Bière bar sat between a cinema and a shoe shop on Rue 22 novembre, in the old heart of Strasbourg, well away from the modern hub of EU buildings to the north. Allsop was already seated and nursing a half-full glass of beer when Sean entered. Before he was allowed to sit with him, he was searched by one of Allsop's guard detail. There were no other customers in the small bar and the barman quickly dropped a glass of beer in front of Sean, before returning to his spot behind the wood panelled counter.

'Sorry about that. I had to make sure you weren't wearing a wire,' Allsop said, grinning through his tobacco-stained teeth.

'Why do you need all this security?' Sean asked.

'You'll find out.'

'When?'

'Tomorrow.'

'Then why meet tonight?'

'To give you some background.' Allsop lifted his arm to order another beer. With his other arm, he deftly dropped a USB stick onto Sean's lap. Taking the hint, Sean slipped it carefully into his pocket. 'We're being watched, but we can't be heard,' Allsop added, lifting his eyebrows.

'So what's on the stick? Why not just email it to me?' Sean asked.

'My emails are being read, no matter what I try to do to stop it. Read it and we'll talk tomorrow: 7 p.m. in the lobby of the Hotel D. Anna Faustein will be with me.'

'Where are we going?'

'You'll find out tomorrow. Now just ask normal interview questions and make notes. In half an hour you can go.'

'Are you having an affair with Anna Faustein?'

'Blimey! If that's your standard interviewing technique, I'd hate to see your interrogation style. The short answer is no, I'm not. We're just very close friends and Anna has far better taste than that.'

'Why should I believe you?'

'First, Anna is a beautiful, intelligent, thirty-eight-year-old woman and I'm a pot-bellied, fifty-seven-year-old man, who's never been good-looking, or particularly intelligent for that matter. Second, I don't care whether you believe me or not. What's important to me is that my wife and children believe me, and they do.'

The interview lasted another twenty-five minutes. Sean asked questions about Allsop's political beliefs, his childhood and other background information. Allsop's responses were animated, interesting and eloquently delivered, and despite the nagging warnings in Sean's head, he found himself warming to the gregarious character. If he was lying and his outward image was a façade to hide deeper, more sinister, objectives, he certainly did it well. Sean didn't once detect the obvious signs of lying which all good reporters were trained to spot. His answers were direct, detailed and offered without pause. They were also very well thought out. Allsop clearly wasn't the extremist loony the British media liked to portray him as. In fact, he was far from it and possessed an intellect that would rival any in British politics.

When the interview finished, Sean shook Allsop's hand warmly and left through the front door of the small bar.

Back out on Rue 22 novembre, he scanned the area, before putting up his umbrella and walking back towards the small hotel, where Clive and Liz would be waiting. He hadn't thought it necessary for Liz to come, but she'd insisted and he wanted to avoid any chance of an argument.

During the walk, he had a feeling that he was being watched, but figured that it was probably just the power of suggestion playing tricks with his senses.

Then, when he turned onto the quiet street that his hotel was on, he saw a flicker of light reflected from a shop window and turned around sharply. A man wearing a long raincoat, standing in a bus shelter, had just lit a cigarette. He looked at Sean, but didn't move and Sean turned away, continuing into the dimly lit street.

Ten metres or so into the street, he could see the hotel lights in the distance and quickened his pace. The sudden appearance of footsteps behind him made him speed up more, until he was almost running. But when he turned to see who was following, he saw nobody. The nagging feeling of somebody's presence still with him, he broke into a run, then a sprint, until he reached the door of the hotel.

Breathing heavily, he pushed on the handle. It was locked.

'Damn,' he remembered that the small hotel secured the door at 8 p.m. and fumbled in his pocket for the key that he'd been given. Again he heard movement behind him and swung around sharply, but as before, there was nobody there.

Trembling slightly, he pushed the key into the lock and opened the door, stepping quickly inside as the warm air from the lobby rushed over his face. Instinctively, he turned around to scan the area surrounding the entrance to the hotel. His eyes instantly darted to a point behind the trees on the opposite side of the road, where he thought something moved, but it was just a cat. Shaking his head at his paranoid state, he quickly locked the door and went to his room.

One of the fundamental principles of democracy is that the people set laws to govern themselves. In practice, this means that the members of parliament, elected by the people, suggest new laws, and these laws are voted upon by the other members of parliament.

In the EU, the elected members of parliament do not have the power to initiate any legislation. Instead, this task falls solely upon the unelected European Commission.

Chapter Five

Wednesday, 23rd September. Strasbourg, France.

Liz downloaded the contents of the memory stick to her hard drive. There was only one file, numbered, but not named, and she opened it quickly.

'It's in German,' Sean said, looking at the thick block of text over Liz's shoulder.

'I think it's translated later on,' Liz replied, scrolling through sixty-three pages of German text, before the language changed to Greek. Six languages and 400 pages further on they finally came across the English version.

The dense text filled the screen; each paragraph was over one page long and punctuation was minimal. 'Bloody hell! The words might be English, but they don't seem to mean anything. What is it?' Sean asked.

'There aren't any headings, but I reckon it's an excerpt from a bill in the European Parliament,' Liz commented.

'Excerpt? Its sixty pages long,' Sean said frowning.

'I think they can stretch into the thousands of pages,' Liz replied.

Clive joined in, looking over Liz's shoulder. 'Who could read thousands of pages of this pseudo-English legal mumbo-jumbo and make any sense of it?' he said.

'Nobody; that's the point. Allsop told me that they pass hundreds of bills every day when Parliament is in session. There's no way any of them could be on top of the content, even if they had an army of readers,' Sean commented.

'So the EU is passing laws that nobody has actually read?' Clive frowned again.

'Except the people that drafted them, of course,' Sean replied.

'Who drafts them?' Clive asked.

'The European Commission,' Liz answered.

'Is it only me that thinks that's rather dangerous: a group of unelected people writing laws that nobody ever reads, which bind whole nations to their contents?' Clive asked.

'Allsop actually admitted that the members are rarely across the bills. There are just too many. In practice, the leader, or a nominated person from a political party, raises their hand with their thumb up or down, indicating how the other members of the party should vote,' Sean said.

'Wow! That puts a lot of power in the hands of the party leaders. They could get their members to vote for anything if they haven't read it!' Liz exclaimed.

'That's nuts. Why hasn't this been made public? I really don't think people know how it works. In fact, I doubt they even know that there are political parties in the EU,' Clive commented.

'To be fair to Allsop, he has tried to let people know, but the media just portray him as a crank, so nobody listens,' Sean said.

'Hmm. I don't trust all this Euro nonsense,' Clive huffed.

'We should try to read this, so that I'm ready for the meeting tomorrow. Allsop said it would be the scoop of my life, so there must be something juicy in it,' Sean said.

Almost four hours later, at 1 a.m., they had all completed their respective reading.

'What do you make of it?' Sean asked.

'It's hard to tell. The language is so confusing. It's clearly something to do with EU bonds and the potential for default,' Liz started.

'Clive?' Sean turned.

'Absolute gobbledegook. I may as well have read the German version,' Clive shrugged.

'It seemed to me like a series of measures that could be taken at the discretion of the Commission, should a member state default on a loan from the EU,' Sean suggested.

'Did any of the measures seem odd?' Clive asked.

'Not really. Some were a bit overbearing, such as forcing budgetary cuts in the country that's defaulted, but that's nothing more than they've already been doing,' Liz said.

'There must be something else; something we're missing. Why was Allsop so secretive about it? Other than having the ability to bore whole nations to death, it seems pretty innocuous,' Clive said.

'We need to read it again,' Sean said, 'more carefully this time. There must be something sensational in there.'

'It's late. You're not meeting him until seven tomorrow. Let's get some sleep and do some more research in the morning; maybe try to put some context to it. Ten o'clock okay with you, Clive?' Liz asked.

'Yep. I'll come to your room.'

Finally alone with Liz, Sean reached out and pulled her towards him.

'I'm too tired, sorry,' she said, turning away.

The European Union administration is made up of four major bodies:

- The European Parliament: The body which houses the European Members of Parliament (MEPs).
- The European Commission: The administrators of the EU; essentially the European Civil Service.
- The European Council: The forum for the heads of state of the member countries.
- The Council of the European Union: A fluid group made up by the department ministers of the member states, who gather based on subject matter.

These four powerful EU bodies are locked in a constant power struggle with each other, for control of the ever-expanding EU.

Chapter Six

Thursday, 24th September. Strasbourg, France.

Sean woke with a start, as loud rapping on the door broke his deep sleep. 'Who is it?' Liz called out, rubbing her eyes.

'Liz, it's Clive. Let me in.'

'It's only nine, Clive. We said ten. What do you want?' Sean said, glancing at the clock on the side table.

Pulling on a hotel robe, Liz made her way to the door.

'Allsop's dead!' Clive said quickly, pushing through the door held open by Liz.

'What?' Sean snapped out of his daze.

'Apparently suicide: an overdose of painkillers.'

'That's rubbish. He's not the type and when I left him he was positively jovial,' Sean said.

'They're saying that he was a long-time drug user and was taking anti-depressants,' Clive countered.

'Crap!'

'I agree. He doesn't fit the profile of either a junkie or a suicide risk. My guess is that he was murdered, but the local police seem to have already concluded that it was suicide.'

'Why would they do that?' Sean asked.

'I don't know, but we'll see what the coroner has to say,' Clive added.

'Could it be something to do with the information on the USB stick?' Liz suggested.

'Maybe. He obviously thought there was something interesting on it,' Clive replied.

'We need to find Anna Faustein. She was meant to come with us tonight. Maybe she knows what's going on,' Sean said.

'She's staying at a place on Rue des Couples, the Cour du Corbeau, I think it's called,' Clive said. 'But she'll have the media all over her, given her relationship with Allsop.'

'Let's try anyway. If she knows that I met with Allsop last night and knows what he gave me, she might talk to us,' Sean said.

'Could you put me through to Anna Faustein's room please?' Sean asked the hotel operator after looking up the phone number.

'I'm sorry, sir. Frau Faustein checked out this morning,' she replied with a strong French accent.

'She's gone. We should try the Parliament.' Sean turned to Liz and Clive, who were seated in the small hotel room.

It took ten minutes in a taxi heading north before the historic buildings of old Strasbourg were replaced by shimmering, state-of-the-art glass buildings of monumental proportions, lining the banks of a wide canal. The EU campus, in stark contrast to the busy downtown area, seemed to move at a leisurely pace, with wide grass verges and narrow rivers flowing through it. The Parliament building itself was a statement in modern architecture. Its colossal rounded exterior blended steel and glass seamlessly into its elegant structure, its huge circular tower seemingly unfinished. Sean remembered reading an architecture article that said it had been purposely left that way to symbolise the unfinished nature of the EU.

'Well, at least I know how they spend all the bloody money,' Clive said, staring up at the impressive visitors' entrance to the Parliament building.

Without stopping to look, Sean raced into the lobby and quickly approached a woman standing behind a long marble reception counter. 'I'd like to speak to Anna Faustein. How can I reach her?'

The receptionist spoke in clear English. 'All of the members are in plenary at the moment. Do you have an appointment with Frau Faustein?'

'No,' Sean said, 'but it's important.'

'Then you must call her office and make an appointment,' the receptionist replied.

'Do you have a phone number?' Sean asked.

'I'm sorry. I can't give you that information.'

'Do you at least know whether she came in this morning?' Sean let his frustration show.

'No, I don't have that information, sir,' the receptionist countered his angry disposition.

'Damn!' Sean said as he walked back to Clive and Liz, who were admiring the enormous glass atrium. 'No help. We can't get in to see her. I'll just have to wait to see if she comes out.'

'We could take the tour? Then we could at least see if she was in the debating chamber,' Liz said, pointing to a sign announcing '*visitors tours*'.

The early hour meant that they soon managed to get onto a tour. After clearing security, Sean immediately asked whether they could go into the viewing gallery for the plenary session, but was told that they would get there in about an hour. Agitated by the slow progress, they stayed at the back of the group of tourists, making no attempt to look interested, although it was hard not to be impressed by the internal architecture of the building, with its expansive central atrium, modern wood panelling and twisting metal staircases. *Whoever built this wasn't on a tight budget,* Sean thought.

'We're here,' Liz said, as the sign for the plenary viewing gallery appeared and the guide told them to stay quiet.

'Do we know who we're looking for?' Clive asked.

'She should be in seat 262,' Liz said, looking at a large curved chart on the wall.

When they entered the plenary debating chamber, the contrast between the outside of the room and the inside couldn't be more emphatic. Gone was the warmth of the wood panelling, gone was the glass and the twisting metal and all that was left was a circular featureless room, with a dark blue carpet and white walls. Above it, the viewing gallery stretched all the way around and was filled with the same cold grey chairs as the chamber itself. *I wonder if this was purposely designed to be less elaborate than the rest of the building, because this is the area that is always seen on TV and they don't want to portray an extravagant image?* Sean considered.

Having been into the British Houses of Parliament a number of times to witness the proceedings, Sean had expected the same level of heated debate here. But there was no such debate, just the monotone voice of somebody reading from a script in German. Most of the members were wearing headphones, obviously listening to a translation. Then the speaking stopped and a few members seated near the front raised one hand with a thumbs-up. Soon a large electronic screen displayed the result of the vote.

'Motion adoptée,' the speaker in the centre of the bench at the front stated.

Almost immediately, the same monotone voice returned and before Sean could locate seat 262, the same process happened again.

'Motion adoptée,' the speaker said again.

'She's not here. Her seat's empty,' Clive whispered.

Sean instinctively stood to leave, but Clive pulled him back down. 'You'll get arrested if you're caught wandering the corridors here. We'll have to stay with the tour.'

During their wait, another tour group entered the chamber. The collection of people took their seats quickly and began to observe the proceedings below, except for one man. He studied the members chart carefully before sitting down, slightly away from the others. He was dressed in a blue business suit, which made him stand out compared to the jeans and t-shirt-clad tourists in the rest of the group. Then, after quickly glancing around the chamber, he focussed his attention on Sean.

'Did you see that?' Sean whispered to Clive.

'Yes, I saw him when he came in; he's no tourist.'

'I don't suppose we could take a sneaky photo?'

'No chance,' Clive responded quickly.

After a few minutes, the odd-man-out stood quietly and moved a few seats closer to Sean. Then he repeated the move again and again, until he was only a few seats away.

It was another forty-five minutes before the tour guide indicated that they should leave. When the group stood to file back into the expansive lobby area, the suited man joined their group.

'Stay behind him,' Clive whispered to Sean and Liz, as he stepped out in front of him.

When they made their way back through the twisting steel and glass, down to the ground floor, Clive stayed just in front of the suited man, while Liz and Sean stayed behind him. At one stage, when he reached into his pocket, Sean tensed ready to pounce on him, but it was just to get a handkerchief.

After they passed through the security barrier, Clive rejoined them, but not before he'd taken a picture of the suited man.

'What now?' Sean asked.

'Let's just head out to the taxi rank, and see if he follows us. He can't be armed or he wouldn't have got through the security checks,' Clive said.

The warm sunshine felt good on Sean's face when they walked out to the pavement, where a long line of taxis were waiting. Behind them, the suited man came through the door, seemingly not trying to hide the fact that he was following them. Then when they climbed in a cab, he took the one behind.

After searching a few screens on his iPhone, Sean hit the link to a number. 'Ah hello, my name is Sean McManus, I'm a journalist from the UK and I was meant to have a meeting with Frau Faustein today, but she isn't in the Parliament, or at her hotel. Could you tell me where she is, please?' He heard some muffled speaking in the background.

'I'm sorry, sir. I don't know where she is. Please leave a number and I'll pass on your message.' Sean quickly passed on his number and hung up.

'Her constituency office doesn't know where she is either,' he said to Liz and Clive.

'That doesn't sound good,' Liz replied.

'We need to find her. We need to know what Allsop was onto that got him killed,' Sean said, after checking in the rear window and noting that they were still being followed by the same taxi.

'And to warn her that she's in danger, if she doesn't already know,' Liz said.

'Don't jump the gun. She could be the killer,' Clive added.

That hadn't crossed Sean's mind but, as usual, Clive was right. What if Anna Faustein had killed Allsop and gone on the run, maybe because she knew he'd passed the USB to him? If so, it wasn't her that was in danger, it was him, and by association, Liz and Clive. He looked back at the following car again quickly, now with more fear of its purpose. 'He's still there,' he said.

'I know. Just let him follow us; there's nothing we can do at the moment,' Clive said, calmly reassuring Sean.

'I don't think we're just going to bump into her on the street. We should go back to London and try to make sense of everything. She could be anywhere,' Sean suggested.

'Makes sense,' Clive replied.

'Would your mum be okay to keep Praew for a few more days?' Sean asked Liz.

'I think so. Why?'

'Just a precaution, until we know what's going on.'

When they pulled up outside their small hotel, the following taxi stopped. Clive quickly sheltered Liz into the doorway and Sean followed behind. When he turned to close the door, the taxi behind sped away, with the passenger still in it.

The doctrine of supremacy places EU law above national law; it has been ruled upon many times by courts in the EU and in the UK. Each time, it was held that EU law takes precedence.

The reason cited for these decisions: as the member state parliaments agreed to join the EU, then they *voluntarily ceded their sovereignty.*

Chapter Seven

Thursday, 24th September. Strasbourg, France.

'We need to get out of here fast. Get your things and let's go to the airport,' Clive said.

It took Liz and Sean less than five minutes to grab everything they had and return to the lobby, where Clive was already waiting for them.

'Terry's bringing the car around,' Clive said. 'When I give you the nod, run and get straight into it.' Clive was scrutinizing the area opposite the hotel.

'He's here. Go!' Clive instructed.

Sean stepped out of the door first and took Liz by the hand, sheltering her from the road. As they reached the bottom of the small flight of steps, an ear-shattering bang rang out in front of them. Instinctively, Sean pulled Liz to the ground and pushed her behind a parked car.

When he rolled to the side to see what had happened, he saw that an old jeep had rammed into the back of Terry's car and smoke was billowing from its grill. Just then a gunshot split the air and Sean heard it ricochet off the wall next to the door where Clive was crouching. When he looked back to the jeep, a man was leaning out of the window gripping a pistol, taking aim.

Clive rolled onto the ground and down the steps, to join Liz and Sean. 'We need to go out the back way,' he said.

'What about Terry?' Sean said.

'He's got two men covering the position; they're closing in on the car now. He'll be okay, but all hell is about to break loose here, depending upon how many of them there are. When the shooting starts, you need to be ready to get back into the hotel.'

Both Sean and Liz nodded their agreement. Their lives had been saved by Clive in the past and their trust in him was unquestionable.

It was impossible for Sean to see what was happening, but as predicted, staccato gunfire soon started, emanating from the direction of the jeep.

'Now!' Clive said.

Pulling Liz up and using his body to shelter her, Sean started to run. The door was only a few metres away, but the gunfire was becoming more intense. Resisting the urge to look around, he dashed straight for the door as two loud cracks came out, sending bullets in their direction. He was holding Liz so tightly that he almost carried her up the steps and into the lobby, before diving onto the tiled floor.

'Are you okay?' he asked Liz.

'Yes, but I'm scared.'

Just then, Clive came crashing into the lobby and dived onto the floor next to them. 'Right, slide on your stomach to the back door. I'm just going to check what's going on here. I'll see you there in a few seconds.

Following Clive's instructions they held their bodies as close as they could to the cold tiles and shuffled across to the rear of the hotel. On the way, Sean glanced into the dining room where they'd eaten breakfast. Four of the hotel staff were huddled together in the corner, taking shelter.

In no time at all, Clive joined them by the rear door. 'Terry's guys have dealt with them, but I'd guess back-up might be on the way and we need to get out of here before we have to explain all of this to the police.'

'What about Terry?' Liz asked.

'He looks fine; a few cuts from what I could see, but he's walking. He's a pro though and he'll already be heading out of France with his guys, so we need to get moving.'

Leaning out of the rear door, Clive scanned the area at the back of the hotel. 'It looks clear. Let's go.' He stood and walked out of the door first, followed quickly by Liz, Sean still holding her hand as tightly as he could.

Once outside, they sprinted in the opposite direction from the hotel, as police sirens started to fill the air. Then at a main road, they slowed their pace and joined the throng of shoppers on the pavement. After walking about 200 metres along the busy street, Clive flagged a taxi.

'Kehl, s'il vous plaît,' Clive said.

Again Sean marvelled at the speed of Clive's thought process. Kehl was a German city just on the other side of the Rhine from Strasbourg. It would be way too soon for any cross-border police force cooperation.

The short journey over the border into Germany took just fifteen minutes before Clive told the taxi driver to stop. Once out of the car, they walked back in the direction they had driven, before Clive went into a car rental outlet. 'I saw it when we passed earlier, but I didn't want the taxi driver to know where we were going,' he said.

It wasn't long before they were speeding away in the rented Volkswagen Golf. To Sean's surprise, Clive turned straight back into France, just north of Strasbourg and headed towards Metz. 'Channel tunnel,' he said, seeing Sean's expression.

'What about the car?' Liz said.

'Least of my worries right now. I can always send somebody back with it.'

Six hours later, Clive pulled the rented car up outside Sean and Liz's Fulham flat. 'I'll see you in the morning in my office. Get some sleep,' he said, before pulling away.

Once inside, Liz called her mother and asked if Praew could stay a few more days, then climbed into bed beside Sean. She sidled over to him and put her arms around his waist.

'I love you,' she said, before falling asleep on his shoulder.

The functioning of the European Union is governed by a series of treaties. In order to change an existing treaty, or bring a new treaty into effect, a unanimous vote of the European Council must be obtained. Neither the European Parliament, nor the Council of the European Union, have any power to block or approve treaty changes, or add new treaties.

Chapter Eight

Friday, 25th September. London, England.

The news was filled with the death of Nick Allsop. MPs spoke highly of his commitment, avoiding actually saying that they agreed with his views. The police were still saying that it was a suicide and experts in male depression were dragged onto the TV screens, all seemingly *knowing* why Allsop took his own life.

Sitting around the small wooden meeting table in Clive's office, Sean, Liz and Clive tried to work out what to do next.

'I had a visit from the police this morning, who said that they were helping the French police with a shooting incident in Strasbourg and the hotel had given them our names. I just said that we were caught in the crossfire of some local gang war and I got you out of the back door. I know the investigating officer well, and I think he believed me. They didn't come to see you, did they?' Clive asked.

'No,' Sean said shaking his head.

'That's good. The other good news is that Terry's alive and well. He got back into England about the same time as us,' Clive said. 'The bad news is that there's still no sign of Anna Faustein. She's not at her office in Brussels, her office in Munich, or at home. She's just vanished.'

'Probably dead, given what we went through,' Sean added.

'Maybe, but as I said, we shouldn't ignore the possibility that she killed Allsop and put them onto us,' Clive responded.

'You know, I was getting to quite like him. He was very charismatic, you know, and surprisingly intelligent,' Sean said.

'For a Nazi,' Liz added.

'Did you get anywhere with that mumbo-jumbo he left us? It must be the key to why he was killed and why somebody tried to kill us,' Clive suggested.

'Not really, we got—' Sean was interrupted as his phone rang. After looking at the screen he chose not to answer. 'I don't know the number,' he said.

'Answer it,' Clive insisted.

Sean picked up the phone again. 'Hello?'

The faint voice on the other end of the line was tinged with a German accent. 'Hello, can I speak to Sean McManus, please?'

'Speaking.'

'Mr McManus, It's Anna Faustein. You left a message at my office. We need to talk.'

'Okay, that sounds good,' Sean said.

'Not on the phone. I'm in London. Can we meet?'

'Okay, where are you?'

'Meet me in the lobby of the May Fair Hotel in one hour.'

Suddenly the line went dead and Sean relayed the conversation to the others.

'What if she *is* the killer? How did she know that you were back in London?' Liz said.

'Why would she contact me if she was?' Sean asked.

'To kill you before you publish the contents of the USB?' Liz questioned.

'Publish what? It'd take me a year to understand it first,' Sean laughed.

'Well, somebody tried to kill us all for it,' Liz noted.

'We can cover you when you meet her in the hotel. Then bring her here. We'll make sure you're not being followed.' Clive said.

At thirty-eight Anna Faustein was young for an MEP. Her short blonde hair was covered with a large floppy hat and she wore tight jeans and a long woollen jumper pulled down to her thighs. She was looking around the lobby, nervously assessing the people coming in and out of the doors, when Sean approached her from the side, having entered via the door from the bar. 'Frau Faustein?' he said quietly.

She immediately swivelled to the side, as if touched by a cattle prod. 'Hello… er, Mr McManus?' she said, looking at him, her eyes dancing with fear.

'Yes, are you okay?' Sean asked.

'I'm scared. They killed Nick,' she said, still assessing the people coming and going from the lobby.

'Why come here, not to the police?' Sean asked.

'Nick said that he trusted you, and that's more than I can say for the French police,' she said. 'I'm sorry, but I had nowhere else to go.'

'Come with me,' Sean said calmly.

'Where to?'

'Somewhere safe,' Sean added. He nodded to Clive and they left the lobby of the hotel, walking quickly towards Piccadilly, then turned left onto Dover Street. Within five minutes they were seated around Clive's meeting table.

'Please call me Anna,' she said forcing a smile, when Liz addressed her as *Frau Faustein.*

'Anna,' Sean said. 'You said *they* killed Nick. Who did you mean?'

She shook her head. 'I don't know; whoever is perverting the legislation.'

'Perverting the legislation? You mean they're changing the bills after they've passed Parliament?' Liz asked.

'No… well, sort of. The translations are not always the same as the original version of the bill,' Anna said.

'What do you mean?' Sean asked.

'It's very subtle in the wording, but changes some powers in the bills.'

'Is that what was on the USB stick that Nick gave us?' Sean asked.

'Yes, the original version was in German and that's the version that will become law. But the English, Swedish, Danish and Polish translations have been interpreted slightly differently from the original.'

'How so?' Liz asked.

'There's a single line about halfway through the text in the original version that clearly gives the President of the Commission the authority to invoke Article 7 of the Treaty on the Functioning of the EU, if a member state defaults on an EU debt obligation. In the four translated versions that permission is more vague, and although the power is granted, it seems to require European Council approval. The actual wording difference is very subtle and very clever, so nobody could obviously point to fraud, but when scrutinised, the meaning is quite different.'

'What's Article 7?' Liz asked.

'It's the mechanism by which a member state can be temporarily suspended from the EU,' Anna replied.

'That seems fair. People are getting tired of constant bailouts that aren't repaid,' Sean said.

'Why shouldn't they be suspended if they don't pay?' Clive said.

Anna frowned. 'Maybe they should, but should that much power rest with one person, especially one who doesn't face election?'

'Probably not, but isn't it just to cut out bureaucracy and get quick action?' Liz asked. 'After all, we are talking about countries that are in default on their debts, and quick action could be vital to stop the situation slipping further.'

'Hmm… whether it's the right thing to do or not is irrelevant. It certainly doesn't justify the means, changing the translations like that,' Sean said. 'Why only the four languages though?'

'Because they're the languages of the members most likely to object to a bill like this, and block it. In general, they're the countries that are opposed to anything which strengthens the power of EU, or pushes it closer to federalization,' Anna answered.

'It seems like a pretty minor risk to the countries mentioned, none of which are at risk of debt default,' Sean said.

'Maybe, but we don't know how many other clauses there are like this. This is just the one that we found.' Anna's expression conveyed her seriousness.

'She's got a point, Sean. If this was just something small, why would they need to kill Allsop?' Clive said.

Sean noted that Clive didn't mention that they were also nearly killed. He'd said that he'd use it at an agreed time to measure the response of Anna Faustein, in an attempt to gauge her surprise.

'Exactly,' Anna agreed.

'*If* he was killed, that is. The police are still saying that it was suicide. Do you have any idea who might be involved?' Sean asked.

'There would have to be a few people, but it wouldn't work unless somebody senior in the Commission's translation services directorate was involved, maybe even Henrik Blom, the Commissioner himself.' Anna shrugged.

'Blom? He sounds Swedish. Why would he change his own country's translation?' Liz asked.

'He's a staunch pro-federalist and for those people, Europe comes first, country second. He doesn't agree with his own government's sceptical views,' Anna answered.

'It's a good place to start. Do you think he's capable of killing somebody?' Clive asked.

Anna lifted her shoulders again. 'Maybe,' she said quietly.

'Well, it looks like the Belgian police just want to sweep this under the carpet, so I think we should take a closer look at it,' Sean said.

'Agreed. I didn't particularly like Allsop, but if he was murdered then he deserves justice,' Clive said. 'And, of course, I'd like to know who was shooting at us, and why,' he added.

Sean studied the features on Anna's face carefully.

'What? You mean somebody tried to kill you?' she said, but Sean couldn't tell whether she was lying or not: her shock seemed genuine, but it was easy to fake.

'Yes, somebody took a few pot shots at us in the city,' Clive said, adding no more detail.

'Liz, what do you think?' Sean asked.

'Well, it's a major change from our original plan, but I agree: he deserves justice if he was killed. One proviso though, if it gets too dangerous, we pass our findings to the police and get out.'

'Agreed,' Sean said.

The EU doesn't operate in any specific language. All members and bureaucrats present in their native language, and all bills are presented in the language of the originator.

The EU employs an army of people to immediately translate everything into the twenty-four official languages of the European Union. With a spend of over €1.5 billion per year on translation services alone, the EU is the largest employer of translators in the world.

Even so, the number of facts 'lost in translation' are a constant source of debate among member states: for example, 'frozen semen' was recently translated into French as 'frozen seamen'; and 'out of sight, out of mind' was translated as 'invisible lunatic'.

This list of translation errors goes on ... and on ... and on, and is often less funny and more important than the above examples.

Chapter Nine

Friday, 25th September. London, England.

'Do you feel that you could go back to work, with protection of course?' Clive asked Anna.

Carefully scanning the three people at the table, Anna seemed to be assessing whether she could trust them. 'I could, but I'm scared. Everybody knew that I was close to Nick. If Blom had him killed, then he'd probably guess that I also have the information.'

'We can provide you with round-the-clock security; professional men. You'll be safe,' Clive encouraged.

'Okay,' Anna said, hesitating slightly.

'There are still a few things I don't understand: firstly, why didn't Allsop just expose this in the Parliament, or go directly to the media?' Liz said.

'To expose this one instance in the Parliament before the reading yesterday was his back-up plan, but remember he thought there may be many more instances which hadn't been found. And he did go to the media: you.'

'Okay, the other thing that I don't understand is why he wanted to meet Sean again the night after the first meeting? Surely he could just have put this information on the memory stick? We could easily check it. Was he onto something else?' Liz asked.

'He wanted us to both meet somebody, a whistle-blower in the translation services directorate that brought this to his attention. Apparently, he has proof of who might be behind it,' Anna replied.

'Did he tell you who it was that he was meeting? Or who this person had fingered?' Clive asked.

'No. Unfortunately neither. I knew he suspected Blom, but that's all I knew.'

'Why me? Why not one of the thousands of political journalists that line the streets of Strasbourg?' Sean asked.

'Because they'd never print Nick's comments. They didn't like him much. They too have a vested interest in seeing the EU grow stronger. It makes their jobs more important.'

'Is there anybody who doesn't have a vested interest in this circus?' Clive asked rhetorically.

'Only me,' Anna said, holding his stare.

Chapter Ten

Monday, 28th September. Brussels, Belgium.

On the two-hour train journey to Brussels Midi from London's St Pancras station, Sean took the seat next to Anna. Liz had chosen to stay in England to meet with the lawyer about Praew's immigration status, and work on the background research into Blom, while Clive was already in Brussels with Terry's team, working out the lie of the land.

Anna looked different from the day they'd met in the lobby of the May Fair hotel, when she'd been scared and tired. A weekend's rest, a change of clothes and some make-up had transformed her from the frightened little girl Sean had first seen, to the image of the modern career woman. When he sat down, their eyes made contact and he noticed the deep blue sparkle of her irises, before he quickly looked away, embarrassed by the brief interchange.

'*Frau:* that means you're married, doesn't it?' Sean asked.

'It did. I'm divorced.'

'Any children?' Sean asked.

'No, just me. Too much time working and not enough time playing. It's why my marriage broke down. I was just never home.'

'Some time apart could strengthen a relationship though,' Sean said, speaking more about his own situation with Liz than Anna's.

She picked the change up quickly. 'Liz is very beautiful. Have you been together long?'

'Only six months.'

'That's very quick to be living together and supporting a child.'

'Yes, more circumstantial than anything. We worked together on a story and I was badly injured. Liz looked after me and nursed me back to health.'

'And the child?' Anna asked.

'A long story, but we're fighting a losing battle to keep her in the UK. If she gets deported to Thailand, she'll be sold straight back into the horrific life we rescued her from, and I won't let that happen. She's a really sweet girl, who's seen too much of the bad side of life already, and she needs a break.'

'Maybe I could help? I am an MEP after all; that must be useful for something. I could lobby the European Court of Human Rights to force the British Government not to deport her,' Anna said, tilting her head to one side and looking into Sean's eyes.

She looked older than her thirty-eight years and her short hair made her seem stern, but she had attractive features and a lean body. 'I may take you up on that, if our current plans fail,' he said.

'Why did you become an MEP?' Sean asked, changing the subject.

'Ambition, I guess. It's very hard to get ahead in domestic

politics in Germany. I think you call it *dead men's shoes*. I was young and I believed in the EU passionately, so … '

'What happened to make you change your view on the EU?'

The question caused Anna to pause, seemingly considering her response. 'It wasn't what I thought it would be. Instead of the shining light of change for good in Europe, it's become a forum riddled with political infighting and an unquenchable thirst for power.'

'And Nick Allsop?' Sean prodded.

'I met Nick in my first year; he was very good to me. He also seemed to be the only person in the Parliament that didn't have a separate agenda to expand his power base, and he was the only person that was prepared to criticise the Commission openly. He was a good man and a loyal friend.'

'Were you in love with him?' Sean asked.

'Yes. No. Maybe. We weren't having an affair if that's what you mean. He was very dedicated to his family.'

'Was he a Nazi?' Sean asked.

He'd expected that Anna would be shocked by the question, but she wasn't, she simply held his stare. 'No. He told me that you'd asked him about his past and the alleged neo-Nazi ties. Strangely, I think that's why he trusted you. When Nick first became an MEP he had a reputation for being a racist. It wasn't true, but given that his party is seen as right of centre, people naturally believe it when he's called a racist. Out of some perverse idea of patriotism, he agreed to make contact with some neo-Nazi groups and pass information to MI6. His reputed racism gave him some credibility with the groups, so they accepted him readily.'

'And what happened?' Sean probed.

'He made contact with a few and passed the information to

MI6, then suddenly people started to disappear and Nick didn't know who he trusted less: the security services or the Nazis.'

'He said they were still watching him.'

'Somebody was. He said they looked and acted like MI6, but in truth, he wasn't sure.'

After the train pulled in to Brussels, they made their way quickly through the busy, cave-like Midi railway station and out over the cobbled footpath, where they got into a taxi. When they turned off the central ring road, Sean was surprised by how rundown the area was, so close to the magnificent Baroque Palace. The buildings were covered in graffiti and at least half looked empty. Then slowly, they began to get cleaner and newer. Another kilometre and they were driving between massive steel and glass structures, with EU flags hanging from every lamppost and draping from every building.

Anna kept an apartment on the Avenue du Maelbeek, overlooking Parc Leopold. On the other side of the park, the huge towering glass and marble structure of the EU Parliament building dominated the skyline.

When they arrived, Terry was waiting for them at the main door and informed Anna that he had already checked the apartment out, noting that it hadn't been entered or damaged. Clearly relieved, Anna blew out a gasp of air and made her way inside, watched carefully by her protection team.

Happy that Anna was safe, Terry then escorted Sean the fifty metres or so to the Sofitel, where they'd booked rooms for the stay. Clive was waiting for them and once Sean had checked in, they met in the lobby for a coffee. A large map was laid out on the table and Sean was quickly taken through the key places.

'The hotel is in Place Jourdan,' Clive said.

'Which is the only sign of civilization in the EU Quarter. The whole place was a ghost town yesterday,' Terry added.

'Most of the politicians and lobbyists go home for the weekend, I think,' Clive said.

Fifty metres away and visible from the hotel, Anna's apartment building sat inside the edge of the park. The European Parliament was just 200 metres away on the opposite side of the park, and the Berlaymont Building, the home of the Commission, and where Blom's office was located, was just one kilometre away.

'We think he keeps a weekday apartment here,' Clive pointed to the map, 'in a new tower on Rue Belliard, but he commutes each week from Stockholm.'

Following Clive's finger, Sean studied the map. Rue Belliard was between the hotel and the Commission. Everything they were here to watch was contained in an area no bigger than one square kilometre.

When Clive had finished, Terry took over the conversation. 'I've assembled a team of six men: three for round-the-clock protection of Anna; and three to assist with the surveillance of Blom. I'll float between the two and coordinate activities.'

Can he really always be as happy as he looks? Sean thought, as he examined Terry's smiling face. He was in his early forties, lean and strong, and had an as-yet-undiscussed military background. During the BW investigation, he'd saved Sean's life more than once and Sean trusted him without reservation.

'Blom's at work in the Berlaymont Building now. Beyond that we don't know, as we can't get in. I've got people on the door. They'll know as soon as he leaves.' Terry continued.

'What if he leaves by car?' Clive asked.

Terry raised his eyebrows at the comment. 'It's covered,' he said, shaking his head at Clive.

'And Anna?' Sean asked.

'Two men outside, one inside. She'll be okay,' Terry replied.

Brussels is a city divided by two languages: French and Dutch. It is now geographically divided between Belgian Brussels — vibrant and filled with historic buildings, shops and tourist attractions — and the EU Quarter, to the east of the centre, dominated by huge glass and steel edifices to the new order, completely soulless and deserted outside office hours.

Chapter Eleven

Monday, 28th September. Brussels, Belgium.

Sean spent the day getting to know the area around the Berlaymont Building, their hotel, Anna's apartment and Blom's apartment. The Berlaymont Building itself was a massive glass and steel structure, built in the shape of a Las Vegas casino, with four independent wings attached to a central core. Outside, twenty-eight EU flags, one for each member country, flew from high stainless steel posts. *That's odd, why aren't they the countries' own flags? That would make more sense,* Sean thought. Then he was reminded of something that Allsop had said.

'The EU is the new dictatorship and it wants to make sure all remnants of the old states are wiped out.'

Suddenly his comment made sense.

Sean thought about the number of EU flags he'd seen flying from the buildings in the rest of EU Quarter; they were *everywhere,* and he couldn't remember seeing *any* national flags, not even the Belgian flag. The only comparison he could think of was Nazi Germany, when the red flag with the white disk and black swastika, had flown from every building in the country. The thought made him shudder. *Was Allsop right? Was there something more sinister at work?*

The British had always viewed the EU quite comically in Sean's opinion, commonly believing that that they voted on the names of sausages or the shape of a banana. But walking through the new mega-city, which was under permanent construction to house the rapidly expanding EU bureaucracy, the reality was obviously something entirely different, and much more serious.

Before Sean could take a closer look at some of the other huge EU buildings, Terry's voice came over his concealed earpiece.

'Blom's on the move. He's just leaving the south door of the Berlaymont now.' Sean could almost see Terry grinning as he spoke.

Once Sean had located the south door, he scanned the area looking for his target, as a blonde man in his late fifties exited the glass doors. His leather courier bag looked like a woman's handbag as it sat against his enormous frame.

'He's huge,' Sean said, as he observed the lumbering blonde-haired frame of Blom stooping to get through the door of the building.

'He's walking. Probably heading home,' Terry's voice appeared again.

'Anna's just arrived home safely too,' Phil, one of Terry's men and another veteran of the BW investigation, added.

'Great. Let's stay alert,' Clive said.

Lurching into a jog, Sean caught up with Terry, who was walking thirty paces behind Blom. They followed him to his apartment building, where Sean left Terry to keep watch and then made his way along the leafy street which bordered Parc Leopold, looking down over the ornate lake and the weeping willows surrounding it. Just above the treetops, the sky was punctured by three glass towers, which jutted out from a massive reflective glass building that Sean had visited earlier: the European Parliament building.

The entrance to Anna's apartment was just a small doorway with a keypad to enter apartment numbers. Once in the hallway, Sean was surprised by how utilitarian the communal spaces were. The white floor tiles and grey walls seemed more suited to a hospital than an apartment block.

Inside, Anna's apartment was just big enough to fit in a small sofa, a tiny dining table and a kitchenette along one wall. *MEPs' expenses mustn't be all they're cracked up to be!* Sean thought. Seeing Sean, the bodyguard left the apartment, choosing to stand guard outside the door instead; offering them some privacy. Anna had just showered and wore a white towelling robe, pulled tight at the waist, with her hair covered by a towel stacked up like a turban.

'I'm sorry. I can come back later,' Sean said.

'No, it's fine,' she replied, pouring a glass of wine and offering Sean one, which he gladly accepted.

'Anything of interest happen today?' Sean asked.

'No, I did as you said; just got on with work as normal. Nothing out of the ordinary at all,' she said, sitting on the small leather couch in the living room and curling her legs underneath her body. Sean couldn't help but think how much younger she looked like that. Gone was the impressive façade of the MEP and just the girl was left, lost and scared again.

'Blom's in his apartment,' Sean said.

She just nodded her understanding, gesturing for Sean to join her on the couch.

A pang of guilt shot through him as he sat on the small couch, close enough to Anna that he could smell the soap on her body. He glanced down at the freshly moisturised skin between the folds at the top of her robe and then looked up quickly, blushing as she traced the movements of his eyes.

She smiled, intimating that she wasn't offended by his looks. 'It's been a while since an attractive man looked at me that way,' she said, leaning forward.

'I'm surprised at that,' Sean said.

'I don't mix with many people my own age. Some of the other MEPs hit on me, but I'm not interested in them: they're either too old, or too fat; and always too conceited.' She looked straight into Sean's eyes, letting him know that it wasn't how she felt about him. Then she looked down, drawing Sean's eyes with hers. He noticed that the front of her robe seemed looser now, exposing her breasts almost to the nipple.

Sean looked up again quickly.

'Liz will never know,' Anna said, still looking into his eyes.

'I can't,' Sean said turning away. 'It just wouldn't be fair on Liz.'

'The world isn't fair, Sean,' Anna said, as she pulled her robe apart and took the towel from her head. Her small breasts were now completely exposed and her large pink nipples were standing erect. She was breathing heavily as she stood and pulled on her belt, slipping the robe off her shoulders onto the floor.

Sean took in the athletic shape of her body; her frame was lean and strong, like a gymnast and she was completely hairless.

A loud rap on the door made Sean jump from the sofa. Pulling her robe back on, Anna opened the door and gave Sean a suggestive glance.

'Sean, is your radio off? Clive's been trying to get hold of you. Blom's on the move again,' the bulky bodyguard said, as he walked in to the apartment. Standing behind him so that he couldn't see her, Anna licked her lips with her tongue provocatively.

Sean ignored the gesture and fumbled around inside his jacket pocket, while trying to conceal his erection, before he switched the radio back on. 'Clive?' he said.

'Sean, don't ever switch that thing off again. Blom's in a restaurant in Place Jourdan. He's just joined three other people for dinner.'

'Okay. On my way,' Sean said, relieved to have an excuse to leave the small apartment.

As he walked out of the door, Anna parted the bottom of her gown and showed her vagina to him. 'Later,' she mouthed silently.

Blom was sitting at a round table in the window of a small restaurant, tucked into the corner of Place Jourdan, adjacent to Sean's hotel. His huge frame overhung the sides of the flimsy wooden chair and he dwarfed the three other men seated with him. A bottle of red wine and some bread crowded the small circular table between them.

The meeting appeared to be far from convivial. Blom's dinner companions seemed to be arguing vociferously, pointing at each other, mouths open in anger. For his part, Blom didn't seem to be joining in. He merely glanced from one man to the other as the heated argument continued.

Pulling out his phone, Sean quickly took a photo of the group and emailed it to Anna: *Any idea who they are?*

The reply came almost immediately:

From left to right: Alain Picquering, MEP, France, Leader of the Socialist Movement Party of Europe (34% of the EU vote); Ruud Ten Harkel, MEP, Netherlands, Leader of the Democratic Alliance of Europe Party (21% of the EU vote); Hans Glass, MEP, Austria, Leader of the European Freedom Front (9% of the EU vote). Strange that they would be dining together. They hate each other!

Sean: *64% of the total vote, wow! Any legitimate reason they'd have to meet?*

Anna: *Not that I can think of. They go out of their way to make sure they're never on the same subcommittees.*

The group in the small restaurant continued their animated dinner for a further two hours. When it was over, Blom left alone, carrying an A4 manila envelope. He made his way across Place Jourdan and then turned into the Sofitel, making straight for the bar.

'Looks like he's a drinker,' Clive said, as Blom downed two whiskies in quick succession.

After downing a third whisky, Blom glanced at his watch and ordered another, which this time he sipped at for ten minutes, before he looked out of the window onto Place Jourdan and asked for the bill.

Leaving the bar, he walked out of the revolving door at the front of the hotel and then straight across the road into the car park that centred the small square.

'He's going to a car. John, bring the Audi around,' Terry said over the mic.

A chauffeur-driven black Maybach was parked in the centre of the square with its engine still running. The chauffeur sat in the driver's seat looking forward, but darkened glass prohibited a view into the rear of the car. Without hesitating, Blom walked straight to the rear door and pulled it open, exchanging a few words with the passenger before climbing in. The moment that the door was open allowed Sean a brief glimpse of another man in the car, but he couldn't make out any features.

Resting his shoulder on the bonnet of another car, Clive was taking photographs rapidly using a long zoom lens, but cursed, noting that he also couldn't get a decent view of the other passenger.

After spending less than a minute in the car, Blom squeezed his body back out onto the car park and closed the door behind him. Almost immediately, the Maybach started to pull away, virtually scraping Blom's side.

'He's left the envelope in the car,' Sean said.

'Terry, follow the Maybach. We'll stay with Blom,' Clive said.

Terry quickly ran over to the waiting Audi and jumped in. Two seconds later, he was heading in the same direction as the black limousine.

Hunting for a clue, Sean and Clive followed Blom, as he made his way back to his apartment on Rue Belliard, via three bars, where he downed two whiskies in each.

The Café Brussels was a large café in the centre of Place Jourdan, with seats outside overlooking the square. Clive ordered drinks for the three gathered people and began the discussion about what they'd seen, some half an hour earlier.

'They're still following the Maybach and it seems to be heading towards Germany. Terry sent the plate through. It's German, but we don't have any way of checking who owns it. Any ideas?' He turned to Anna.

Looking down at the table Sean purposely tried not to make eye contact with Anna, who was now dressed in tight jeans and a woollen jacket.

'The plate's from Leipzig, but that's all I know,' she replied.

Sean couldn't help noticing how her demeanour had changed since the time in her apartment. She had quickly shifted from a steamy temptress to a calculating professional. 'You said that it was odd that the three party heads met with Blom. Why?' he queried.

'Just that they make no secret of their animosity towards each other. They have a very different set of beliefs.'

'Really? Even on the EU?' Sean said.

Anna paused to think briefly. 'No, you're right. They're all staunch federalists, but Ten Harkel is virtually a communist, while Glas is extremely right wing. They have nothing else in common.'

'Do you know any of them well enough to ask why they met together and with Blom?' Sean asked.

'Yes, when I first became an MEP, I was a part of the Democratic Alliance of Europe Party, so I had a number of meetings with Ten Harkel.'

'Where's this going, Sean? I'm not sure Anna should be sticking her neck out like that. They'll know that she was close to Allsop and if they're involved in some way … ' Clive said.

Anna interrupted. 'It's okay. I know him well enough to ask and I'm sure he's not connected to anything to do with Nick's death. He has some strange political views, but he's not the type to go to extremes.'

'Okay, then it's worth asking, I guess. We should know who Blom met in the car park before tomorrow as well,' Clive conceded.

When they left the café, they walked Anna back to her apartment. Sean was glad to have Clive with him, although Anna still managed to discreetly tell him to join her later, opening her eyes wide when making the offer.

Hoping that Clive hadn't noticed the brief interchange, or if he had, he'd understood that it wasn't welcome, Sean walked back to the Sofitel and went straight to his room, showering quickly before calling Liz, who he told nothing of the events in Anna's apartment.

During the call, Liz updated him on her research. 'Blom is fifty-six years old: a Swede from Gothenburg, but now living in

Stockholm. He's been married for twenty-two years and has three children. He was a senior figure in the Swedish Government before taking on the role at the Commission, where he's been for seven years. His upbringing and education were fairly standard: middle-class, good university, etc. His politics are considered just left of centre and he's never been involved in a scandal… that I can find, that is.'

'He sounds pretty dull,' Sean said.

'A grey man, like all of them,' Liz replied.

Describing the situation in detail, Sean quickly filled Liz in on the events in the car park.

'Weird, but unless you know what was in the envelope and who the other person was, it doesn't mean much.'

'I know. We're working on it. How's Praew?' Sean said.

'She got an A for her maths homework, she's so pleased and I'm so relieved.' Sean could almost feel Liz's passion over the phone.

'That's great. Can I talk to her?'

'She's in bed, sorry. But I'll tell her you congratulated her.'

'Anna said she might be able to help with the Home Office.' Sean felt his stomach tighten even mentioning her name.

The line went silent briefly. 'Really? Why? She doesn't know us,' Liz said.

'I know, but she's an MEP and may have some influence,' he said, surprised by Liz's response.

'I don't like her, Sean. There's something about her.'

'She's okay. She's just trying to help,' Sean said.

'We'll see. Be careful around her,' Liz warned.

Sean shivered. *Could she know? Did she sense something?*

Chapter Twelve

Tuesday, 29th September. Brussels, Belgium.

'Terry finally called at 5:30 a.m. He followed the car to a house on the outskirts of Leipzig. I've forwarded the photos to both Liz and Anna, to see if they know who the passenger is,' Clive said, before slurping on a coffee.

'It's seven now, only six in London. Liz won't be up yet. Have you heard from Anna?' Sean asked.

'She's joining us for breakfast. She'll be here any minute.'

When Anna entered the breakfast room just a few minutes later, dressed in a dark blue pinstriped suit and carrying a black designer briefcase, Sean noticed again how her image changed: one minute the vulnerable shy girl; next the temptress; then the formidable business woman, hard and unapproachable. After pouring herself a coffee and grabbing a croissant, she joined them at the table.

'Do you know the person in the photos I sent you?' Clive asked.

'Yes, unfortunately I do,' she said. 'It's Ulrich Wagner, one of the less satisfying by-products of German re-unification. He owns steel mills across the old East Germany, and is reputed to be one of Germany's richest men.' She paused to take a sip of coffee. 'Mr Wagner holds some very unhealthy political ideas.'

'Such as?' Sean asked.

Considering her response before speaking, Anna placed her coffee back on the table and lowered her eyes. 'You have to understand that East Germans were trapped in time following the Second World War, unable to communicate with the outside world and fed a diet of communist propaganda. Many of them have very outdated ideas about Europe and the wider world.'

Sensing that Anna was holding back, giving the politician's answer rather than the direct response, Sean pressed further. 'And what are his views?' he said quickly.

Following another sip of coffee, Anna lifted her head, looking straight at Sean. 'He believes that 1945 was only the end of the second battle of the war for Europe; 1918 being the end of the first battle.'

'Jesus Christ!' Clive exclaimed.

'So he thinks there'll be another war in Europe?' Sean asked.

'Not exactly. He believes that we're still at war and have been since 1914. Not an armed war anymore, but a quiet war: one which he believes Germany will ultimately win and take its rightful place as the leader of Europe.'

'Is he a Nazi? Why hasn't he been arrested?' Clive asked.

'Yes, he would also be considered a Nazi, but we don't arrest people for their opinions in Germany,' Anna said.

'So he doesn't condone violence then?' Sean queried.

'On the contrary, he openly advocates it. But he believes that Germany has been made too weak by the treaties signed at the end of both World Wars, so it's incapable of mounting a third military attempt at domination. He does, however, think that Germany has been winning the ceasefire, and that it can win the war by using its financial and political influence.'

'Why would an EU Commissioner agree to meet somebody like that?' Sean asked.

'I don't know, but I understand why it was done so secretively. If any EU official was seen in the presence of Wagner, it would be political and career suicide.'

'Do you think the people that Blom met with earlier could be part of some conspiracy involving Wagner?' Clive asked.

'No, in the case of Ten Harkel and Piquering. Wagner would consider France an enemy and the Netherlands as neutral at best. Only Glas, as an Austro-Hungarian, would be thought of as an ally.'

'Austro-Hungarian?' Sean questioned. 'Isn't that a bit outdated?'

'People like Wagner don't use the same map of Europe that we do. In his mind, Germany stretches all the way east to the Russian border, and Austria-Hungary forms virtually all of its southern border, stretching south to Montenegro and east to Romania. France is always the enemy, and the Netherlands are sometimes neutral, but never an ally.'

'You said people like Wagner: does that mean there're more of them?' Sean asked.

Anna smirked. 'Yes, a lot of people in Germany and elsewhere in Europe believe the same, particularly in the East. But Wagner stands out because he's wealthy and powerful.'

Glancing at her watch, Anna made her apologies and left for work, followed closely by Phil, while Sean and Clive continued their discussion. They agreed that Terry should stay on Wagner for a little while and watch him from a distance.

They were updated on Wagner's movement by Terry and received various snippets of background from Liz during the day, but nothing out of the ordinary. Wagner had gone to work in an office block in central Leipzig and hadn't left, other than to have lunch, which he did alone. Liz had uncovered lots of newspaper clippings, but all were in German and she hadn't yet had them translated. Though some of the photos showing him wearing a military style uniform, similar to the SS uniforms of the Third Reich, were unnerving.

At 7 p.m., Sean collected Anna from her apartment to join him and Clive for dinner. When he arrived she was dressed in jeans and knee-high boots, with a leather jacket tied at the waist, again showing her chameleon-like ability to change her image. Now she looked young and trendy, not the efficient business woman of the morning. Sean was beginning to wonder just how many outward personalities Anna could portray.

When they stepped out to cross the road to Place Jourdan, she linked arms with him and smiled at him affectionately. Again, guilt shot through his veins, and he was glad they were meeting Clive. *Have I got anything to feel guilty about though?* he thought. The only thing that he was guilty of was not telling Liz about Anna's advances. *But our relationship is just so brittle at the moment.* Sean feared that a revelation like that could be the straw that broke the camel's back.

It was a warm night and they meandered slowly across the road, catching up on the events of the day. Then, just as they crossed the central line, Sean felt a sudden powerful thump in his back, forcing him forward and onto the ground. Almost immediately, Anna fell beside him with a thud, as she landed.

At the same time, right behind him, Sean heard a crunching bang and looked over his shoulder. The sight of Phil's body being thrown into the air, landing headfirst some twenty metres further along the road, churned his stomach.

With screeching tyres, the vehicle that had hit Phil stopped some fifty metres further on, then the white reversing lights came on as it accelerated backwards towards them. Scrambling to his feet and pulling Anna up, Sean wondered how he hadn't heard the car approaching, then he suddenly realised that he still couldn't hear it: it was a Prius, running silently on electric power. He ran towards Phil to pull him from the road, but he was too late, the car got there first and ran straight over him, crushing his chest as the tyres bounced over his ribcage.

'Run!' Sean shouted to Anna as he dived out of the way and the car continued in her direction.

Responding quickly, Anna started to run awkwardly in the opposite direction. *Clearly she doesn't run often,* Sean thought.

The car gained ground quickly as she ran clumsily away. With less than twenty metres to go to the corner of Place Jourdan, the car mounted the kerb taking out a post box. Seeing the collision just behind her, Anna ran onto the road, but the car followed, just metres behind her. Then, just as it was about to hit her, Anna dived athletically to one side and onto the verge of the park, rolling herself into the grass.

As the Prius stopped, Clive came sprinting around the corner and ran to Anna, just as Sean reached her. Seeing that she was okay, Clive jumped forward, running towards the Prius. When he was just five metres away from it, it shot away silently, turning left at the end of the park.

Leaving Anna trembling with Clive, Sean sprinted back in the direction of Phil. When he reached him, his body was twisted into an awkward position, with his spine bent at a ninety-degree angle below his rib cage. Sean dropped onto his knees and carefully lifted his blood-covered head. His lifeless eyes stared back at Sean without any recognition.

Chapter Thirteen

Wednesday, 30th September. Brussels, Belgium.

The remainder of the previous evening had been spent with the Belgian police. Sean had stopped short of implicating Blom or Wagner, because he knew there was just no evidence and, upon Clive's advice, Anna had done the same.

'They were definitely after you,' Sean said to Anna, who was sitting in his hotel room wrapped in a blanket, still shaken from the experience. 'If they'd been after me they'd have stopped when they passed me.'

'Have you called in sick?' Clive asked.

'Yes. I said I'll be back in a week or so,' she replied.

Reluctantly, Sean agreed that Anna should go to London and stay with Liz for a while. He was yet to tell Liz, which wouldn't be easy following her comments about Anna.

'We need to take a good look at Ten Harkel. He was the only person that Anna spoke to yesterday beyond her normal activities,' Clive said.

'Are you okay to carry on after what happened to Phil?' Sean asked.

'I won't do anything *but* carry on, until I find the bastards that killed him,' Clive replied.

'It'll only be for a week or so,' Sean said to Liz on the phone.

'I don't care. I don't like her. There's something fake about her,' Liz replied.

Knots formed in Sean's stomach. He hated to put Liz in such an awkward position, especially given their precarious situation, but he felt obliged. 'She's a politician. They're all fakes,' Sean said. 'Please. She's scared and has nowhere else to go.'

A loud sigh came from Liz. 'She's got one week and then she's out,' she said, hanging up.

'Thanks,' Sean said into the dead line.

'Terry's just called. Wagner's on the move and he thinks something's going on. There were a lot of people at his house today before he left,' Clive said.

'What?' Sean said, snapping quickly out of the daydream he'd been in since the call with Liz.

'He thinks we should get over there?'

'What? Where?' Sean said shaking his head.

'Prague. Wagner's just crossed into the Czech Republic, on the road to Prague. He's not sure that it's the final destination, but if we get there, John can collect us and take us wherever.'

The short flight to Prague landed at 5 p.m. When John collected Sean and Clive at the airport, in the same blue Audi they'd followed Wagner in, he looked tired and unkempt. 'I've not been able to shower yet, smart arse,' he said, as Clive intimated that he stank.

'They're out at an old steel mill about half an hour away. Terry's still there. We should pick him up on the radio when we get close. There's a vantage point on a hill overlooking the yard and there's a lot of activity down there,' John said.

'What kind of activity?' Sean asked.

'Better you see it for yourself; it looks like they're setting up for something big,' John replied.

After about twenty minutes driving through the rolling hills outside Prague, John pulled the car over onto a dirt track, which led up the side of a densely wooded hill. 'This is as close as we can get. The other side's crawling with guards. From the top we can get a good view.'

'Terry,' Clive said over the concealed radio.

'Welcome to the 1930s,' Terry replied.

'What?' Clive said.

'You'll see.'

Intrigued by Terry's comment, they ran quickly up the footpath to the top of the hill and linked up with him, as he lay in a prone position, peering through a bush. The activity below drew Sean's gaze and he quickly looked down, through the trees into the huge factory yard. The area was teeming with people, scurrying around, setting out staging and equipment. Then a lone figure began to test a PA system from the stage.

'Test ein, zwei, drei,' the voice sounded out.

From their vantage point they could hear the sound system clearly.

'Why are they speaking German? Why not Czech?' Clive asked.

'Maybe it's something to do with that,' Sean said, as two huge vertical blue flags were unfurled on the stage behind the podium. In the centre of each flag a white circle with a black swastika centred in it was surrounded by a ring of gold stars.

'Fucking hell!' John commented on the unfurling of the combination of the EU and Nazi flags.

'Does this remind you of anything?' Clive said.

'The Nuremburg rally?' Sean replied.

'Precisely, and that flag clearly ties this lot back to whatever's going on in the EU.'

'Blom,' Sean added.

'Yep, it would seem so.'

Two more hours passed before the daylight started to dwindle and the powerful floodlights were turned on. The surge in the activity level below signified that something was about to happen. It was impossible to count, but at least 2,000 men and women stood in block ranks facing the huge stage. They were all dressed identically in brown Nazi uniforms, bearing blue swastika armbands.

On the stroke of 8 p.m. the hoard fell silent, then, from behind a curtain on the left of the stage, a slight man appeared and walked quickly to the podium. Unlike the crowd, he was dressed in a full-length black leather coat, topped with a leather peaked military cap, curved down at the sides. Sean squinted through the binoculars to see his face, but it wasn't Wagner.

'*Meine Damen und Herren ...* ,' the speaker started, as Sean reached into his pocket and pulled out his phone to video the proceedings.

'*Es ist mir eine Ehre, Ihnen Ulrich Wagner, Irren Führer vorzustellen.*' The announcement boomed out and from behind the same curtain, Wagner stepped out wearing full military uniform, complete with lines of medals. The noise that greeted him was cacophonous, as the gathered crowd cheered and clapped.

'I don't speak German, but did he say *Führer?*' Clive asked.

'I think so,' Sean said, concentrating on his filming.

'Bloody hell!' Clive said, as the massed ranks performed the Nazi salute and shouted *'Sieg heil,'* in unison.

Wagner's speech lasted twenty-two minutes and used up the memory capacity on three phones. Having seen enough, Sean, Clive, Terry and John started to make their way down the hill in the opposite direction from the rally.

'Wait,' John said, dropping to one knee and pulling Sean and Clive down with him. 'I heard something.'

They held their breath listening for another sound. Then it came again: a broken twig under a foot, then footsteps through the woods, as four soldiers carrying machine guns came up the hill from the direction of their car.

'Sie sind hier,' one of the soldiers shouted.

'Shit! I think they're onto us,' Terry said. 'We'd better get out of here.'

'What about the car?' Clive asked.

'I guess they've found that and that's why they're coming this way.'

Staying low, they scurried down the hill in the opposite direction from the soldiers, getting ever closer to the rally. The noise of their movement had alerted the soldiers to their position and they followed behind, gaining ground all the time. Sean could hear their boots cracking through the branches behind them as he followed Terry's movement in and out of the trees, so they that couldn't get a clear shot.

When they reached the bottom of the hill, hundreds of parked cars lined the road in front of them and there were at least twenty more armed guards lurking around the gates to the factory. When he looked up the line of cars, Sean noticed that the vast majority had German plates, even though they were in the Czech Republic.

Indicating to the others to stay still, John quickly crawled out from the edge of the forest and hid behind an old Audi. When he was happy that he'd not been seen, he beckoned for them to follow.

Only a matter of seconds after Sean had crouched down behind the car, the four soldiers that had been following them emerged from the woods, holding their weapons at the ready. They had come out onto the path, roughly 100 metres away from where they were hiding, and were scouring the area, looking for the intruders.

'What now?' Sean whispered to Terry.

'Wait here,' the reply came.

Terry rolled onto his side and slid along the car, using the shadow cast by the floodlights to hide from the soldiers. He quickly fiddled with the lock and after only a few seconds, he was inside the vehicle, beckoning the others to get in.

Following the same manoeuvre, using the shadow of the car to hide from the soldiers, one by one they climbed into the old Audi. Once inside, Sean was told to stay down in the footwell in the back of the car, but before he could get in position, he saw people moving out of the gates towards their cars. First it was just a trickle of people, then more, until they filled the road. When the first of them reached their cars, they started to change out of their Nazi uniforms.

'They're going back to Germany. The swastika's illegal there,' Clive said.

After ripping off the plastic cover under the steering wheel, Terry played with some wires that he'd pulled down. Then suddenly there was a small spark and the engine started. The noise made the soldiers turn in their direction and point their weapons, but it was too busy: they couldn't shoot into the crowd that was filling the area quickly. Taking the opportunity, Terry pulled out into the throng of people and beeped his horn, moving through them as they parted in front of the car. Shouting and pushing people out of the way, the soldiers tried to get to them.

When they were clear enough, Terry accelerated hard, forcing the last few people to dive out of the way. Lifting his head, Sean looked out of the rear window as the soldiers stopped giving chase, and instead commandeered a new looking BMW 5 series from a man dressed in a full brown uniform.

Out on open road, the old Audi's engine screamed as Terry took the car to its limits, but through the trees, Sean could see the lights of the BMW making up ground quickly. The Audi was just too old.

'They're gaining on us,' he said.

'We can't outrun them in this heap of shit,' Terry said, swerving the car round a tight bend.

Stabilising himself with the door handle, Sean quickly looked behind again. He could still see the lights; they were less than a kilometre behind.

'Get ready to jump out,' Terry said suddenly.

'What?' Sean started, but stopped when Terry slammed the brakes on and skidded to a halt in a dirt lane, just around a sharp corner.

'Out!' Terry shouted.

Without thinking, Clive, John and Sean jumped out of the car and ran into the edge of the dense woodland by the road.

When they stopped, Sean saw that Terry had turned off the lights on the Audi and had spun the vehicle around to face the road. The lights of the BMW were approaching quickly through the trees, the engine straining as its tyres screeched around the tight corners at high speed.

Just as the BMW approached their position, the engine revved hard and the tyres spun on the Audi. It shot forward in the direction of the BMW, blocking the road, but still moving forward, as Terry rolled out of the driver's door and into a ditch.

When the BMW came hurtling at full-pelt around the corner, the driver had no time to react as he saw the Audi coming in his direction with its lights turned off. The crunching collision smashed the Audi clean off the road, with the BMW jammed onto the front of it, in a tangled mess of glass and twisted metal. Two of the soldiers were hurtled forward through the windscreen and onto the road, before a burst of flames spread throughout the two wrecked cars.

Springing to his feet, Terry quickly ran forward and collected the machine guns from the dead soldiers in the road, then joined the others.

'Fuck me, Terry! This isn't actually the war you know,' Clive said, surveying the carnage on the road in front of them.

In response, Terry just smiled and passed John a machine gun. 'Captain Hook here can't handle one anymore,' he said winking. 'Now let's get the hell out of here before One Ball back there misses his friends.'

It took them over two hours to reach the outer suburbs of Prague on foot, staying away from the roads. When they arrived, they dumped the guns in a river and found a taxi to take them to the airport.

None of them had spoken about what they'd seen; their time taken by moving quietly through dense woodland to avoid discovery.

'What the hell did we just see?' Sean said.

'I don't know, but it's terrifying to think that kind of thing goes on today,' Clive said.

'We need to get Anna to translate exactly what he was saying,' Sean added.

'I think we should head back to London to regroup anyway. It's moving too quickly and we're not keeping up,' Clive suggested, to unanimous agreement.

Nazi symbols and uniforms are illegal in Germany, but are openly displayed in many other countries, particularly in the former communist eastern states.

Because of this, German Nazis often hold meetings in bordering EU countries, where they can wear their uniforms without fear of arrest.

The Schengen Agreement, which removed physical borders between most EU countries, ensures that they are not at risk of being caught when returning to Germany.

Chapter Fourteen

Thursday, 1st September. London, England.

When Sean arrived home late at night, Anna greeted him like a long-lost friend, hugging him tightly; a little too tightly. As he pulled away, Liz backed off into the bedroom and slammed the door. *Shit!* He quickly made his apologies to Anna, who just shrugged and blew him a kiss, then went into the bedroom to join Liz.

'I don't know why she did that,' he said, climbing onto the bed and putting his arm on Liz's side.

Liz turned away from him and pretended to be asleep. A few minutes later, when he climbed into bed, he thought he could hear the sniffle of tears and tried again to console her. But she just pushed his hand away roughly.

'I'm sorry, Liz, but there's nothing between us,' he said to her back, before giving up and falling asleep himself.

In the morning they both took Praew to school and managed to put on a happy act until she walked through the school gates. She beamed a beautiful smile, so proud of her achievements so far.

As soon as she disappeared into the playground, Liz turned to Sean, her smile gone. 'You slept with her, didn't you,' she said.

'No, I didn't,' Sean responded, looking straight at her.

'I can tell… the way she looks at you.'

'I think she has a crush on me, but it's not reciprocated… honestly,' Sean pleaded.

'Promise me that you haven't even kissed her.'

'I promise. I wouldn't cheat on you,' Sean said honestly. Even though Anna had tried to tempt him, the one thing that stopped him was the thought of cheating on Liz. She'd been so good to him and he loved her so much. He just wished he could make her understand, but he couldn't find the right words.

'I want her out of the flat,' Liz said, rubbing her tongue against her teeth.

'We agreed one week. She's scared. Somebody tried to kill her.'

'Which is another reason I don't want her there. What about Praew? What if they come after her? What about the Home Office? We can't be considered good carers if we put her life at risk. I want her out tomorrow, or you go with her.'

Liz's ultimatum took Sean by surprise. He'd known that the discussion about Praew or him was coming and he'd been dreading the moment, but this wasn't how he'd expected it to come about.

'Is this about Praew and the things your lawyer said?' he asked in a more reconciliatory tone.

Tears started streaming down Liz's face as she turned to face him again. 'I don't know what to do. It's awful. I thought if I got angry with you it'd be easier for you to leave me,' she said.

'Liz, I love you, and seeing you like this is killing me. Praew's as much my responsibility as she is yours. We have to face it together and find a solution that we can both live with,' Sean said, pulling her into his shoulder.

'I know. I'm an idiot. Sorry. I just don't know what to do.'

Seeing Liz in this state churned Sean's stomach. She was the most together person that he knew and she'd been reduced to a blubbering wreck by this ludicrous situation. 'Promise me that you'll just be open about everything in the future. Then we can decide together,' he said, stroking her hair.

Nodding her agreement, Liz continued to cry. 'It's just not fair,' she said.

'I know, but we'll find a way through.'

After a few minutes Liz pulled herself together and stopped crying, lifting her head from Sean's shoulder. 'I still don't like her,' she said, wiping the tears from her cheeks.

'Okay, tomorrow,' Sean agreed.

'Good. You know she hinted that you'd been intimate with her to me before you came home, and then I saw you hugging her like that, what was I supposed to think?'

Sean was taken aback briefly. *Why would Anna hint to Liz that they'd been intimate? Besides some brief flirting, nothing had happened.* 'Liz, I swear nothing happened between us. I'd never do anything to hurt you.'

'Then why would she say it had?'

'I really don't know. I think she's recently divorced and lonely.'

'Well, she's not having you,' Liz said, reaching out and pulling Sean into her again.

Clinging onto her waist, Sean looked into Liz's dark eyes. 'I love you,' he whispered.

Back at the flat, Sean made a point of sitting as far away from Anna as possible and of making open gestures of affection towards Liz, who returned the same. By the time Clive and Terry arrived, the tension between Liz and Anna was palpable and Sean hastily gathered the group around the dining table to watch the video clips of the rally from the previous evening.

Watching the proceeding again made what they'd seen the previous night seem somehow more real. But Sean still found it hard to believe that this kind of thing still went on in Europe. All but Anna were overtly disturbed by the Nazi show of strength.

'What was he saying?' Clive turned to Anna.

'Just the usual Nazi rhetoric: blaming the Jews, the Romas and the Muslims for the problems in Europe, and saying that the time is coming; that they'll soon be in power; and they'll be able to right the Jew-led wrongs of the last 100 years.'

'Aren't there laws against that? Isn't it inciting racial hatred?' Sean asked.

Anna shook her head. 'In Germany, yes, but in the Czech Republic, no. That's why they have the rallies there. Most of the people attending were probably German though.'

'Yes, there were a lot of German plates and the people were getting changed before driving back,' Sean said.

'So Wagner can do this and just get away with it? What about all the armed militia there?' Clive asked.

'As long as they're used for private security, it's allowed.'

'What if we released the video on YouTube?' Sean asked.

'You could, but it'd just be one of many. Wagner doesn't hide from his Nazi ideology; he actively promotes it,' Anna responded.

'It's true. There's stuff all over the Internet on him, including videos at rallies like this one,' Liz added, not looking at Anna.

'What about that flag? The combination of the EU and Nazi symbols,' Clive asked.

'It's nothing new and people will just write them off as cranks,' Anna countered.

'So we're no closer to finding out who killed Phil and Allsop, and who tried to kill Anna and us. And we don't have a thing we can write about.' Sean exhaled loudly.

'I wouldn't say that. You've got pictures of Blom getting into Wagner's car in a quiet car park at night in Brussels, carrying an envelope, then leaving later without it. That should be enough to stop Blom,' Anna said.

'Yes, but as far as a story goes, and without more detail, it's a bit circumspect,' Sean said. 'It's more like a paparazzi job.'

'Really? It'd be big news in Sweden and the mainstay EU countries. People in Britain may not be so interested, but they're not the target market,' Anna said.

Momentarily, Sean crossed eyes with her. She was staring straight at him and he immediately wished he hadn't, as she took the opportunity to raise her eyebrows provocatively. Acting instinctively, he looked away and stroked Liz's hand, but he knew that the brief interchange hadn't gone unnoticed. 'It'll probably pay well, but I don't feel good about destroying somebody's life. Not without doing more checking,' Sean said.

'He's definitely involved. He has to be, and he did meet with Wagner. That couldn't be innocent,' Anna said.

'In truth, we only saw the car, not Wagner himself,' Sean replied.

'We know he was there, just as I know Blom is behind all of this,' Anna said, raising her voice slightly.

'She's right. The priority needs to be to stop this insidious mess that Blom is behind. People are getting killed. I know you'd rather find out more and make it the perfect story, but this time, I think you'll just have to publish a scandal piece and be done. If this Wagner character has some influence over a key EU official, lord knows what damage could be done,' Clive added.

It was nothing more than Sean expected from Clive:

intelligent as he was, he was still a policeman at heart, and stopping crime was always his first priority.

'Liz?' Sean asked, looking for a more balanced view.

'I'm not sure. I'll defer to your judgement,' she said.

'Sean, you really need to publish this, not just to stop Blom, but also to allow me to return to a normal life and go back to work. Otherwise, I'm a prisoner,' Anna pleaded.

'It's only half a story though. What about the others? What about Phil and Allsop? We haven't solved their killings,' Sean said, shaking his head, still unconvinced.

'Please, Sean, if nothing else, do it for me.' Anna reached out and put her hand on his.

As soon as he felt Anna's touch, Sean immediately withdrew his hand and looked at Liz, making sure that she knew he hadn't made the gesture.

'Are you happy that we don't follow up on Phil's death, Clive?' Sean asked, beginning to think that he was losing the argument.

'I'll keep the pressure on the Belgian police, but this is separate to that,' Clive responded.

'Please, Sean,' Anna said.

'Just do it, Sean. Then we can all get our lives back to normal,' Liz said, glaring at Anna.

It went against all Sean's instincts, but now he was the only one defending further work, and Liz had obviously realised that it was an opportunity to get rid of Anna for good. 'Okay, sod it!' he reluctantly agreed. 'I'll pad the story out a bit and take it to some editors. They'll probably ask for more, which I don't have, but it'll get published in a tabloid.'

Still unable to make any connection between Phil's or Allsop's death and Blom, or the attempt on Anna's life and Blom, Sean decided that it was just something he'd have to put down to experience and move on. There was too much at stake to do anything else. He wasn't about to lose Liz over any story, no matter how important.

Early in the afternoon, he crafted a short piece entitled EU COMMISSIONER LINKED TO NAZI LEADER and attached a few of the more telling photos: one of Blom getting into Wagner's car with the envelope; one of him getting out without it; and one of Wagner speaking at the rally in the Czech Republic. He wasn't happy with the story, because it left too many *why* questions unanswered, but he settled for it the way it was, and didn't offer any speculation beyond what the images showed, protecting his legal position. He didn't even mention the corruption in the translation department.

It took him less than two hours to sell the story to four newspapers in different countries, all with national exclusives. Even he had been surprised by the price he attained: at €20,000 per country. After costs, and splitting half with Liz, he'd still have €15,000 which would allow him to buy back 15% of the company from Liz.

Even though the story was a financial success, it still didn't leave him with a good taste. It was just an assassination, nothing else. Maybe Blom deserved it, Anna seemed sure, but to Sean it was an unfinished piece and that was something every good journalist hated.

Chapter Fifteen

Friday, 2nd September. London, England.

The piece hit the news in morning. By midday, Blom had resigned from his post in the Commission amid the scandal, which had broken out into a wider discussion about the extent of the powers the unelected European Commission held.

Anna was interviewed by the *BBC News* at Heathrow airport, before catching a flight back to Brussels. She commented that the power in the EU should be devolved from the state member cronies of the Commission, to the real elected representatives of the Parliament. Shortly afterwards, the British Prime Minister said much the same, renewing his commitment to EU reform.

Within a few days, the Commission President had also resigned, citing unacceptable changes in the power balance between the Parliament and the Commission.

Sean wasn't surprised when Clive announced that he was going to Brussels to visit the Belgian police regarding Phil's death. He was convinced that Blom was behind it and he wanted them to investigate it. While there, he also attended the coroner's hearing on Allsop, which confirmed the suicide theory that the police had put forward.

The European Commission was created to fulfil the role of the EU civil service. But unlike the UK Civil Service, which is politically neutral and its employees are legally barred from political party membership, the European Commission is led by its own political president and a group of 28 political commissioners, who each occupy a cabinet post.

This group of unelected political leaders is responsible for all of the EU's resources, including: the initiation and drafting of every EU law, and the management and allocation of the whole EU budget.

In the world today there are a number of states that follow the same system of governance and are ruled by unelected political leaders: The People's Republic of China and the Democratic People's Republic of Korea (North Korea) are just two.

PART TWO

Chapter Sixteen

Sunday, 24th January. London, England.

Kissing Liz on the cheek gently before standing and straightening his bow tie, Sean walked steadily through the tables, shaking hands before he climbed onto the stage to accept his outstanding journalism award: his second in just twelve months, albeit from a different organisation. Last time, he'd been in hospital and unable to attend the ceremony, or make a speech. This time, after clearing his throat, he thanked everybody that had helped him in his investigation of Lyle Walsh, the Baptist priest from Cornwall, who had since been arrested for a number of crimes, including extortion and embezzlement.

Then he turned his attention to what he really wanted to say and spoke about the plight of a thirteen-year-old Thai girl, sold into prostitution by her father at twelve and brutally raped every night for a year, until she was finally rescued by a loving British couple. Now the Home Office were trying to force that couple to return the girl into the same plight. He didn't mention any names, just the outline facts, but he knew that the room was filled with journalists and it would be followed up by at least one of them.

All the way home to their Fulham flat from the Mandarin Oriental hotel in Knightsbridge, Liz held onto his arm, leaning her head on him gently. 'That was very selfless of you, to use your time in the spotlight to help Praew, rather than further your own career,' she said.

Suddenly feeling good about himself, Sean bent his neck forward and kissed her on the forehead. 'It's the least I can do. You've been jumping through all the hoops with the idiots at the Home Office, while I've been gallivanting around having fun, chasing errant priests.'

A smile broke out on Liz's face. 'You were right about him,' she said.

'Yes, a nasty piece of work.'

'I can't believe his followers still supported him through the trial,' Liz said, as they arrived at the flat.

Sean took her by the waist gently as she stepped out of the cab. 'Praew's staying at your mum's, isn't she?'

'Yes, why?'

'Then how would you like to have kinky sex with a multi-award-winning journalist?'

'I can't think of anything I'd rather do more right now. Who were you planning on bringing over? I quite fancy that guy on *ITV News*,' Liz giggled, letting Sean pick her up and carry her into their apartment.

Waking up late in the morning and feeling the effects of the previous night's festivities, both in and out of the home, Sean pulled on a pair of boxer shorts and stumbled into the kitchen, where Liz was cooking eggs and bacon. 'That smells fantastic,' he said, sitting at the dining table and flicking on the TV.

Searching the stations, he quickly found the news, where the anchor was reporting on a fire in a warehouse, somewhere in East London. Sean looked down at the scars on his stomach and chest and thought about how much his life had changed in the last year. The elephant was still in the corner in his relationship with Liz, and they only had a few months left before they needed to make a decision, but they hadn't discussed it since that day in the car, both acknowledging that if they couldn't change it, then it was better left unsaid.

In a way, Sean thought that the Damocles sword that hung over their relationship had strengthened their bond, with both of them seeking to get the most out of it before the sword inevitably fell.

'Oh, what's that bitch been up to now?' Liz said, looking at the TV, where Anna Faustein was speaking to a reporter outside the European Parliament building in Strasbourg.

'Ms Faustein, why have the three parties merged?' the reporter asked.

'It's just a further evolution of Europe and a move to greater democracy,' Anna replied.

'Really? But doesn't it put a lot of power in one party: some 65% of the vote?' the reporter questioned.

'Yes, but we're democratically elected representatives of the people, rather than the unelected bureaucrats in the Commission,' Anna said.

'Why do you think you were chosen to lead this new mega-party, when you're a relatively unknown backbencher, and might I say, a lot younger than your peers?'

'I think the party sees in me a person that can lead them into the future, into a new Europe with closer and closer union between members.'

The interview broke off and the picture returned to the main anchor in the London studio. 'That was Anna Faustein, the newly appointed head of the Federal Party for Europe.'

Pulling a puzzled face, Sean switched the volume down as the weather came on. 'That's a bit strange, don't you think? When we met her, she was a staunchly anti-federalist backbencher. Now, only a few months later, she's the leader of a newly formed pro-federalist party, with 65% of the EU voting power.'

'What are you suggesting?' Liz asked.

'I don't know. It's just odd, that's all.'

'I hope you're not thinking of contacting her. Last time you had anything to do with her it nearly ruined our relationship.'

Liz's fiery reaction was anticipated and Sean sat back in his seat, formulating his response carefully. 'Liz, you know nothing happened, and look at us now: we're better together than we've ever been. I just smell a rat, that's all. Isn't that my job?'

Joining Sean at the table, Liz placed his greasy breakfast in front of him. 'What is it that you think she's up to?' she asked.

'I don't know, but I'd like to ask her a few questions about her sudden about-turn.'

'Okay, but I'm coming with you,' Liz said.

'I think we should doorstep her; give her no time to prepare,' Sean suggested.

'How? She'll be surrounded by the media now.'

'Let's use Clive again. He can watch her and let us know when an opportune chance appears.'

'Look at you, spending our money now that you're a 50% shareholder,' Liz laughed.

It had been a pleasing moment for Sean when he'd netted enough money from the Walsh piece to pay back Liz, and leave a little more to carry on. They still weren't far from bankruptcy, but they were at least on the right side of the line. 'Do you think we can't afford him?' Sean asked, misinterpreting Liz's response.

'I was joking silly. I think we should use Clive. He'll probably catch that bitch eating children, or something equally nasty.'

Chapter Seventeen

Monday, 1st February. Brussels, Belgium.

Both Sean and Liz had decided to leave it a week before travelling to Brussels, as they had a few things to follow up on the Walsh piece, and anyway, they wanted to allow some time for the hype around Anna to die down.

Travelling ahead with Terry to set up camp and establish a pattern for Anna's movements, Clive was glad to be back on the case, as he felt the death of Phil was still unresolved, his efforts with the Belgian police having fallen upon deaf ears.

'She's not in the same apartment anymore. She keeps a large house on Avenue de Lothier in the Woluwe St Pierre district, and either she's won the lottery recently, or she's living above her means. When I say a large house I mean a 16,000 square foot mansion, in the best district in Brussels,' Clive said, nursing a beer in the same café in Place Jourdan where they'd met previously.

'Can we get any background checks done on her: family money etc.? She wouldn't get a place like that on an MEP's salary.' Sean frowned.

'Already onto it. We should have some information tomorrow,' Clive answered.

'What's she been up to?' Sean asked.

'Working mostly. She's been at her offices until dinner each evening, then she dines with a steady stream of politicians, both national and EU. We've got pictures of everybody she's met with outside of work and home, but nobody out of the ordinary,' Terry reported.

'How about the house?' Sean asked.

'Ten foot high walls with barbed wire on top, permanent security on the gate, flat land… There's no way we can find out what's going on inside. Some cars come and go, but they all have privacy glass so we don't know who's in them, and unfortunately, my contacts don't stretch into the Belgian police, so we can't find out who owns them,' Clive said.

'How does she get to work?' Liz asked.

'This is where I think there's a chance: she runs,' Clive smiled.

'Perfect. Why just a chance?' Sean queried.

'Firstly, she's fast, and can probably outrun you if she wants to.'

Memories of the clumsy way she'd run away from the car in Place Jourdan crossed Sean's mind. Even though she was wearing heels it hadn't been the gait of somebody used to running, especially not somebody Clive considered *fast*. 'Are you sure? She seemed rather awkward on her feet before.'

'There are a lot of things about this Anna Faustein that don't compute with the timid woman who showed up in London. The second reason that the running route might not work is that she has her car follow her and can get in and leave at any sign of a problem,' Clive said.

'That's odd. I thought she was a bit chameleon-like before,

changing from the lost girl to the independent businesswoman in minutes. But why the act?'

'I don't know, but I'm telling you that the lost girl is long gone and she's now a woman who's in charge. It's in her walk, in the way she speaks to people. She's a formidable woman,' Clive said.

Before he left the hotel the next morning, Liz held onto him tightly. 'You know I don't like you being around her, Sean. She tried to steal you from me before and didn't even have the courtesy to hide it.'

'I know, but she's got no chance. I have the two most beautiful women in the world already. Why would I need another?' he said.

The journey from the hotel to the interception point only took ten minutes before Sean had to climb out of the warm car. He waited by a hedge, outside the park on the Avenue de Marquis Villalobar, in the faint light that emitted over the high walls from the mansions lining one side of the street. From his position, it was just possible to see the corner where Terry was hiding, ready to signal Anna's arrival. Banging his feet on the gravel path, trying to keep the blood flowing in the subzero temperature, he rubbed his arms up and down his sides in the heavy tracksuit, worn with a beanie hat, so that Anna wouldn't recognise him from behind when she approached.

In a weird way he was excited about seeing Anna again. He'd rekindled his relationship with Liz, partly as a result of her flirting, but that wasn't what it was: he knew the sensation; it was the thrill of the story; the chase for the elusive information that made the difference between a great story and a hollow report. And with Anna Faustein, Allsop and Blom *et al.*, he knew he had unfinished business. Now, Anna's sudden rise to fame gave him the perfect opportunity to re-open his enquiries.

Two quick flashes of a torch indicated that Anna was approaching, so Sean started to run at a steady pace along the gravel path that ran adjacent to the park. He was glad to be running, letting the feeling come back into his extremities as the blood flowed to them, and it wasn't long before he could hear Anna's footsteps approaching, then the lights of her car lit up the footpath in front of him. Three other runners had passed while he waited, so the sight of another person wouldn't be anything of concern for Anna, or her security.

Her controlled breathing suddenly came into earshot, as she moved up quickly behind him and her steps were fast and light on the gravel. Then, in no time, she passed him, striding away quickly.

'Anna,' he called out.

She spun around quickly and instinctively moved towards her car, then squinted. 'Sean?' she said. 'Is that you beneath that stupid hat? Have you been following me?' she smiled and leant against the car.

'Hi, Anna, I was hoping that I could ask you a few questions?' Sean said, suddenly feeling a little silly.

'You can if you can keep up with me. I have an early meeting,' she said, as she started to run again.

Sean quickly scrambled to catch up.

'You do know that the normal way to get in touch with me is to arrange a meeting through my office? Jumping out of the bushes near my house is a little weird,' she called out over her shoulder.

When he finally drew level with her, he was panting. 'Sorry. I didn't think I'd be able to get in to see you,' he said, lying to cover his embarrassment.

'Are you writing a piece on me, Sean?' Anna said, grinning.

'Maybe. It depends whether there's anything worth saying.'

'Oh well, I'd hate to be considered boring. Maybe I'll just make up some juicy bits for your readers.' She raised her eyebrows suggestively at him.

For some reason, Sean had expected Anna to be hostile towards him, but he was now unable to fathom why. They'd parted on good terms and agreed on an approach to the translation issues. Then it dawned on him: it was Liz. Because *she* held Anna in such contempt, Sean had somehow translated that into Anna thinking the same about him. Something that was obviously wrong, given her friendly reaction to his approach. He wondered whether she'd feel the same when he started to ask her questions.

'How did you go from an anti-federalist backbencher, to the head of the largest federalist party in Europe, in just five months?' he asked, between breaths.

'It's just politics, Sean. A woman has to do what she has to do,' Anna laughed, still breathing comfortably.

'What about your loyalty to Nick?'

'That was a sad episode, but I've moved on.'

'That doesn't sound like the caring Anna I met five months ago,' Sean said, surprised by the remark.

'Well, maybe I'm not that Anna anymore,' she said.

'What happened to your apartment? How can you afford such a grand house?' Sean switched tack quickly as Anna quickened her pace.

'My divorce settlement came through and I decided to treat myself. Besides, I live in Brussels full-time now, following my promotion, so a small apartment just wasn't suitable.'

'Do you ever think about who might have killed Nick?' Sean asked.

Slowing her pace a little, she turned to look at Sean. 'The coroner said it was suicide, didn't you hear?'

'I did, but I still don't believe it. Do you?'

'I don't know,' she said, slowing to a walk. 'I just don't have time to think about it anymore. Things are going well for me now and I want to make sure it stays that way. Raking over old memories won't help.'

Standing still on the footpath with her hands on her hips, she looked up and down Sean's body. 'You're in good shape considering your injuries,' she said.

'The physio regime was pretty brutal.'

'I see that your career is blossoming too. Congratulations on the award,' she smiled.

'How do you know about that?' Sean asked.

'I like to know what my friends are up to. That's what you are, a friend, aren't you? I'm assuming that you didn't come to Brussels to dig up dirt on me?'

'No, of course not, and yes, we're friends. I just wanted to ask how you had suddenly become so successful, that's all.' Sean forced out a fake laugh, feeling as if he'd somehow let her down by doubting her.

'I'm just lucky, I guess: only in work though, not in love. Are you still with Liz?' Anna shrugged.

'Yes,' Sean said, too quickly.

Suddenly, Anna stepped forward until she was only a few inches from him and looked up, her eyes searching into his. 'That's a pity. We could do great things together, you and I. Look me up if it all falls apart,' she said and kissed him on the lips.

When Sean moved back instinctively, Anna laughed, before turning away and running down to her car. 'Sorry. I've got a meeting. Next time, just call me and we'll meet for dinner,' she said, as she climbed into the rear seat of the black limousine and it sped away in the direction of the EU Quarter.

Chapter Eighteen

Monday, 1st February. Brussels, Belgium.

'So that's it? A complete waste of time?' Liz said in a satisfied tone.

'I'm afraid so. Everything she said seemed perfectly legit,' Sean said, sipping on a cappuccino in the small café, back in Place Jourdan.

'The sudden money?' Clive asked.

'Divorce settlement,' Sean replied.

'That's not surprising,' Liz added.

'How about the sudden change of political stance? Did she mention that?' Clive asked.

'Yes, she just said it was politics. She openly acknowledges that she's ambitious and that she did it to get ahead. To be honest, I don't think any of them have really deeply held views. It's all about their own careers, and they just say what makes them popular,' Sean said.

'Was she annoyed about being doorstepped?' Liz asked.

'No. In fact, she made a joke of it and said that in future I should just call,' Sean said, shaking his head. 'To be honest, it was embarrassing.'

'So, she wasn't angry at all?' Clive asked.

'No, she was anything but,' Sean said, avoiding eye contact with Liz.

'I think we're barking up the wrong tree. If she was hiding something, she wouldn't be so open,' Clive said.

'I agree. Much as I'd like to think that she's a fire-breathing witch, hell-bent on world domination, I think you're right: she's just an overly ambitious bitch. Perhaps that's what makes her so dislikeable,' Liz said.

'Okay, I guess we should find somebody else to write about then,' Sean conceded, frustrated by the lack of progress on his unfinished piece.

'How about Blom?' Clive suggested.

Both Liz and Sean looked quizzically at Clive. 'He quit and went back to Sweden,' Liz said.

'I still think he had something to do with Phil's murder,' Clive said. 'Losing his job wasn't quite the punishment I had in mind for him, if we can prove that he was involved, that is.'

Glancing at Liz, Sean tilted his head to one side, silently asking her what she thought. Liz shrugged her shoulders back in an equally silent reply.

'Okay, what do you suggest?' Sean asked Clive.

'I think we should visit him in Sweden and ask him a few questions,' Clive answered.

'You're not a policeman anymore, Clive. He doesn't have to cooperate, you know?' Liz said.

'I know. That's why I'm taking Sean. It's better cover,' Clive responded.

'Okay, what the hell. I've never been to Sweden. But you owe us for the flights if he just slams the door in your face,' Liz laughed.

'Done,' Clive agreed.

Chapter Nineteen

Tuesday, 2nd February. Stockholm, Sweden.

When the plane broke through the clouds on its descent into Stockholm's Arlanda airport, a sea of fresh white snow blanketed the city, making it look like some kind of fairy tale kingdom. Sean held Liz's hand as they landed and drew up to the terminal. It was 11 a.m. and they were due to fly back to London at 5 p.m. the same day, giving them very little time to find Blom and interview him.

Once again, Sean had chosen not to call ahead, in case it sent the corrupt Swede underground, or worse, brought out a welcome party of his Nazi friends. Walking out of the airport, they rented a car and made straight for the apartment that Liz's research had identified as Blom's current home.

Just over an hour later they crossed a bridge onto an urban island close to the centre of the city. The faded concrete block on Tantogaten, in the Södermalm district of Stockholm, had a smattering of poorly stocked shops underneath, and looked as if it was well overdue for demolition. At least half of the small windows overlooking the busy railway line were boarded up with plywood. As Terry pulled up by a group of teenage children with their hoods up, Clive and Sean climbed out onto the pavement.

'It looks like somebody's had a rapid fall from grace,' Clive said.

When they entered the apartment building, the smell of urine permeated the concrete stairwell and Sean held his nose trying to block out the foul stench, as they climbed to the tenth floor.

'1045, right?' Sean said, as they walked along the dimly lit corridor, with litter strewn all around it.

When they reached apartment 1045, other than the fact that there was a light on inside, a person could be forgiven for thinking that it was empty; abandoned by a group of squatters. Paint was peeling from the wooden door in large strands, and the small window looked as if it hadn't been cleaned in years. Clive quickly stepped forward and pushed the bell twice, then moved back, keeping Sean behind him.

'I hope he doesn't recognise you. I don't fancy having a tussle with a guy his size,' Clive said.

It had crossed Sean's mind that Blom might have researched him as the journalist who ruined his career. But that was something they'd just have to deal with if he had.

It took two more rings before Blom finally appeared in the hallway. Sean could see his lumbering frame moving slowly towards the door, through the opaque glass panel. When he finally opened it, he seemed to move in slow motion.

'Ja?' Blom said, stooping to look through the doorframe. He was wearing an old blue towelling robe wrapped around a vest, with dirty slippers and he hadn't shaved for days.

'Mr Blom, could I ask you a few questions?' Sean said, stepping out from behind Clive.

'Who are you and why do you come here?' Blom said in

English, showing no emotion on his face, the rancid stench of freshly drunk vodka emitting from his mouth.

'I'm a journalist writing a piece on some people at the EU and I wondered if you could give me some background.'

'I don't work at the EU anymore and I don't like journalists. Go away,' Blom said, still without a trace of emotion.

'We're looking into the death of a man in Brussels. He got knocked down near Place Jourdan,' Clive said.

'I already spoke to the Belgian police. I had nothing to do with it. Ask them.'

'Do you know Anna Faustein well?' Sean asked.

'No. Why?' Blom replied.

'Because we think that whoever killed the man in Place Jourdan, was really trying to kill her,' Sean answered.

'Probably a jealous boyfriend, I heard that she's a slut. What's it to you anyway?'

'The man that died was a good friend of mine and I'd like to know why he died,' Clive said, leaning forward and staring at Blom.

Suddenly Blom seemed to soften and he looked closely at Clive's face, obviously considering his next move. 'I'm sorry. Come in,' he said, showing them to a threadbare couch in his living room, while he dropped his mammoth body into a decrepit armchair. A half-drunk bottle of vodka sat on the side table next to him. 'How can I help you?' he folded his arms.

'This murder happened the day after you met with Wagner and it was very close to where you met. We think the two things might be related,' Clive carried on.

'If they are related, it's not via me. I didn't even know Wagner before I met him in the car.' An ironic expression crossed Blom's face.

'Then why meet him?' Sean said, somewhat puzzled.

'You wouldn't believe me if I told you,' Blom replied.

'Try me,' Sean countered.

'I met Wagner because I was doing a favour for somebody.'

'Okay, who?' Sean asked.

'Hans Glas, the fucking Austrian prick!' Blom seethed.

'I'm sorry. I don't follow,' Sean said.

'I had dinner with Glas and some other spineless MEPs earlier that evening, and Glas asked me to take some documents for a house he was selling to a car in the car park.' He looked up at the ceiling, clearly cursing something.

'The car that Wagner was in?' Sean asked.

'Yes, but I didn't know it was Wagner. Glas said it was his daughter's ex-husband and he didn't want to see him, that's why he asked me to take the papers.'

'Didn't you think that it was strange to meet in a car like that?' Clive asked.

'Yes, but he said it was urgent and, well, I didn't really have a choice. I owe Glas money; a lot of money. I did look at the papers before I delivered them and they were just as he said, house transfer documents, so I decided what harm could it do. And I've regretted that stupid decision every moment for the last five months.'

'What did you do when you saw Wagner?' Sean asked, still sceptical about Blom's version of events.

'Nothing. I didn't know who he was and he claimed to be Glas' daughter's ex-husband, just as Glas had said. He had a German accent; it made sense.'

'Why did you get in the car then? You could have just passed the document through the window,' Clive queried.

'Because he asked me to and offered me a shot of single malt. Unfortunately, I have a weakness for alcohol,' Blom admitted.

Surprisingly, Blom's story was starting to stack up, and Sean felt a welling of self-doubt building inside him. *Did I destroy a man's life in error?* he thought. 'Why did you owe Glas money?' he asked, fighting the growing sense of panic.

Again Blom shook his head ruefully. 'I have a gambling problem and I owed other, more dangerous people, money. Glas, I thought, had helped me out. Obviously I was wrong.'

'Why didn't you tell people this when the story broke about Wagner?' Sean asked.

'Because somebody made some very nasty threats against my family if I said anything, so I just left as quietly as possible.'

'Who made the threats?' Clive asked.

'I don't know. He was German and I assumed he worked for Wagner, so I thought the threat was credible. As you can see, my family left me anyway after what happened. My wife said she couldn't live with a Nazi, it would put too much shame on the children. The only thing left for me now is to make sure Glas doesn't get the family house.'

'You mean you still owe him money?' Sean asked.

'Yes, when I left the Commission I lost all of my income and the loan from Glas was secured against my house,' Blom replied.

'But he hasn't tried to repossess it?'

'No, he uses it to punish me. I receive a small unemployment benefit from the Swedish Government, three quarters of which I pay to Glas. It doesn't even cover the interest on the loan, so Glas holds the threat of taking the house from my wife and children over me.'

'Does your wife know?' Clive asked.

'No.' Blom shook his head.

Now beginning to feel sorry for the huge Swede, Sean was starting to think everything he'd said was believable and studying his current surroundings, he had little reason to lie. 'Why would Glas want you out?' he asked.

'I don't know, but the German representative took my post in the Commission, so maybe it was something to do with that.'

'Could it be anything to do with this?' Sean opened his laptop and showed Blom the excerpt from the bill that Allsop had given him, pointing to the sentence that mentioned Article 7 of the TFEU, and then the Swedish translation that Anna had pointed out.

'What is this?' Blom's face contorted with confusion.

'It's an excerpt from a bill that went through the European Parliament in September, before you left,' Sean said.

Pushing his rimless glasses up his nose, Blom studied the text more carefully. 'I recognise the bill, but this translation, no. I don't understand. It wasn't like this the last time I saw it.'

'Could it have slipped through without you noticing,' Sean continued.

'Possibly. I wasn't across everything. But this is dangerous,' he said.

'Anna Faustein said the same,' Clive added.

'What would she know? She probably never read a bill in her life. None of them do.' Blom raised his hands dismissively.

'What's dangerous about it?' Clive asked.

'If a member state is suspended, they can't vote in any of the forums until the suspension is lifted.'

'Rightly so,' Sean said.

'Yes, but if all of the power to suspend them rests with the Commission President, it could be misused.' Blom seemed less of the drunken wastrel now and was genuinely concerned about the bill.

'How so?' Clive asked.

'The majority of the members have long wanted to remove the unanimous vote of the European Council required for a treaty change. If they can somehow suspend the dissenting members for long enough to pass a unanimous vote of those left, to change the voting laws to simple majority, then European federalization could march forward without the brakes applied,' Blom responded, his eyes conveying the seriousness with which he spoke.

'I'm not a politician. If federalization does move ahead quickly, where would that leave the UK?' Clive asked.

'Like Idaho,' Sean said in a glib tone. 'We'd have no more say in the running of our country than Idaho does in the US. The British Government would be relegated to managing garbage collections.'

'It's true,' Blom added. 'In a federal Europe, the British vote would only be 8.4% of the total. It's too small to have any impact.'

'The British people won't surrender their sovereignty that easily. We'll leave the EU,' Clive said indignantly.

The impromptu outburst made Sean chuckle. He'd never seen Clive as the patriotic type; he was too clever and too considered.

'I'm sorry. Forgive me for being rude, but the United Kingdom gave away its sovereignty in 2008, when it ratified the Treaty of Lisbon. All that's left now is to tidy up the details,' Blom said.

'We can still leave,' Clive said, clearly still agitated.

'Yes, that's true, and Lisbon makes a member's right to leave the union clear.'

'Good,' Clive added for effect, as if he could personally invoke the UK's exit from the EU.

Thanking Blom for his openness, Sean stood to leave, but Blom didn't stand.

'You're Sean McManus, aren't you?' he said, staring at Sean's face.

The words temporarily paralysed Sean, but Blom didn't look angry, he seemed to be just asking a simple question. 'Yes,' he said, wondering whether he should have lied.

Standing quickly Clive positioned himself between Sean and Blom, but the enormous Swede didn't stand to cause trouble.

'Why did you hide in the car park and take photos of me that night?' Blom asked.

In the circumstances it was a very relevant question and Blom deserved an honest answer. Blom had been targeted because of the excerpt given to him by Allsop. *Was Allsop somehow involved with Glas? And was that why he'd been killed?*

'Nick Allsop gave us the excerpt I showed you and we assumed that you were involved in the changes, so we followed you,' Sean said truthfully.

'Allsop? But he killed himself before I finished?' Blom frowned.

'We think he was murdered,' Clive butted in.

'And you think I was involved in that also? I actually liked Nick. He was a difficult man, but he had integrity, something which is rare in the halls of power at the EU.' Blom raised his eyebrows.

'I did, but I don't anymore. Who do you think would want both Allsop and Faustein dead? Assuming the two are related that is,' Clive asked.

Deep in thought, Blom again shook his head. 'Glas seems to be the obvious choice if everything is related. He was certainly the person that finished my career, but I don't know why,' he said.

Sean thanked Blom for his time and shook his hand firmly. Then, just as he was leaving, Blom said. 'Keep me informed. I'd like to know how this turns out. Despite what you see, I would like some vestige of my life back. And if I can be of any help, please contact me.' He handed Sean a slip of paper with his phone number and email address scribbled on it.

In the car on the way back to the airport, Sean explained the conversation to Liz and Terry, and asked Clive whether he still believed Blom was involved in the deaths.

'No, I don't think so. He seemed genuine enough to me and his reasons for dropping off the letter were plausible. Besides, he has nothing left to lie for,' Clive responded.

'Where does that leave us?' Liz asked.

'Hans Glas would seem the obvious target,' Sean said.

'Agreed,' Clive commented.

Quickly searching her phone, Liz scrolled through a number of screens. 'He lives in Braunau-am-Inn, in Austria.'

'That rings a bell, but I'm not sure why,' Sean said.

'I think we should go there,' Clive suggested.

'Why?' Sean replied.

'To get some background on Glas. I doubt he's the same person at home that he is in Brussels.'

'Okay,' Sean said. 'Makes sense, I guess. Liz?'

'I'll go home. I don't want to leave Praew with Mum for too long, in case the Home Office come snooping. I can do the background work from there.'

'Done.' Sean nodded his head.

Chapter Twenty

Tuesday, 2nd February. Braunau-am-Inn, Austria.

After flying to Munich, they took the short drive east towards Braunau, crossing the Inn River into Austria at Simbach. 'This is the same route Hitler took in the Anschluss in 1938,' Terry said.

The comment surprised Sean. He saw Terry as more the action type rather than a history buff. 'Really?' he said.

'Yep, he was born here and apparently wanted to show off upon his victorious return,' Terry replied, as they drove into the main village square, with its colourful traditional buildings and cafés spilling onto the street.

That's it, Sean thought, suddenly realizing where he'd heard the name of the town before. *It's Hitler's birthplace.*

Quickly turning off the elongated square, they pulled up outside a small hotel, unloaded and checked in. Once in his room, Sean checked his email. Liz had sent some information on Glas.

Hi Sean,

Sorry I didn't want to come to Braunau, but at the moment Praew comes first, and frankly, it didn't seem like the right place to go. I think the real story is in Brussels.

I did a bit of background work on Glas while I was at the airport. He's 80! Born in Braunau and has lived there his whole life. Didn't go to university, worked as a butcher and then entered politics at the local level by becoming the Mayor of Braunau. Then became an Austrian MP as a member of the Freedom Front of Austria (a far-right group focussed on immigration and Austria First etc.). He served 24 years in the Austrian Parliament before losing his seat to a socialist MP. Two years later, he appeared as an MEP and has been one for 12 years. There are a lot of news clippings on him, but they're nearly all in German. I tried to translate a few using an online translator, but there was nothing of great interest, just the usual political meetings. One thing I did find odd was that the Freedom Front is strongly anti-Europe.

I found an address for him in Braunau too: 27 Münchenerstrasse.

I hope this helps.

Love Liz xx

Sean responded quickly.

Liz,

Thanks, that really helps. I'll let you know how it goes, but I'm with you: I don't really know why we're here. Clive's never let us down in the past though. Pass my love to Praew.

Sean x

After settling in, Sean joined Clive and Terry in a traditional *Bierkeller* for dinner. On the way there, he noticed a large boulder with a polished brass plaque, outside an empty building. The sign was in German, but he thought it claimed to be the birthplace of Adolf Hitler, marked like a tourist attraction.

'Why are we here, Clive? Wouldn't our time be better spent in Brussels following Glas?' Sean said.

'He comes home every Thursday evening and stays until Monday. In the meantime, we can do a little background checking on him. If he's up to anything unusual, I bet it's here, not there, where he's in the public eye,' Clive said.

It seemed logical, Sean conceded. He shouldn't have questioned Clive's logic, which was always sound.

After a couple of very large beers and a pork-knuckle dinner, Sean was falling asleep in his seat. Making his excuses, he decided to leave Clive and Terry in the beer cellar, while he returned to the hotel to get some sleep.

When he made his way out into the square, a group of youths had gathered around the fountain at its centre. He paid them no attention, but as he got closer, Sean noticed that they were skinheads, wearing 1980s' style ska clothes and Doc Marten boots laced up over their calves. They were drinking schnapps from the bottle and pushing each other around boisterously. A knot tightened in his stomach as he passed them, avoiding eye contact.

'Hey,' a voice shouted out from behind him, just after he'd passed.

Ignoring it, Sean kept his head down and continued walking.

'Hallo, Blondie, ich spreche mit Dir' the same voice called out.

Without understanding the words, Sean knew they were directed at him and again he just continued walking, picking up his pace.

Then one of the youths appeared in front of him from nowhere, forcing Sean to stop. The intruder was in his late teens or early twenties and had a muscular build, with a completely shaven head. He had the words '*Ich hasse Juden*' tattooed over his right ear. Even with his limited knowledge of German, Sean knew that it meant '*I hate Jews*'. Four other members of the gang soon gathered in front of him, as Sean stood still, looking for a way out.

'Bist Du taub?' the first of the group shouted at Sean.

'I'm sorry. I don't understand you,' Sean said.

'Er ist Engländer,' the first youth said and then shouted to the group that was still by the fountain. *'Roland, er ist Engländer.'*

Responding to the call, a young man in his mid-twenties came over from the fountain. He also had a completely shaved head and wore a green fishtail parka. Sean could see that he had tattoos all over his neck, but one stood out: it was just four characters, BR18, but it took pride of place in the centre of the elaborate artwork. 'So, *Engländer*, what do you make in the birthplace of the *Führer?'* The rest of the gang parted to allow the speaker to enter. By the deference they gave him, Sean could tell that he was the leader.

Pulling his hands out of his pockets slowly, Sean prepared

himself for a fight, quickly assessing his best option to get away. When a young couple came out of a café opposite the statue and looked at the group gathered around Sean, he quickly waved his hands in the air. 'Help!' he shouted. But the couple just lowered their heads and walked away.

'They are scared. They won't help you,' the skinhead leader said.

'What do you want?' Sean asked.

'I want to know why a fancy Englishman like you is in Braunau, the home of the *Führer?*'

'I'm just passing through. I have no business here,' Sean said.

'I don't believe it. There is nowhere to go from here for people like you. Why are you here?' the leader pushed.

'As I said, I'm just passing through,' Sean said a little more forcefully.

'Ich glaube er ist ein Jude, hast Du seine Nase gesehen?' the first of the gang interrupted causing the leader to smile.

'He thinks you're a Jew. He says you have a Jew nose. Is that true? Are you a Jew?' the leader spat out the word 'Jew' like it was dirt.

'No, I'm not. But, why would that matter?' Sean said, somehow feeling obliged to ask the rhetorical question of why it mattered.

Smiling sadistically, the leader pulled a flick knife from his pocket and opened it, pointing the blade towards Sean. 'Because if you are a Jew, you will soon be a dead Jew.'

Remembering how he'd fought David Findlow on the beach in Tuscany, Sean watched the blade of the knife intently. But he'd made mistakes in that fight and had been stabbed twice in the process. He hoped that the skinhead leader wasn't as skilled a fighter as Findlow, as adrenalin forced his senses into overdrive.

'Sieh Dir seinen Pimmel an,' the first gang member said, pointing towards Sean's groin.

'You say you're not a Jew. Prove it. Show me your dick. If it has the skin taken, I'll cut off the rest,' the leader said.

Panic welled in Sean's body. Even though he wasn't Jewish, he had been circumcised, but convincing one of these thugs that it was for medical reasons would be impossible. He balanced his weight between his two feet, preparing himself for the imminent lunge of the knife.

'Open your trousers,' the leader said, edging forward, wielding the knife in Sean's direction.

'No. Now let me go,' Sean said forcefully, in a last attempt to negotiate his way out of the fight.

Seemingly angered by Sean's resistance, the leader jabbed forward with the knife. But Sean was ready for it and moved back, comfortably out of its reach. This seemed to anger him more and he tried again, this time more aggressively, but Sean glanced his hand away with his forearm and the knife passed aimlessly by his side.

Seeing an opportunity while the leader was off-balance, Sean instinctively pushed him back and ran to his side, colliding with one of the other gang members, knocking him to the ground with his shoulder. It worked! A space opened up in the group and he charged through the gap, picking up his pace to a sprint.

Heavy footsteps pounded against the cobbles behind him, but Sean knew that he would be able to beat them in their heavy boots and the gap grew quickly.

As the noise behind him grew fainter, he continued to sprint in the direction of the hotel, with relief starting to make its way into his thought process. Just then, he felt a hard crack on his shin and he tumbled forwards onto the cobbled footpath, rolling three times before stopping face-down on the cobbles. When he looked back to see what he'd run into, he saw a leg with a Doc Marten boot, extended from a shop entrance.

Without warning, the boot's owner pounced on Sean, trying to pin him down, but Sean lashed out with his fists and knocked the young skinhead off him, springing back to his feet. As he scrambled to run again, the other skinheads arrived and grabbed him roughly by the coat and hair.

Still fighting and trying to escape, Sean was frog-marched by the group of youthful skinheads back to the leader, who hadn't given chase and was swigging schnapps from the bottle, still playing with the long flick knife.

'*Zieh ihm sein Hosen aus,*' he instructed his followers.

Terror was shooting through Sean's mind as he tried to get free, but it was no use: he was held still by four people, while a fifth undid his belt and pulled his jeans down to his knees, then the same youth pulled down his boxer shorts.

'*Keine Vorhaut. Jude,*' the undresser said.

'So, after all, you are a Jew,' the leader said.

Abject panic replaced any other feeling Sean had felt when the youth that undressed him dropped to the floor and held onto his legs. He was now held by five people. Escape was impossible.

'Now I'm going to cut your Jew dick off, so you won't be able to make any more Jew pigs,' the leader said, stepping forward and grabbing Sean's penis with his free hand.

'HELP!' Sean screamed at the top of his voice. 'HELP!'

'Hey!' he heard a shout from over his shoulder, but the leader didn't release his grip.

Suddenly Sean heard footsteps running towards them. 'Hey, let him go!' Terry's familiar voice shouted.

As Terry arrived, the leader stepped back, releasing his painful grip on Sean's penis and holding up the knife towards Terry.

'*Noch ein Engländer,*' the first skinhead said.

Taking his chance, Sean tried again to struggle free, but he was still held firmly in place.

'Let him go,' Terry said, stepping forward aggressively.

'Why? Are you going to fight us all? Jew pig!' The leader laughed, swinging the blade of the knife in Terry's direction.

Before he could finish his sentence, Terry reached out and grabbed the leader's wrist. Then in one swift movement he spun under the leader's arm, twisting it around his back and pulled the knife from his hand.

The leader cried out with pain as Terry forced his arm up past his shoulder blades and with his other hand, put the knife to his throat. 'Now tell them to let him go.'

Without the need for a translation, the other members let loose their grip on Sean, who hastily bent down and pulled up his trousers. Then, out of the corner of his eye, he saw another one of the gang reaching for a knife. Before he could open the blade, he fell forward at the knees and onto the cobbles. Clive stood behind him and put his foot back on the floor, as the other members of the gang moved away.

Moving Sean and Clive behind him, Terry threw the leader to the ground, keeping hold of his knife, as the leader scrambled to his feet and backed away.

'That was a mistake, Englishman. You don't know who we are,' the leader said.

Terry smirked. 'Really? You look like a bunch of idiotic children to me. Now fuck off, before I really get annoyed!'

'We'll find you Englishman, and your Jew friend,' the leader said, as he backed away, still facing Terry.

'I'm shaking in my fucking boots. This is your last warning. Fuck off!' Terry said, raising the knife again.

Grinding his teeth in anger, the leader turned and walked away quickly towards the other gang members.

'Thanks. You don't know how relived I am to see you,' Sean said feeling his crotch.

'Just kids,' Terry said, dropping the knife into a storm drain.

Just kids? Sean wondered what kind of people Terry had dealt with in his military career to classify this dangerous gang as *kids*.

'I don't know. I've seen their type before. Kids yes, but there's usually something more; some kind of club that they belong to, with far more sinister people behind it,' Clive added.

Back at the hotel, Sean called Liz and filled her in on the night's events.

'Come home. It's not worth it. There's something creepy about the Nazi undercurrents in this investigation. That's the third time it's come up,' Liz said immediately.

'I know. It's a like a time warp. I thought this lot died off a long time ago.'

'Sean, if it is some secret Nazi thing you've stumbled on to, it's dangerous and I'm worried. I'd rather you just did boring business reporting.'

'Come on. We knew that there'd be risks when we set this up. Clive and Terry are looking after me. And believe me, Terry isn't a man you'd want to cross; he didn't even blink when he fronted eight angry skinheads. Clive said he's some kind of ex-special forces, but doesn't like to talk about it.'

'Hmm. Be careful and don't take any unnecessary risks,' Liz said. 'And call me often, so that I know you're okay.'

'I will. How's Praew?'

'She's great. Loving school,' Liz replied.

'Anything from the Home Office?'

'No, but I'm sure they'll be snooping around some time.'

Braunau-am-Inn is a small town in Upper Austria, nestled on the banks of the River Inn, which forms Austria's border with Germany. There, on 20th April, 1889, Klara Pölzl gave birth to a male child. She and her partner Alois Hitler named their new son Adolf.

The quaint town of Braunau-am-Inn is now a mecca for so-called *Hitler tourism*.

Chapter Twenty-One

Tuesday, 2nd February. London, England.

Liz hated lying to Sean. She felt her throat tense as she told the lie, but she knew that he had enough to deal with already and committed to telling him the truth when he got home… if she could find the truth that was.

When she had collected Praew from school before, she'd waited at the gate for her to come out. Each day previously she'd emerged from the same door, beaming with pride at her achievements… but not today. Today, she'd emerged through a different door and scurried quickly across the playground, avoiding the other children.

'What's wrong?' Liz asked her.

'Nothing,' she said, taking Liz's hand.

'Why did you come out of a different door?' Liz questioned.

'No reason,' she said smiling.

At home, Praew had been more withdrawn than usual. She didn't want to discuss her day at school and curled up on the couch next to Liz, watching TV.

'Did something happen to you at school today?' Liz asked.

Eventually, after persistent questioning, Praew looked up. 'Okay,' she said, folding her arms. 'It's nothing, but some boys called me names and sang a silly song to me. It really doesn't matter; it's just names,' Praew said, tears forming in her eyes.

A sudden rush of anger came over Liz. 'What were the names?' she asked.

'Nothing really, it's silly,' Praew said.

'It's not silly if it upsets you, Praew. What did they say?'

'I feel stupid getting so upset by it. They called me "slant eyes" and they changed the words to a Coldplay song, singing that I was *"All Yellow"*.'

Liz felt her heart beating against her chest. They'd purposely enrolled Praew in the school because it claimed to have a lot of international students and they thought that she wouldn't experience any racism, the way Liz had in her school when her parents had moved to the UK. 'Who were they?' she asked, stroking Praew's hair.

'Some older boys,' Praew said.

'How old?'

'Fifteen.'

'English?'

'No, Russian,' Praew said.

'Is that all they said?' Liz asked, straining to hide the rising anger she was feeling and keeping her voice mellow, so as not to startle Praew.

When Praew didn't speak, but bowed her head noticeably, it indicated to Liz that there was more. 'Praew, darling, it's not your fault. They're horrible people. What else did they say?'

'They called me Thai whore and asked me to suck their dicks for £10,' she said, wiping the tears away.

After all Praew had been through with the Russians that had people-trafficked her to the UK, then forced her to have sex with violent old men, while she was near-starved to death and kept locked in a grubby room, naked and cold; to think that she was now being abused at a school, which sold itself as not tolerating racism, incensed Liz to her core! She knew that Praew was tough, she'd needed to be to survive, but she could see that this had really hurt her, maybe even more than the treatment at the brothel. She'd been so happy in the school, made new friends and had really settled in. Liz thought that she was finally starting to believe that life could be better; that she wouldn't always be surrounded by people that wanted to hurt her. Then this. This was ruining it for her, killing her first chance of a good life; a life without fear.

'What about your friends? Did they see it? Did they try to help you?' Liz asked.

Praew screwed up her face. 'No, they were scared. It's not their fault.'

'I know, darling.'

'One boy tried to stop them. William. I sit with him in geography.'

'Oh, that's nice. What happened to him?'

'They punched him,' Praew said. 'He's only small and not a good fighter, but he's very kind and clever too,' she added.

'Did any of them touch you?' Liz asked, suddenly dreading the answer.

'One boy grabbed my bum, but that's all. It didn't hurt and I kicked him on the leg.'

'Good! I hope it really hurt him.'

'It didn't. He just laughed,' Praew said, attempting a weak smile.

'Did you tell a teacher about it?' Liz asked, still controlling the rage that was bursting inside her.

'No, it'd just make it worse. They're not scared of the teachers. Their families are very rich and they do what they want.'

'What are their names? I'm going to talk to the head teacher,' Liz said.

Praew sat up immediately and looked into Liz's eyes. 'Please don't. You'll make it worse. They'll pick on me all the time if you do.'

The fear Praew showed almost made Liz burst into tears, but she pulled Praew into her chest and held her tightly. 'Okay, darling, I won't. But you have to let me know if it gets any worse, Okay?'

'Okay,' Praew agreed, smiling properly for the first time since she'd got home.

After she'd put Praew to bed and spoken to Sean, Liz started work, but she wasn't researching elderly MEPs from Austria that might have Nazi ties. Her work was much closer to home: she was looking for Russians who sent their children to Praew's school.

Chapter Twenty-Two

Thursday, 4th February. Braunau-am-Inn, Austria.

A whole day had passed since the altercation with the youth gang and Sean's nerves were starting to recover, but not to the point where he felt safe wandering the streets alone. He, Clive and Terry had spent the day tracing the life of Glas: they'd visited the impressive wooden chalet on the edge of town that he called 'home', and watched as his wife cleaned the steps, and welcomed what they assumed were her children and grandchildren. She just looked like an ordinary grandmother going about her daily chores.

Then they watched his constituency office in the centre of town: people came and went for the hour they stayed, but nothing stood out. In the evening, they dined in a small Italian restaurant on the German side of the river, hoping not to run into the skinhead gang from the previous night. It was a good decision and they managed to get a good night's sleep in preparation for the following day.

Today was the day Glas was due to arrive from Brussels. Clive's intelligence said that he usually left Brussels at midday and made the journey by train. If they were correct, Glas would arrive at 5:15 p.m.

As the red regional OBB train pulled into the platform at Braunau station, Sean scanned the doors, waiting for Glas to emerge. But only three people got off when the doors opened and none were over forty; none were Glas. When he stood to leave, a door opened at the far end of the train, first class, and an old man stepped carefully onto the platform. Sean instantly recognised the man who had dined with Blom in Place Jourdan, but if they were looking for the leader of a plot to take over Europe, he seemed an unlikely candidate.

Although spritely for his age, he was still an old man and didn't project the image of ambition that would be required for something so daring. He was dressed in a long traditional Austrian overcoat, thick rubber-soled shoes, and on top of his head he had a traditional trilby style green hat, with a feather coming out of the headband. Walking at a steady pace, he went into the train station and passed straight through, out onto the street, where his wife was waiting for him in a green Volkswagen Golf. Without greeting her, he placed his suitcase into the boot and climbed in.

Across the car park, Sean slipped into the rental car where Terry and Clive waited.

The short drive to Glas' house took less than five minutes on the quiet streets of Braunau. Once Glas was inside the house, Terry pulled the car to a point beyond the entrance and they waited for him to come out again.

At 7:30, Glas emerged from the side door of the chalet and went into his garage. Seconds later he pulled out in an old black

Mercedes 600, causing Terry to laugh. 'Well, if we're looking for a future dictator, he's already got the car,' he said.

Following the three-minute drive into the centre of town, Glas stopped right in the middle of the town square in a no-parking zone, then proceeded to clamber carefully out of the car. Without locking the door, he walked into the same beer cellar in which Sean, Clive and Terry had eaten dinner on the first night.

Continuing past the old vehicle, Terry pulled around the corner and parked in a parking space, away from the main square. When they rounded the corner into the square again on foot, Sean saw that some of the youths from the first night were hanging around the fountain again. Lifting the collar on his jacket, he tucked in behind Terry, as they went through the ornate carved door of the historic *Ratskeller.*

The smell of beer, sausages and sauerkraut filled his nostrils as he went through the inner door and into the warmth of the hall. He immediately spotted Glas in a booth against the far wall. The elderly MEP was with three other men of roughly the same age. All four wore traditional Austrian dress, complete with lederhosen, and four large beers sat on the table in front of them. They were talking energetically, with Glas waving his arms in the air, between gulps of beer.

An hour or so later, the four old men then took up positions on the band podium and started to play their various traditional instruments, with Glas on the accordion. It was all Sean could do to stop himself from laughing.

Obviously not sharing the same reservations, Terry began chuckling at the sight and swinging his beer to the *umpah* music. He turned to Clive. 'Are you sure? They don't exactly look like terrifying master criminals at the moment!'

'Do you think that Blom might have given us a bum steer?' Sean laughed.

'Don't get too cocky. He might be packing an Uzi in those leather pants,' Clive chuckled.

After playing three sets, and drinking three litres of beer, which Sean considered quite a lot for an eighty year old, Glas bade his musical friends farewell and walked unsteadily out of the bar. Once outside, he staggered across to his car and literally fell into the driver's seat.

'For a politician, he doesn't seem to have much respect for the law,' Clive said.

As he drove away, Terry sprinted around the corner to get the car, but then, all of a sudden, Glas stopped, next to the large fountain that dominated the main square.

'Shit, he's pissed and he's going to have a go at those thugs. We may need Terry,' Clive said.

About ten metres from the fountain, Glas wound the window down on his old Mercedes with his left hand and said something to the youths. But rather than rush forward aggressively, as Sean had expected, the leader of the youths walked to the car window, alone, and began a conversation with Glas. In the scenario — old man wearing funny pants meets skinhead gang leader — this wasn't how Sean had expected it to turn out.

The leader of the group appeared to be positively deferential towards Glas, nodding at the old man's comments, while seemingly being told off. Then Glas handed him a piece of paper, which the leader pocketed quickly and moved back from the car. Glas then closed his window and sped away, careering around the corner at the end of the long town square, swerving onto the wrong side of the road as he did.

'Let Glas go. Let's follow the skinheads,' Clive said, watching the gang, as Terry pulled up to them.

They stayed in the car, watching the group of youths from a safe distance, while the leader gathered three other members of the gang and walked in the opposite direction from them, then turned off the square. Carefully trying not to be seen, Terry pulled forward to the corner, where they had a clear view down the street that the group had turned down. The four skinheads climbed into a beaten old pickup truck; all four of them squashed onto the single bench seat in the front.

When they pulled away, Terry followed from a distance, just keeping sight of the rear lights, but not close enough to be discovered. A few minutes later, they turned onto the main road that ran along the riverfront and drove north. The battered old pickup truck stayed on the same road for around ten minutes, before pulling off and stopping outside a small cottage, nestled in a hamlet of just a few houses.

Pulling in, Terry stopped the car and turned off the headlights.

In front of them, the four skinheads jumped out of the vehicle clumsily and walked to the rear, where they pulled various tools from the back: a pickaxe handle; a lump hammer; a saw chain; and a something that looked like a scythe.

'Something nasty's going down,' Clive said.

As quietly as possible, they got out of the car and ran to the fence of the small cottage, using the high hedge as cover. A chill ran down Sean's spine when the leader of the group banged on the door using the pickaxe handle.

A few moments later, a small boy answered the door and then quickly tried to slam it again, but the leader put his foot into the open space, pushing the boy aside and entering the hallway, followed quickly by his three fellow gang members.

'Shit!' Terry said, as he ran forward, towards the house.

Struggling to keep up, Sean and Clive followed and caught up with him at the front window of the house. Inside, a young couple in their thirties, stood in front of their two children, shielding them from the group of thugs. The leader was pointing the pickaxe handle at the father and shouting, but the father didn't respond. To his side, one of the other gang members was taunting his wife with the scythe, prodding at her breast and side with the sharp rusty point. The two children, who were both under ten, huddled together with tears streaming down their round cheeks.

Suddenly, the leader swung the pickaxe handle around and struck the father on the kneecap, producing a stomach-churning scream of pain, as he fell to the floor. Yelling at the leader, his wife immediately bent down to help, but as soon as she reached him, she was pulled back viciously by the hair and thrown to the floor.

'Okay, that's enough,' Terry said, as he stood and knocked on the window.

Startled by the noise, the leader turned to face him, just as Sean and Clive also stood. A look of utter incredulity crossed the leader's face, as he registered the three unexpected visitors. After a few short words to the father, who was on the ground, clutching his knee, the leader moved into the hallway and then opened the front door.

As the door swung open, the leader thrust the pickaxe handle wildly forward making huge swathes in the air until he was in the garden. Laughing at the manoeuvre, Terry simply stood back and watched him, until his three companions joined him on the compact lawn. In his peripheral vision. Sean saw the father push his wife and children out through the back door and into the car, before he limped to the front door to see what was happening.

In the garden, the four skinheads were holding their weapons up at the ready, but keeping their distance from Terry, clearly wary of his confident posture.

'What's wrong? Scared?' Terry taunted, with his hands on his hips.

Sean stepped forward to help, but was quickly pulled back by Clive. 'If he needed help he'd ask. It's still not a fair fight yet. There'd have to be at least ten of them,' Clive smiled, as if enjoying the spectacle.

'What are you doing here, Englishman? Go now and you can live. Stay and we'll have to kill you,' the leader said, brandishing his weapon again.

The display amused Terry and he laughed loudly again. 'And how exactly do you think you're going to do that? All I can see is four idiotic creeps with farm tools that they don't know how to use,' he said.

Terry's confidence was clearly unnerving the leader's other gang members and they were backing away towards the gate slowly. When he noticed that he was being left alone, the leader also started to back away. Once he'd reversed through the gate, he stopped and made a pistol shape with his fingers, pointing it at Terry, before pretending to shoot him.

If it was meant to be a warning to Terry, it didn't work. He made a comical joke of being shot, before lurching forward towards the gate causing the skinheads to run away to their truck.

Once the thugs had gone, the father fell to the floor clutching his knee again. 'Thank you,' he said in English.

'What was that about?' Clive asked.

'My son got into a fight at school with another boy: the grandson of a powerful man and he sent this gang to take revenge.'

'Really? All this over a playground fight?' Clive asked.

'This family are people who don't like to lose at anything, let alone a fight,' the father said.

'Don't tell me: the Glas family,' Sean said.

The man's eyes closed momentarily. 'Yes. You know them?'

'Not really. What can you tell us about them?' Sean asked.

The father dropped his eyebrows suspiciously. 'I'm sorry, who are you? Why did you come to my house?'

'I don't blame you for being suspicious, but we're not here to harm you. I'm a journalist and I'm looking into Hans Glas' life,' Sean said, holding up the palms of his hands.

After surveying the three strangers on his lawn, the father nodded and was joined by his wife and children. 'We only moved to Upper Austria six months ago from Klagenfurt, in the south, so we don't know much.'

'We know that the Glas family act like they own Braunau,' his wife said. 'The old man drives around in that stupid Mercedes, the type the African dictators drive, and just ignores all road signs and parks anywhere he likes, and the local police do nothing about it.'

The image of him parking in the main square and then staggering to his car drunk came to Sean's mind. 'Why is that?' he asked.

'Because he has powerful friends: the *Bürgermeister* — sorry, mayor — is his close friend. They play music together in the beer hall,' the wife added.

'The only reason they let them play is because they dare not tell them they can't, and they really are all bad musicians,' the father said.

'Why did your son get into a fight with the Glas boy?' Clive asked.

The father said a few words to his son in German and the son replied quickly. Then the father began to translate, but he didn't need to; they'd all understood the German. 'Because he called him the son of a Jew pig and my wife a Jew whore.'

'Are the family openly anti-Semitic?' Sean asked.

The father shook his head. 'I'm not sure about the old man, the MEP. I think he tries to stay out of it because of his position, but his son, Joseph Glas, is nothing more than a street criminal. Also, we're not Jewish, but it's just what they call somebody when they want to start a fight.'

'I think it would make sense if you went away for a while, in case those thugs come back,' Terry said.

'We were already thinking of moving back to Klagenfurt. Braunau is a strange place,' the father said.

'In what way?' Sean asked.

'Because it's the birthplace of Adolf Hitler, it attracts some weird people. They come here to revere the memory of Hitler, not to condemn it,' the father said. 'There are a lot of neo-Nazis in this area. Before we moved here, we thought that it was just nonsense; that people today didn't hold such extreme beliefs, but unfortunately it's true. Most of the visitors here are from the former Soviet-backed countries, and they openly show their Nazi loyalty.'

'The four young men that were here, are they part of some fascist club?' Clive asked.

'I think so. They have an old farmhouse by the Lachforest, near Ranshofen, where they seem to live. We were told by friends to stay well away from it.'

Clive took directions to the house and they stayed with the family until they had packed some bags and left the small cottage, bound for Klagenfurt.

'What are you thinking?' Terry asked Clive on the way back to their hotel.

'I think we should pay their club a visit tomorrow,' Clive said.

Despite fighting against the Nazis in the Second World War, with the loss of over twenty million lives, Russia and Ukraine are still believed to hold the largest numbers of neo-Nazis in Europe.

Chapter Twenty-Three

Thursday, 4th February. London, England.

Liz stared at the screen on her laptop. Having narrowed her search down to six boys that were in the right year in Praew's school, one name stood out from the page and scared her; Nikolai Koryalov. She had reviewed brief notes on Vladimir Koryalov that she'd made when she suggested him as a target for their first investigation and noted that he had two children: a fifteen-year-old boy, Nikolai; and a twelve-year-old girl, Ekaterina. She kicked herself for not checking where they went to school.

Nikolai's Facebook page was easy to find, and like most teenagers who used Facebook, regardless of the age policy, he hadn't protected it in any way, wanting the world to see how great he was. He was a good-looking boy, with dark brown hair, cut in a modern style, and his tall slim body was well-dressed in expensive designer street wear. The comments on his profile were in a mix of languages: some Russian, some English and some French. When she opened the photo albums, Liz was surprised by the extravagant lifestyle on show for such a young boy: there were photos of him in St Tropez on a superyacht, drinking champagne, accompanied by bikini-clad women that were clearly much older than him; then more in Courchevel, in a lavish ski chalet, again drinking champagne, with a bevy of older women; then he was driving a Ferrari… in London. One thing that was common in each photo, other than the constant presence of women in their early twenties, was that there were no adults present.

Although Liz had also grown up in a very wealthy family, her childhood had been very different from the one on display here. A quiet and educated English father and a traditional Korean mother had seen to it that the benefits she gained from the family wealth had been strictly focussed on education and manners. She couldn't imagine how much trouble she'd have been in if she'd been seen behaving like Nikolai Koryalov.

Continuing to scan the photos, she found an album from the UK. Nikolai was in a nightclub with two other boys of roughly the same age. The table in front of them was filled with bottles of vodka and mixers, as the three teenagers grinned into the camera. Liz pushed the mouse over their faces: Vadim Dementyev and Arkady Belov. She clicked on Vadim's profile first. Although he claimed to have *previously* attended Praew's school, the same way Nikolai had, it was clear he was a pupil there. Arkady's profile was the same: a *previous* pupil of Praew's school.

Could these three be Praew's bullies? They certainly fitted the profile: Russian; rich; and they looked to be out of control.

She turned her attention to Vladimir Koryalov, a previously unknown colonel in the in the SBP, the Russian Presidential Security Service, who had suddenly appeared in London with billions to spend. The exact origins of his money were the subject of much speculation, but the strongest rumour was that it was actually the President's money, and Koryalov was merely a trusted guardian, investing it for the President, ready for his future life outside Russia.

After studying an online image of him, she flicked back to his son's Facebook page and searched the photos. She had to search hundreds before she found one with Vladimir Koryalov in it, giving her proof that Nikolai was indeed his son. She expanded the image on her screen. They were in a restaurant and Nikolai was holding a bottle of Petrus towards the camera. In the background, his father was deep in conversation with another man, but Liz didn't recognise him.

That afternoon, she arrived early to collect Praew and stood in a position that gave her a good view of all of the exits from the school. At 3:45 on the dot, the bell rang and hordes of children suddenly started to pour out of the exits, wrapped in coats, with schoolbags slung over their small shoulders.

There were so many children, Liz was struggling to assess them all, then through the door on the far right, Nikolai Koryalov emerged, followed by Vadim Demetyev and Arkady Belov. The three of them had either already changed out of their school uniform, or didn't wear it in the first place. They were walking slowly across the playground, pushing each other around. It was obvious that other children went out of their way to avoid them, stepping aside until they'd passed by.

On the other side of the building, Praew came out of the door carrying her bag in front of her body. Liz could see that she was scanning the playground, but she wouldn't be able to see the boys among all the other children, she was just too short.

As Praew walked carefully across the tarmac, Liz calculated that she was on a direct collision course with the three Russian boys. Rather than step forward, she pulled back and hid from view behind the gatepost. If they did run into each other, it would give her the proof she needed; the proof that she'd identified the right boys.

As she grew nearer to them, Praew caught sight of the group of boys and slowed her pace. *I'm right. It's them.* Then Belov suddenly saw Praew and pointed her out to the other boys. They immediately started making their way towards her, but, when she saw them, Praew began to run in the direction of the gate. Just as she arrived at the gate, the boys arrived behind her.

'Hello, sucky fucky time. Thai whore,' Dementyev shouted.

'Ready for my big Russian dick?' Belov added.

'No, she's not,' Liz stepped forward from behind the post and grabbed Praew. 'Now leave her alone or I'll have you expelled,' she said.

Koryalov moved forward to within two feet of Liz. 'Look boys, the Thai whore has a Thai whore mother. You want some big Russian cock in the sideways cunt of yours, whore?' he said, grabbing his crotch and pushing it towards Liz.

Her pulse was racing as she moved Praew behind her. The other mothers collecting their children avoided eye contact, pulling their children away quickly. 'First, little boy, you wouldn't know what to do with it; and second, I doubt it's as big as you think it is.' She held her stare, fighting the fear pulsating through her body.

Koryalov blushed. He obviously hadn't been expecting Liz to stand up to him. 'You want to try it, bitch?' he said, looking to his friends for affirmation.

'Yeah, stick it to her, man,' Belov said.

'When you get rid of your acne and don't smell like a fight in the Brut factory, you can talk to me politely, until then, stay well clear. And if you even so much as utter a word to my daughter again, I'll cut your minute Russian dick off your spotty Russian body. Do you understand?' Liz took a step towards him.

Koryalov instinctively stepped back. 'You don't know who you're messing with, cunt!' he said.

Liz smiled. 'Really? You can tell Colonel Koryalov that we know where his money comes from. Now get in your car and fuck off!' Liz pointed to the blue Bentley limousine that had pulled up by the kerb.

Koryalov didn't take his eyes from Liz as he walked to the car and climbed in, followed by his two friends.

'Bitch cunt!' he shouted out of the window as the car pulled away.

Liz lifted her hand and wiggled her little finger at him, indicating that he had a small penis. The gathering of children that were watching laughed and repeated the gesture.

After the car pulled away, Praew stepped around and held on to Liz tightly. 'Thanks, but it really wasn't necessary,' she said, craning her neck backwards, looking up at Liz's face.

Stroking her hair gently, Liz looked down at Praew inquisitively. 'When I was at school some people bullied me and called me names like "chinky". They used to pull their eyes with their fingers and make them thinner. It used to really upset me. I was desperate for my parents to do something, but they just said it was something I had to deal with myself and I had to stand up to them.'

'I'm sorry. If I was there I'd have beaten them up for you,' Praew said, pulling Liz tighter.

'If they bother you again, you need to tell me,' Liz replied.

'They won't,' Praew said confidently.

The comment puzzled Liz and she looked down frowning.

'I already fixed them,' Praew smiled, showing her teeth.

'What? How?' Liz asked.

'I did what Dad would do. William filmed them taunting me and pushing me around and we posted it on YouTube and tagged it to their Facebook pages. By now everybody in school and all their Facebook friends will have seen it, and soon they'll have no friends.'

Stunned by what she'd said, Liz considered Praew's words for a while, then a smile broke out on her face. 'That's brilliant!' she kissed Praew on the forehead.

Chapter Twenty-Four

Friday, 5th February. Braunau-am-Inn, Austria.

The icy wind bit into Sean's face as he waited for Terry to pull the car around to the front of the hotel. A fresh layer of snow covered the ground and wedged itself against walls and doorways in deep drifts. Despite being chilled to the bone, Sean was beginning to feel a renewed sense of optimism that they weren't chasing shadows and that here was indeed a good story somewhere in the information they'd uncovered. But what it was, he was still unsure.

Ranshofen was a small town adjoining Braunau, with a large forest taking up its southern border. Progress was slow in the deep snow, but they were soon passing the huge aluminium-smelting works that the father from the previous evening had told them to look out for. They were deep into the dense woods when Clive pointed to his right. 'That's it. Pull past. We'll walk down,' he said.

Luckily there were no other cars on the road in the fresh snow and Terry pulled the car off the street, into a nearby layby.

The house they were looking for was supposed to be at the end of a long dirt road, hidden in the forest.

Rather than walk up the road, they made their way slowly through the forest, keeping the dirt track in sight. About 200 metres in, Sean saw what they were looking for: an old decrepit farmhouse, set in a clearing in the woods, surrounded by a high barbed-wire fence. Terry quickly indicated that they should stay low and be quiet, as they crept nearer to get a better view.

When they got closer to the fence, they could see people moving around inside the farmhouse through the filthy windows. The gate to the house was also high, with barbed wire on top and locked with a thick chain. A large red sign attached to the wire read *"Betreten verboten"*, which Sean assumed meant *'no trespassing'*. The image, which accompanied the sign, of a man hanging from a noose, was more disturbing though.

As Sean stepped forward, he felt the ground give way slightly and a large stick broke under his weight. The crack of sound shattered the previous silence and Sean, Terry and Clive froze, holding their breath, hoping that it hadn't been heard inside the farmhouse.

Only seconds later their hopes were broken and two Dobermans came running from a kennel on the front veranda, barking loudly.

'Was ist los? Blöder Hund.' A man that Sean recognised as the first to approach him in the square a few days before, shouted out, stumbling through the door. Even though it was only 9 a.m., he was drinking from a schnapps bottle.

The dogs were salivating and jumping against the wire fence, only thirty metres from where Clive, Sean and Terry lay in the snow, hiding behind the foliage.

When the youth produced a key from his pocket and started

to walk towards the gate, Terry got to his knees. 'He's letting them out. Let's go.'

Reacting immediately, Clive and Sean sprang up and started to run in through the woods towards the car, with Terry following behind them. The deep snow was slowing them down though and Sean fell twice within twenty metres.

'Halt!' a voice shouted out behind them.

The car was only 100 or so metres away, when the gate opened and the dogs were released.

'They're going to catch us,' Sean shouted.

'Keep going. Dobermans are thin; they're not snow dogs. They'll struggle with this stuff as much as we will,' Terry said, pulling Clive up from the snow.

When Sean looked back, he realised that Terry was right: the dogs were sinking into the snowdrifts and making heavy work of it, but they were still gaining ground. Summoning up every bit of strength he could to speed up, Sean tumbled again and rolled into the deep snow, instantly righting himself and carrying on.

The car was only thirty metres away, but Sean could hear the snarling of the dogs just behind them. They weren't going to make it.

'Keep going!' Terry shouted, as he turned to face the dogs.

Acting instinctively, Sean turned around as the first of the dogs jumped up at Terry, then the second bit into his leg; tearing through his jeans.

'Go!' Terry shouted, as he fought the first dog, letting the other bite his leg without hindrance.

'Get the car,' Sean shouted to Clive, as he sprinted back and grabbed the second dog by the neck, pulling it from Terry's leg. Thick red blood squirted into the snow as the teeth came free.

'Pull its front legs apart,' Terry shouted, still grappling with the first dog.

The second dog jumped up at Sean, knocking him onto his back. He fumbled with his arms at full stretch on the dog's neck, stopping it from biting his face, but the snow was making it impossible to get any kind of grip, as the dog lunged downward again; this time its lower teeth scraping Sean's cheek. He knocked its head upwards with his forearm, protecting his face.

Undaunted by the hard smack to the head, it lunged again, saliva dripping from its teeth. Sean swung his leg up, striking it hard in the testicles with his foot. A painful yelp replaced the aggressive growl and Sean took the opportunity to grab its two front paws. His hands were slipping from the cold wet fur, but then, summoning all his strength, he managed to get a firm grip and pulled them apart.

The bone breaking sound as the dog's rib cage parted was vile and the injured animal fell to the ground, whimpering, helpless in the deep snow.

Turning to Terry, Sean jumped up again. He was trying desperately to grab the dog's legs, but his blood-soaked hands were just slipping helplessly from its fur. His face was almost fully covered by its salivating mouth, as it increased the pressure, biting deep into his flesh and blood was gushing from his leg. He glanced over his shoulder to see the approaching skinheads, no more than fifty metres away.

Repeating the move he had made on the previous dog, Sean kicked it hard in the testicles, causing it to immediately release its grip and turn to face him. As it did, he heard the same sickly bone break and whimper… Terry had finally pulled its legs apart.

The snow around Terry was blood red, and he continued bleeding heavily from cuts to his head, neck and leg. Taking his weight, by looping his arm around him, Sean started to drag him towards the car, where Clive had the doors open and the engine running. Finding strength that he didn't think he had, Sean managed to get Terry into the car, just as the first of the group of skinheads arrived.

As the bald-headed youth charged forward, Sean swung his fist wildly in his direction, connecting with his jaw. He didn't feel the impact; his hand was numbed by the cold, but it had the desired effect as the youth fell backwards into the snow, allowing Sean enough time to get into the car and lock the door.

Two more skinheads battered into the side of the car, banging on the window, but it was too late, Clive spun the wheels and pulled the car away, leaving them yelling and kicking out at the small vehicle.

'He needs a hospital. He's losing blood fast,' Sean said.

'We can't take him to Braunau. You heard what they said last night,' Clive replied.

'What about over the bridge into Germany: Simbach-am-Inn?'

Acknowledging Sean's suggestion, Clive forced his foot to the floor, speeding the car along the road in the snow.

In the rear of the car, all three wounds were bleeding heavily and Sean tried to stop each in turn, trying to keep Terry still, as the car skidded from side to side on the slippery surface. 'How's he doing?' Clive asked, as he swerved around another corner.

'Losing consciousness,' Sean said.

'Don't let him sleep,' Clive said.

Following Clive's warning, Sean tried to talk to Terry, who in turn was trying to speak, but bubbles were coming from the wound to his neck and no sound came out.

As the car screeched across the bridge over the River Inn,

Terry's head dropped to the side. Sean slapped him on the arm, trying to wake him, but he couldn't; Terry wasn't responding and he quickly felt for pulse, but couldn't find one.

A sign with a red cross on it, saying '*Krankenhaus*' made Clive swerve to the right off the main road. Two minutes later, he pulled into the emergency entrance of a hospital and jumped from the car.

Two staff members ran from the door and helped Terry onto an A&E bed, before wheeling him inside and straight through to the emergency theatre, followed closely by Sean and Clive. When they arrived at the theatre, they were abruptly halted and told to wait outside.

'Damn!' Clive said, as he took a seat in the corridor and felt his prosthetic hand. Further down, Sean fingered the cuts on his face and paced up and down the sterile hallway.

'You should get a tetanus jab for those,' Clive said, pointing to Sean's face.

'I'll wait until I know how Terry is,' Sean said.

When he turned to walk up the corridor again, two policemen rounded the corner in front of him, accompanied by a theatre nurse.

'Say nothing. We were taking a pee in the woods and got attacked,' Clive whispered.

'Why were we there?' Sean asked.

'Skiing, and got lost.'

Sean quickly nodded his agreement.

'Excuse me. I believe you speak English? May we ask you some questions about your friend?'

'Yes, okay,' Sean said.

The policeman apologised for his poor English and took a brief statement from both Clive and Sean. When Sean mentioned where it had happened, the policeman stopped writing. 'Near the *Nazi* house?' he asked, pulling a look of disgust.

Sean shook his head and shrugged. 'I saw a big factory, but nothing else.'

After about half an hour of questioning, they were told to wait with his colleague in the hospital, while he made a few enquiries. The second policeman stayed in the corridor with Sean and Clive, but indicated that he didn't speak English, so they didn't communicate further.

Two hours later, his colleague returned. 'The Austrian police can't find any blood, or dogs where you indicated, but they could have taken them back into the compound. And it's snowing again, so any traces could have been covered,' the policeman said.

'Didn't they go into the compound?' Clive asked.

'No, they didn't have a warrant,' the policeman replied.

'So what? Surely if there's reasonable suspicion they could enter?' Clive said, his voice strained with frustration.

Eying Clive suspiciously, the policeman nodded his agreement. 'If it was me, I'd have gone in, but we have no jurisdiction there and the Braunau police, are… well … '

'Well?' Clive asked.

'Respectful of these fringe groups.' The policeman chose his words carefully.

Before Clive could speak, a doctor walked out of the theatre pulling a mask from his face. 'Are you the people who brought him in?' he asked in English.

'Yes,' Sean said, turning to face him.

'He's alive, but only just and if he makes it through the coming days, he's going to need major plastic surgery. Unfortunately, he lost a large part of his face.'

An image shot into Sean's mind of Terry's ever smiling face.

'We're going to transfer him to intensive care in Munich this afternoon. The nurse will give you the details,' the doctor said, before speaking to the policeman in German and walking away.

Before they were allowed to leave, their passports were photocopied and copies given to the police.

'I hope he gets better,' the policeman said, with a genuine expression of concern on his face.

'Does he have a family?' Sean asked, as he and Clive sat down again.

'No, nobody. He's had a tough life has Terry. He really doesn't deserve this.'

'I'll ask Liz to meet us in Munich to look after him, while we get the bastards responsible,' Sean said.

On the drive back to their hotel, Clive didn't speak.

'What's wrong,' Sean asked.

'One of my friends died in Brussels; one is nearly dead here and the Austrian police won't even go into a fucking property. Well if they won't do their job, I'll do it for them!'

They pulled up outside the front entrance of the hotel and saw that their bags had been packed and placed on the doorstep. Clive immediately stormed into the hotel, as Sean struggled to keep up.

'What's the meaning of this?' Clive snarled at the portly manager.

The owner quickly appeared from the office. 'Please Herr Miller, we don't want any trouble. We ask that you leave our hotel quietly.'

'Why?' Clive shouted.

'The police came here. I think it's for the better,' the owner said.

Jumping up, Clive leant over the desk to get as close as possible to the owner. 'Tell your friends at the police station that I'll make sure every last one of them loses their job before I'm finished. And as for you, you're not worth the effort, you snivelling worm.' He then spun around to Sean quickly. 'Let's get out of this shithole before I hurt somebody.'

Back in the car, they made their way over the bridge to the hospital.

'I guess that means *they* know who *we* are?' Sean said.

Clive nodded. 'Yes, but we're no closer to knowing who *they* are.'

Chapter Twenty-Five

Friday, 5th February. London, England.

The previous evening, after Praew had gone to bed, Liz watched the YouTube video she'd posted. The image was a little shaky but clear enough to see what was happening. It showed Praew standing in a featureless corridor putting things into her locker. Then, out of nowhere, Koryalov, Belov and Dementyev appeared in the shot behind her.

Belov pushed her against the locker, holding her there. 'Hello, Thai whore. I'm ready for my sucky fucky time,' he said.

Praew pushed back and elbowed him in the ribs. 'Leave me alone,' she said.

'What's wrong? You don't like good white meat?' Dementyev added.

'Get lost!' Praew shouted and moved to the side, trying to escape.

Then Koryalov stepped forward. He was at least two feet taller than Praew and he pushed her against the locker, pinning her with his hand on her throat. 'I'm going to fuck your little Thai cunt, whether you like it or not,' he said, as the other two jeered, egging him on.

In a swift movement, Praew raised her knee hard into his groin and his grip on her throat released. As he moved backwards, she pushed him onto the floor, before running in the opposite direction from the camera.

'You're dead, yellow cunt!' Koryalov shouted after her.

When Liz closed the screen on her computer, she wept uncontrollably, her chest heaving up and down. 'Why can't this little girl just get a break in life?' she said to herself. 'It's just not fair.'

That morning Praew came down early for breakfast, with a broad smile stretched across her face.

'You look lovely today,' Liz commented, trying to act happy for Praew's sake.

When Praew reached for the toast, she was grinning from ear to ear.

'What is it?' Liz asked, surprised to see her so happy.

'1.4 million hits,' Praew said.

'Sorry, I'm not with you. What do you mean?' Liz shook her head.

'Our YouTube Video went viral. It had 1.4 million hits last night.'

'Shit! Sorry. What does that mean?' Liz apologised for swearing.

'Well, apparently, thousands of people have sent them hate mail.'

'Good. They deserve it.' Liz said.

During breakfast, Liz told Praew that she'd seen the video and was horrified, but thought she'd been very brave and that she was proud of her.

'William must be very brave too. That was a special thing he did for you, and I'd like to thank him,' Liz said.

'You can. I said he can come over one day for dinner, if that's okay?'

When she saw the glint in Praew's eye, indicating that William might be more than just a friend, Liz smiled properly for the first time that day. 'Of course it's okay, darling. This is your house just as much as anybody else's. Any time you want to have friends over, that's fine.'

'Thanks,' Praew said, grabbing another piece of toast, before heading to her room to get ready for school.

'Be really careful today, I don't want those boys to retaliate against you. Are you still sure you want to go in?' Liz said, as they rounded the corner of the street that the school was on.

'I do. I think it'll be better now,' Praew replied, reaching into the back seat of the car for her schoolbag.

'What the—?' Liz exclaimed, as the school came into view.

Outside the school gates a large crowd had gathered and Liz could see two TV news crews, talking to people that were trying to enter the gates. She slowed the car and took in the view.

'That's her; the kid from the video,' she heard somebody shout.

Immediately, both film crews turned their cameras towards Liz and Praew and the reporters started to run in their direction. Reacting quickly, Liz sped up as much as she dared, without risking running anybody over. Then when she was clear, she sped away and headed for home.

'I'm guessing you've earned a day off,' she said.

'Wow! I didn't expect that,' Praew said.

When they were safely back in the flat, Liz turned onto the *BBC News*. The headline read: POLICE INVESTIGATE RACIAL AND SEXUAL HARASSMENT AT PRESTIGE LONDON SCHOOL.

'A YouTube video of a girl being racially and sexually harassed at one of London's best schools has attracted the attention of the police this morning,' the anchor said, before the screen switched to a reporter at the school gates.

'Yes, John. The video showed a thirteen-year-old girl of oriental origin being victimised by three fifteen-year-old boys, believed to be from Russia. After it was posted late yesterday afternoon, it soon went viral and, as we count, has received more than 2 million hits.'

'Is the girl okay?' the anchor asked.

'We can't name her, but she arrived at school this morning with her mother and then left when she saw the cameras,' the reporter responded.

'What about the three boys?' the anchor asked.

'We spoke to the headmaster. All three have been suspended from school until further notice, but that's the least of their worries. The police are conducting an investigation into their behaviour as well. We spoke to the investigating officer this morning and this is what she had to say.' The screen switched over to a woman, making a statement to the camera.

'The Metropolitan Police take this kind of abuse very seriously indeed, and given the obvious evidence in this case, it's more than likely that criminal charges will follow.' The camera switched back to the anchor, who moved onto another piece.

'Wow!' Liz said. 'You did cause a stir. Well done. I'm proud of you.'

Throughout the morning they watched updates on the news and Liz ignored the doorbell to the flat, as it rang constantly. When she looked out of the window, the pavement was lined with journalists. 'I wish Sean was here,' Liz said. When the Police arrived to interview Praew, she invited them in, but still refused the press an interview.

It was at around 1 p.m. that Praew was mentioned by name for the first time and an association made to Sean and Liz. The video had received over 10 million hits and had spawned a whole group of YouTube videos categorised as 'Shame your Bullies'. *BBC News* was now calling it a 'movement'.

At 2 p.m., following the announcement by the police that the three boys would be charged for common assault, sexual assault and racial harassment, a journalist mentioned Praew's immigration situation. He'd obviously made the link back to Sean's speech at the award ceremony and put two and two together.

A chill ran down Liz's spine as they explained the little information they had been able to gather on Praew's background.

When the call came through from Sean asking her to go to Munich to look after Terry, she jumped at the opportunity to get away.

Chapter Twenty-Six

Saturday, 6th February. Munich, Germany.

'Bloody hell! I'm going to need to give you three permanent security,' Clive blew out after Liz explained the situation in the UK. 'You got Vladimir Koryalov's son expelled from school and charged with assault?' he added laughing. 'Well done, Praew. That was really brave,' he added.

'I'm really proud of you for standing up to them. How did you come up with the idea?' Sean said, seating Praew on his knee.

'I just thought about what you'd do in the same situation,' she said, looking up at Sean. 'I knew I couldn't fight them, so I needed another way.'

'Beautiful and a genius,' Sean said, kissing her on the forehead.

'The police said that, if found guilty, they're going to ask the Home Office to deport the three boys from the UK and issue permanent banning orders for them,' Liz said.

'Maybe it'll help with our case,' Sean replied.

'Maybe,' Liz responded in a non-committal way. 'How's Terry?' she changed the subject.

'He's stable, but still on life support,' Clive said, looking out from the small bakery by the fountain in the Karlsplatz. The area was busy with shoppers, traipsing through the melting snow.

'I'll take Praew to see some of the museums and then go in to see him this afternoon,' Liz suggested.

'Thanks, it's really appreciated,' Clive said.

'Ich möchte Deutsche lernen,' Praew said, smiling broadly. 'That means, I'd like to learn German,' she added.

A bright smile broke across Sean's face and he kissed her gently on the forehead again. 'Such a clever girl,' he said. 'Did you tell Uncle Clive about your A in maths?'

'He doesn't want to know about that now. He has more important things to think about,' Praew beamed.

'Terry is safe in there, isn't he?' Liz asked.

'Yes, I think so. We may only be sixty miles away from Braunau physically, but we're eighty years away mentally,' Clive said.

'Do you really need to go back there?' she asked.

'Yes. We need to find a link to Glas and then work out why he was trying to kill Anna, when he killed Phil in the process,' Sean said.

'I understand, but be careful,' Liz replied, looking at Clive.

'We should be back by midnight,' Clive said.

The drive back to Braunau took just over an hour and when they arrived, Clive drove through the main square, where the skinhead gang were in their usual place by the statue, congregated around the leader, who was holding onto a teenage girl in a mini-skirt.

Without stopping, they drove straight through Braunau and turned right for Ranshofen. 'It's Saturday night. They'll all be out causing trouble,' Clive said.

They soon pulled in to the same layby as they had the day

before and parked the car discreetly out of view from the road. Clive took some tools from the boot and they scurried though the woods again towards the farmhouse. When they reached the fence, there were no lights on in the house and the densely wooded area was very dark.

'They won't have had time to replace the dogs yet… I hope,' Clive grinned.

Within two minutes, he'd cut a hole in the fence big enough for them to crawl through, and Sean scrambled quickly through the soft snow, across the yard to the front of the house, where he was joined by Clive just a minute later.

'I've had a look through the windows. I can't see anybody,' Clive said, pulling a set of locksmith's tools from his bag and playing with the lock on the door. A few moments later, they were in.

A rotten stench filled Sean's nostrils as he entered the kitchen: empty beer and schnapps bottles littered the bare floorboards, while half-eaten takeaway was just thrown into a corner.

Grimacing at the filth, they crept through the kitchen and into the lounge, where two threadbare couches sat at right angles facing an old TV, above which a black-and-white poster of the Nuremberg rally clung to the wall. It was the only part of the room that wasn't covered in fascist graffiti. The letters 'BR18' were painted in large black letters above the poster.

'I saw that tattooed onto the leader's neck,' Sean whispered.

Clive examined the writing. 'Probably the name of the gang,' he said, then pointed to the stairs in the corner of the room, indicating that they should head that way. When they reached the top, it was pitch-black and Sean reached into his pocket for the torch Clive had given him.

The first bedroom along the corridor was taken by Clive, so

Sean automatically took the next. Waving his torch around the room, he took in the disgusting sight. Like downstairs, the floor was covered with empty alcohol bottles. A filthy foam mattress was pressed into one of the corners, with three dirty sleeping bags thrown onto it and the walls were covered with the same type of graffiti as downstairs. Backing out of the door, Sean quickly moved onto the landing and pulled the handle down on the next door… it was locked.

Moving back down the dark corridor, he found Clive in another bedroom, which was much the same as the first he'd seen. 'There's a locked room back there,' Sean whispered.

Clive quickly came out and used his tools to open the lock, before gently pushing the door open. When Sean shone his torch into the space, it wasn't like any of the other rooms; it was clean, tidy, and had a new carpet. A double bed was pushed against the far wall, with a picture of Adolf Hitler riding in an open-topped car over the bridge linking Simbach to Braunau, during the Anschluss; Hitler's annexation of Austria into Germany. The other walls had more pictures of people wearing Nazi uniforms. Taking his phone out, Sean quickly took photos of the space and moved on.

When he looked inside the traditional wooden wardrobe, he found a Nazi SS uniform hanging in a laundry bag. The black uniform was clean and well-pressed, with polished silver buttons. It was very different from the scruffy skinhead uniform the leader was wearing now.

Moving quickly around the room, he opened a drawer in the wardrobe and scanned the contents. There was a collection of Nazi war medals and some other bits of Nazi memorabilia, but nothing of much interest. Noticing that the base of the drawer was lined with paper, Sean wondered whether the leader was some kind of schizophrenic; portraying an external image of filth and disorder, yet carefully arranging his private life.

As he was closing the drawer, he noticed that the paper was slightly uneven, so he carefully pulled out the memorabilia and placed it on the top of the drawers. It took a little fiddling to get his nail under the edge of the lining paper, but when he lifted it, he found an A4 envelope and opened it carefully, revealing three sheets of paper. 'Clive,' he whispered, 'you need to see this.'

'What is it? It looks like an organisation chart. Take a picture of it and put it back,' Clive said.

They spent a few more minutes, looking through the dilapidated farmhouse and taking pictures, before sneaking back through the hole in the fence and returning to the car.

'Can you make anything out on the chart?' Clive asked.

'Just the heading '4R18', the rest is too small. We'll have to wait until I can upload it to my computer.'

'Glas' house next. That might not be quite as easy as this one,' Clive said.

Ten minutes later, they pulled up outside the wooden chalet owned by Glas. It was 9 p.m. and the lights were all off.

'Looks like there's nobody home,' Sean said.

'Either that, or they're in bed,' Clive responded.

Staying out of sight, they parked the car a few hundred metres away and made their way back to the house quickly on foot. There were no security fences to negotiate this time and they were soon outside the back door, where Clive again fiddled with the lock and opened it within minutes.

The inside of the house was dimly lit by the orange glow from the street lamp, so they didn't need torches. The decor was traditionally Austrian, with chunky wooden furniture, red-checked curtains and a terracotta stone floor. As they made their way through the ground floor of the house quietly, there was nothing unusual; just a typical old people's house, cluttered and badly decorated.

When they reached the stairs, Clive went up first, carefully testing each tread to make sure it made no sound, followed by Sean, placing his feet in exactly the same spots.

At the top, Clive waited, pushing his finger to his lips to hush Sean. From a room at the end of the landing, the faint sound of snoring came through the open door. After telling Sean to stay put, Clive quickly looked in each room, except the one where the snoring emanated from, and rejoined Sean, pointing down the stairs.

When they were back in the kitchen, Clive whispered, 'Something's missing. There was no office. I'd expect an MEP to have a home office.'

'Cellar?' Sean suggested.

Clive nodded and searched around for a door, but couldn't find one.

'Maybe outside?' Sean said.

Silently creeping around, they made their way back out onto the terrace and down into the garden below. There, beneath the high terrace, was an old style wooden door. Again Clive picked the lock and opened it. The inside was black and lightless, so he quickly turned on his torch, which revealed stone steps leading down into a damp cellar.

A musty smell hit Sean as soon as he entered the corridor and he shivered at the sudden drop in temperature. In front of him, four doors led from the dingy space into the cellar chambers. Following the same process, Clive took the first, while Sean took the second. When he opened the thick wooden door, the beam from his torch highlighted a pile of old junk: broken rusty bikes, children's toys and other rubbish was piled to the ceiling, and he quickly exited and moved on to the next room.

When he opened the door, he caught sight of a chunky wooden desk, *bingo,* he thought, *the office.*

As the light from the torch lit up the small space, he noticed that the desk didn't have a computer on it, but did have an elaborate pen and ink holder: *an old man's office,* he thought. Then he shone the beam up to the wall behind the desk, where a large framed black-and-white photograph hung. The picture depicted Hitler, shaking hands with a small child, held up by a man wearing an overcoat with a Nazi armband. Underneath, the writing said:

Der Führer wird von Josef Glas und sein Sohn Hans begrüßt, als er triumphierend tritt Österreich am 12 März, 1938, Braunau-am-Inn

Translating the message in his head as best he could, Sean came up with: Josef Glas and his son, Hans, meeting Hitler in Braunau, in 1938.

My god, Glas actually met Hitler, and he's obviously proud of it. He spun around quickly to get Clive, but he didn't need to. As he turned, Clive walked into the office with his hands held high above his head. Behind him, Glas held a shotgun close to his back. He shoved Clive forward with the barrel and closed the door behind him.

The sight of such an old man brandishing a shotgun brought images of *Mr Magoo* cartoons to Sean's mind, but any comparison between the cartoon character and the real-life one ended with age. Glas held the weapon confidently and gritted his teeth in anger.

'*Warum bist Du in meinem Haus? Was suchst Du?*' Glas said moving the weapon between Sean and Clive.

'I'm sorry. We don't speak German,' Sean said.

'Ah, den Engländern aus Ranshofen,' Glas nodded, then switched language. 'Why are you in my house? What are you looking for?'

'I'm a journalist investigating a piece on neo-Nazis,' Sean said.

'This doesn't give you the right to break into my house in the night.'

'No, it doesn't,' Sean said. 'But why do you hide the fact that you're a Nazi from the European Parliament?'

'What makes you think I'm a Nazi?' Glas extended the gun angrily.

'That is you meeting Hitler in the picture, isn't it?' Sean said, pointing to the picture above the desk.

'Yes, but as you can see, I was just a small boy.'

'But it still takes pride of place on your wall,' Sean added.

'Enough. I'll call the police,' Glas said.

'You won't, because you'd have to show them all of this,' Clive swept his arm around the room, highlighting the pictures of various people in Nazi uniforms. In each corner of the room, behind the desk, red flags with white circles and black swastikas were presented facing the desk.

'Then I'll kill you here… for trespassing.'

'You won't do that either. You may get one of us, before the other gets you, but you won't get both. So any attempt to fire your gun will be suicide on your part. Plus, it'll also bring the police, and disgrace your family.'

'The police do as I tell them,' Glas snarled.

'I don't think a double murder will be left to the local police, do you?' Clive said calmly.

The comment unsettled Glas and he looked uncertain, indecision written across his face. 'What do you want?'

'Just to ask you a few questions, then we'll leave you alone,'

Sean said. He didn't wait for a response from Glas. 'Why did you set Blom up with Wagner?'

'So that's who sent you here: Blom, the neutral.' Glas renewed his grip on the gun.

'The neutral? You do know that the war ended a long time ago?' Clive said, picking up on the odd language.

Glas laughed loudly. 'You think I'm crazy because I say the war is still going on. Let me tell you, it's your blindness and the ignorant triumphalism of the British people that doesn't let you see the real war. Just because it's now fought with bank notes and legal acts doesn't make it any less a war. And, it won't be any less deadly now that victory is in sight.'

Glas' comments worried Sean: he wouldn't be making them if he planned to let them go. He immediately tensed his muscles, ready to pounce at the right opportunity.

'Why did you try to kill Anna Faustein?' Clive asked, still intent upon finding the person responsible for Phil's death.

'Faustein? Ich?' Glas looked confused. Before he could continue, Sean took the opportunity and leaped forward pushing the barrel of the gun into the air. With his left hand making sure it was safely pointing away, he pushed Glas to the floor easily and took the gun away from him.

'I asked you a question,' Clive said.

Looking up from the cold stone floor and shaking his head, 'I don't know what you're talking about,' he said.

Leaving Sean with the gun, Clive picked Glas up from the floor and sat him in the chair behind the desk. Then he scanned the room for any phones or other communication devices, but there were none to be seen. Taking the key from the lock, he placed it in the outside of the door, indicating to Sean that they should leave.

Before they left, Sean took a photo of Glas in the chair behind the desk, making sure he got the photo of Hitler and the two large Nazi flags in the frame.

'We've got to go,' Clive said hurrying up.

Ignoring the reminder, Sean looked straight at Glas. 'Blom doesn't owe you any more money. Do you understand,' he said aggressively.

'But … ' Glas started.

'Not buts,' Sean interrupted. 'In the morning, you'll send him a letter forgiving him all of the debt and wishing him well for the future. If he doesn't get that letter by Thursday, on Friday morning, every newspaper in Europe will be carrying this photo.' Sean turned around the screen on his phone so that the old man could see it.

Glas gritted his teeth, but didn't respond.

'Agreed?' Sean pushed.

Finally, Glas begrudgingly nodded his head in agreement and Sean turned to leave.

Once outside the office, Clive locked the door, but left the key in the lock. 'I'll leave a note on the table telling his wife where she can find him,' Clive said, before he took the gun from Sean and wiped it clean.

Quickly climbing the stairs out of the basement, they scurried through the garden back to their car. Within five minutes they were across the bridge and back into Germany.

'What do you think he meant when he said they were close to victory?' Clive asked.

'God knows, but I really want to find out,' Sean said.

Chapter Twenty-Seven

Sunday, 7th February. Munich, Germany.

The breathing apparatus covering a portion of Terry's face did nothing to disguise the extent of his injuries. Special bandaging stretched from his forehead to his chest and was changed at regular intervals by a team of nurses, as machines monitored his every life sign.

Moving next to the bed, Praew held onto his hand, checking for any signs of movement in his face. She stayed there for a whole hour, but was disappointed when he failed to respond.

'Let us know if he comes around, please,' Liz said to the nurse before leaving the intensive care ward.

'Of course,' the nurse nodded.

'I wish British hospitals were that good,' Liz said to Praew as they walked back out onto the street.

The snow was piling up on the street and Praew gripped tightly onto Liz's hand for the short walk back to the hotel near to the hospital.

'What did they say about having him moved to London?' Clive asked.

'Basically no; he's not well enough to be moved yet,' Liz answered.

Taking in the news, they found a table in a café, which joined the lobby of the hotel, ordered three coffees and an orange juice and Liz immediately produced her laptop. 'I had a look at the pictures last night. Look at this.' She turned the screen around to reveal the organisation chart that Sean had photographed in the skinhead farmhouse.

After pulling out his glasses, Clive studied the chart carefully. 'Far more organised than it was years ago,' he said, still reading.

'What do you mean?' Liz asked.

'When we were looking at Allsop, there were quite a few neo-Nazi groups, but there was no command structure: each was an autonomous organisation and quite small. Now it looks like they're grouping together under a common leadership: this 4R18.'

'The first two pages seem to be all on one level, including Glas: *Regionaler Markführer*, which means regional leader,' Liz commented, then zoomed in on some so that Clive could see them more clearly.

'So Glas is just an underling: one of hundreds of other regional chiefs?' Clive said.

'Yes, it looks like it, and I think the BR in BR18, means Braunau, which would make sense, look at all the other initials: they must be names of towns,' Liz said, then scrolled up two pages, as the org chart first went to six people on a level, then to two. Next to one of the two boxes, the name '*Wagner*' was written in blue ink. In the box his title was *Kriegsminister.* 'It means Minister of War,' Liz said.

'So he's not the boss? That's interesting,' Clive commented.

'No,' Liz replied, then highlighted the box on the same level as Wagner's, which was named *Propagandaminister*, with a handwritten name: *Dorsch?* 'I assume the question mark by the name means the writer wasn't sure,' she said.

After they'd taken the page in, Liz scrolled up to where just one box sat above Wagner's and the Minister of Secret Police. The printed title in the box was *Vizekanzler*, but there was no handwritten name by it. 'Vice Chancellor, if you hadn't already guessed,' Liz said.

'Then,' Clive pointed up the screen as Liz scrolled up further. *Führer und Reichskanzler der Vierten Reich* was typed in a large box at the top, again with no name beside it.

'The Leader and Chancellor of the Fourth Reich,' Liz added.

'The Fourth Reich? What are these guys up to?' Clive blew out a rasp of air.

'I don't know, but if you go back down the chart, they seem to have hundreds of divisions, and not just in Germany or Austria, but right across Europe, including the UK, Russia, the Ukraine etc.,' Liz said, scrolling down to the bottom of the chart. 'See LO18, under the UK? I'll bet that's London and MA18… Manchester,' she added.

'It's massive,' Sean said, almost scared by his own words.

'Why do you think he was filling in the names?' Clive asked.

'I don't know. I've been asking myself the same thing. It's almost as if he was investigating them,' Liz suggested.

'Maybe he's undercover police?' Sean said.

Clive was staring off into the distance and then looked back at Sean. He was moving his head up and down slightly. 'I think you may be right. He speaks English, so he's obviously educated and on three separate occasions he took the least violent option: he hit the father on the knee rather than the head; he backed away from a fight with Terry in the square, even though he outnumbered us four to one; then the same again at the father's house. Not exactly the behaviour of a racist thug, is it?'

'Then there was his room; it was much cleaner than I expected,' Sean added.

'Look at the page next to the Vice Chancellor's box and the Chancellor's. It's marked with deep pen dots. He was obviously frustrated about something,' Liz said.

'He's trying to piece the organisation together,' Clive said. 'We need to know why.'

It is estimated that there are over half a million active neo-Nazis in the world today.

Police forces across the globe have reported a growing level of organisation and interconnectivity among their ranks.

Chapter Twenty-Eight

Monday, 8th February. Braunau-am-Inn, Austria.

The light was fading as Clive drove the car over the bridge into Austria from Simbach-am-Inn. Sean had offered to do the driving, but Clive had insisted, Sean assumed so that he could prove he was still physically capable, despite his prosthetic hand. The sight of the onion-domed church tower sticking out above the roofs of Braunau sent a nervous shudder through Sean's spine. Isolating the leader of the skinhead gang wouldn't be easy, especially without Terry around.

'What if we're wrong? What if he's just the local leader of a group of neo-Nazi thugs?' Sean said.

'Then we'd better be prepared for a fight,' Clive replied.

'How confident are you that he's not one of them?' Sean asked.

'Fifty-fifty I'd say,' Clive shrugged.

Not really the odds Sean wanted to hear as they parked the car in a side street off the Stadtsplatz, the elongated main square where the skinheads hung out. Their position gave them a good view of the fountain and they waited. It was around eight when the first of the skinheads arrived. Then more came, until their number swelled to around twenty. The leader wasn't with them and they seemed particularly boisterous, egged on by the first of the youths Sean had encountered the previous week. He was chastising people as they walked by, following them and making childish faces, intimidating them, as his gang jeered and laughed.

Sean could sense that the policeman in Clive wanted to do something, but he just stayed in the car, watching, as his ire clearly swelled.

By nine-thirty, the leader still hadn't arrived and Clive was becoming increasingly agitated by the loutish behaviour of the skinhead gang. 'Where are the police? Look at the way he's goading that couple; they're terrified,' Clive said.

Another half an hour passed, but still the leader didn't show.

Then, just as Sean thought Clive was about to burst with anger, Glas' black Mercedes 600 appeared at the far end of the square. 'I thought he'd be back in Brussels,' Sean said.

'He is. His wife's driving,' Clive replied, as the car pulled closer.

Then they caught sight of him, the skinhead leader, sitting in the front seat of the car, being driven by Glas' wife. When the car stopped at the statue, the leader kissed Frau Glas on the cheek and climbed out. The boisterous activity died down quickly, as the first thug re-assumed his position as deputy and the leader walked over and leant against the fountain wall.

'That's weird. She kissed him like she was his mother. I think we've got it wrong about him,' Sean said.

'Maybe, but I still don't understand why he had the org chart, if he's not trying to piece the organisation together,' Clive responded.

'It could just be homework. You know, studying the organisation before some kind of promotion?' Sean suggested.

'Yes, but why the dots on the page showing his frustration at not knowing the ultimate leaders? If it was some kind of studying, they're the last names he'd forget.'

'You're right. We need to talk to him,' Sean concluded.

'You know what to do,' Clive said.

Knowing what to do, and actually doing it are gulfs apart, Sean thought, as he mentally rehearsed Clive's plan. He would walk into the square and get the attention of the thugs, keeping enough distance that he'd be able to outrun them for long enough to get across the river into Germany, where they hoped the police would be more helpful, if needed. They were hoping that, as before, the leader wouldn't join in the chase and Clive would pull the car up alongside him, using the fake pistol he'd bought from a toyshop to get him into the car. Then they'd catch up with Sean on the agreed route to Simbach. It sounded simple, but they both knew that a lot could go wrong and the consequences if it did were unthinkable.

Tentatively climbing out of the car, Sean made his way to the corner of the square. The fountain was about eighty metres away and Clive had warned him not to get closer than fifty metres to the gang, as he needed a good head start for safety. Plucking up his courage, he stepped out of the shadows of the side street and walked straight towards the statue. He could feel every movement of his body as his heart raced in anticipation of what was to come.

After ten metres, nothing happened, so he slowed his pace deliberately, counting down the distance between him and the skinheads. *65, 64… 58, 57… 46, 45…* He was too close and he knew it… *40, 39. Way too close. 36, 35 ...*

'Hey, das ist der Engländer,' he heard one of the group shout

and point in his direction. He stopped no more than thirty metres from the group, waiting for the chase to begin, tensing his muscles ready to run.

The break came from the side of the group, from the same youth he'd confronted on the first night again. Sean turned and started to run, pushing his speed faster, while trying to avoid slipping in the snow.

When he glanced over his shoulder, as expected, the group was giving chase. Knowing that he needed to conserve energy, he ran at three-quarters pace past the car, where Clive was crouched down in the driver's seat, hiding. The gang were now about forty metres behind him and not gaining ground, so he continued at the same pace, allowing something in reserve in case he got into trouble.

When he approached the sharp corner onto the river road, still coasting ahead of the angry group, his confidence was growing. Suddenly, as he attempted to round the corner, he felt his feet lose their grip on the cobbles and he slid across the pavement, falling headfirst into a snowdrift. Behind him, the gang gained ground quickly. He rolled out of the drift and onto the firm ground, righting himself as quickly as he could.

Just as the first of the skinheads reached the corner, he started to move away again, the thug's outstretched hand failing to connect with him. As he picked up his pace again, he looked back to see the skinheads falling at the same spot that he'd slipped.

Somehow, they managed to right themselves more quickly than he had, and had gained some twenty metres, so he increased his pace and started to pull away, thankful for Clive's advice about holding something in reserve, as the thugs struggled to keep up in their heavy boots.

When the lights on the bridge came into view, just 300 metres in front of him, with the gap to the gang growing to about forty metres or so behind, he started to feel confident he could get there before them and maintained his pace.

Then, with just seventy metres to go, he heard the sound of an engine revving hard, when he glanced over his shoulder, he saw the pickup truck the thugs had used some nights before, skidding around the corner. A bolt of panic shot through his body and he picked up his pace to a sprint, pushing towards the bridge as the truck got closer.

Thirty metres before he reached the bridge, the truck pulled alongside him. One of the skinheads was leaning out of the window, hurling abuse at him, but steel street posts stopped the truck from mounting the kerb and Sean just carried on running, ignoring the abuse, hoping that they didn't have weapons.

Just then, Clive's rented car shot past on the bridge road, skidding to a halt ten metres onto the bridge. Right behind it, Sean flung himself around the corner and onto the bridge, while the truck slid sideways in the snow as it hit the junction. When Sean reached the car, he jumped into the rear seat and before he could close the door, Clive hit the pedal again, with Sean's legs still dangling onto the street.

The wheels spun in the snow, trying to get traction, as the truck rammed the rear of the car, sending it careering forward. The violent crash threw Sean into the footwell and he lost his grip on the seat, suddenly slipping backwards out of the open door.

Somehow, Clive managed to regain control and steer to the centre of the road, with the truck still pushing at the rear.

Sean rolled to a halt against the railings of the bridge. When he looked back, he saw that the skinheads had stopped at the edge of the bridge, watching the car chase. When they saw Sean, they started to sprint in his direction.

A loud cracking sound came from the rear of the car, as the bumper was ripped from the frame and the truck swerved free.

Sean sprinted as fast as he could towards the German side of the bridge, with the group of skinheads behind giving chase, then suddenly in front of him, the truck stopped and started to turn around.

A signpost above the truck read; *Willkommen im Deutschland. Clive was right! They won't cross into Germany.*

As the truck straightened up on the bridge, it was about thirty metres ahead of Sean and the skinheads on foot were about the same distance behind him. He was trapped.

Chapter Twenty-Nine

Monday, 8th February. Braunau-am-Inn, Austria.

Sean glanced down at the freezing River Inn below the bridge. It was tearing underneath at a fast rate, boosted by the snowfall. He'd be dead in seconds if he tried to jump in.

The three skinheads from the truck were now out of the cab and walking towards him. Closing in from the other side, ten skinheads were approaching, also now at walking speed.

Sean looked for a gap between the two groups, but there wasn't one. The only way out was the river, where he was sure that he'd end up anyway if the skinheads had their way.

When the two groups reached a point just five metres away from him, they stopped and formed a semi-circle around him. Sean felt behind him for the handrail of the bridge. It was cold and wet, but its touch meant that he was close enough to the edge.

The deputy leader took control of the group, centring himself in the semi-circle of neo-Nazi thugs. Hatred welled in his eyes as he pulled out a knife from his coat and theatrically licked the blade. 'For your dick, *Engländer*,' he said in heavily accented

German. The other skinheads laughed at the comment, grabbing at their crotches.

Sean made a quick decision. There was no way he was going to let the skinheads cut off his penis; he'd rather take his chances in the freezing river. He swivelled around and climbed onto the stone wall that separated the road from the river. The drop was only five or so metres to the water. He'd survive the fall, but probably not the ice-cold glacial water.

The deputy suddenly stopped, a sadistic grin crossing his face. '*Springen*, English. *Kaltwasser.* Dead,' he laughed, mixing up the two languages.

Sean looked down at the rushing water again, plucking up his courage. Then, as he twitched his leg muscles to jump, the Volkswagen, shot past the parked truck on the bridge revving hard and heading straight at the group of skinheads.

As they turned, Sean took the opportunity and ran along the wall of the bridge, jumping over the small stone pillars, every step dicing with the icy death that waited for him below, but getting away from the angry mob.

The Volkswagen continued to drive straight at the skinheads who were now running for cover. Then just before it reached the first of them, it hit a handbrake turn and skidded around to face in the other direction. Seconds later it was by Sean's side and slowing down. Sean quickly leaped down from the wall and dived into the rear seat, slamming the door behind him as Clive floored the accelerator and sped away.

Once they cleared the bridge, Clive slowed down to a normal speed. 'That was close,' he said.

'Too close,' Sean agreed, then he looked at the unconscious leader in the passenger seat and frowned.

'He resisted arrest,' Clive said grinning.

'Shit, Clive! what if he *is* a policeman?'

'Then he should be a better fighter,' Clive laughed. 'Don't worry, it's just a little trick Terry showed me. He'll come around soon.'

A few miles outside Simbach on the road to Munich, Clive pulled the car over into a layby. 'Let's wake up laughing boy here,' he said, and reached out of the car door for a handful of snow, which he promptly rubbed into the gang leader's face.

'*Was ist … ?*' the leader shouted, coming to, staring at Clive.

'Calm down. I'm not going to hurt you,' Clive said. '*He* might though,' he pointed at Sean.

After looking back at Sean, the leader slumped into his seat, realizing that he was outnumbered. 'What do you want, Englishman? Why do you keep coming back to Braunau?'

'Because somebody killed my friend, and I'd like to know who,' Clive said.

'Then why bring a journalist with you?' the leader asked, looking at Sean. 'Yes, I know who you are Mr McManus,' he added.

'Then tell us who you are,' Clive said.

'My name is Roland Glas. The man whose house you broke into is my grandfather,' the leader said casually.

It obviously wasn't the answer Clive had been expecting, as Sean saw his jaw drop slightly.

'So it was *your* brother who had the fight in the playground with the child from the cottage?' Sean filled in the gap quickly.

'No, it was my brother's son. They are new to town and don't know people yet, so they were confused, if that's what they told you.'

'Why did you only hit him on the knee?' Sean asked.

'Because he didn't deserve any more. My nephew is a horrible child and a bully. I felt sorry for the family.'

'But you still went there, why?' Clive asked.

The question seemed to annoy the skinhead leader and Sean scrutinised his face as he turned away from Clive. He was young, but somehow possessed the presence of an older person and he clearly wasn't scared of Sean or Clive, somehow knowing that they would eventually let him go.

'What's this?' Sean said, passing him a copy of the organisation chart that they found in his room.

It certainly gained a reaction as the leader's eyes opened wide at the sight of the paper. 'I see you didn't just break into my grandfather's house.'

'What is it?' Clive said.

'As you can see, it's an organisation chart.'

'For which organisation?' Clive pressured.

'The Fourth Reich,' the leader said.

'Is it real?' Sean asked.

'Very real,' the leader replied.

'Why were you filling in the names?' Clive asked.

Silence. The leader didn't speak.

'Are you an undercover policeman?' Clive asked.

The question seemed to shock the leader and he looked down, clearly grappling with something. 'No, I'm not,' he answered.

'Then why are you trying to find out who all the people in the organisation are?' Sean interrupted.

Again, silence, but then the leader seemed to change his mind. 'Go back to England where you'll be safe. You're prying into things that will get you killed,' he said.

'Not without answers regarding my friend's death,' Clive pushed.

'Okay, what do you want to know? But after I tell you, you must leave and never return to Braunau. Agreed?'

Clive considered the deal briefly. 'Agreed,' he said.

'Okay, who are you really?' Sean asked.

'As I said, Roland Glas. Hans Glas really is my grandfather.'

'Then why are you researching the organisation?' Clive asked.

'Because I'm helping the German security services,' he answered.

'The police?' Clive asked.

'Not exactly.'

'You work for the BND?' Clive said, raising his eyebrows.

'What?' Sean frowned at the question.

'It's the German Federal Intelligence Service. Don't ask me what the letters stand for,' Clive answered.

'*Bundesnachrichtendienst*,' the leader said. 'And no, I don't work for them. As I said, I'm just helping them.'

'Why?' Sean asked.

'Because my family is a bunch of dangerous lunatics. Before I went into the army, I thought it was pretty harmless. But when the BND approached me, I realised that it was more; that it was growing like a cancer and needed to be stopped.'

'Why you?' Sean asked.

'Because my family name gave me an easy in; I was already trusted. My great-grandfather was the first to welcome Hitler into Austria in 1938, and he went on to rule Upper Austria with an iron fist for the Nazis, until the end of the war, when he was killed by his own people.'

'And your grandfather?' Sean asked.

'He used the wealth stolen by my great-grandfather to buy power, and has always been very proud of the family connection to Hitler. Believe it or not, being a person who actually met Hitler gives him some kind of celebrity status in this group.'

'Why did he become an MEP?' Sean asked.

'We don't know, but something changed in the Nazi groups when Wagner appeared, throwing his money around. They became more organised and started to put people into positions of power.'

'What are they up to?' Sean said.

'That's what people like me are meant to find out. Unfortunately, I can't even find out who's in charge above Wagner. What we do know is that activity has been building, and so has the Nazi rhetoric about seizing power.'

'What? Nazis taking over Germany or Austria again?' Sean narrowed his eyes in disbelief.

'We think their ambitions are greater: the whole of Europe,' the leader said.

'That's nuts. How will they do that?' Clive said dismissively.

'Again, we don't know. I agree it sounds unbelievable, but there are some very powerful people involved, and people like that don't usually waste their time on things that have no chance of success.'

'Can't you just ask your grandfather about it?' Sean said.

The leader looked at him suddenly wary. 'I'd be dead before I left the room. My grandfather might look like a harmless old man, but he's in this up to his neck, and he isn't a stranger to making people disappear. Be careful of him: you're already on his hit list.'

'Who is Dorsch? It says he's the Propaganda Minister,' Sean asked.

'He's a Bavarian businessman, heavily involved in providing private security contractors to war zones like Iraq and Afghanistan.'

'There was a question mark by his name?' Sean asked.

'Yes, I'm not sure. My grandfather met with him in Braunau

a couple of times, and he has the resources, so I made an assumption. It could be wrong of course.'

'One last question: all of the divisions on the org chart have letters and then 18 after them. What do they mean?' Sean asked.

'The letters are the name of the district: BR is Braunau; KO is Köln; and so on. The 4R is the Fourth Reich.'

'And the 18?' Clive asked.

'The first and eighth letter in the alphabet, AH, for Adolf Hitler. It's a common symbol of Nazism. They use it, or 88 for Heil Hitler, so as not to provoke the police so openly in certain countries.'

'Thank you,' Clive said when they dropped Roland Glas back at the bridge in Simbach. As he walked away, Sean considered the bravery of the decision made by the lonely figure stumbling over the snow-covered bridge. If he succeeded he'd lose all his family; if he failed he'd lose his life.

Chapter Thirty

Monday, 8th February. Munich, Germany.

'They know who you are? How?' Liz exclaimed.

'I assume through the Austrian police following Terry's injuries,' Clive said.

'That means they probably know where Terry is as well,' Liz said.

'Yes, but I don't think he's in any danger. We're not a threat to them yet. We don't know anything, so I doubt they'll come after us,' Clive replied.

'What do you propose we do now?' Liz turned to Sean.

'I think we go after Dorsch. Going up the org chart makes more sense than going down,' Sean answered.

'Okay, but I can only stay in Munich until next Sunday. Praew needs to go back to school next week,' Liz said.

'That's okay. Dorsch lives in Munich anyway, so we'll work from here,' Sean agreed.

Following a night's sleep and a visit to the hospital, where Terry was still in the same condition, they began their research into

Stefan Dorsch. Again, nearly all of the information was in German, but putting the text through an online translator gave them a general idea of what it meant.

Dorsch was forty-seven, single, and lived in an apartment in central Munich, close to his business offices on Prannerstrasse. In his twenties, he'd apparently been a mercenary, selling his services to any number of violent dictators across Central and Northern Africa. Then, after the Gulf War, he'd suddenly emerged as one of the leading security contractors in Iraq. Now his company provided heavily armed security to businesses and individuals working in Iraq, Afghanistan and a number of African states.

The photo of him that Liz had found showed that he was lean and muscular, with a chiselled face that looked younger than his years. His closely cropped grey hair was balding in the middle and he had a scar on his left cheek. *He even looks like a mercenary*, Sean thought.

'We may need a bigger team to keep an eye on him,' Clive said.

'How many?' Sean asked, mindful of the exorbitant costs of Clive's men.

'Two should do it: one for the office; one for the home,' Clive said.

'Okay,' he shrugged.

'I'll have them here later today,' Clive said.

'Did you see anything that might show a political allegiance yet?' Sean asked Liz, who was sorting through screens on her computer.

'Nothing. Everything's about his business, which appears to be doing very well. They say he's a billionaire.'

'That's two billionaires already: Dorsch and Wagner. It makes you wonder who the two people above them are,' Sean said.

'And what kind of resources they've got,' Clive added.

'Well, we know Wagner seems to have revived the whole of the Hitler Youth, and Dorsch actually does have a private army for sale, or otherwise,' Liz said.

Roland's words were echoing in Sean's mind: *People like that don't get involved unless they think that there's a chance it will succeed.*

'Bloody hell, Sean! You're a like a magnet for dangerous psychopaths,' Clive said.

'What are we looking for?' Liz asked.

'Where he goes; who he meets with; anything that'll lead us to the person next up in the chain of command,' Sean said.

'Are we saying that Glas isn't responsible for Phil's death now?' Liz questioned.

'Well, I wouldn't discount that he's involved in some way, but he's not calling the shots and he did seem genuinely surprised when we suggested that he tried to kill Anna Faustein,' Clive said.

They caught their first glimpse of Dorsch later that afternoon, when he walked from his offices back to his apartment complex. In real life, he looked far less threatening than in the photos. He was dressed casually in jeans and a thick padded bubble jacket, with a woollen hat covering his head. Instead of a suitcase, he carried a designer over-the-shoulder messenger bag across his chest. Even through the thick clothes, his athleticism was apparent, as he strutted through the streets quickly.

'He looks fairly normal,' Sean said to Clive, who was walking beside him.

'That's the thing with the real psychopaths: they hide it well. Remember David Findlow?' Clive responded, reminding Sean of the CEO of BW Corp, who had looked like a Hollywood film star, until he took off his clothes to reveal a body covered in sadistic tattoos. 'The ones that openly show it are usually just mindless thugs, like the skinheads, who are usually scared of their own mothers, whereas,' Clive pointed towards Dorsch, 'people like him are scared of nobody.'

A shiver ran down Sean's spine as he examined Dorsch further. He walked bolt upright and dead straight, confident that people would move out of his way, which they did, without him even needing to adjust his fast pace.

'The German police have a name for people like him. They call them "Tie Nazis", whereas they call people like the skinheads "Boot Nazis": the officer corps and the cannon fodder,' Clive said, as they watched Dorsch enter his apartment building.

Back at the hotel Liz was sitting at the desk with her computer screen open. 'You need to see this Sean,' she said as Sean entered the room.

'What is it?' Sean said, making his way over to her.

'Is that Stefan Dorsch?' She pointed to the screen where a bald man was sitting at a dining table in a restaurant.

'It's a bit pixelated, but I think so why?'

Sweeping her fingers across the track-pad, Liz expanded the screen to show the person that Dorsch was dining with. 'What? So Dorsch knows Vladimir Koryalov,' Sean said pulling a confused face.

'But there couldn't be any kind of link to 4R18… he's Russian. Maybe it's just a coincidence.'

'There're a lot of neo-Nazis in Russia so I wouldn't discount the possible Nazi link. But any link to us must be pure coincidence, he couldn't know that we were thinking about investigating him and the incident at Praew's school would have to be unrelated,' Sean concluded.

'I may have told his son that we knew where his father's money came from,' Liz admitted, somewhat sheepishly.

'If he told his father that would certainly throw the cat among the pigeons, but it doesn't explain this. When was the picture taken?'

'It looks like it was taken recently. It was added to Nikolai Koryalov's Facebook page last Wednesday, if that means anything?' Liz shrugged.

Sean shook his head. 'I can't see it. It must just be a coincidence. It's not the most remote idea that two European billionaires would know each other. It's still a pretty exclusive group who have that kind of money.'

Nodding her head in agreement. Liz closed her laptop.

The two new men that Clive brought in were of a very similar ilk to all of the others Sean had met, two of whom were now dead: Colin in the BW case and Phil in this investigation. With Terry still on the critical list, it made Sean wonder whether it was worth it this time. In the BW case thousands of lives had been at stake; this time, he still hadn't identified the real risk.

'Pete and Steve. They've all got such simple names,' Sean commented.

A smile broke out in Clive's face suddenly. 'Some investigator you are. You didn't think they were their real names did you?'

'No… well, actually yes. I just hadn't thought about it.' Sean felt like an idiot.

The prompt arrival of the two highly trained security guards made Sean realise again why they paid Clive's exorbitant fees. They simply couldn't do it by themselves. He watched the two muscular young men as they unloaded their surveillance equipment quickly and efficiently, while they grilled Clive, Sean and Liz about the target. It was only when they asked about Terry that they showed even the remotest of human emotions. It was clear that Clive had worked with them on many occasions before and knew what to expect from them.

'Both ex-special forces,' Clive whispered to Sean. 'Believe it or not, outside work, they're pretty good fun.'

It was indeed hard to believe. They looked so serious, but on the odd occasion that he'd seen Clive let his hair down, metaphorically speaking, he too had been able to transform himself from one of the most controlled men Sean had ever met, into a fun-seeking hedonist. *Maybe it's because they experience so much danger, so when they let go, they really make the most of it; just like soldiers on leave from a war zone,* he thought.

It was midnight before Pete woke Clive and Sean. 'He's on the move. Steve's with him,' he said.

'Where?' Sean asked.

'He's on foot and heading south. Here.' He pointed to a map on his phone. 'He looks kinda scruffy, so I doubt he's off clubbing,' Pete added.

Quickly clipping in his earwig device, Sean listened to Steve's commentary.

'Let's go see what he's up to,' Clive said.

Grabbing coats, they ran quickly down Landsbergerstrasse and over to Prannerstrasse. When they rounded the bend, Steve was 200 metres in front of them, walking quickly, close to the buildings. Sean could just see Dorsch another 150 metres or so ahead of him, walking at the same aggressive pace he had done earlier.

'Any security following?' Steve asked.

Pete scanned the area around them. 'Nothing visible and they'd have to be mobile, so I'm guessing not.'

'That's odd,' Clive said.

'What?' Sean asked.

'How many billionaire heads of security firms do you know that would walk the streets of a major city like Munich at night, without some kind of security close by?' Clive responded.

'Maybe he doesn't want anybody to know where he's going,' Sean suggested.

'Exactly,' Clive raised his eyebrows. 'Don't lose him, Steve,' he said.

After a few more minutes' walking, the streets were suddenly deserted. Long empty offices and warehouses lined each side of the wide street.

'He could be leading us into a trap?' Sean said.

'I don't know how he'd know we were here though. Any sign that he knows he's being followed?' he asked Steve.

'No. He could just be good though,' Steve replied.

In the distance, Dorsch suddenly turned off into what looked like a side street between two warehouses. Steve automatically sped up in order not to lose him.

'Bollocks!' Steve said over the radio.

'Have you lost him?' Pete asked.

'No, worse than that,' he said.

'What?'

'He's gone straight into a gay sauna. I'm going to have to take my radio off before I go in, nowhere to hide it in there,' he said.

'Be careful. It could be a cover for something else. We'll stay around the corner. Let us know when he comes out,' Clive said.

'And remember… you're just in there to follow him,' Pete added, grinning broadly.

'Fuck you!' the reply came swiftly from Steve.

A few metres further on, they found a quiet spot in a car park and hid between some large rubbish bins, waiting for Steve's signal that Dorsch was leaving.

'Not where you'd normally expect somebody with his political views to be hanging out,' Sean said.

'We don't know whether he's involved yet. Remember Roland said he wasn't sure; that he'd just put two and two together,' Clive replied.

'You're right. I guess this is probably good evidence that he's *not* involved. As far as I can remember, Nazis don't have a very high opinion of gay people.'

An hour and a half later, Steve's voice re-appeared on the radio. 'He's out and coming your way,' he said.

'And?' Clive asked.

'It wasn't a cover. It's exactly what it said on the tin and our friend participated… heavily, shall we say,' Steve replied.

'You can tell me all about it later, darling,' Pete laughed.

Less than two minutes later, Dorsch rounded the corner in front of them and started making his way back in the direction that he'd come from. Pete stood and followed, while Sean and Clive waited for Steve.

Within ten minutes, Dorsch was back in his apartment and Sean, Clive and Steve returned to the hotel, leaving Pete on watch. Back at the hotel, Steve filled Liz, Sean and Clive in on the events inside the sauna.

'It seemed to be a regular thing for him. He was too familiar with the surroundings for it to be his first time and he seemed to know what he wanted, while lots of other people just stood around watching.'

'What was that?' Liz asked.

'Is that really relevant?' Steve said, obviously reluctant to go into details.

'I don't know. It could be,' Liz replied.

'Okay, he went into a darkened room where a leather swing was hanging from the ceiling, climbed into it and let seven men have anal sex with him, while he gave fellatio to three others,' Steve said.

'Sounds submissive? Odd, given who he is,' Liz said.

'Not really. It's a fairly common thing I've seen over the years. Powerful man during the day is turned on by submissive fetishism at night,' Clive said.

'What's his body like? Covered in tattoos?' Sean asked.

'See for yourself,' Steve said, producing his phone. 'I managed to get a couple of snaps over my shoulder in the changing rooms, before I had to put it in the locker.'

The two images of Dorsch's naked body showed that he was extremely well-toned, with veins pushed out over hard muscles, but he didn't have a single tattoo in sight. Three large round scars covered his chest.

'Bullet wounds,' Steve said, pointing them out.

'Brilliant,' Sean said, as he saw the sign for the sauna above Dorsch's head. 'That should give us something to talk to him about.'

'What?' Liz curled her lip.

'I figure that he obviously wants to keep this quiet, so we can use it to push him for a name,' Sean replied.

'What if he's completely innocent and his only crime is that he's a closet homosexual?' Liz asked.

'Then we won't expose him,' Sean said.

'And if he is involved?'

'Then it depends on what he tells us.'

Chapter Thirty-One

Tuesday, 9th February. Munich, Germany.

The point chosen for the interception was at the gate to the old city near the end of Prannerstrasse, close to Dorsch's office. They knew that he usually passed through the ornate stone structure at around 7:30 a.m. on foot, and he didn't appear to have any kind of security.

It was still dark and bitingly cold as Sean positioned himself against a large stone pillar of the gate, making sure he couldn't be seen from the other side. Pinned to the wall, he looked down Prannerstrasse, which was lined with traditional Bavarian style four-storey buildings, some of which were new copies of the original style and some that had survived the Second World War bombings. The gate was located at the far eastern end of the street, wedged between two newer buildings.

At 7:25, bang on time, Steve told Sean that Dorsch was on his way. He instinctively checked that the mic was firmly attached to his ear and pressed himself harder against the freezing cold stone of the gate pillar.

'Now!' Clive prompted over the mic.

Sean stepped out directly in front of Dorsch. 'Stefan Dorsch?' he asked quickly.

Dorsch immediately adopted a defensive pose, readying himself for a fight. *'Ja?'* he said, shifting his weight between his front and back feet.

'Could I ask you some questions, please?' Sean queried.

Dorsch's stance softened slightly. 'That depends on the questions,' he said in English, 'and upon who you are,' he added, carefully scanning the surrounding area.

'I'm a journalist from the UK. I'm doing some research into MEPs,' Sean said.

'Then what do you want with me? I'm not an MEP.'

'Do you know Hans Glas?' Sean asked.

'Ah, okay. Yes, I do. Why?'

The response took Sean by surprise. He hadn't expected him to be so open about it. 'We know that you met with him in Braunau. Why was that?'

'I have a training camp in Upper Austria and he's the local MEP. It's good to keep the bureaucrats onside in Austria; the administration there can be very difficult if not.'

'Do you know that he's a Nazi?' Sean asked.

The question seemed to surprise Dorsch. 'No, I didn't. Is he?'

Either he's a good actor, or he's genuinely unaware of Glas' Nazi association, Sean thought.

The threat having passed, Dorsch's demeanour had now relaxed completely and he stood square to Sean. 'Is this going to take long? I have to get to work,' he said, moving towards his office.

Stepping sideways, Sean followed him. 'Do you know Ulrich Wagner?' he asked.

A slight tell-tale twitch crossed Dorsch's face. 'I don't know him, but I know who he is, and yes, I *do* know that *he's* a Nazi.'

'Did you know he was involved in something called the Fourth Reich?' Sean asked, as Dorsch picked up his pace.

'No. Look where's this going? I'm a busy man, Mr … ?'

'McManus,' Sean said. 'Are you a senior figure in the Fourth Reich?' Sean quickly got to the point before Dorsch went into his office.

The question stopped Dorsch on the spot. 'Are you suggesting that I'm a Nazi? You print that and I'll sue you so badly that you won't eat for ten years.'

'Are you?' Sean asked, as Dorsch started walking again.

'Look, Mr McManus, this interview is over. If I see you again you'll be hearing from my lawyers.'

The comment surprised Sean a little. He'd become so used to physical threats, that a legal threat seemed so benign. 'Maybe I'll just publish this then. I wonder what your Nazi friends will make of it,' Sean said, holding out his phone with the picture of Dorsch in the gay sauna on the screen.

Before Sean could react, Dorsch had grabbed the phone and twisted Sean's arm up his back. Then he spun him around and pinned him against the wall by his neck. 'Where did you get this?' Dorsch asked, saliva bubbling from his mouth.

'I followed you into the sauna and saw you have sex with seven men,' Sean said.

'What are you going to do with it?' Dorsch increased the pressure on Sean's neck, cutting off the supply of air to his lungs. But Sean didn't attempt to fight back; he just held his breath and waited.

Then, suddenly the pressure was released, as Dorsch was sent flying backwards onto the pavement grabbing at the air. Steve and

Pete stood over him, crouched and ready for him to make a move. But Dorsch didn't move, seemingly knowing that his two assailants were professionals and that he'd be wasting his time.

'To answer your question, I'm going to send it to every newspaper in Germany… if you don't start talking, that is,' Sean said, rubbing his neck.

Dorsch looked again at Pete and Steve, assessing his chances in a fight. 'Okay, but not here. In my office. It's just over there.' He nodded his head in the direction of his office building.

'No, somewhere more neutral. Come with us. If you make any attempt to get away, we'll publish the photo,' Clive said.

The walk back to the hotel by the main train station took a little over five minutes. Dorsch was flanked by Steve and Pete and made no attempt to run or speak. Clive and Sean walked behind. Once in the hotel, they went to Clive's room.

Dorsch was positioned on a seat by the desk, well away from the door, with Pete and Steve on either side of him, ready to react, should he try anything. Clive sat on the edge of the bed.

'Okay, how much do you want?' Dorsch said, pulling his mouth to one side.

'This isn't about money,' Sean said, surprised at Dorsch's statement.

'Then what is it about?' Dorsch responded, equally surprised, obviously assuming that it was some kind of extortion attempt.

'As I said: the Fourth Reich. Are you involved in it?' Sean said.

'You followed me and took these pictures just for that? Do you know that those pictures would ruin my life? In my business, it's not good to have such tendencies,' he said, his German accent very clear.

'You mean homosexuality?' Sean said.

'If that's what you want to call it,' Dorsch answered.

'Well what would you call it?' Sean asked.

'A kink; nothing more. I like anal sex, but I'm not attracted to men.'

'Okay,' Sean said, then changed back to the real subject of his interview. 'Well, are you involved in the Fourth Reich?' Sean asked again.

Before he spoke, Dorsch looked Sean up and down making him feel as if he was being strip-searched. 'No, I'm not, but I do know more than I said earlier.'

'How?' Sean asked.

'I was approached by them: first by Glas, then by Wagner. They tried to recruit me, would you believe?' Dorsch said, with a wry grin.

'I don't understand. Why is it funny?' Sean said.

'Firstly, as you know, I have sexual tendencies which don't exactly fit their view of the ideal German; and secondly, I'm actually Jewish.'

Sean frowned. 'But Dorsch isn't a Jewish name.'

'No, my grandfather changed our name before the war to avoid being interned by the Nazis. I'm not a practising Jew, so nobody would know now. It's just my heritage.'

'So when they approached you, why didn't you go to the authorities?' Sean continued with his questioning.

'And say what? They hadn't broken any laws. Everybody knows that Wagner's a Nazi, and Glas… well, he's nearly dead anyway.'

'Why do you think they approached you?' Clive asked.

'I don't know, maybe because I have over 8,000 highly trained soldiers at my disposal.'

'What did they want you to do?' Sean asked.

'They asked me to take a cabinet post in this so-called Fourth

Reich. I thought it was all a bit crazy to be honest. They said that they'd organised over 400 once disparate Nazi groups from Moscow to London; that they now had a membership of over 300,000; and that they were preparing to restore the Fatherland to its rightful place in Europe.'

'300,000 people! Didn't that make you think it was more serious?' Clive asked.

'Not really. I didn't believe them and I'm sure most of their so-called membership is made up of disillusioned children, playing on the Internet.'

Maybe not. Sean thought about the number of divisions on the org chart.

'Did they tell you who ran the organisation, or who their deputy was?' Sean questioned further.

'No. I remember that they said the Vice Chancellor was somebody high up in the EU, but they didn't say who, and frankly, I didn't believe them, so I didn't push it. Then they started to babble all kinds of nonsense, so I just switched off.'

'What do you mean?' Sean asked.

'Well they started to talk about bloodlines and the natural heirs to the European throne. I really just wanted to get away from them, so I didn't question it any further.'

'Bloodlines? You mean like descendants of Hitler?' Clive said.

Dorsch shrugged. 'Hitler, the Kaiser, Attila… who knows and who cares? They're all crazy. I wanted no part of it.'

'Is there anything else you can tell us about them?' Sean asked, laughing.

'No, that's about all I remember. Now, will you erase the photos?'

Before responding, Sean thought about Dorsch's answers. He'd been cooperative and he seemed believable. 'Yes, I'm sorry. That's not how I normally go about an interview.'

'Thank you. And if you want my advice, forget these idiots. They're nothing but a bunch of misguided fools, goose-stepping around in Nazi uniforms and carrying on. It's embarrassing.'

The interview over, Steve showed Dorsch to the door and let him out.

'Do you believe him?' Sean asked Clive when Dorsch had gone.

'I'm not sure. He could just be a good liar.'

'There is one part of his story we should be able to test. He said his grandfather changed their name before the war. Liz is pretty good at digging through that kind of thing. I'll go and get her. If he is a Jew, it's pretty certain he wouldn't get involved with this lot.'

Chapter Thirty-Two

Tuesday, 9th February. Munich, Germany.

Sean left the room they had used to interview Dorsch and made his way down the corridor to his own room, knocking loudly on the door to wake Liz, who quickly opened it for him. To his surprise she was already dressed, and Praew was with her. 'Look at this,' she passed her iPad to Sean.

The page was opened on the *BBC News* app and the headline immediately caught Sean's eye: UNITED KINGDOM DEFAULTS ON EU LOAN. A shiver ran down his spine. 'Do you think this is it? What they've been planning?' he said.

'Read on,' Liz replied.

The rest of the article outlined the technical default by the United Kingdom and nine other members of the EU. 'So, they haven't actually defaulted on a payment of debt, it's just a technicality. That can't be too bad,' he said.

'That's what I thought, until I read this.' Liz clicked over onto another website, which had an analysis of the default. Sean read that the loan wasn't a loan from the EU Central Bank to the UK;

it was the other way. But one of the thousands of technical clauses in the loan required the buyers to hold certain levels of euro reserves; in fact, these levels were so high that the only way the UK could comply would be to adopt the Euro as its own currency and drop Sterling. Of course, the UK Government had refused to do this when the default was notified by the European Commission. It stated that: 'its interpretation of the clause was that it only applied to countries whose currency was already the euro'.

The European Court of Justice had ruled on the clause last week and upheld the Commission's view that it applied to *all bond holders*.

'Couldn't they just sell the bonds?' Sean asked.

'Apparently not: they're fixed term and not transferrable.'

'What about the other countries?'

'All of the Eastern European ones want to be in the euro anyway, but don't qualify yet. That only leaves Denmark and Sweden, and they're in exactly the same boat as the UK.'

'Bugger! So what now?' Sean said, shaking his head.

'The UK Government has been given a week to make a plan to get back in compliance with the loan; i.e., agree a time to transfer to the euro, or face other penalties, which as you know could now mean suspension.'

'Do you think that they *know* it could mean suspension?' Sean frowned.

'I haven't seen anything that says that; in fact, the opposite. Most commentators are just talking about a fine and more provocation for the UK to leave the EU.' Liz replied. 'How did it go with Dorsch?'

Sean quickly explained the outcome of the interview.

'I'll see what I can do, but if he'd hidden his identity well enough to fool the Nazis prior to the war, I doubt there'll be anything to uncover now,' Liz replied. 'Let's go and talk to Clive. This is all getting very complicated and I think the urgency may have just been stepped up, given the news on the default,' Liz said.

When Sean and Liz arrived at Clive's room, he was alone. Steve and Pete had decided to follow Dorsch to see if he made any interesting moves. Sitting on the bed, Sean quickly explained the situation at the EU to Clive.

'Amazing that we haven't heard anything sooner, if there was a court case,' Clive responded.

'I guess everybody thought it was just bureaucracy at work and that it would amount to nothing. There are constant challenges by member states in the EU courts that never get reported,' Liz said.

'How serious do you think this could be?' Clive asked.

'I don't know, but it's clear that the UK, Sweden and Denmark can't quickly rectify their default. I still find it hard to believe that they'll actually suspend them, based on a technicality, using some dubiously worded translations,' Liz said.

'Hmmm, I'm not sure. It depends who's behind it and what their end game is,' Sean added.

'What do you think it could be?' Clive asked.

Sean considered Clive's question briefly. He was quickly coming to the realization that they really didn't know anything, and that all the information they'd gathered had no definite links. 'I really don't know, but I think we need to work out what we've got before we make our next move.'

Clive immediately produced a piece of blank paper. 'Agreed.' He drew a circle in the centre of the page, but then stopped. 'You know, I don't even know what to put in the centre of the page. Are we investigating the corruption in the EU primarily; the murder of Allsop and Phil; or the Nazis and Glas?'

It was a relevant question. So far all of the work seemed to add up to three independent enquiries with only tenuous interconnection. 'I think you have to put the EU corruption at the centre,' Liz said. 'To me, it's the common link.'

Clive wrote 'EU corruption' in the centre circle, then drew more circles, orbiting the centre. Working in a clockwise direction he wrote: 'Glas' in the first; 'Wagner' in the second; '4R18' in the third; 'Allsop' in the fourth; 'Faustein' in the fifth; 'Dorsch' in the sixth; and 'Blom' in the seventh. Then using different colours he started to join the circles. First, Glas, Blom, Faustein, Allsop and the EU were linked. Then, 4R18, Wagner and Glas, with a dotted line to Dorsch. Finally, he drew a line between Glas, Blom and Wagner, indicating a separate link.

'I drew that because I think it's the only link we understand more about,' Clive said. 'The set-up of Blom meeting Wagner was obviously a plan to get Blom out of the way and replace him with somebody else.'

'Who was he replaced with?' Sean asked.

'Gunther Matthias; a German who was previously responsible for budgeting,' Liz answered.

Clive immediately added another circle for Matthias. 'He has to be involved somehow,' he said.

'What about what Dorsch said? That the Nazis have a senior figure in the EU?' Liz added.

Clive added a dotted line from Matthias to 4R18. 'He's certainly a senior figure,' he said.

'But what would that achieve: one commissioner, who's appointed by the German Government?' Sean asked.

'Hmm, I don't know. You know, we really don't know enough about the internal struggles at the EU to work out what's going on here and the motivations behind it,' Liz said.

'We could ask Anna?' Clive suggested.

'She's part of the system. We need somebody more impartial,' Liz said quickly.

'What about Nathan Shaw? When he left the *Daily* he went to Brussels to work as the EU correspondent for the *Economic News*? He's one of my LinkedIn connections. I know he's a bit of a prat, but he may well be able to help,' Sean said.

'A bit of a prat? That's an understatement! But if we have to, at least he should be independent,' Liz responded.

Sean managed to contact Shaw and set up a Skype call quickly. When he'd worked with Sean at the *Financial Daily*, Shaw had been a real pain; he'd arrived straight from university with an attitude that he was better than everybody else because he came from a privileged background. But he'd soon learned that nobody in the news room cared about his parents, and that he had to prove himself to get ahead. After a bit of work from Sean, he'd turned himself into a competent reporter, but still couldn't get along with the rest of the team, and eventually left. In his current role as a political reporter, his family contacts were important and he'd thrived.

When his face appeared on the small screen of Liz's laptop, he hadn't changed much in the four years since Sean had seen him last: his hair was still slicked back against his head tightly, and his gaunt face looked as if he hadn't been fed in years.

'Hi, Nathan,' Sean said.

'Hey, McManus. How may I be of assistance?' the pompous voice replied.

Sean wasn't about to tell him anything about the investigation in case he stole the story, so he carefully fed him some snippets. 'A piece I'm working on has some EU element and I thought you may be able to shed some light on a few of the subtleties.'

Shaw laughed loudly. 'Maybe. But I thought you'd have given up political reporting after your last attempt?'

'What?' Sean was genuinely bemused.

'The Blom piece. Clearly it was a set-up. Blom's an alcoholic and a gambler, but he's no Nazi,' Shaw continued to laugh.

'But he met with Wagner. How was it a set-up?' Sean didn't disclose that he knew that Blom had been set up by Glas.

'I'm sure that was staged for your benefit. Why do you think that whoever was feeding you information didn't go to one of us?'

'I don't know,' Sean replied, a sudden jolt of panic entering his mind.

'Because we'd have seen the politicking behind it and not reported it,' Shaw continued to laugh.

Suddenly, Sean felt a heavy weight on his chest. Shaw was saying that it was *he* who'd been set up, to finish Blom's career. Had somebody been playing them all this time; pushing him into a position for their own gains? 'Who'd do that? Why?' he said.

'Who gained most from Blom's removal?'

'Matthias?' Sean suggested.

Shaw pulled a face. 'But he just got transferred to another directorate, so he didn't really gain anything. I'd say the real winners were the Parliament in general. Following the scandal, their powers were increased quite a lot at the expense of the Commission. And then there's the new Commission President; he only got an opportunity because the old one resigned, following your scandal piece.'

'So who would want to increase the powers of the Parliament?' Sean asked.

'The federalists, of course! That gives you about 250 million people to work with. What you have to understand about the EU is that it's divided by a power struggle between the state governments, represented by the two councils, and the Parliament, represented by the MEPs. Keeping more power with the councils is something supported by the sceptics, like the UK, while the federalists would rather see the power given to the Parliament to act like a real state, independent of the member governments.'

When Sean thought about Shaw's comments, they made sense, but it didn't fit with the view he'd formed of what was going on. 'What about the Commission? Isn't the real issue that unelected officials in the Commission were being given too much power?'

Shaw pursed his lips. 'Not really. Although the Commission acts like it's in charge, it's really just a pawn, controlled by others. But whoever controls the Commission controls the EU.'

'And who controls the Commission?'

Shaw laughed again. 'Well, until recently the state governments, via the councils, but the scandal from your article, and more importantly, the way the new President came to power, has shifted that balance towards the Parliament. In fact more specifically towards one party.'

'What was that about the President?'

'In the past, the selection of the Commission President was the sole domain of the European Council, but the Treaty of Lisbon added that the candidate must be approved by the Parliament. This, in effect, gave the selection power to the Parliament.'

'Well, isn't that a good thing? It sounds like it; the elected members taking power from the unelected bureaucrats?'

'That depends on your point of view, old boy. If the Parliament takes control of the Commission, the EU truly frees itself of member state government interference, and the EU becomes a real federal state… with a Parliament elected by the people in control of the resources and laws. It means the end of national sovereignty in Europe.'

'From what you've just said, isn't it already there?'

Shaw tilted his head slightly. 'Not quite. Almost, but luckily, the various treaties still limit the power of the EU, and the heads of state still have to unanimously adopt new treaties.'

A knot formed in Sean's stomach. He knew that the default on the loan gave the Commission President power to suspend member states, which would allow them to change the unanimity requirement for a treaty. Where his thinking had been wrong was that he'd been led to believe that this was a power-push by the Commission. The real winners, however, would be the Parliament; more specifically one party in the Parliament. *Damn! I've been played,* he thought.

During his investigations, he'd only encountered three members of the parliament: Allsop, who was dead; Glas, who was involved somehow, but as a peripheral player; and Anna Faustein, who had transformed herself from a lowly backbencher to the most important person in the Parliament… and if these changes were made, the most important person in Europe.

'Thanks, Nathan. That was really helpful,' Sean said quickly.

'Is that all you wanted, old boy?' Shaw said.

'Yes, thanks,' Sean said, desperate to get off the call.

After disconnecting the call, Sean turned to Liz and Clive. 'We've been set up,' he said, the colour draining from his face.

'How? By whom?' Liz asked.

'Anna Faustein,' Sean conceded.

'How did you get there?' Clive said.

'She was the person that steered us towards Blom, then stopped us looking further. She was the one that seeded the idea that the Commission was getting out of control and needed to be stopped... and she's the one who's gained most from it,' Sean said.

'So, you're suggesting that she had Allsop killed and staged the attempt on her own life, when Phil was killed, just to push us in a certain direction?' Clive said.

'Yes. Then she got us to back off. She never expected us to visit Blom and go after Glas,' Sean said. 'I can't believe I've been so stupid. I should've seen it.' He cursed his own naivety.

'It all fits. She was the one person who knew what Allsop was on to, and then her sudden appearance in London,' Liz said.

'And the Nazi link?' Clive asked.

'She could be the Vice Chancellor of 4R18. Dorsch said it was somebody high up in the EU. If she pulls this off there'll be nobody higher,' Sean said.

Pulling out a red pen, Clive drew three circles around Anna Faustein's name on the page, making it stand out from the other names, acknowledging that he agreed with Sean's analysis.

'My god, if you're right, that means Europe could be being governed by a Nazi as soon as the next few weeks,' Liz commented.

'Days!' Sean corrected.

'But the UK will just pull out, surely?' Clive suggested.

'I don't think we'd have a choice, but I still don't like the idea of a Nazi being in charge of Europe,' Sean said.

MEPs are elected in local elections by claiming to be members of a domestic political party, i.e., Conservative, Labour, UKIP, etc, and by claiming to represent local and national interests in Brussels.

However, when those same MEPs attend the European Parliament, they swear their allegiance to a different, transnational, party and cast their vote based upon the view of their transnational party leader.

This system effectively blocks any local or national interests in the EU Parliament and ensures that the real power lies with the huge transnational political parties.

Chapter Thirty-Three

Tuesday, 9th February. Munich, Germany.

It was 10 a.m. in the morning when the hospital called to say that Terry was awake and that his vital signs were improving rapidly. Sean, Liz and Clive broke off their discussions, collected Praew, and ran to the nearby hospital. When they arrived, Terry was sitting up in bed, still connected to a drip, but the ventilator was gone. Through the bandages, Sean saw the recognition in his eyes as they came over to the bed. Praew immediately held his hand gently and smiled. 'I knew you'd be okay,' she said.

'He's improved a lot overnight,' the doctor said as he entered the room behind them.

'Enough to travel to London?' Liz asked.

'If things go well today, he should be able to be moved tomorrow. We've contacted the NHS and they've found him a bed in the Chelsea and Westminster Hospital.'

'That's great,' Sean said.

'I'll go with him and make sure he's looked after. It means I can get Praew back to school as well,' Liz added.

Two hours later, they sat down to lunch at a café on Landsbergerstrasse. 'We could just take what we have to the British Government?' Clive said.

'We don't have anything to take but speculation. They'll just laugh at us. Besides, who would we go to see?' Sean replied.

'I still have some contacts, but you're right. I'm not sure where I'd start with this story,' Clive nodded.

'I think we really need to decide what the story is that we're chasing. Is it that the Parliament is trying to take over the EU and federalise Europe by the back door? Or that the most powerful person in that parliament may be a Nazi?' Sean said.

'Surely it's both,' Liz said.

'That'll spread our resources thin,' Sean replied.

Liz shrugged. 'I can go back to Grandpa for more money.'

'Not yet. Let's see how we go with what we've got,' Sean said defensively. He'd only just managed to buy half of the business and pay back the debts to Liz's grandfather; he had no intention of going back so quickly to where he'd started.

'Okay, so we head for Brussels with Pete and Steve, and it's all eyes on Faustein,' Clive said.

'Yes, tomorrow, but in the meantime, her constituency is here in Munich. Maybe we can dig up some background info on her?' Sean suggested.

Within a couple of hours, Liz had found a former residential address for Anna. It now appeared to be occupied by her ex-husband, Bertram Faustein. 'We'll go and take a look,' Clive said.

'At least we know that *Faustein* is her married name. Have you found a maiden name?' Sean asked.

'Not yet. The data's in German and I'm having to translate it all through a translator, so it's pretty time-consuming. You go with Clive and I should have more when you get back,' Liz replied.

Landsberg-am-Lech was a medium-sized town in Munich's commuter belt. The cobbled main square was triangular in shape and surrounded by colourful traditional Bavarian buildings. A fresh smattering of snow covered the rooftops, but it had melted on the ground.

'It says we're here,' Clive said, pointing to the GPS in the rental car.

Carefully scanning the area around them, they parked the car just outside the pedestrianised square. Above the narrow boutiques that lined the street, small apartments made up the second storey of the buildings. Sean counted down to number 32. 'That's it,' he said, and walked down to the front of a small florist's shop.

Next to the entrance to the shop a small yellow door led to the upstairs apartment. 'It looks tiny; not exactly the home of a man who's just made a massive divorce settlement,' Clive questioned.

Nodding his agreement, Sean quickly leant forward and pressed the doorbell.

'What are you doing? If we talk to him, Anna might get wind of it,' Clive said quickly, pulling Sean's hand away from the doorbell. But it was too late; he'd already pressed it.

'We're out of time on this one, Clive. We need to take the direct route,' Sean replied. 'Besides, it's only 3 o'clock; he's probably still at work.'

An answer to the bell soon proved Sean's theory wrong. '*Hallo?*' a voice said over the intercom.

'Mr Faustein? Do you speak English?' Sean asked.

'A little,' the quiet voice came back.

'We'd like to ask you a few questions about your ex-wife, Anna,' Sean said.

'We're divorced. I have nothing more to say,' Faustein replied.

'I know, but you may still be able to help,' Sean tried to counter the initial resistance.

'Please go away, or I'll call the police,' the heavily accented reply came, this time more forcefully.

Frustrated by the response, but not willing to explain things to the police, Sean stepped back from the small entranceway and walked down the street.

'What do you make of that?' Sean asked, when Clive caught up.

'Either he's being harassed by the press constantly and is sick of it, or he's scared of Anna and won't risk speaking to the press?' Clive suggested.

'He could just be a private, angry man,' Sean said.

'Let's see what happens next; that should give us a few clues,' Clive said, walking into a small café with a view of the door to Faustein's apartment.

Before the waitress arrived at the table with two steaming cups of coffee, a silver BMW 7 series pulled up outside Faustein's apartment. Two men in their thirties, dressed in black suits were sitting in the front seats of the car. In the rear, an older man, dressed in a traditional Bavarian jacket was speaking to them. Then, the door opened to the apartment and a gaunt man in his mid-forties stepped out of the door.

'Let's go,' Clive said and pulled out ten euros from his pocket, dropping them on the table next to the untouched coffee. Keeping an eye on the BMW, they exited the café and made their way quickly to the rental car, trying not to attract the attention of the people in the BMW, which was pulling away, with Bertram Faustein now inside.

'He didn't look well at all,' Clive said as he followed behind the BMW at a safe distance. When it twisted and turned its way through the narrow historic streets, they followed, always far enough away that they wouldn't attract attention. In no time at all, they were out of the pretty Bavarian town and turning onto the main road south, towards Garmisch-Partenkirchen.

The road was relatively busy, so Clive tucked in a few cars behind the BMW. Then, no more than five kilometres outside Landsberg, it pulled off the road. To avoid being spotted, Clive pulled the car past the turn-off and stopped a few hundred metres further on, on the hard shoulder.

'Looks like a disused construction site. I don't like the look of that,' Clive said, climbing out of the car.

Following on quickly, Sean joined Clive on the side of the road as they started to run in the direction of the site. They made their way through a wooded area by the road, then, about fifty metres in, they arrived at a high mesh fence. Sean instinctively dropped to the floor when he saw the silver BMW, copied immediately by Clive.

On the other side of the fence, in a small clearing that looked like it had been cleared for some forgotten construction, the two younger men were holding the undernourished Faustein. The older man was asking him questions, spitting aggressively as he spoke. When Sean saw the panic in Clive's face, he wondered what was troubling him.

'What's wrong?' Sean asked.

'That,' Clive said looking at the scene in front of them, helpless to stop it.

The older man had produced a small pistol and was holding

it to the head of Faustein, who was now pleading for his life. Sean quickly pulled out his phone to film the scene. But before he could hit record, without warning, the man pulled the trigger.

A stream of blood shot backwards from Faustein's head, as he crumpled to the floor, dead. Without any hesitation, the two younger men dragged the body to a hole in the ground and rolled it in.

'Fuck!' Sean said, as the same two men went to the boot of the BMW and collected two shovels, quickly returning to the hole and starting to fill it in on top of Faustein. The older man cleaned the gun carefully, then tossed it into the hole with Faustein's body.

'We've got to get out of here before they do,' Clive whispered, grabbing Sean's arm.

Sean didn't move; his body was paralysed with fear at the scene he'd just witnessed. 'Come on,' Clive said, intensifying his grip.

Feeling the pressure on his arm, Sean suddenly snapped out of his daze and backed away from the fence with Clive. Once out of the woods, they sprinted down to the car, where Clive made a U-turn and headed back in the direction of Landsberg.

'What now?' Sean asked, still shaken by the execution.

'It'll take them fifteen minutes or so to cover that body well enough, so we've got ten minutes.'

'For what?' Sean asked.

'To search Faustein's apartment.'

After what Sean had just witnessed, the last place he wanted to go was to a place where the same men could well follow, but he trusted Clive's instinct; it hadn't let them down before, and he stayed quiet.

It took Clive a matter of seconds to pick the lock to Faustein's door. Once inside, they both ran up the narrow staircase, which led straight into the small dark lounge room. There were only three rooms in the apartment: a bedroom; a lounge/kitchen; and a small bathroom. Clive scanned the area, looking for something. 'Look at the family pictures; none have Anna in,' he said.

'Could just mean a bad divorce,' Sean said.

Clive quickly opened a bureau style desk that sat against the wall and started flicking through the few papers that were there. Then, after finding nothing of interest, he moved into the bedroom. The room was tiny and stank of sweat and cigarettes as Sean entered. A traditional wooden wardrobe, wedged into the corner, barely had room for the doors to open, as Sean pulled at the wooden handles.

'You need to see this,' he said to Clive.

The only clothes in the wardrobe which were actually hung neatly were covered by a transparent plastic cover. The brown Nazi shirt had a small metal badge attached to the collar with an inscription, *LL18*. 'Landsberg-am-Lech Adolf Hitler,' Sean said. 'It looks like Mr Faustein was a member of the same club as Glas and Wagner.'

'Then why kill him? Was it just coincidence that we were here?' Clive said.

'What if he knew too much, and was no longer of any use to them? Then when he called to say that we'd visited, they decided that they couldn't take the risk anymore,' Sean said.

'That could be right. Following his divorce, he could be a liability if Anna is involved and he knows about it.'

The sight of the uniform somehow made Sean feel less guilty about the murder and he helped Clive continue to search the room. He looked under the bed and in the small chest of drawers, but found nothing.

'We need to get out of here. If they think he knew something, they may well be heading this way,' Clive said.

Their search complete anyway, Sean went back into the lounge and moved towards the stairwell. Before descending he took one last look around the spartan room. There was something wrong and he knew it, but what was it? Then his eyes were drawn to the shabby two-seater couch; one of the cushions was crumpled and dented in the centre, the other was flat.

'What are you doing? We've got to go,' Clive said, as Sean pushed past him and went back into the room.

Ignoring him, Sean lifted the cushion and found a blue cardboard envelope style folder, bulging with papers. 'Okay, let's go,' he said, putting the folder under his arm.

As they reached the halfway point on the stairs, Sean froze: the distinctive shape of the silver BMW 7 series was pulling up outside the door. He leaned forward and grabbed Clive's shoulder, pointing through the small window above the architrave.

'Did you see another way out?' Sean said.

'No,' Clive replied, in a sombre tone.

Chapter Thirty-Four

Tuesday, 9th February. Landsberg-am-Lech, Germany.

'Stay close,' Clive said as he stepped down the remaining stairs.

With his pulse racing, Sean followed one stair behind. He heard the two front doors of the car open and then slam shut. Then footsteps approached the door.

'Head down, shoulder in,' Clive whispered, as the key entered the lock right in front of them.

As soon as the door had swung open Clive rushed forward with his head down, smashing his shoulder into the first of the two men, Sean charged out behind, repeating the move on the next man, until both fell to the floor beside the BMW.

Clive grabbed Sean by the coat and pulled him away, virtually pushing him into the rental car, as the older man climbed out of the BMW and the two stunned assailants got to their feet.

The first shot from the BMW hit the steering wheel of the rental car, as Clive spun the wheels away and skidded around a corner into the pedestrianised square. Within seconds, the BMW followed with its tyres screeching as it hit the cobbles.

Fighting to stay in control on the cobbles, Clive guided the car through the old archway at the top of the square and back onto the road, quickly flinging it right into the oncoming traffic. He swerved deftly around one car, then another, before he turned left into a side street and floored the pedal again.

'Call Liz,' Clive said, while still driving at full speed. 'Tell her to get Terry and get out of there. They know who we are and they'll be coming for them.'

Just then, the BMW entered the street about 150 metres behind them. 'This thing doesn't have the power, but it's more nimble than that,' Clive said, as he swerved right into a narrow street filled with houses, then screeched left into the next street.

Holding onto the door handle as the car swerved left and right through tight spaces, continually increasing the gap between them and the BMW, Sean called Liz. 'Come on, Liz,' Sean said, as the phone rang. But she didn't answer and the call went to voicemail.

He quickly dialled again, with the same result. 'Bollocks!' he said and dialled again. But still there was no answer. 'I'll try again in a minute.'

'Try Pete or Steve,' Clive said.

Sean quickly dialled the number he had been given for Steve.

'Hey, Sean,' the answer came on the first ring.

'I can't explain everything now, but we need to get Liz, Praew and Terry out of harm's way as quickly as possible,' Sean said.

'Shit, we're about 45 minutes away. We've followed Dorsch to a small village north of Munich,' Steve said.

'Damn!' Sean exclaimed. 'Can you get back as soon as possible? We'll see you in Munich. If you get there before us, could you get Terry out of the hospital?'

'We're on our way,' Steve said. 'Stay in touch.'

As they screeched past a sign for the *Autobahn* in the direction of Munich, Clive seemed to get even more from the small Volkswagen. When Sean looked at the rev dial, it was sat on 7,000 revs. The small engine was tearing itself apart to maintain the high speed in low gear.

A few minutes later, they hit the Autobahn at 175 kilometres per hour and when Sean turned, there was no sight of the silver BMW. Clive's manoeuvring had thrown them off in the back streets of Landsberg.

Settling into his seat, Sean quickly tried Liz again… but still no answer.

In the thirty minutes that it took them to get to Munich, Sean called Liz's phone forty-five times, but she didn't answer any of the attempts. Clive bumped the car onto the pavement outside the hotel and before he could fully stop, Sean jumped out and ran through the foyer to the lift. He hit the back wall of the small space as he ran in so hard, swivelling athletically to hit the button for the seventh floor. Panting with impatience as the lift went through its processes. On the seventh floor, he sprinted to the door of the room he and Liz shared and put the card in the lock, opening it aggressively.

Liz's things were still strewn around the room, but there was no sign of her. Sean immediately ran to the next room, the one occupied by Praew, and started banging heavily on the door, but nobody answered.

Confusion infused with panic ran through his body as he ran back to the lift and went to the ground floor, pushing past some people at the reception counter. 'Have you seen the Asian lady and girl that were staying in rooms 701 and 702?' he asked the receptionist, panting heavily.

The receptionist didn't say anything, clearly thinking. 'Yes, about an hour ago, they went out of the door together. In that direction, I think.' He pointed to the right. 'Is anything wrong?'

'No,' Sean shook his head and sprinted back out of the revolving door to the car, where people were walking around it on the pavement making angry comments to Clive, who just ignored them.

'She's not there. Let's go to the hospital,' Sean said.

Pushing into the busy traffic, Clive immediately backed the car onto the road and sped forward towards the hospital. Two minutes later he pulled the car into an emergency waiting spot and they both ran in the direction of the entrance.

They both entered Terry's ward at the same time, banging the twin swinging doors open. Terry was sitting up in bed, all of the tubes and drips were removed, but he was still covered in bandages.

'Have you seen Liz or Praew?' Sean asked.

Terry shook his head.

'Fuck! Where are they,' Sean's tone went up an octave.

'Calm down! We'll find them, but we have to get Terry out of here now,' Clive said firmly.

Biting his lip in frustration, Sean quickly helped Clive bundle Terry into a wheelchair. A few minutes later, they were wheeling Terry out of the front door of the hospital.

'We can't get him in the car. What are we going to do?' Sean said.

'I don't know,' Clive responded, as they passed the rental Volkswagen and ran out of the hospital grounds.

'Wait,' Sean said and ran back to the car, grabbing the cardboard folder he'd taken from Faustein's apartment.

'We may need this,' he said, when he caught up again.

Terry hadn't attempted to move or speak during his enforced discharge from the hospital, seemingly understanding that it was best that he just sit in the chair and stay still.

When they'd extracted 400 euros each from the cash machine, Clive walked into a nearby hotel, followed by Sean pushing the wheelchair.

'We need two twin rooms, please,' Clive asked the receptionist standing beside the grubby counter in the tired reception area. It was a far cry from the room in the hotel they'd left, but it would be safer.

Once they were safely in the room, Clive instructed Sean to go back the other hotel and gather everything he could from their rooms; computers, passports etc. and then come back.

A sense of foreboding was building in Sean as he made his way back towards the hotel. He ran as fast as he could, dodging between the pedestrians, but not hanging around to apologise when he bumped into some of them.

About thirty metres from the hotel door, he stopped suddenly and pressed himself against a pillar, when he saw two men dressed in dark business suits, leaving the hotel via the main door. One of them was carrying Sean's messenger bag, the other was wheeling Liz's suitcase behind him.

As the two men walked away from the hotel, Sean made a quick decision to follow them. Staying close to the edge of the buildings, he walked about thirty metres behind on the busy pavement, keeping them in sight.

A short way along the street, they climbed into the rear of a black Mercedes. Desperate not to lose them, Sean ran into the road and physically stopped a passing cab. 'Follow… er… *schwarz Mercedes*,' he said, pointing to the car the two men had climbed into.

'It's okay, I speak English,' the taxi driver said. 'You must be James Bond,' he added.

Two blocks in front of them and getting away, the black Mercedes turned left onto the main road across the Karlsplatz.

'Quickly, please,' Sean said as the lights were changing.

Possibly sensing Sean's panic, the driver sped through the light on amber and took his place four cars behind the Mercedes. Two minutes later it turned right and drove into the Maximillianspl atz, where it slowed down quickly and made a sharp right turn.

'Shit! I know where this is,' Sean said to himself as the taxi pulled through the arched gate of the old city wall. A hundred or so metres ahead of them on Prannerstrasse, the Mercedes pulled up outside the offices of Stefan Dorsch.

'Pull over here,' Sean said, as he watched the two men climb out of the car and enter Dorsch's office, carrying the things they'd taken from the hotel.

'Bayerstrasse. Hotel Krefelderhof, please,' Sean said, instructing the driver to take him back to the old hotel so that he could see what had been taken.

When he entered the room he and Liz had occupied, it had clearly been ransacked in the search for something. He quickly went to the safe, but it had been opened and the contents taken. Then he made his way to Praew's room, the door wasn't fully closed and he walked into the same scene, clothes strewn everywhere and the safe open. Shaking with fear, he quickly ran down the corridor to Clive's room. It too had been ransacked and there was nothing left but clothes. Then the room Pete and Steve shared; the same.

When he ran back out of the lobby onto the street he paused for a while, checking that he wasn't being followed. He repeated the same procedure six times before he entered the lobby of their new hotel, just three blocks away.

Steve and Pete were already there, having received

instructions from Clive not to go back to the old hotel and Sean quickly relayed what he'd seen.

'We need to go to the police. They've got Liz and Praew,' Sean said.

'No police yet. We need to know what's going on first. If the flatfoots go blundering in there, Liz and Praew will be gone, never to be seen again,' Clive said.

'What could they want with them?' Sean asked.

Clive reached across to the table and lifted the blue cardboard folder. 'My guess is this folder. It must contain something very important,' he said.

Chapter Thirty-Five

Tuesday, 9th February. Munich, Germany.

It was bitterly cold when Liz and Praew left the hotel to return to the hospital, in order to check on Terry. Liz pulled Praew close into her body and huddled her away from the icy gusts of wind, as they both bowed their heads forward.

When they passed Goetherstrasse on the way to Landsbegerstrasse, Liz had already had enough of walking in the cold and she turned to hail a cab. Fortunately, one was just pulling up behind them. Liz helped Praew in to the car and then hopped into the back with her, feeling the sudden relief as the warm air hit her face.

It was only when the car turned right at the end of the street that she started to worry. She chose not to say anything, assuming that they were just being ripped off by a driver not wanting such a low fare, and she didn't want to make a scene over a few euros. But when the car pulled into a darkened car park behind the train station, she realised that something was wrong. She instinctively grabbed at the door handle trying to push it open… but it was locked.

With panic welling up inside her, she lunged forward to grab the driver's hair, but he just knocked her arm away easily, before he stopped the car. As the wheels came to a halt on the tarmac surface, Liz reached out for Praew and pulled her closer to her body. With her other hand she felt around in her pocket for a pen. *If this bastard is going to try to rape us, he's going to regret it!* she thought, rolling her fingers around the thin round implement.

Just as she was preparing to make a second attack on the driver, this time with the pen in her hand, aiming at his neck; her door opened and a burly man, dressed in a black tracksuit pulled her out of the car.

When her body hit the cold tarmac, she screamed at the top of her voice, but her mouth was covered in seconds by a huge gloved hand, before it was taped closed. When her arms were pulled behind her back and tied, she struggled, but couldn't get free. On the other side of the car, Praew was fighting like a wild cat, but she too was subdued easily.

The last thing Liz remembered seeing before a hessian sack was placed over her head was Praew biting her assailant's hand.

The deprivation of the sense of sight made her feel disorientated, as she was pushed forward, held firmly at the top of her arm. She stumbled on a loose stone, then she was forced unpleasantly up a step, into some kind of van. The rancid smell of oil and petrol fumes filled her senses, as her knees were kicked from behind and she fell to the floor, face-down.

Only seconds later, the van started to move and her body bounced up and down against the metal floor painfully, while the hessian scratched at her face. Ignoring the pain, she tried to count the number of times the van turned, in case it was of any later use, but it was hopeless, and she soon lost count. Then suddenly, only a few minutes after they'd started, the van stopped and the engine was turned off.

The two front doors opened and closed again, then footsteps were coming to the rear door. Suddenly a rush of cold air hit her, as the doors opened. Liz lashed out with her feet into the dark space, but she didn't connect with anything.

Two hands suddenly grabbed her, pulling her violently out of the van. Then she heard Praew being dragged out behind her. *At least she's with me.* After being lifted to her feet, she was frog-marched for about five minutes, through several doors and up three flights of stairs, before she was thrown unceremoniously to the floor and strapped to something cold and solid, with her arms pulled at a painful distance behind her back.

Some shuffling a few metres away made her think that Praew was getting the same treatment, then the footsteps that had brought her there disappeared and a door closed just a short distance from where she lay.

Tied up and unable to see or speak, Liz started to cry softly. She was scared, but her tears weren't for herself; they were for Praew, who'd been dragged into yet another deadly situation, which was out of her control. *When would she ever be able to live without fear?* She cursed herself for getting Praew into this situation; then the British Government for wanting to deport her; then Koryalov for bullying her at school. *If anybody in the world deserved a good life, it was her!*

Chapter Thirty-Six

Tuesday, 9th February. Munich, Germany.

Sean opened the blue cardboard folder, while Clive, Steve and Pete discussed the best way to get to Dorsch.

'He couldn't have been there personally. We were watching him and he was thirty kilometres away,' Pete said.

'That doesn't mean his men didn't do it,' Clive said.

'They definitely went into Dorsch's office. That should be proof enough,' Sean added, to the agreement of Pete and Steve. Then he returned his attention to the contents of the file.

There were scores of photographs of Anna and Bertram Faustein. On the back of each one; a date, time and place was written clearly and they were all numbered. Placing them to one side for later review, he turned his attention to the papers. There were a number of official looking documents, but all were in German. Even though he couldn't read them, he had the feeling that they were immigration papers

Pulling out an official looking paper, he scanned the text. It was headed: TRAUSCHEIN, and was marked with the emblem of the Bavarian Government. He quickly keyed the word into a translator on his phone. 'Marriage Certificate,' he said to himself, then started to read the detail.

> *Bertram Elmar Faustein, born 21/04/1975, Landsberg-am-Lech, Bayern, Deutchland. Married Anna Maria Ruiz, born 12/02/1977, Cuiaba, Mato Grosso, Brasilien, on 05/03/1998.*

'Anna's Brazilian?' Sean said, stunned by the revelation.

'What? She doesn't look it,' Clive replied, 'or sound like it for that matter.'

Shaking his head, Sean scanned some of the photos from the pile, noting her long dark brown hair. 'She did, until she cut her hair and died it blonde,' Sean said. 'I guess her skin is quite dark. I just thought she was tanned,' he added.

'What else is in the file,' Clive asked.

'It just looks like immigration stuff: the documents and proof of a real relationship, so that she could get German residence, I guess.'

'Why would that be hidden?' Clive said.

'I don't know,' Sean said, shrugging, 'unless the marriage was a sham of course, just to get a German passport. No MEP would want that to get out. They'd have their passport removed and be deported,' he added.

'If that's all it is, where do the Nazis fit in? There has to be more to it,' Clive suggested.

Sean knew from experience that when Clive suspected something was incomplete, he was usually right. On the BW investigation he had forced Sean and Liz to look beyond the obvious and find the key links between the various players. But

Sean was distracted now, thinking about Liz and Praew, and couldn't concentrate on the detail. He scrambled aimlessly through the remaining documents, but nothing stood out.

'What are we going to do about Liz?' Sean asked.

'We're working on it, but it isn't going to be easy without weapons,' Clive said.

'Can't you get some?' Sean asked, remembering the virtual armoury that they'd taken to Dubrovnik.

'Not at this short notice in Germany,' he replied.

Ten minutes later, Clive broke from his huddle with Pete and Steve and called Sean over. 'Okay, here's the plan ... ' he started.

Chapter Thirty-Seven

Tuesday, 9th February. Munich, Germany.

Liz felt around with her fingers. The cold floor tiles and damp smell made her think that she was in a bathroom. When she heard a movement a few metres away, she made a humming sound through the tape on her mouth. The sound that returned confirmed that it was Praew. In a way she was relieved that Praew was still with her; at least, she hadn't been taken somewhere else. But guilt still riffled through her mind about putting the vulnerable young girl in this situation in the first place. Then a horrible thought occurred to her: *maybe she and Sean weren't suitable parents for such a girl after all. Maybe the Home Office rules were right!*

Trying to banish the thought, she pulled her shoulders forward, forcing her wrists against the pillar that was restraining her, but the thin straps cut into her painfully. Whatever it was that she was tied to was solid and immovable.

Trying something else, she managed to wriggle onto her side and kick out at the surrounding area. When her knee struck something cold and hard, she winced with pain, but still tried to assess what it was by stroking it with her leg. It felt like the side of a bath. Her previous instincts were good: they were in a bathroom.

Carefully assimilating all of the information she could, she also knew that they were still very close to where they'd been taken from, as the drive in the van had been less than five minutes. She hoped the proximity would help Clive and Sean piece together the clues and come to find them.

When her thoughts turned to Sean, a pang of guilt hit her stomach. She knew that she hadn't been treating him well since the lawyer had suggested that Praew's situation would be more secure if she and Sean didn't live together. She had mistakenly concluded in her mind that they had no choice: he'd have to move out and then it would be only a matter of time before their relationship broke down. That conclusion had led her to withdraw from him, to shun his affections, somehow in the belief that it would be better that way; that he might feel it was good that they parted.

Now, in a cold dark space, lost and terrified, clarity came to her. She wasn't willing to lose either Sean or Praew, and if she could get out of the current situation, she'd fight. She wouldn't hide her relationship with Sean from some petty bureaucrats; she'd flaunt it. Sean was and would be a good father to Praew and a good partner to her: he was loyal, caring and trustworthy, and Liz knew that he loved both her and Praew deeply. She knew that he'd risk his own life to protect them. Indeed, he had, a number of times.

She bit the inside of her lip, regretting that she hadn't told him how much she loved him, and told him that they'd get through it together, not apart. Now she'd been kidnapped and taken; possibly to her death!

Chapter Thirty-Eight

Tuesday, 9th February. Munich, Germany.

It was early in the evening and Munich was blanketed by dark clouds. As the freezing night air washed over Sean's face, he reflected upon everything that had happened to him since he'd met Liz and rescued Praew. They had been the best times of his life, even though for most of it he'd been recovering from injury. To wake up next to Liz each morning and watch her as she went about her daily chores gave him more pleasure than anything else he'd ever experienced. And seeing Praew develop from the lost and frightened girl, who didn't speak any English, to the intelligent and thoughtful young lady she was today, full of hope for the future, brought a tear to his eye.

You're not going to take that away from her, or Liz from me, he thought, focussing his anger on Dorsch, as Steve's voice came over the concealed headset.

'He's on his way home. Looks like he's got company this time: one in front about twenty metres; and one behind, about fifty metres,' Steve said.

Sean's muscles tensed. He'd always relied on Clive's men to tackle the more professional criminals they'd encountered. This time it was up to him, Steve and Pete would be otherwise detained and Clive's ability was limited by his injury.

Anger fuelled his body, as he stared out from behind his position, hidden between two vans on the exclusive street where Dorsch's apartment was situated. When Dorsch's first guard passed, scanning the area ahead of him, Sean recognised the guard as one of the two people he'd seen leaving his hotel. It was further proof that Dorsch was the right target. He had Liz and Praew, and scared as he was, it firmed up his resolve to act.

A few seconds later, Dorsch passed, walking the same way he had previously, head held high, as if he owned the world and feared nobody.

'Okay, let's go,' Steve said.

Suddenly acting on autopilot, Sean straightened and shot forward from his position, sprinting towards Dorsch, determined to make the impact heavy enough to floor the German. Pete had drilled into him how important the element of surprise was when fighting a better-equipped enemy.

As he launched himself at Dorsch like a rugby player heading into a tackle, Dorsch turned suddenly, but it was too late, Sean hit him at full speed, arms around his waist and sent him tumbling to the ground. Sean landed on top of him heavily. Then, out of nowhere, Clive appeared, grabbing at the shocked Dorsch's arms as best he could, trying to secure him. Sean grabbed his legs and pressured them to the ground, as the muscular Dorsch struggled.

Out of the corner of his eye, Sean could see Pete grappling successfully with the first bodyguard and securing his arms. Then he glanced the other way, where Steve was also winning his struggle with the unsuspecting guard.

Just then, Clive's prosthetic hand slipped from Dorsch's arm and he flipped over onto his side, sending Clive onto the ground next to him. Sean rammed his knee into Dorsch's groin hard, but the blow didn't even seem to affect him.

Moving his body skilfully, Dorsch wrapped his legs around Sean and pulled him over, righting himself in the same move. Now he was above Sean, sitting on his chest, arms ready to strike.

When Clive kicked out from the floor at Dorsch's head, he deftly moved away from the blow and punched Clive firmly in the testicles, producing a painful shriek. Undeterred, Clive came back again, as Dorsch used the palm of his hand to strike him cleanly on his solar plexus. The blow sent Clive falling to the floor, gasping for air and clutching at his chest.

Seeing his chance Sean lashed out and stuck Dorsch hard in the neck, it was something that had been done to him and he knew how debilitating it was. The blow landed directly upon Dorsch's Adam's apple, but failed to move him. He quickly returned his attention to Sean, twisting his body in a way that used his legs and arms to pin Sean down.

The position of Dorsch's leg under Sean back was arching it painfully and Sean was terrified that it would snap his spine.

'One move and I'll break your back,' Dorsch said in English. 'Now, what do you want?'

The question was ludicrous and if he could have moved, Sean would have ripped Dorsch's heart out with his fingers, for even suggesting that he didn't know why they were there. 'Fuck you! You know what we want. Where are Liz and Praew?' he shouted.

'What? What are you talking about?' Dorsch's face contorted.

'I saw your men leaving the hotel with our things. Don't try to bullshit me,' Sean snapped back.

Just then Pete and Steve arrived, panting heavily from their respective fights.

'Come near me and I'll kill him... one more step,' Dorsch said.

Both Pete and Steve stopped. It was obvious to Sean that they both knew that the hold Dorsch had on him wouldn't take much manipulation to be fatal.

Still eyeing the two ex-special forces' men carefully, Dorsch turned his attention back to Sean. 'Yes, my men went to your hotel when you were out, to steal your computers and other things; just to make sure that you kept your side of the bargain regarding the photos. I don't know anything about the people you mentioned. I assume that's the names of the woman and girl you're travelling with?'

His mind racing trying to correlate Dorsch's response, Sean studied the German. If he did kill him, it would be murder-suicide as Pete and Steve would be upon him immediately. If he had Liz and Praew, it would be a far better bargaining tool. So why was he denying it?

The sudden realization that Dorsch was telling the truth hit Sean hard. He felt a rush of helplessness, as if he was drunk. 'So you didn't kidnap them?'

'No.'

'Then who did?' Sean's voice reflected his despair as he smashed his hand onto the ground.

'Tell them not to attack me and I'll let you go,' Dorsch said, nodding towards Steve and Pete.

Now back on his feet, Clive nodded his agreement, still holding his chest. Steve and Pete immediately backed off a few metres, but Dorsch didn't let his grip go upon Sean. 'Please, go and get my men first,' he said.

Obviously realizing that they weren't in the strongest of positions, Clive again nodded his agreement and Pete and Steve went in opposite directions to free Dorsch's men.

A minute or so later they both returned, holding pistols to the head of Dorsch's guards.

'Let them go,' Dorsch said, wriggling, causing Sean to let out a cry of pain as his back bent further.

Before letting the guards go, both Pete and Steve, quickly took the bullets out of the pistols and passed them back to the guards, pushing the two burly mercenaries away as they did.

Suddenly, Sean felt the release of the tension in his back and Dorsch spun out of his hold and stood up to face Clive. Straightening his back, Sean quickly stood and joined Clive, Pete and Steve, facing the three mercenaries.

'Before this goes any further, I just want to check your hard drives, then you can have your computers and passports back,' Dorsch said, but then his expression softened. 'But did you say that somebody had been kidnapped?'

'Yes, my girlfriend and our thirteen-year-old daughter,' Sean said.

'Who'd take them and why?' Dorsch's face reflected his disbelief.

'The Nazi group we mentioned to you earlier. They're more serious than we thought, and they know we're investigating them,' Clive said.

'Really? That idiot Glas and Wagner? They didn't seem up to it to me.'

'Yes, them and others. The organisation's quite big and straddles a number of countries,' Sean said.

Dorsch held his lower lip in thought. 'Come with me. Maybe I can help.' When he moved towards his apartment door, nobody followed.

'Look, you can either trust me and accept my help, or try to find them yourself,' Dorsch said.

Sean looked at Clive, requesting his opinion.

'Okay,' Clive said.

Chapter Thirty-Nine

Tuesday, 9th February. Munich, Germany.

Liz had no way to determine how much time had passed since they'd been left in the bathroom. It felt like hours, but she suspected that it was far less. Her senses were playing tricks with her mind; the depravation of light making time pass more slowly.

Her arms were aching from being tied behind her back and her body was bruised from the van ride, but otherwise she was fit and well. The occasional shuffle close by her let her know that Praew was still there.

Just as Liz was adjusting her position again to try to relieve some of the pressure on her arms, she heard a door open in a room close by, then voices. She listened carefully to the words of the people that came into the adjacent room. There appeared to be three of them and, if she wasn't mistaken, they were speaking Russian.

Everybody they'd encountered during the investigation so far had been from an EU country, but Liz knew that there were plenty of neo-Nazis in Russia. Her thoughts turned to Praew; her life had been tormented by Russians. First, the people traffickers that had kept her as a prisoner in a squalid brothel, then the boys at school, now this.

The three men in the next room seemed to be enjoying themselves, laughing and joking, but there was something odd about their voices. A champagne cork popping startled her, then another and another. The voices suddenly got louder as the drinking started. Half an hour later, three more corks and the voices went up, louder again.

As she listened to the party in the adjacent room, it suddenly dawned upon her. The voices weren't of men, they were younger, boys even. It was hard to tell through the thick Russian language, but certain syllables were too high-pitched and lacked the gruff voice an adult would use.

What going on? Children? It can't be... can it?

Footsteps suddenly started to move towards the bathroom, then without warning, the sack was lifted from Liz's head. As her eyes came into focus, she saw Nikolai Koryalov lifting the sack from Praew's head. When Praew caught sight of the young Russian, her pupils narrowed with fear.

In some circumstances it would have been a relief to know that your captors were fifteen-year-old boys, but to Liz it made things worse. These three boys knew no boundaries and hadn't yet matured enough to understand right from wrong. The fact that they commanded more resources than most adults could ever dream of meant nothing. They were still adolescents, and they were drunk, making them extremely dangerous.

'Hello, Thai whore. Did you think you could get me expelled from school and charged by the police and get away with it?' He pushed his hand onto Praew's face and pulled her cheeks together. 'Now, you'll have to suck my cock, and I'm not even going to pay you for it, you ugly yellow cunt.' Koryalov slurred his words slightly, as he let go of Praew's face.

Belov and Dementyev were at the bathroom door, drunk and laughing at Koryalov, who held a half-empty bottle of Cristal in his hand, like a wannabe rock star.

Liz instinctively lashed out with her leg, but it failed to connect and she fell against the tiled floor heavily.

'Don't worry mamma slut, your filthy yellow cunt will get some big Russian cock too,' Koryalov said, grabbing at his crotch, much to the amusement of his friends.

Dementyev said some words in Russian to Koryalov. With her limited understanding of Russian, Liz thought he told him to hurry up and that his father would be there soon. If it was true, that Vladimir Koryalov was on the way, Liz knew that she had only a short time to get away.

The sight of the three young boys laughing at their vile threats made Liz think of young boys that were given weapons in Africa and the Middle East, then told to commit atrocities that no adult ever would. It was that lack of a moral brake that made power in the hands of children so dangerous.

Another thing was really worrying her: Sean would be looking for the Nazis, Glas, Wagner, etc. He wouldn't suspect that Koryalov had them followed from England.

Leaning on the wall behind the toilet, Koryalov suddenly unzipped his jeans and pulled out his penis. The jet of urine splashed against the seat and hit his shoes as he swayed from side to side, trying to steady himself. When he'd finished, he wiped the end of his penis on Praew's forehead. The sight made Liz vomit in her own mouth. When she was forced to swallow it again because of the tape covering her mouth, the acid burned at the back of her throat.

'What's wrong, mamma whore? You want it first, is that it? Or is it that you've never seen such prime Russian meat and you can't wait to get your dirty yellow cunt onto it?' Koryalov's words were getting more slurred and his eyes were narrowing into an evil expression.

Pushing himself away from the toilet, he moved over to Liz and forced his penis into her face, just under her eye. She moved away as best she could and tried to kick him, but he just laughed and moved back, taking another huge swig of champagne, before he threw the bottle against the wall, smashing it, and then turned his attention to Praew.

Reaching down clumsily, he grabbed her t-shirt and ripped it open from the neck down, exposing her small breasts. Praew didn't move, paralysed with fear, her eyes glazing over with tears.

Her insides burning with pure hatred, Liz struggled against the ties again, but it was no use, she watched on helplessly as Koryalov grabbed at Praew's vagina though her jeans. 'That's the problem with you yellow cunts: no tits! But I bet this is nice and tight,' he said, grabbing again at her vagina.

Still Praew didn't move, abject terror etched across her face.

Chapter Forty

Tuesday, 9th February. Munich, Germany.

The seven men filed one by one into Dorsch's sumptuous apartment, where Carrera marble lined the floors and walls of the oversized entrance.

'This way,' Dorsch said as he walked through a high oak doorway.

Every sense in Sean's body was on full alert, pumping adrenalin, ready for the attack at any stage. He scanned the large office, looking for something to use in a fight. But deep down he somehow felt that he could trust Dorsch. *Was he just a good actor?*

'Do you know where and when they were taken?' Dorsch said, seating himself behind a desk with four large screens surrounding it. Out of the corner of his eye, Sean saw the two bags the guards had taken from their hotel earlier.

'Take them if you want them,' Dorsch said, noticing Sean's eye movement, 'but I think this is more important.' His face was stern: he was clearly a man scared of nothing; a skilled fighter and a deadly adversary; but there was still something about him that was telling Sean to trust him.

'Look, Mr McManus, I know you don't trust me, and frankly, given my previous experience of you, I'm finding it hard to trust you, but you've just told me that a woman and a thirteen-year-old girl have been kidnapped. Through my business I've been involved in the safe return of hundreds of kidnap victims and the one common factor in them all is that time is of the essence.'

He's also very intuitive, Sean thought.

'What about the police?' Sean suggested, as he had to Clive.

'The easiest way to ensure they end up dead. Now, where and when, please?' Dorsch said with authority.

'Between four and five; somewhere between the Krefelderhof Hotel and the Schwarbig Hospital,' Sean said.

'Okay, we'll start at the hotel. Two people per screen and I'll take this one. Watch out for them.' Dorsch played with the keypad of his computer and suddenly each of the four screens lit up with a street image. A clock in the corner read 16:00. Then the images started to move.

'You have access to the Munich Police CCTV?' Clive asked.

'Yes, large amounts of money can sometimes be very useful,' Dorsch said, without looking away from the screen.

The image Sean was watching showed a view of the entrance to the Krefelderhof from about twenty metres away. He focussed intently in the screen, trying to rid his mind of any morbid thoughts about what could be happening to Praew and Liz.

'There. That's them,' Pete said after twelve minutes of watching his screen.

His heart bouncing against his chest wall, Sean looked across quickly at the frozen screen. Liz and Praew were holding hands, huddled together against the cold, bowing their heads into the wind.

Dorsch quickly hit a key and the image started to move again. A tear formed in the corner of Sean's eye as he watched the two figures making their way along the road slowly, clearly battling the cold weather. *It's my fault. They wouldn't be here if it weren't for me and my bloody ambition!*

As they passed out of view from one camera, Dorsch hit a few more keys and another camera showed them from the front walking towards it. Suddenly they stopped and Liz waved for a taxi. Sean watched as they climbed into the cream-coloured Mercedes.

'Go back to the last camera,' Clive asked.

When the screen flicked back, they saw it clearly; the taxi was there. It had been following behind them, waiting to be flagged.

'Get the details of the taxi. I'll follow the cameras through,' Dorsch said.

Clive quickly wrote down the number plate and vehicle identifier, before Dorsch flicked to the next camera. The image showed the taxi pull to the end of the road that the hotel was on, and then turn right.

'That's not the direction to the hospital,' Clive said,

Each time the screen changed, Dorsch, managed to skilfully locate the taxi moving slowly through the streets. Then it turned off between two buildings and disappeared.

'*Scheiss!* No cameras down there,' Dorsch said.

'Then we have to get there. That must be it. That must be where Liz and Praew are,' Sean said, his voice shrill with panic.

'Wait. Keep watching it for a while,' Clive said.

Less than four minutes later, a black Volkswagen van emerged from the side street. 'That could be them,' Clive said.

Immediately after the van, the same taxi pulled out of the street… minus its two passengers.

Dorsch quickly flicked to another screen and they watched as the black van passed through the Königsplatz. Then another screen as it passed through Maximilliansplatz.

When they watched it turn right into the street where Dorsch's apartment was, where they were actually standing right now, Sean stiffened. *Is this just a game? Is this how Dorsch gets his kicks, by leading us on like this?*

Giving a subtle look towards Pete and Steve, putting them on alert, Clive clearly thought the same.

Leaning forward slightly, Sean wrapped his fingers around the stem of one of the monitors, ready to smash it into Dorsch's face when the pretence ended.

When the next camera picked up the van driving past Dorsch's apartment, he relaxed his grip and focussed on the screen. Another camera then showed it pulling into the parking garage of an apartment block, just fifty metres further along the same road that Dorsch lived on; on the same side.

'They're just here?' Sean said.

'It looks that way,' Dorsch replied.

'Is that too much of a coincidence?' Clive said suspiciously.

'This is the most expensive street in Germany. Whoever it is that has them has money. And if you have money in Munich, this is where you live,' Dorsch replied, shrugging.

'Wagner?' Sean said.

Dorsch quickly hit a few buttons on his computer, producing a list of names with numbers next to them. 'There's no Wagner listed as an owner of an apartment there, but that's not to say he doesn't rent one.'

'How the hell … ?' Clive started to speak.

'I own a security company and I like to know who my neighbours are,' Dorsch interrupted.

Leaning over his shoulder, Sean scanned the list of names quickly. He gasped as his eyes were drawn to one name. Reaching down, he lifted a letter opener and pushed it to Dorsch's temple.

Waving his security guards away, Dorsch kept his head still. 'What now, Mr McManus?'

'Vladimir Koryalov, you know him,' Sean said, pressing the point of the knife against Dorsch's skin.

'Yes, he's a client of mine. But how would you know that?' Dorsch replied.

'I saw a photo of you having dinner with him on his son's Facebook page.'

'As I said, he's a client. He has extensive operations in Africa and we supply armed security to his plants and executives. But, how do you know him?' Dorsch asked.

Sean kept the knife in place. 'His son attends the same school as my daughter and they had some problems,' Sean answered.

'What kind of problems?'

'My daughter got his son charged by the police and if he's found guilty, he'll be banned from the UK permanently.'

'Nikolai. Damn,' Dorsch said.

'What is it?' Clive asked.

'Koryalov's fortune is entirely dependent on his UK residence. If he has to leave because of his son, he'll also lose all his money, as it actually belongs to the Russian President.'

'So that's true?' Sean said.

'Very, but it took me a lot of work to find it out. I like to know who my clients really are. Tell me is your daughter the only witness to the offence that Nikolai committed?'

'No, it's all over the internet. There's a video.'

'Hmm,' Dorsch said, thinking. 'He must think that he has a way around the video evidence and is looking to get rid of the eye witness.'

Sean let the blade drop away from Dorsch's temple. 'What do you mean. Is he going to kill them?'

'As I said, I like to know who my clients really are and Vladimir Koryalov is a cold blooded killer, but something doesn't fit. If he wanted them dead, he'd have killed them on the street. He certainly wouldn't take them to his own apartment, leaving a trail any half-witted policeman could follow.'

'So what do you think it is?' Sean asked.

'A trap maybe… but for who?'

'Could he be linked to 4R18?' Clive asked.

'It's not beyond the realms of possibility. He may well know Wagner from the old Soviet Union days.'

'Too coincidental,' Sean said. 'What if he doesn't know who the other eyewitness is? He'd need to get Praew to tell him before he killed her.'

'If there's another eyewitness that would make sense,' Dorsch said. 'But it means we'd better be quick, god knows what he'll do to your daughter to make her give him the name.'

'Can you get us into his apartment?' Clive asked.

Dorsch laughed suddenly. 'Without even breaking in. My company set up the security for him, so I have all the access codes. Just one minute.' Dorsch clicked a few more keys and then scrolled through some screens of data. 'Well, somebody's there. The alarm was deactivated yesterday and hasn't been re-activated since.'

Every sense in Sean's body was on maximum alert, his instinct was still telling him to trust Dorsch, but the coincidences were stacking up. Anyway, he had no choice for now, he'd go along with it, but one of his eyes would never leave the German. He slid the paperknife into his belt and stepped back from Dorsch's chair.

After saying a few words in German, one of the guards walked out of the office. Two minutes later he returned with four browning pistols.

'Could you give them their ammunition back now, please,' Dorsch said to Steve and Pete, as the guards handed out the loaded weapons.

Sean had only ever held a gun once before and that time he'd wanted to shoot, but it was taken away from him by Terry before he pulled the trigger. The dead weight of it reminded him again of that moment.

'Only use it if you have to,' Dorsch said, obviously reading Sean's surprise at being handed a gun. 'And try not to shoot me,' he added.

Chapter Forty-One

Tuesday, 9th February. Munich, Germany.

Liz struggled again against her restraints as Koryalov tugged violently at Praew's jeans. She screamed as loud as she could through the tape, but just muffled noises came out.

'Shut her up, man. She's stopping me from getting hard,' Koryalov said to Belov, as he finally pulled Praew's jeans over her feet.

For some reason Praew still wasn't fighting back, which was unlike her. When they were confronted by Finlow, she'd fought hard, kicking and biting. *Maybe she's given up hope?* Liz thought, tears welling in her eyes again and hatred coursing through her veins.

When Belov copied Koryalov by sticking his penis in her face, Liz butted him in the testicles sending him backwards crying in pain. Just then, she thought she saw a glint of happiness in Praew's eyes. *There's still hope!*

'You'll pay for that, whore!' Belov said, regaining his composure. He slapped Liz hard across the face with the back of his hand and then grabbed at her breasts through her pullover. 'The older slut's got better tits,' he said, as Liz saw the sadistic lust in his eyes.

The sight of Belov's out-of-control lust sent a jolt of fear through Liz's body. They'd passed the point of no return: they were out of control and anything could happen. Liz wriggled and squirmed to get away, but couldn't. As he continued to grope at her breasts, she looked over to Praew, where Koryalov had ripped her white kickers from her body, leaving her naked and tied to a radiator.

The fifteen-year-old Russian pawed at Praew's body: first her breasts, then her vagina, but Praew didn't move, or try to resist. Liz, on the other hand, twisted and turned, fighting the groping of the hapless Belov at every possible opportunity. When he tried to copy Koryalov again and rip her top, the material proved too strong for him and he just returned to groping at her breasts and grabbing between her legs.

Belov was young, drunk and stupid, but Liz wondered how long she'd be able to fight him off for, especially if Dementyev joined in.

On the other side of the room, Koryalov had removed his jeans and underwear. His erect penis was sticking out beneath his shirt.

When he started masturbating and pushing his penis into Praew's face, Liz vomited again into her own mouth, almost choking on the sickly fluid. But still Praew didn't move.

'She wants it, man. Thai whore! She loves it,' Dementyev said, saliva bubbling from the side of his mouth.

Buoyed on by his friend's shouts and numbed by the alcohol. Koryalov's thrusting became more pronounced and he was knocking Praew's head back with each thrust.

'Stick it to her, man. Fuck her in her in her yellow cunt and dirty arse. You know she wants it,' Dementyev carried on.

Koryalov was losing control as he continued to masturbate, pushing his penis into Praew's face.

Belov was leaning over Liz, groping clumsily at her and she waited until the right moment and pushed her knee up hard into his groin, sending him to the floor by the bath screaming.

As he fell, out of nowhere, Praew's hand was suddenly free. As quick as lightning, she ripped the tape from her mouth and grabbed Koryalov by the testicles. Then she opened her mouth and clamped her jaw onto his penis, biting hard.

Koryalov, let out a high-pitched scream and hit Praew on the side of the head, but she didn't let go, biting harder. Suddenly her other hand was free and she scratched at the boy's skin, while he hit her again and again on the head. But she still didn't let the grip with her teeth go.

Dementyev moved forward to help, but as he passed, Liz stretched out and kicked him on the kneecap. Then, when he fell, she kicked him in the head.

Losing his balance, Koryalov suddenly fell backwards into the corner of the bathroom. Still Praew didn't let his penis out of her mouth, instead she sprang up and on top of him athletically and grabbed his testicles with her left hand, while she gouged at his eyes with the other. With a final swipe and a gasp, Koryalov passed out on the floor and Praew finally let his blood-soaked penis out of her mouth.

When Liz caught sight of it, the limp piece of torn flesh was bleeding heavily from the end and was deeply severed in two places.

Praew stood to face Belov and Dementyev, with blood running from her mouth. Both quickly backed out of the bathroom away from her, fear spreading across their faces.

Seeing them back away, Praew quickly found something to cut Liz's ties with and removed the tape from her mouth. Once free, Liz put Praew behind her and went into the living room to deal with Belov and Dementyev. The sight of Liz coming into the room with hate strewn across her face and Praew behind her, brandishing a pair of scissors, made Belov and Dementyev turn and sharply exit out of the front door of the apartment, abandoning their friend in the bathroom.

As she heard the footsteps running down the hallway, Liz turned to Praew and held her tightly. 'Thank you. You're so brave and I love you so much,' she said.

After she'd put Praew down, Liz looked through the door of the bathroom. Koryalov was unconscious in the corner, losing a lot of blood through his penis. Wondering why she was even contemplating saving his life, she quickly searched through the bathroom cabinet and found a bandage. Making a loop, she tied bandage around his penis at the top completing a tourniquet. The bleeding stopped almost immediately.

'That should keep him alive,' Liz said.

'He doesn't deserve to live!' Praew replied, gathering up her clothes from the bathroom floor.

'Don't worry. That tourniquet, while it'll keep him alive, will almost certainly render the rest of his penis useless with gangrene or the like, and they'll have to amputate it at the hospital.' Liz smiled.

'Good. He deserves it.'

After Praew had washed her mouth thoroughly and dressed in her jeans and a jumper that she found in the wardrobe, she joined Liz back in the main bathroom. Liz was watching Koryalov as he slowly came to.

'We'd better get out of here before his father arrives. We need to find Sean and Clive, they'll know what to do. How did you get your hands free by the way?' Liz asked.

'It's a trick I learned in the Russian place in London. They used to tie us up at night and I couldn't sleep with my hands like that, so I learned to make my hand smaller than my wrist and slip it through the ties.'

As they moved towards the main door, it suddenly burst open and Belov came stumbling back into the apartment.

Chapter Forty-Two

Tuesday, 9th February. Munich, Germany.

'The apartment takes up the whole top floor. When you come out of the lift, you'll be in a corridor with a large double door at the end. Wait there if you get there before us, we'll take the stairs. I've disabled the security cameras,' Dorsch said to the team assembled in the lobby of Koryalov's apartment building.

Clive, Sean, Pete and Steve went to the lift. When it opened on the third floor, they stepped out into a grand entrance hall.

One minute later, the door to the fire exit opened and a teenage boy was pushed through, followed by Dorsch, then another boy, followed by his two guards.

'What the—?' Sean said.

'These two were running away from something. I'd like to find out what,' Dorsch said. He grabbed Belov by the ear and pushed him forward to the security pad, where he entered the code. When the door clicked open, Dorsch shoved Belov into the apartment first.

'Aarrrg!' the shout came out. It was a girl's voice. *Praew,* Sean thought, pushing his way forward. As he stepped through the door behind Dorsch, who had his pistol drawn at the ready, he saw Praew collide head first with Belov. A cracking sound came from his ribs as he fell to the ground screeching in pain.

'Sean, thank god!' Liz shouted.

Momentarily confused, Sean grabbed Praew and pulled her close to him as Liz reached him and flung her arms around his neck. Behind them, Dementyev was pushed into the room by one of Dorsch's guards, then Clive and the team filtered in. Upon seeing Liz and Praew, Clive suddenly broke down, tears forming in his eyes and Praew instantly moved over to comfort him. The sight made Sean realise just how close Clive had become to them, and just how good a friend he was.

'It's okay, Uncle Clive, we're fine,' she said, wrapping her arms around his shoulders.

'What the hell happened here?' Dorsch exclaimed when he looked into the bathroom.

'It's a long story, but that boy's called Nikolai Koryalov and he and his friends kidnapped us and tried to rape us,' Liz said.

Seemingly unshocked, Dorsch nodded his head. 'He won't be raping anyone again,' he said, examining the tourniquet.

'Are you okay?' Sean said, still holding Liz.

'I'm fine. Praew saved me yet again,' she said, tears streaming down her cheeks. 'His father's on the way though.' She pointed at Koryalov.

'Let my guys deal with this mess. You come back to my apartment. If Vladimir Koryalov's after you, you'll need to be protected.' Dorsch said.

Liz frowned at Sean, clearly not understanding where Dorsch fitted in. 'It's okay. He's on our side,' Sean said.

'Deal with them? You can't kill them! They're children!' Clive pulled Dorsch to one side and whispered to him.

Dorsch laughed. 'Even evil mercenaries like me don't kill children. But if I'm right about his father, he's going to come looking for us. If he has to get his son to hospital first, it might just buy us enough time.'

'So you're just going to give them over to his father? Is that wise?'

'Nikolai's not seen me and the other two don't know me, so his father won't be looking for me. Along with the injuries to his son, it'll give us a couple of days,' Dorsch explained, to Clive's nodding head.

Clive quickly explained the situation to Sean.

'What about the police?' Sean said.

'And explain the teeth marks on his penis, the fact that we broke into his apartment, didn't report a kidnapping, and illegally accessed police CCTV footage? We'd spend longer in prison than them.'

'What happens in a couple of days when his father does come after us?' Sean said.

'Then we'll deal with his father too,' Dorsch replied, overhearing the remark, with a determined look on his face.

Chapter Forty-Three

Tuesday, 9th February. Munich, Germany.

Back in Dorsch's apartment, Pete made his excuses and said that he needed to check that Terry was okay. Before he left, Sean took his phone and deleted the image of Dorsch in the gay sauna. Pete nodded his quiet agreement and Steve also deleted his copy. Dorsch had proved himself trustworthy, so it was the reasonable thing to do.

'I can't thank you enough, Herr Dorsch,' Sean said, still holding Liz and Praew's hands tightly.

'Please, call me Stefan. And it looked to me as if these young ladies didn't actually need any help.' Dorsch smiled at Liz and Praew. 'The next time I need soldiers, I may send for them.' He smiled.

Praew giggled and threw a mock punch into the air. Liz had explained what had happened in the bathroom on the short walk between the two apartments. Given this, Sean was pleased to see her spirits so high, her resilience never ceased to amaze him. The experiences she'd had in her short life would condemn most people to a lifetime of counselling, but Praew just seemed to soldier on, parrying the blows she been dealt like a champion boxer.

By comparison, Liz was visibly shaken by the incident and from her narrative. It seemed that the fact that her captors had been fifteen-year-old boys had disturbed her most. 'You can reason with an adult, but fifteen-year-olds haven't mastered the art of reason yet, especially drunk ones,' she said.

'Now, you said you had some problems with the Nazis?' Dorsch asked.

'We may have kicked that particular hornets' nest, yes. Why?' Clive said.

'Call it loyalty to my country, or my inherited religion, but I'd like to help… if I can, that is.'

'Why? You intimated earlier that you weren't interested,' Sean asked.

Dorsch sighed. 'Tonight's little escapade made me think. I've done a lot of bad things in my life — killed people that perhaps didn't deserve to die, and worked for people that perhaps didn't deserve to live — it felt good to do something worthwhile for a change.'

'What are you offering?' Clive asked.

'Myself and my resources. For instance, you said you had a critically ill friend in Munich. You can use my plane to transport him to safety, if you wish?'

'That's very generous of you, thank you.' Clive smiled.

'And the rest of my services?' Dorsch asked.

'Which are?' Clive queried.

'Not dissimilar to what your two friends do,' Dorsch said. 'And I'm very good at it.'

'I learned a long time ago never to turn down a genuine offer of help,' Clive said, extending his arm. 'Welcome to the team.'

'Okay, please prepare your friend for his journey. A private ambulance will collect him from your hotel in two hours. Where will the flight be going?'

'Aberdeen,' Clive said.

Sean remembered that the hospital where Clive had been treated anonymously following his shooting was in Aberdeen. *He must be planning to send Terry to the same place.*

'Okay then. I think we should all get some sleep. It's been an eventful day. Why don't we meet here at 8 a.m.?' Dorsch suggested.

'Done,' Sean said. 'And thank you again.'

On the short walk back to their new hotel, Sean asked Clive whether he trusted Dorsch.

'Yes, I think so. He had no reason to help us out like that if he was involved with the Nazis,' Clive responded.

Nodding his agreement, Sean filled Liz in on the events of the day at Faustein's house and the contents of the folder.

'Brazilian? I wouldn't have picked it. She seemed as German as bratwurst to me,' Liz said. 'My head's still spinning at the moment, so I won't be able to sleep. Perhaps I'll spend some time on the Internet; see what I can dig up on her.'

At that moment, Sean realised that it was the first time they'd looked at Anna properly, as a real target of their investigation. He wondered what Liz might find.

'I'd like to help. I'm not tired either,' Praew said.

'That's wonderful, darling. I'd love to have a clever assistant researcher like you,' Liz kissed Praew's forehead and Sean noticed that she beamed with pride.

Forty-five minutes later, just fifteen minutes after Liz had settled down to work, she climbed in bed next to Sean.

'I'll do it in the morning. I'm suddenly tired after all,' she said, snuggling into Sean's shoulder.

'I'm so glad you're safe. I don't know what I'd do without you,' Sean said.

Liz suddenly lifted her head and looked into Sean's eyes. 'I'm sorry if I've been distant since the lawyer told me about Praew. The situation tonight made me realise that I love you more than anything, and I won't let them come between us. We'll fight them together.'

Sean dropped his head down to hers and kissed her passionately on the lips. The intimate lovemaking that followed felt like it was their first time, as they gazed intensely into each other's eyes, silently committing to the words they had just spoken.

When they'd finished, Sean rolled onto his back. 'Would it make any difference with the Home Office if we were married?' It was never the way he intended to propose and he hadn't prepared; there was no ring, but in that moment it felt right: to him, there would never be a better time.

Liz instantly sat upright on the bed. 'Are you saying what I think you are?'

'Yes, I think so,' Sean replied.

'Then my answer's yes. Not because of Praew — and by the way I checked; it won't help — but yes, because I love you with all my heart and I want to spend the rest of my life with you.'

Chapter Forty-Four

Wednesday, 10th February. Munich, Germany.

When Sean and Liz went to wake Praew in the morning, she looked like she'd had a tough night's sleep. There were bags under her eyes and her hair was strewn around like spaghetti.

'Are you okay, darling?' Liz said, gently stroking her face.

Praew's eyes opened half way. 'Is it morning already?' she said, turning over.

'Didn't you sleep well?' Liz asked.

'Yes, but not for long enough. I was working until four,' she said, tilting her head to the side.

'We've got some news for you,' Liz said quietly as Praew sat up and rubbed her eyes. 'Sean and I are getting married.'

'Yippeee!' Praew jumped up and first held Liz, then Sean. Then they all sat on Praew's bed and talked about how Sean had proposed.

'Not very romantic, Dad,' Praew said, pulling a face.

'Perfect for me, darling,' Liz replied. 'Now, you said you'd been up working half the night. Did you find anything interesting?'

Praew pulled a long face. 'Not really. Well, I don't know; something, but I think it's a bit silly.'

'I'm sure it's not,' Liz encouraged her.

Reaching down to the side of the bed, she pulled up her laptop and flicked open the screen. After making a few keystrokes, she turned it around so that Sean and Liz could see it.

The screen showed an article from a UK newspaper, dated November 2012. The heading read: ADOLF HITLER'S FINAL RESTING PLACE.

The article went on to describe a controversial theory that Hitler didn't kill himself in his Berlin bunker in 1945, but instead escaped to Argentina and from there to Brazil, where he grew old and died aged ninety-five. But not before he'd married a local girl and had two children.

Impressed by her ability to link all of the facts together, Sean smiled at Praew. She'd done very well. He knew that there were literally hundreds of crank conspiracy theories about Hitler's escape to South America, along with Mengele and Eichmann, who'd been found there in later years. But he wasn't about to discourage Praew.

When he read the next paragraph, his stomach knotted tightly. *This* theory claimed that Hitler had lived in a small mining village close to the Bolivian border. Nossa Senhorra do Liveramento was a satellite town of the state capital of Matto Grosso, Cuiaba.

Feeling a sudden sense of urgency, he went back to his own room and grabbed the blue cardboard file from Faustein's apartment, extracting the marriage certificate. He read the details again: *Anna Maria Ruiz, born 12/02/1977, Cuiaba, Mato Grosso, Brasilien.*

Shaking his head, he passed the form to Liz.

'You can't be serious?' Liz said, giggling.

'I know, but Dorsch did say that the 4R18 mob believe that their leader has some kind of bloodline to Hitler.'

'She's too young to be his daughter,' Liz said.

'Granddaughter perhaps?' Sean said.

'No, it's nuts. Mossad would have found him years ago. He died in Berlin, in 1945.'

'You do know that nobody ever found his or Braun's body?' Sean said.

'You're beginning to sound like a conspiracy theorist,' Liz laughed.

'Don't you see? It doesn't matter whether we believe it or not. If the nut cases in the 4R18 believe it, it gives them a powerful rallying cry.'

Not laughing anymore, Liz bowed her head in thought, then lifted it nodding. 'My god, you're right. If those deranged morons think that they're following Adolf Hitler's granddaughter, they'll wreak havoc.' She turned to Praew. 'Well done. This is very important and I'd never have found it,' she said.

Praew's face lit up brightly at the compliment. 'It was easy really,' she grinned.

'We need to get Clive and get over to Dorsch's,' Sean said, standing up.

Clive grinned when he spoke about the theory to Dorsch, obviously embarrassed to be spouting such nonsense. But Dorsch's response surprised Sean.

'Why do you think it's so crazy? I've heard much less likely conspiracy theories, like the 911 plot etc. At least with this one, there's a genuine lack of credible evidence for the official story.'

'So you think it could be true? That Anna Faustein could be Hitler's granddaughter?' Liz questioned.

'I think it's unlikely, but I can't see why it's implausible. Like most people, I'd require some kind of proof, DNA etc.'

'And what would you do if you got that proof and found that she was Hitler's offspring?' Sean asked.

Dorsch smiled. 'If she lived in a farmhouse in South America, or even Germany for that matter, and didn't bother anybody, then I'd do absolutely nothing. It's not her fault who her grandfather was. But, if as you say, she's involved in some secret conspiracy to gain power in Europe, then I'd find a way to stop her.'

'Good. Then we're in this together,' Sean said.

'My plane came back early this morning. Your friend has been delivered to the hospital in Scotland. We can talk on the way to the airport about what we do when we get to Brussels,' Dorsch said.

'And what we're going to do about Koryalov,' Sean replied.

'Thank you for getting Terry to safety,' Clive added.

Initially, Sean was concerned that Clive wouldn't like the way Dorsch was taking over events. But if he was, he certainly didn't show it, and he seemed quite happy to go along with things for now.

On the way to the airport, Sean received a text on his phone and grinned. 'Blom got the letter,' he said.

'That's good, at least it's one thing off his plate. Poor guy,' Clive responded.

The general aviation terminal at Munich airport was two kilometres away from the regular terminals. When the two black Mercedes limousines pulled up outside the glass structure, a uniformed doorman opened the door for Sean and they quickly made their way inside.

Unlike the only other time Sean had flown on a private jet, he wasn't packed into a wooden crate and the formalities were completed very casually in the terminal building, before they made their way straight onto the plane. As soon as the door was closed, Dorsch nodded discreetly to the stewardess and they began to taxi away from the terminal building.

The cream leather and polished walnut interior of Dorsch's plane was a world away from the cramped economy flights that Sean was used to. As soon as they'd levelled out, Dorsch joined Clive, Liz and Sean around a meeting table, while the stewardess showed Praew onto the flight deck.

'There's one thing I still don't understand. Even if Faustein is a Nazi, the rest of her party isn't, nor the rest of the EU. It's not as if she's goose-stepped in there in her SS uniform and declared that she's Hitler's granddaughter. So what impact can she really have?'

'I don't think we're talking about revolution: just small steps with a large cumulative effect,' Liz said.

'Like what?' Dorsch asked.

'I don't know: how about a law that overrides the German ban on Nazism and the swastika, passed under the guise of an EU human rights and freedom of expression law. As a consequence of which, German Nazis start to wear their uniforms in public, and start to release propaganda appealing to the genuine insecurities of people worried about mass immigration?' Liz countered.

'Nobody will listen to those idiots,' Dorsch said.

'Really? As far as I can tell, the popularity of the far right is growing quickly in every European country, even the traditionally communist France. It wouldn't be a huge leap to call them Nazis. All they need is a uniform,' Sean added.

'And let's not forget it happened before, less than 100 years ago, in a similar febrile political environment as now,' Liz said.

'Carried out on a Europe wide scale, with expansion of the EU's military and police capabilities, which is already happening. Nation states will be helpless to stop it,' Sean said.

Dorsch fell silent, looking out of the window briefly as the plane continued its ascent. 'Okay, I think I get it. You must understand that it's not easy to be German and talk about Nazis. In most of us the sense of guilt is still very strong.'

'We need to form a plan to watch Anna Faustein around the clock,' Clive said, taking control again.

'Last night you said that you had evidence of where Koryalov's money came from,' Sean said to Dorsch.

'Yes,' he nodded.

'Could I see it?'

'Yes, it's on my hard drive. I'll email it to you, but why?'

'I think it may be the key to getting him off our back,' Sean said as the plane began its descent into Brussels.

Despite the constant appearance of conspiracy theories claiming that Adolf Hitler escaped to South America following the Second World War, none have ever been proved. And despite extensive searching, Hitler was never found.

However, the officially accepted theory that Hitler committed suicide in his Berlin bunker on 30 April, 1945, has, equally, never been proved, and rests solely on the testimony of one man: Rochus Misch, Hitler's personal bodyguard, and the closest thing Hitler had to a friend.

A skull fragment found at the bunker site, which had long been thought to be Hitler's, and which represented the only physical evidence of his demise there, was subjected to DNA testing in 2009. It turned out to belong to a woman!

Chapter Forty-Five

Wednesday, 10th February. Brussels, Belgium.

The large house that Dorsch had rented for the team on Chemin de Putdael, in the Woluwe St Pierre district, was less than half a kilometre from the grand mansion in which Anna Faustein now resided. It was chosen by Dorsch for that reason, and for its high fences and walls, offering privacy to its inhabitants.

When two plain white vans arrived filled with military hardware, Sean realised why he wanted the privacy.

Within hours, Dorsch and Clive had organised surveillance teams to monitor Anna's house and the doors to the Willy Brandt Building, where her office was located.

'She's on her way out, walking, heading through the park,' Steve's message came.

'She's heading towards the gate at Place Jourdan. You can pick her up there,' the next message came though a few minutes later.

'Got her,' Pete's voice came over the radio clearly.

'She's turned into an apartment building by the park.' Pete's voice again came through.

'It's where she used to live. Maybe she still has an apartment there?' Clive said.

'She's carrying a suit bag. I'll wait over the road and watch the door.'

'Her apartment is on the ninth floor, the last one on the right. You should be able to see the light come on if she goes in there,' Sean said, then quickly looked at Liz for a reaction. He'd never told her that he'd been in Anna's apartment. Luckily, she didn't seem to notice his remark and the radio fell silent for a few seconds while everybody waited.

'Yep, light's just come on. I can't see her though, the angle's too steep.'

A few more moments passed.

'The light's gone off. Either she likes the dark, or she's on her way back out,' Pete said. 'Okay, she's out and walking towards Place Jourdan, without the suit bag.'

'She's gone into a small restaurant on the corner and joined two other people. You should be able to see them now.'

The screen in the centre of the table lit up with the scene from the restaurant, filmed by one of Dorsch's men on his phone.

'They're MEPs from her party,' Liz said, flicking though her computer screen.

Two hours later, the confirmation that she was on her way home came though.

After one of Dorsch's men confirmed that Anna was in her Woluwe St Pierre house, Clive, Liz, Sean and Dorsch sat around the makeshift operations room they'd established in the dining room of the rented house.

'What's the apartment number in that building? If she's dropping clothes off there, she intends to use it,' Dorsch said.

'903,' Sean answered, again wishing he hadn't said it so quickly.

Dorsch quickly summoned two of his men and spoke to them in German.

'What was that?' Liz asked.

'We're going to get some eyes and ears in that apartment,' Dorsch said.

'You mean bugs?' Liz asked, widening her eyes, looking at Sean.

'Yes, and cameras,' Dorsch responded.

'Is that legal?' Liz asked.

'No, it's highly illegal, but how else will we know what's going on in there? I'd like to get them into her house as well, but it's like Fort Knox and we can't get near her office. That apartment's our only chance, and who knows, she may just have been dropping something off for a friend.'

'I don't like it,' Liz said.

'He's right, Liz. We need something to get a break or we're just going to be watching her through a window for months,' Clive said.

That night, Sean and Liz debated the pros and cons of the spy devices, with Liz in the firm belief that they'd crossed the line and were becoming too much like their targets in the pursuit of the story.

'Aren't the means justified by the end?' Sean protested.

'That's the mentality that leads to rendition and torture,' Liz scolded him.

Admitting that she was right, Sean agreed that there had to be rules. 'Okay, if we don't have anything by Sunday, I'll tell Dorsch that he needs to get them out.'

'What was on the files that Dorsch sent you?' Liz asked.

'Given your last response, I don't think you'll like it. Dorsch somehow has a complete audit trail of Koryalov's wealth, right back to President Volkov. He even has decoded email correspondence between Koryalov and Volkov and it's clear who's in charge. God knows how he got it.'

'I don't think our new friend Dorsch has much respect for privacy laws, we need to make sure we don't get caught up in any of his tactics,' Liz said. 'What are you going to do with the information?'

'I haven't decided. Probably write a piece, it'll make a great story.'

'Well whatever you decide, do it soon, because I think he'll be coming after us when he sees his son's penis.'

The following day was like ground-hog day, even down to the restaurant; the small eatery on the corner of Place Jourdan, which Anna clearly favoured for her evening meetings. This time she met with the new President of the European Commission, Paulo Grossi. It was just the two of them and Sean noted the familiarity they shared as he watched the FaceTime feed from Dorsch's man.

The most senior politician in the EU and the most senior civil servant seemed to be discussing the contents of a piece of paper that lay on the table between them. The conversation wasn't angry and was accented with frequent laughter, but there was something about it that seemed odd.

'Look at the body language. She's giving him instructions,' Sean said. It was subtle, but Grossi was showing some deference to Anna.

'I think you're right. Look at the way he's nodding when she speaks. It's like she's his boss,' Liz agreed.

'Maybe she is.' Clive placed the Nazi organisation chart on the table between Sean and Liz and circled the box for the *Propogandaminister.*

'Jesus Christ! The leader of the Parliament and the President of the Commission, both part of 4R18? If they're working together, they could get anything through,' Sean exclaimed.

'It makes sense. It even fits with their mentality. He's Italian; an ally,' Liz added.

'And who better to head the propaganda war than the President of the EU,' Sean commented.

'But how the hell did they pull it off?' Clive said.

'Powerful friends, from an all powerful political party,' Sean concluded.

Nodding his agreement, Clive circled the box at the top of the organisation chart with a large red question mark by it. 'But who?' he said.

Before they could carry on, Anna grabbed her briefcase and headed out to her car, leaving the papers with Grossi. Two cars then followed both diners back to their respective houses, with nothing of note to report.

The current President of the European Commission belongs to the same transnational political party that controls the European Parliament.

Chapter Forty-Six

Thursday, 11th February. Brussels, Belgium.

Anna didn't run to work as she usually did, but rode in her car very early and went straight to the Berlaymont Building; the Commission's head office.

'I know why she took her car and came in early. It's chaos out here today. There are cavalcades everywhere and half of the EU quarter is sealed off,' Pete said over the radio.

'There's an EU summit today. All the heads of state are in town,' Liz said, before returning to the lounge to join Praew on the sofa.

An hour later, Liz ran back into the operations room. 'She's on the news.'

The screen focussed on a small group behind a podium. Grossi and Anna were among them, waiting for a cue. Then Grossi moved to the podium, with Anna behind him. He began to speak in Italian, but then the English translation came through on *BBC World News*.

'Today it saddens me to announce that we have not been able to reach an agreement with four of our member states — the United Kingdom, Poland, Denmark and Sweden — regarding their breach of the terms of certain EU bonds. To this end I hereby announce, that I immediately invoke the powers granted to me under Article Seven of the Treaty on the Functioning of the European Union, and suspend those states from European Union membership, until this breach is rectified.'

Quickly stepping in when he moved back, Anna took the podium. 'As the leader of the largest party in the Parliament, I am here to say that I, and the Parliament, fully support President Grossi's tough stance on this important matter. It's high time that the heads of member states realise that they cannot just flout EU law without consequence.'

The noise level in the pressroom at the Berlaymont exploded, as every journalist raised their hand to ask questions, while at the same time reaching for their phones to call the office.

'Wow, they've done it! That must have been what the meeting was about last night; putting the final words together,' Liz said, blowing out hard.

Everybody at the house stayed rooted to the screen for the next hour, unable to move. With the press coverage going into overdrive, there was plenty to see as every news channel speculated about the response from the four suspended countries.

At 10:30 a.m. on the dot, the British Prime Minister, Ed Halliday, appeared outside the Berlaymont Building for a press statement, with every single TV channel in the world watching to see how he would react. 'Will he just dismiss it as politicking, or will he react more aggressively?' the *BBC News* anchor speculated.

When the noise from the mob of journalists had quietened down enough that he could be heard, Halliday fronted the microphones. 'Today we have seen a barbarous act from a European Union that has become infested with political infighting and corruption. But I'm here to tell you that we won't stand for it. We won't allow Britain to be bullied by the technocrats of the EU any longer, and if this position isn't reversed, I see no other option than to cancel Britain's membership of the EU forthwith.'

Any speculation that he might just brush the actions of the President aside were gone, and he pushed his way through the journalists without taking any questions.

'Fucking hell! It's real,' Clive said with his mouth aghast.

Like Clive, Sean had been plagued by the constant question of whether what they were looking for was really happening, or whether they were just chasing conspiracies, and whether he was about to make a fool of himself again in the complex arena of European politics. All those doubts were now vanquished, as he stared intently at the TV screen, watching the lonely figure of the British Prime Minister walking away from a horde of reporters.

'Anna's walking out, right into that mess,' Pete suddenly said over the radio.

Back on the TV, a reporter shouted, 'There's Anna Faustein. Do you have anything to say to her, Prime Minister?'

'Holy shit!' Sean said, as Halliday swung around to see Anna walking through the revolving doors.

'I do, and I'll say it to her face,' Halliday said, marching boldly towards her.

When Anna saw him coming she stopped and looked back at the door, but it was already too late: she was on camera; she'd have to face him. The scene was electrifying as Halliday strutted up to her, chased by a crowd of journalists. As he reached earshot, he immediately started to yell at her, waving his finger. But there was no sound, the sound crews had been blocked out by the traditional journalists in the race to keep up.

When the telescopic sound poles finally started to receive the conversation, they caught Halliday's angry words. 'It's a fucking disgrace. I don't know when that slimy bastard was even given the power to do it. And as for you, you can stick your fucking European Union up your arse, because we're leaving.' Swivelling around like a soldier, Halliday marched away, chased by the reporters, until he climbed into a waiting car.

Holding a hand up against her face, Anna did the same, refusing to comment on the way.

'Good on him! I didn't think he had the balls,' Clive said.

'I agree. I'd switched my allegiances, but I might even vote for him now,' Sean added.

'That'll be a wasted vote. Last I saw he was ten points down in the polls. He's got no chance with the general election so close. Farrell will win hands down and *he's* just about stupid enough to comply with everything the EU wants,' Liz said.

'Anna's gone into the Willy Brandt Building. I guess she'll be in there for the rest of the day as usual,' Steve said over the radio.

For the next eight hours, Sean and Liz were glued to the TV, switching between news channels. Sean thought he'd heard the sound bite 'You can stick your fucking European Union up your arse, because we're leaving', at least 400 times.

Every station was now reporting the results of an online poll that had been conducted throughout the day by one of the main political pollsters. Halliday had made a seventeen point swing in his approval rating and was now easily the clear favourite to win the May election.

'Seems they all think like you,' Liz said, poking Sean. 'A few expletives and suddenly he's cool again.'

FROM ZERO TO HERO IN A DAY, the *Sky News* headline read, with a large picture of Halliday scolding Anna next to it.

Chapter Forty-Seven

Friday, 12th February. Brussels, Belgium.

They were distracted from the TV at 6:45 p.m. 'She's out again. You could set your watch by her movements,' Steve said.

'She's heading through the park on foot,' the next update came through.

'I'll pick her up at the gate, but stay with her until then,' Pete said.

Five minutes later Pete announced that he had her in sight. 'I bet she goes to the same restaurant,' Pete laughed.

'Wait a minute. No, she's going to the apartment.'

Running into the operations room, Dorsch immediately clicked a few keys on his computer and the screen in the centre of the table lit up with six live images: four depicting different shots of the inside of Anna's apartment; one of the corridor outside; and one of the lift entrance.

The sight of the small couch where Anna had propositioned him made Sean twitch with guilt.

Then there was movement: first, on the camera by the lift, as

Anna exited, walking brusquely; then, the corridor, as she pulled out the keys and opened her apartment door. Once inside, she kicked off her shoes and went into the kitchen, where she opened a bottle of wine. After drinking a glass quickly, she looked at her watch and went into the bedroom.

She hastily inspected the contents of the suit carrier that was hanging in the wardrobe, without getting it out. Then she started to undress.

'This is wrong,' Liz said, shaking her head and looking at Sean.

'Okay, you watch and tell us when she's decent,' Clive said.

Reluctantly, Sean, Clive and Dorsch stood and moved around the table where they couldn't see the screen. All eyes were focussed on Liz.

'What's happening?' Sean asked.

'She's taken all her clothes off and is masturbating with a huge dildo.' Liz smiled.

'Ha ha!' Sean said.

'Okay, she's gone into the bathroom and she's having a shower. I can't believe you put a camera in there,' Liz looked up at Dorsch.

Some time passed while Anna showered and dried her hair. 'I bet she just uses the place to get changed when she has a function. There's sure to be some kind of banquet tonight with all the big knobs in town,' Liz commented.

'Maybe, but keep watching,' Clive said.

'Okay, she's back in the bedroom now, naked. She's getting her clothes out of the suit bag.'

Then Liz's eyes bulged as she tried to focus on the screen. 'Oh! I may be wrong, but I don't think that's the usual attire for a state banquet.'

'What is it?' Sean asked.

'Some kind of dominatrix outfit I'd say.'

Unable to resist, Clive, Sean and Dorsch all moved back around the table.

'Perverts,' Liz exclaimed.

'It looks like she's expecting company. Look at that whip,' Dorsch said.

Sean wasn't sure whether he was just commenting, or that he genuinely admired it.

After laying out the leather clothes on the bed, Anna carefully dressed herself and pulled on thigh-high patent leather boots to complete the image, before walking into the small lounge, dimming the lights and pouring herself another glass of wine.

Five minutes later, there was some movement in the corridor.

'Did you see anybody come into the building, Pete?' Clive asked.

'No, not a soul for the last half-hour,' Pete replied.

'That's weird. Either he lives in the same building, or there's a back way.'

When the new entrant knocked on Anna's door, they watched as she checked her outfit and picked up the whip before opening it.

'Wow,' the deep male voice said before he entered, clutching a bottle of champagne. He was wearing a beanie hat pulled low onto his head and a long heavy black coat.

'I thought I'd put on a special treat for you tonight, you naughty boy,' Anna said.

'She's speaking English,' Liz commented.

'Did you mean it when you said you wanted to put something up my arse?' Anna said in a provocative tone.

The four people surrounding the kitchen table in the house froze.

'No, it can't be,' Sean said.

Then Anna pulled the beanie from her guest's head, revealing the grey hair and manicured face of Ed Halliday, the British Prime Minister.

'How did he get in there?' Clive exclaimed.

'The coat. the hat. I'm guessing he gave his security the slip and came in through a rear door somewhere,' Dorsch said.

'More importantly, what the hell is he doing there after today's events?' Liz added.

'We need to be ready to speak to him on the way out. This is just about the only chance I'll ever get to question a Prime Minister,' Sean said excitedly.

'I'll stay here with Liz and Praew. You two go,' Clive said. 'We'll keep you informed.

Dorsch quickly grabbed a pistol from the cupboard and indicated to Sean that they needed to move. Once outside, a driver was waiting for them.

'What's happening, Liz?' Sean asked, as the car sped out of the gates.

'Wouldn't you like to know. Let's just say that he won't be saying much for a while. She's just gagged him with a mouth ball. I'll let you know if anything relevant happens, but I'm not providing a running commentary of the sex.'

In less than ten minutes Sean and Dorsch had joined Steve outside Anna's apartment building. 'Keep an eye on the door. We'll see if there's a rear entrance,' Dorsch instructed.

'Anything new, Liz?' Sean asked, as they ran around the side of the ugly concrete building and through the garbage collection area.

'Lots of *new* things. You'd be surprised! But nothing *relevant*,' Liz replied.

'It's here,' Dorsch said, pointing to a dark enclosed entrance, at the rear of the building. We'll hide there by the bins,' he said.

They waited for another hour and a half, before Liz finally spoke. 'Well, I'm glad that's over. I was starting to feel sorry for him,' Liz said.

'Has he said anything yet?' Sean asked.

'No, they're lying next to each other on the bed, exhausted. With good reason I might add. Wait, they're finally speaking. Can you hear them?' Liz said.

'Yes, just about,' Sean replied.

'It looks like I'll be calling you Mr Prime Minister for a lot longer then,' Anna said.

'Yep. I can't believe it worked so well and so quickly,' Halliday replied, laughing.

'They planned it! I can't believe he'd do that. Jeopardise the whole country for his own political gain,' Liz shouted.

'When will you tell your party that you don't intend to leave the Union?' Anna asked.

'After the election, when you've removed the suspension… as we agreed. It's only a few months. We can string it out until then. Besides, I quite enjoyed being a national hero today. I'm sure I'll get the opportunity to build on that in the next few days,' Halliday gloated.

'You'd better get going before you're missed,' Anna said.

'You're right. Bloody security. They spoil my life,' Halliday joked.

'He's getting dressed. And it will ruin his life when his wife and children find out,' Liz said.

The vile stench of the rotting garbage filled Sean's lungs, as he and Dorsch crouched down behind the garbage bins and waited, watching the secluded doorway.

Chapter Forty-Eight

Friday, 12th February. Brussels, Belgium.

'He's leaving now, using the stairs. Get ready,' Clive noted.

Sean tensed and flicked his tongue around his dry mouth. Accosting a Prime Minister wasn't something that he should take lightly, even if he was leaving a clandestine sex rendezvous. He studied Dorsch. So far, after only a few days as part of the team, the German billionaire had shown little respect for the law.

'We can't assault him,' Sean whispered.

'Then how will we stop him?' Dorsch replied.

'If he doesn't stop of his own accord, we have to let him go. Assaulting a Prime Minister is going too far.' Even though he was whispering, Sean made sure his point was firm.

'Okay,' Dorsch agreed, pointing in the direction of the door, as the shadowy figure emerged into the darkened yard.

As soon as Halliday was clear of the entrance, Sean sprung to his feet. 'Did you have a good time in there, Prime Minister?' Sean asked.

Clearly stunned by the approach, Halliday stopped and looked around, looking for an alternative route, but there was only one way out of the yard and that meant he would have to walk past Sean and Dorsch. When he saw that there were two of them, he turned and started to fumble for the key in his pocket, trying to head back into the building. But Sean ran forward to a spot only two metres away from him.

'Can I ask you a few questions?' Sean asked.

Ignoring Sean and looking away, Halliday continued to search for his keys. When Dorsch joined them, Sean could see the panic growing in the Prime Minister's face.

'We're not going to hurt you Prime Minister. We just want to ask you a few questions,' Sean said, blocking Dorsch's advance with his body.

Suddenly stopping his key search, Halliday turned to face Sean. 'Who are you and what do you want with me? I can have my security here in seconds and you'll spend a long time in prison,' he said aggressively.

'For what? Asking questions? I didn't think that had been criminalised yet. But since you ask, my name is Sean McManus, and I'm a British journalist.'

'The journalist from the BW affair?' Halliday said.

'Yes, that's right,' Sean acknowledged, knowing that it would help Halliday understand that he was in no physical danger.

'Look, I was just visiting a friend in this building, and I didn't think it was fair to bring half of the world's media with me,' Halliday said, regaining his composure.

'Oh, that's nice of you. Who's your friend?' Sean asked.

'It's an elderly lady: an old friend of my mother.'

'Really? That'll make a very nice personal interest piece on you. Would you mind if we interviewed her?'

'I'm afraid that she's quite frail and I wouldn't want to disturb her again.'

Dorsch made a loud tutting sound and Sean again moved to block him out.

'That's funny, I've never considered Anna Faustein old or frail.' Sean lifted his eyebrows, making the point.

Halliday bowed his head like a schoolboy caught lying. 'Okay, you've caught me. I came here to continue my argument with her on behalf of the British people. I wanted to make sure I got my point across.'

'Ha!' Dorsch exclaimed in frustration.

Even Sean would have to admit that the Prime Minister was a convincing liar. His face showed no signs of false statements: his eyes were open and made contact with Sean's, even though that was the second blatant lie he'd told. Sean quickly switched approach. 'Why are you lying to me?' he asked.

'I'm not lying to you, and quite frankly, I'm offended by that comment.'

This time Sean laughed at the fake indignation displayed by Halliday. He'd seen the same face on TV thousands of times, telling lies to millions of people, in the deluded belief that they trusted him.

'Why are you laughing?' Halliday said, the tone in his voice sharpening. 'Now, if you don't mind, I've got to get back to my hotel,' he added.

Sean thought quickly. He had to stop him from leaving, but the only way was to incriminate himself. 'I'm laughing because I have video footage of you partaking in some rather interesting activities with Ms Faustein. I doubt many people will see it as continuing the argument, although it was apparently quite aggressive.'

The comments made Halliday freeze and turn around to face Sean. 'What do you want, Mr McManus? To break up my family, ruin my life? I have some interests that I share with Ms Faustein. Should I be persecuted for that?'

'Tell him to ask his wife,' Liz's voice popped up over the earpiece.

The speed of Halliday's transition from denial, to lying, to pleading forgiveness was unbelievable. Sean pressed further. 'I'm not a tabloid muck-raker, Prime Minister, so if it was just the sex I could probably overlook it. But the problem I have is that it's more than that, isn't it? You conspired with a German MEP to deceive the British people, in order to get votes.'

'And how do you know that?' Halliday said.

'Surprise surprise! We were listening, as well as watching. Now get to the point,' Dorsch interrupted.

'You know that spying like that is illegal? If you try to use it against me in any way, I'll make sure you spend a long time in prison,' Halliday said.

Sean knew that it was coming; the point when Halliday stopped playing games and started to make threats. The problem he had was that Halliday was right. Any attempt by Sean to use the information would automatically incriminate him, and given that the target was the British Prime Minister, it wouldn't take a great leap of imagination for the prosecution to manipulate the charge into one of espionage.

'It seems we're at somewhat of an impasse, Mr McManus. You have information that I don't want published, and you *can't* publish it. So, please, get out of my way. You may be able to destroy my life, but you'll be destroying your own in the process.' Halliday moved to push past Sean, but Dorsch put his arm out and stopped him.

'What about me, you arrogant pig? How are you going to stop me publishing it?' Dorsch said, looking even more threatening than normal in the dim light. Sean could see that Halliday was scared by the sudden outburst and the sight of Dorsch blocking his way.

'The same will go for you: a long term in prison,' Halliday said, less confidently than before.

Sean was going to stop Dorsch, but maybe he had it right.

'First, you don't even know who I am; and second, I'll just put it on YouTube anonymously. I don't need to publish it like a journalist. By the time you get out of your bed in the morning, it'll be all over the world, and if your wife doesn't put a hatchet in your head, the British people will put one in your career. You think anybody will give a shit where the video came from?'

Impressed and a little intimidated at the same time, Sean realised that Dorsch hadn't become a billionaire by mistake.

Suddenly, Halliday looked like a deer caught in the headlights. Sean could tell that he wanted to go on the counter-attack and make some threats, but each time he went to speak, he stopped, obviously realizing that he was cornered, with no realistic way out.

'You bastard!' He looked at Sean, finally with real sincerity in his eyes. 'It was just a little spin; something to boost my votes for the election. It was Anna's idea and I thought it was brilliant. There's no real harm done. We'll get back in, once the election's over, and everything will be back to normal.'

'Back to normal?' Sean shook his head. 'You do know that she suspended you so that she can change the voting structure? So, when you get back in, you'll have no power to block anything. She played you so that you wouldn't take it too far. She's probably done the same to all the others, so that they think it's just a political game, rather than a real threat to sovereignty.'

'What? No, that's impossible,' Halliday said.

'No, it's not. Think about it,' Sean replied.

After a few moments of silence, Halliday put his hands over his face. 'Fuck! What've I done?' he said. 'If they change the voting structure, we'll have to leave. We can't be part of a Union that we have no say in.' Halliday was talking to himself and didn't expect input, as the implications of his actions hit home.

'You do know that Anna Faustein's a neo-Nazi?' Sean said.

His earpiece suddenly exploded with Liz's voice. 'Sean, I thought you said you weren't going to mention that! What if he's the leader of the bloody Fourth Reich?' she exclaimed.

Aware that he'd taken a gamble, Sean wanted to see Halliday's reaction when he was down, when he wasn't thinking as quickly as normal.

'What?' he looked at Sean, removing his hands from his face. 'But she's the head of an EU party. They're not Nazis.' He shook his head.

'They're not, but she is. We think she's secretly trying to manipulate EU legislation to make the environment right for a Nazi resurgence across Europe,' Sean said.

'It wouldn't take much,' Halliday admitted, clearly without thinking.

'What?' Sean replied quickly.

'I shouldn't have said that. Sorry.'

'What did you mean by it?' Dorsch said angrily.

Halliday looked at the angry Dorsch and then faced Sean. 'Our intelligence services are reporting massive growth in neo-Nazi organisations. They're presenting a more moderate image, attracting more respectable voters. They play very heavily on the issues created by the financial crisis, and it's working. It's only a matter of time before a far-right party wins a general election in a European country. Then god help us, because pretty much all of them are just fronts for neo-Nazi groups.'

'Doesn't it seem odd to you that they'd use the EU as their vehicle? Most nationalist parties are completely against the EU and would scrap it,' Sean said, genuinely looking for Halliday's experienced political opinion on a question that had been troubling him throughout the investigation.

'It depends what they see as their nation. If they conform to Hitler's ideal of one Europe under Nazi control, then it makes perfect sense.'

Nobody spoke for a little while as the reality of Halliday's words sunk in. Throughout the investigation Sean had never thought there was any real risk of the Nazis actually taking over the EU; he'd just thought they were positioning themselves to influence it. Halliday obviously thought differently, and Sean had to bow to his superior knowledge.

'What are you going to do?' Sean asked.

'I'm going to play Ms Faustein at her own game. I'll play along like everything's going as planned, then I'll put a vote to the British people and with the right push, they'll vote to leave the EU. It's our only option if we want to remain a sovereign nation.'

'What about the Nazis?' Sean asked.

'That's for you to deal with. If I say anything it'll just look like sour grapes and I'll look like a crank. You have to get firm proof and then publish. It's the only way.' Halliday looked into Sean's eyes: he was the politician again, negotiating his way out of a difficult corner. But this approach suited Sean. He still wanted to get his story, even if he didn't mention Halliday's involvement.

'Can I rely upon you for help if I need it?' Sean asked.

Halliday considered the question briefly. 'Yes, as long as you destroy everything you have on that tape and promise me that you'll never try to publish any of the events of tonight.'

It was Sean's turn to think. Halliday would have no way of knowing if the information had been destroyed, or whether Sean would stick to his word about not including him in his piece. But Sean still believed in honour and if he made a promise, he'd keep it… as long as Halliday kept his side of the same bargain. 'Okay, it's a deal. How do I get hold of you if I need you?' Sean asked.

'Contrary to common belief, I actually have a mobile phone. Very few people have the number and it's often with my private secretary, but I do have one.'

Sean took out his iPhone and keyed in the Prime Minister's private number.

'Gentlemen, I trust we have an accord?' Halliday questioned both Sean and Dorsch.

'Yes,' they said in unison, although Sean could sense Dorsch's reluctance.

'Okay. Then I really do need to go.' Halliday walked past Sean and around the corner, disappearing into the dimly lit park.

Chapter Forty-Nine

Friday, 12th February. Brussels, Belgium.

The conversation around the large, oak dining table was vibrant as each discussed the events of the evening.

'We still don't know much. Anna could be either the leader or the number two,' Sean said.

'Stefan's info said that the number two was high up in the EU, so that would make it likely that it's her,' Liz added.

'But Wagner also said that the person they call the *Führer* is also in some way related to Hitler, so she could be either,' Dorsch countered.

'Yep,' Sean agreed. 'Either way, we don't have a shred of evidence that we can use against anybody.'

'We do know three of the four, assuming that we're right about Grossi, that is. We should put round-the-clock surveillance on all of them,' Clive said.

'We're already watching Faustein and Grossi, but I can have men on Wagner by the morning,' Dorsch said.

'Good, then let's pick it up tomorrow. I don't know about you, but I'm exhausted,' Sean said.

When Sean climbed into bed, Liz was sitting up waiting for him, clearly not in the mood to sleep.

'I can't believe you just let Halliday off the hook like that,' she said.

'Do you think I should have hung him out to dry?'

'Well, yes, but that's not actually my point. You'd caught the British Prime Minister — a married man with two children — indulging in kinky sex with a German MEP whom he'd publically rebuked just hours earlier. Then he admitted that it was all a sham to fool the voters.'

'Yes,' Sean nodded.

Liz shook her head. 'By anybody's measure, that would be the scoop of a lifetime. Given that it'd be your *second* scoop of a lifetime, it would propel you from a guy that might have got lucky once, to a global rock star; you'd be a journalistic legend.'

'Yes,' Sean nodded again.

'Look, I know the Nazi and EU story is probably more politically important, but as far as readability and public outrage, the Halliday story would trump it every time. I know you'll say that there are legal issues etc., but we could get around those.'

'You're probably right,' Sean admitted.

'Then why did you let him off?' Liz asked, her face contorted. 'I thought that's what you wanted: recognition; career success. I always thought you were really ambitious.'

'I am, and you're right,' Sean agreed.

Sean's apathy was getting Liz frustrated. Her face wracked with confusion. 'Then why? I don't understand,' she said, quietly, almost despondently.

'I did it for Praew,' Sean said.

'What? What do you mean? What's Praew got to do with it?' Liz said, her tone picking up, but her confusion increasing.

Sean smiled. 'From now until the general election, I have the British Prime Minister in my pocket. When the time's right, I'm going to give Mr Halliday a call on the mobile number he gave me, and ask him to put pressure on the Home Secretary to approve Praew's residence application.'

The words hit Liz like a train crash and her face suddenly lit up. 'Oh my god, Sean, you're a genius! He'll never be able to refuse.' Then she stopped smiling and looked at him seriously. 'Are you sure? I mean, this is it — everything that you've ever dreamed of, right there in your hands — and you're going to give it away for Praew?'

Sean lowered his head and stared into Liz's eyes. 'There's nothing in the world I wouldn't give away for you and Praew. So yes, I'm certain.'

Chapter Fifty

Saturday, 13th February. Brussels, Belgium.

Sean and Liz were woken early in the morning by Clive.

'Anna Faustein's up and heading in the direction of the airport. Dorsch's guys are on her. They'll find out where she's going and we'll follow in his plane.'

'I'll stay here with Praew and if you don't come back by Sunday night, I'll take the train to London. I need to get her back to school,' Liz said.

'You can't do that. What about Koryalov?' Sean asked.

'She has to go back some time. We can't just hide forever.'

'I know, but let's deal with Koryalov first.'

Staring helplessly at Sean, Liz pleaded. 'Okay, but do something soon. I'll stay here and do some home schooling with her for now, but ...'

'Good, you'll be safer here with Dorsch's men,' Sean agreed, climbing out of bed and heading for the shower.

Ten minutes later he was in the back of a Mercedes S Class, with Clive, Steve and Pete, being driven to the private terminal at Brussels International Airport. There was no traffic so early on Saturday morning and they pulled up outside the hanger less than fifteen minutes later. Dorsch was already inside, waiting for them at the reception counter.

'She's flying to Berlin. I've got people waiting for her there, but we'll get there before her anyway. Her flight doesn't leave for another half an hour.'

The flight to Berlin took just over an hour and they were soon sitting outside the main passenger terminal at Tegel airport. The 1970s' curved concrete façade swept away into the distance as Sean peered through the darkened glass window of the Range Rover that had collected them. Dorsch was in the front passenger seat and Clive was in the rear with Sean. At the other end of the terminal, Pete and Steve were in another car with two of Dorsch's men, waiting.

'She's coming through now,' the voice of another of Dorsch's men said from inside the terminal. 'She'll be at the south side door.'

When Anna strode out of the glass doors of the terminal building pulling a carry-on suitcase, she looked as confident as ever, dressed in a neat black business suit and carrying a thin, black, leather briefcase. To Sean though, she looked different: she was now the target. 'She must be going to a meeting. That's not how she dresses outside work,' he commented.

A black BMW 7 series arrived at the kerbside next to her and a uniformed chauffer quickly jumped out to open the door. Anna didn't wait, opening the door herself before climbing into the limousine.

Both cars followed the BMW through the streets of north Berlin for fifteen minutes, before they came out from under a bridge and curved right, onto the ultra-modern *Moltkebrücke*, which spanned the River Spree. On the other side of the river, the BMW slowed and indicated to turn right. Both of Dorsch's cars continued through the curve to the left and didn't stop.

'Why aren't we following?' Sean asked.

'That's the Bundeskanzleramt; the home of the Chancellor. We can't stop around here,' Dorsch said. 'We'll put one car in either direction and pick her up when she leaves. At least we know who she's meeting.'

It would be normal for a person in Anna's position to meet with the German Chancellor, but Sean's mind raced. *Could that be who we're looking for... the Führer?'*

'I don't suppose she could be... I mean Dorfman... the *Führer?'* Sean said

'I've given that some thought. She's from a party linked to Faustein's party and although she claims to be from the centre of politics, it's not the way she acts. She runs the country like a dictator and takes no prisoners. I wouldn't be surprised if she was involved in some way,' Dorsch said.

Instinctively, Sean picked up his phone and called Liz. 'Hi, Liz, could you get me as much background as possible on Gretal Dorfman?'

'The German Chancellor?'

'Yes. Anna Faustein's just gone into her residence.'

'My god, Sean, be careful. Give me a few hours and I'll see what I can come up with.'

When Sean clicked the phone off, he was still processing things in his mind. 'It doesn't really make sense though; a national head of state making the EU irreversibly more powerful than the state. They're the people who stand to lose the most,' he said.

'That depends on whether she's pulling the strings in the

background. She probably has the ability to vote Faustein in or out as party leader, it's an effective means of control,' Dorsch said.

Images of the news articles that Sean had read over the years, which claimed that the German Chancellor was really in charge of events at the EU, suddenly sprang into Sean's mind. He'd always written them off as nonsense, because he couldn't see how it could work, but that was before he understood the power of the transnational political parties and their links to national party leaders.

'They'd need to be confident that they had the right person before they transferred the overt power like that. Whoever it is would have to be beyond corruption; totally loyal to the cause,' Sean said.

'Like the granddaughter of Adolf Hitler?' Clive suggested.

The two other passengers suddenly fell silent.

'Surely not! Surely that's nonsense!' Sean said quietly.

But the others didn't speak.

The European Peoples Party (EPP) is by far the strongest party in the European Parliament. It also boasts 14 of the 28 EU Commissioners as members, including the Commission President.

In a federal Europe, the leading party would also provide the President of Europe, the most powerful person in the world.

The EPP is heavily influenced by the Christian Democratic Union of Germany (CDU); a political party which is led by the current Chancellor of the Federal Republic of Germany.

Chapter Fifty-One

Saturday, 13th February. Berlin, Germany.

Anna's car came back out onto Willy Brandt Strasse two hours later and turned right, towards the centre of Berlin. Following behind, they were soon out of the gleaming modern structures of the government buildings and into some of the few remaining historic structures that had survived the Allied bombing of the Second World War.

After a few minutes, the BMW came to a halt outside a sandstone building with burgundy awnings above its windows. In the distance, the Brandenberg Gate dominated the area and Sean scrutinised the edifice he'd seen on TV so many times growing up. It was something that had become the symbol of the struggle between East and West during the Cold War; the most prominent point on the Berlin Wall.

They'd stopped on the former communist side and Anna climbed out of the car, while a hotel porter took her bags. After stretching her back, she sauntered through the doors of the Hotel Adlon.

'I guess we'll be here for a while,' Clive said, as Anna's car pulled away from the door.

Agreeing with Clive, Dorsch quickly hopped out of the car and returned with some cold drinks and sandwiches, but they didn't need to wait as long as expected for Anna, as within minutes, she ran out of the front door of the hotel and turned left towards the gate, wearing her jogging clothes.

'We can't follow her there. It's pedestrianised. We'll have to go to the other side. You stay here in case we lose her,' Dorsch instructed the other car, as they sped away from the gate to a road that cut through the buildings, out to the western side of the wall.

When they arrived on the other side, tour buses were blocking the view back to the gate. They scanned the area for Anna, but she was nowhere to be seen.

'We've lost her,' Clive exclaimed.

'Wait. Is that her getting into that green Audi?' Sean pointed to a green car on the wide street by the park.

'Yes, it is. She's being cautious. She's up to something,' Clive commented.

When the Audi pulled away, they followed as it headed north on the road towards Rostock. After about half-an-hour's driving, Dorsch's phone rang. 'Wagner's just left Leipzig in a helicopter. We can't follow him,' he said, after the call.

Returning to his phone, Dorsch then made another call and spoke in German. 'My guys are checking out her room in the Adlon. She can't get back there to surprise them now,' he said, following the call.

Thoughts of what Liz would make of Dorsch's lack of respect for the law crossed Sean's mind, but he decided to just let it go.

Another hour and a half passed before they reached the

Baltic seaport of Rostock. When the Audi pulled over by a small roadside café, Anna got out carrying a bag and went inside. The team waited, out of sight in the Range Rover. After about twenty minutes, Anna emerged, but she was no longer wearing her running clothes and had changed into a traditional dirndl, topped off with a long blonde wig. If it was a disguise, it was good. Sean would have walked past her in the street.

The Audi soon sped away, but Dorsch told the driver to wait a minute or so. 'I don't want to be seen, and anyway, I think I know where she's going.'

'Where?' Sean asked, as the Range Rover started to move again.

'Jamel. It's not far from here, but we can't go there.'

'Why not?' Clive said, surprised by Dorsch's sudden caution.

'Because it's a town for Nazis: only Nazis live there; and only Nazis are welcome there. We'd stand out like, how do you say it… the testicles of a dog.'

'We could get some pictures of Anna dressed like that,' Clive said.

The comment made Dorsch laugh. 'Every woman in Germany has a traditional dirndl. I'm guessing that she's wearing it because it fits with the mentality of the Nazis.' They like tradition, anything which harks back to the old Germany,' he said.

With the Audi now well out of sight, they were soon out into open countryside, passing through quaint towns with traditional buildings. When they arrived at the small village of Gressow, Dorsch told the driver to stop, and they parked the car behind a café, hiding it from the road. 'This is as close as we get,' Dorsch climbed out of the car. 'Jamel is less than two kilometres up this road. We'll catch her when she leaves.'

When they entered the small café, the owner said something

in German to Dorsch, who in turn, seemed to be asking questions of the elderly man.

'That's odd. He says that a lot of cars have gone into Jamel this morning. It must be some kind of meeting,' Dorsch relayed.

As Sean was about to speak, the propeller noise from a nearby helicopter disrupted them, smothering the conversation. Sean immediately ran outside and took a photo of it, before it disappeared over the tress, seemingly landing in Jamel. When he returned to his seat, he quickly pulled the photo up on the screen and passed it around. 'I'd bet that's Wagner. What flag is that?' Sean asked about the black, red and white flag with an iron cross in the corner, which was painted across the bottom of the helicopter.

'It's the flag of the Kaiser. Nazi symbols are banned in Germany, so they've adopted this instead. I think you're right. The only person wealthy enough to own a helicopter and bold enough to paint it this way is Wagner. It must be an important meeting,' Dorsch said.

'If it is, they'll all be there: all the leaders,' Clive said, raising an eyebrow.

Taking the hint, Dorsch quickly sprang to his feet. 'Come on. Let's see if we can get a better look.' He ran out to the Range Rover and instructed the driver to stay with the car. Then he pulled out a camera with a zoom lens and two sets of military binoculars from the boot, before passing around three browning 9mm pistols. 'Same rules; don't shoot me,' he said to Sean, grinning.

'Won't the café owner give us away?' Clive asked.

'I doubt it. He called them "fucking Nazi dickheads" earlier.' Dorsch smiled.

Following behind Dorsch, they ran out of the town, through a farmer's field and into a small forest. When they made their way to the other side of the trees, the small village of Jamal came into view, about 300 metres away across open fields. Staying behind the last line of trees, Clive and Sean began to scan the area with the binoculars, while Dorsch assessed their position just using his naked eyes.

A yellow tin sign for the town came into view in Sean's binoculars, announcing it as Jamel, Landkreis Nordwestmecklenberg. Along from the tin sign and closer to the village centre, he saw another, more makeshift sign. It had a series of wooden arrows attached to it, giving distances to other places in Europe, similar to the tourist signs seen in major cities all over the world. When Sean read the arrow second from the bottom, it sent a chill down his spine: *Braunau-am-Inn 855km.* Beyond the signpost, painted onto a rendered wall, a large mural depicted a traditional Bavarian family; all with blonde hair and blue eyes. Even with his limited historical knowledge, Sean knew that it was a copy of a 1930s' Nazi propaganda poster.

The small village was filled with parked cars, and skinheads with dogs roamed around the perimeter of the houses. The irony of the fact that these vicious-looking bald-headed thugs somehow identified themselves with the people in the poster baffled Sean completely. *But then Hitler himself was hardly the prime Aryan example,* he thought.

In the centre of the village, Anna's green Audi was parked by a light blue-coloured house, which was surrounded by guards. Wagner's helicopter sat in a small paddock on the edge of the village, also surrounded by skinhead guards.

'I think they're meeting in that building there,' Dorsch said, pointing to the cream building closest to the woods that they were hiding in. He quickly pulled the camera up and set up a tripod below it, which seemed a bit extreme to Sean.

'It's a laser listening device. It has to be perfectly still and focussed on a window,' Dorsch said, interpreting Sean's expression.

'Sorry, I thought it was a camera,' Sean smiled.

Lifting his eyebrows in a concerned way, Dorsch continued to play with the lens a few times, before stopping. 'It's no use. I need to get closer. Stay here,' he said, before grabbing the equipment and edging across the trees. When he reached the end of the forest, he moved forward towards the town, using a hedgerow as cover.

With Dorsch now so close to the village, Sean felt his pulse race, willing him to be careful. Then he stopped, just 150m from the building where the meeting was taking place and set up the listening device behind the hedgerow. After a couple of minutes of fiddling with it, he turned and gave the thumbs-up.

'What are they saying?' Sean asked.

Pushing his headphones into his ears, Dorsch didn't answer for a while. 'They seem to be judging some kind of beauty pageant.'

'Really? That's it?' Sean said.

'Yes, they've just named some girl from Dortmund Miss Hitler, saying that she's the perfect Aryan.'

'Fucking hell! Are you serious?' Clive said.

'Yes. Shhh,' Dorsch replied.

The radio went silent for a little while again. 'Okay, it's a meeting alright, they've moved on to the next agenda item.'

'Anna's speaking now. They introduced her as the *Vizekanzler*, so we were right about that,' Dorsch laughed.

'Wait a minute. How the hell did he get there? It's Grossi.'

'At least we know that he's involved now. So we know three of the top four people in 4R18,' Sean said.

'Quiet, they're talking about you,' Dorsch said quickly.

'What?' Sean asked.

'They're saying that the Russian failed. They know about Koryalov. They gave him your location.'

'So Koryalov *is* part of this?' Sean asked.

'I don't think so, they just seem to have been using him.'

'But how did they know about us and Koryalov?'

'Wasn't it all over the news?'

'Yes,' Sean said sheepishly.

'Wagner's just said that he'll deal with it himself from now on.'

'Did he say that he knows where we are?'

'Shhh,' Dorsch said again. 'They've just introduced the *Führer*.'

'Who is it?' Clive asked quickly.

'Shhh,' Dorsch repeated, as Sean saw him pushing on the outside of his ear phones. Then he suddenly lifted his head, peering over the hedgerow. 'No, impossible. It can't be… '

The small town of Jamel, in Mecklenberg-Vorpommern, Germany, lies approximately 10km due east of the port of Wismar and is said to be completely inhabited by neo-Nazis.

A sign at the entrance to the town gives its distance to Braunau-am-Inn and another declares it 'Free, Social and National': a slogan used to assimilate it with National Socialism (Nazism).

Chapter Fifty-Two

Saturday, 13th February. Jamel, Germany.

The loud crack of a single, high-velocity round fired from a sniper rifle made Sean dive to the ground. When he looked up to see what was happening, Dorsch was lying prone on the floor by the hedge where he had been crouching. Straining to see, Sean instantly drew the binoculars to his face.

As the field glasses came into focus on Dorsch's body, Sean gasped at the sight of the limp form on the fresh snow. A large patch of red blood had formed around him and the place where his head should have been was just a mess of flesh: the bullet had shattered his skull. Instinctively, Sean stood to run forward, but Clive grabbed his coat.

'What are you doing?' Clive asked.

'Going to help. We can't leave him there like that.'

Reaching up, Clive pulled Sean down to his side and turned his head to face him. 'He's dead. There's nothing we can do for him now and if we don't get out of here now, we'll be next.'

Deep down, Sean knew that Clive was right, but it just didn't feel right to leave him there.

'Look, the only thing we can do for him now is live and bring his killers to justice. If we die too, then they get away with it,' Clive said, without letting Sean's coat go.

The sight of dogs approaching from the village shook Sean back to his senses and he stood with Clive still holding onto him. When he started to move away from the tree line, Clive finally let him go, allowing him to increase his speed. The going was tough, as the ground under foot was filled with air pockets created by the snow. But they sprinted as fast as they could away from the village. Behind them and just arriving at the edge of the small woods, the dogs were making ground fast.

When they exited the treeline, Sean glanced over his shoulder. He could see four dogs just twenty metres away. Digging deep, he mustered up all his energy and dashed across the narrow road. The small café where the Range Rover was parked was only 300 metres away. But it was too far: there was no way they could outrun the dogs.

Sliding into the ditch on the far side of the road, Sean swivelled around and knelt on the floor as the first dog leapt in the air towards him. He pulled the trigger of the pistol twice in quick succession and jumped to the side as the dog dropped onto the road heavily, fighting for breath. In no time at all, the next two dogs were there and Clive was also aiming his pistol at them. The volley of rounds from the two pistols, felled the two animals before they could get to them. Then the fourth dog attacked from the side and clamped onto Sean's leg. He fell to the ground trying to get a shot away, but missed.

Three shots then rang out from Clive's gun and the dog dropped, dead, with its jaw still clamped onto Sean's calf. Its teeth felt like they were gnawing at his bone, even though it wasn't breathing and Clive quickly ran forward tearing at the its head, trying to release its locked jaw.

'Clive,' Sean pointed, where a group of six skinheads had just emerged from the forest on the other side of the road.

Leaving Sean to fight with the dog's jaw, Clive let off two warning shots over the heads of the skinheads, watching as they dived to the ground. 'They're not armed,' Sean said, when Clive scrambled back over to help him, pulling helplessly at the dog's jaw.

'There's only one thing for it. Close your eyes,' Clive said, as he pointed the pistol at the dog's head, close to Sean's calf.

Abject terror filled Sean's mind as he closed his eyes and tensed his muscles, waiting for the pain that would surely come from the move. Then he heard the dull click of Clive's pistol. 'It's empty,' Sean said. 'You're out of ammo.'

'No, it reloaded it can't be, it's just a dud round. Give me yours.' Clive said reaching out.

Turning the muzzle around, Sean passed his pistol to Clive and tensed again, ready for the pain. The loud bang was followed by a shattering feeling, which seemed to reverberate through his whole body. Immediately, Clive was pulling at the bits of loose bone and teeth, getting it out of Sean's leg.

Before he could clear the wound, a burst of machine gun fire came out from the woods on the other side of the road and bit into the ground next to Sean.

Suddenly, two men in paramilitary uniform came out of the woods, brandishing small machine guns. 'They're not very accurate. Move around,' Clive instructed.

Fighting the pain in his calf, Sean rolled around in the grass, as Clive dived to one side and took aim. The three shots from

Sean's pistol missed their target, as the paramilitaries took evasive action.

Seconds later, the next volley of machine gun fire hit the spot where Sean had been lying, just milliseconds earlier.

'Damn!' Clive exclaimed as he discarded Sean's pistol and started to fiddle with his own, trying to get the jammed round out of the chamber. Sean looked at the protruding metal bulge on the end of the barrel of his own pistol... it was out of ammunition.

The gap in hostilities didn't go unnoticed by the paramilitaries and they must have sensed what was happening. Rising to their feet, they started walking forward towards Sean and Clive, weapons at the ready.

While Clive was still trying to unblock his pistol, a shattering burst of machine gun fire suddenly opened up, tearing against the trees behind the skinheads. Confused, Sean turned around and saw the Range Rover speeding in their direction. The driver was holding a machine pistol out of the window and firing indiscriminately in the direction of the attackers.

Seconds later, the car screeched to a halt alongside Clive and Sean. As a second volley of rounds left the machine pistol, they jumped up and opened the doors, scrambling into the front and rear seats.

Before they could pull away, a hail of bullets ripped into the side of the Range Rover and the driver slumped back into his seat, with a trickle of blood running out of his mouth.

Without hesitation, Clive dived across the car, thrusting head first into the well of the driver's side and pushed the accelerator with his hand. The Range Rover shot forward and he shouted to Sean. 'I can't see anything. You steer.'

The Range Rover was veering quickly towards the edge of the

road, as Sean pushed the top of his body through the gap between the driver's and passenger's seat. He grabbed the steering wheel, just managing to correct its course in time.

As he straightened the wheels up, another volley of rounds hit the rear of the car, but Sean felt nothing, not even the pain from the dog bite, as he struggled to steer the speeding SUV down the narrow road.

When they came to a junction, he turned the wheel as best he could, but the car was going too fast and it lifted onto two wheels. Clive suddenly pulled his hand off the accelerator, letting it right itself, before they swerved into a ditch.

With his body hanging between the front and rear seats, laying across Clive's back, pressed down by the dead body of Dorsch's man, Sean grappled uselessly with the steering wheel, as the car bounced through the ditch and then ploughed through a hedge. The bump caused the dead body of the driver to bounce on his back, wedging him tightly between it and Clive, making it difficult for him to turn the steering wheel.

When the car finally stopped bouncing around, Clive suddenly forced the accelerator down again.

'What are you doing?' Sean shouted.

'If we're in a field, we need to keep moving or we'll get bogged. Aim back for the road,' Clive shouted as best he could, still jammed in the footwell.

Fighting with every ounce of strength he had, Sean managed to point the steering wheel at the hedge on the other side of the field, hoping that there was a road on the other side of it.

It was almost impossible to hang on as the car bounced from left to right over the bumpy ground, and the three bodies clattered together painfully, but he gripped his fingers around the wheel and shoved his arm into the spokes.

When they hit the hedge the car lurched into the air, leaving the ground, then it battered heavily into a turf bank on the other side, smashing the bonnet open. The brief glimpse of the road that Sean had been afforded before the bonnet blocked his view, made him think the road was to the left. He pulled sharply on the steering wheel, swinging the car violently sideways.

The unmistakable sound of tarmac appeared under the tyres, 'STOP,' Sean yelled. Almost immediately, his body rolled forward, pressed against the steering wheel by the dead body of the driver, as Clive switched his hand from accelerator to brake.

The car swerved from side to side, smashing Sean and Clive's bodies in the small spaces, before it finally stopped.

Pushing out with his elbows, Sean released the dead body from his back and forced himself up, grabbing Clive's coat, and pulling him out of the footwell as he did.

Before Clive had time to take in the scene, Sean jumped out of the rear door and instantly fell to the floor, his injured leg collapsing underneath him. Gritting his teeth, he stood up and opened the driver's door. Then, putting all his weight on his good leg, he pulled the driver out from the car. In seconds, Clive was by his side and helping him bundle the body into the back of the car. Both of them were covered in blood when Clive took the driver's seat only seconds later and Sean closed the bonnet as best he could, before climbing into the front passenger seat.

'They won't be far behind,' Clive said, as he floored the accelerator.

The battered Range Rover sounded like an old farm tractor as it lurched forward, with parts falling from the bodywork.

As Clive had predicted, it wasn't long before a white pickup truck appeared on the narrow road behind them, followed in quick succession by two similar styled vehicles.

The Range Rover was too badly damaged to outrun the new pickup trucks, and they gained ground quickly. When Sean looked down at his leg, the throbbing pain started to overcome the adrenalin. Blood was still running from the puncture holes where the dog's teeth had perforated his skin. He pulled the belt from his waist and wrapped it around the wound tightly a number of times, applying pressure.

Before Sean could sit up again, the first of the pickup trucks smashed into the back of the Range Rover, sending it swerving across the road. As Clive struggled to control the steering wheel with his one good hand, Sean climbed though the gap into the back seat. He pulled the body of the driver down into the footwell and jumped back up, hitting the small switch to drop the rear seat forward. When it came down, he saw the array of hardware that the car had been carrying.

Most of the boxes were dented and smashed, but then he saw what he'd seen earlier; a small unmarked metal case that he'd watched Dorsch inspect before they went into the woods. At the time he'd wondered why Dorsch thought that he needed the three hand grenades packed in foam. Now he didn't care.

As he stretched out into the boot to grab the case, a huge bang echoed out from the back of the car and the rear windscreen shattered under the pressure of another direct hit from the chasing vehicle. Glass rained down onto Sean's legs, but his face was protected by the parcel shelf. He stretched again and grabbed the grenade box, quickly returning to the front seat, where Clive was still struggling to control the battered Range Rover, which now sounded like the axel was about to fall off.

'How do I work these?' Sean asked, showing Clive the contents of the box.

'Jesus! What was Dorsch planning?' Clive exclaimed. 'It's

simple. Twist off the safety tag and pull out the pin. Make sure your hand is over the handle and tight around the body of the grenade. When you let it go, it starts the timer,' Clive said.

'How long before it goes off?'

'It varies, could be thirty seconds; could be five.'

Shocked at the vagueness of the timing, Sean quickly untied the safety tag on the first grenade. As he pulled it clear, they were struck again by the truck from behind and he dropped it into the footwell. Terror ripped through his body as he quickly reached down and grabbed it, shaking with fear.

'It's okay. The pin's still in. But please don't drop it when the pin's out,' Clive said.

Sean's hands were trembling when he pulled the metal clip out of the grenade. His knuckles white, as he held the handle against the body of the device so tightly, that he could feel the imperfections on the steel casing. Plucking up his courage, he looked around; the rear windscreen had completely gone and the pickup truck was only a few metres behind them, closing in again. Angling his body carefully, he went to throw the grenade out of the rear window. As he released his grip, the grenade sprung forward out of his palm and dropped onto the parcel shelf, rolling around on the shattered glass.

Panic-stricken, he flung himself through the gap between the seats and grabbed at the grenade, but the pickup truck hit the car as he did and it sent him reeling backwards into the back of the driver's seat. Then the driver's dead body landed on top of him. Thrusting upwards, he managed to push off the body and get back into position, but the grenade was gone. Just broken glass lay on the parcel shelf.

Turning to the seat, he felt around with his hands… nothing. Then he saw it, rolling around in the rear footwell. In one move, he dived down and swung his arm up, tossing it out of the rear window, waiting for the explosion… but nothing happened and the pickup truck was closing in again. Then an explosive bang screamed out some 50 metres behind them, and well behind all three chasing vehicles.

'That means they're thirty-second fuses. Sorry I forgot to tell you that they can spring out of the clip. Be careful when you open your hand,' Clive said.

That was only thirty seconds? It felt like an hour! Sean thought as, he reached into the case and carefully undid another safety wire.

'You're going to have to let the clip go and hold onto it for a while. Use your watch,' Clive said.

Nodding his understanding, Sean carefully pulled the pin out of the second grenade, trying to control the shaking in his hands.

'Okay, turn it around and let the handle drop,' Clive said.

As Sean released his grip, the clip sprang away from the grenade, arming it. Sean gulped, watching the second hand count down on his wrist. 25… 20… 15 ... Fear dictating his movements, he threw the grenade out of the back window; again nothing, nothing, then a bang, well behind the cars.

'That's not going to do it, Sean. I'll try to get some more distance, but you need to give it just two seconds, or they'll just drive by.

'Two seconds? I'm not sure my watch is that accurate,' Sean exclaimed.

Clive looked at him seriously. 'I'm not sure how long I can keep this thing on the road. It's falling apart. Just a few more knocks and that's it. Get close to the rear screen and just drop it out of the back on twenty-eight seconds,' Clive said firmly.

Sean prepared the last grenade, clinging to it tightly as he got into position. Every nerve in his body said that he couldn't time it to within just two seconds, and broken glass cut into his knuckles as he spread himself out onto the parcel shelf.

'Tell me at ten seconds,' Clive yelled from the driver's seat.

Taking a deep breath, Sean let the clip ping away out of the rear window. He gripped the rear head rests with his legs, focussing on his watch face. The bonnet of the pickup truck was less than two metres away from him and he could see the sadistic glare of the skinhead driver, as he closed in to ram the Range Rover again. The collision jolted Sean to the side, and he banged his head against a pillar, but he clung on to the grenade, with blood dripping from his knuckles as they scraped across the broken glass.

'How long, Sean?' Clive's shout came as he repositioned himself.

Sean looked at his watch. 'Er... fifteen, I think.' His mind blanked, briefly. 'Yes... fifteen, eighteen... twenty,' he said.

The Range Rover suddenly sped up, jerking Sean across the glass painfully. They were now about fifteen metres clear of the pickup truck. Sean glared at his watch, counting 25, 26, 27... He let the grenade drop from his extended hand. It bounced off the rear bumper and fell into the road.

Just as the pickup truck drove over it, it exploded, lifting the vehicle in the air, Sean covered his face as debris shot forward, but the speed of the Range Rover made sure it didn't hit. When the pickup truck came back to the ground, the two chasing vehicles ploughed head on into it. Two explosions followed as the Range Rover rounded a bend and they sped away from the carnage.

In a real online beauty pageant dubbed *Miss Hitler*, neo-Nazis are seeking to find the most beautiful, anti-Semitic woman in Europe.

Among other qualification criteria, entrants are required to be a Nazi and a woman that hates Jews.

The woman who receives the most 'likes' will be declared the winner.

At last count, 7,000 people had 'liked' this page. One of the leading contenders to win said that, she 'adores Hitler for his philosophy on the ideal society and his willingness to experiment on people'. Another contestant noted that she 'is intently focussed on Holocaust Revisionism'.

Chapter Fifty-Three

Saturday, 13th February. Wismar, Germany.

When the Range Rover limped into the small port town of Wismar, just a few kilometres from Jamel, Clive was careful to stay away from any busy roads, skirting the edge of the port, before pulling into a deserted logging yard.

'It's Saturday. We should be okay here. I'll call Pete to come and get us,' Clive said.

On the call he asked Pete to pick up some medical supplies and clean clothes on the way. 'Berlin's about two hours away. How's your leg?' he asked, when he'd finished speaking to Pete.

'Painful, but not seriously damaged,' Sean said, wincing as he touched the belt, which had effectively stopped the bleeding.

'Pete and Steve should be here about 4 p.m. ish. I'd guess it's about a six-hour drive to Brussels from here, so we should be able to get there tonight.'

'I'll call Liz to let her know,' Sean said, pulling the phone from his pocket.

When he looked at the screen, he'd received a text message from an unknown number.

> *I guess that's the end of our friendship then! We could have had something special, but now you and your slant-eyed cunt will have to go the same way as the traitor, Dorsch. Who, as I speak, is being fed to the rest of the hounds. Run Sean, run, but know this, you can't hide!'*

When Sean studied the message, his first reaction was to respond and tell her to go fuck herself, but he knew that would just play into her hands.

'It's from Anna,' he said passing the phone to Clive.

'How did they know it was us?' Clive frowned.

'Security cameras? Phone cameras when they were chasing us? Who knows. I'd better warn Liz to get out of the house,' Sean said.

'No, wait. I think that's the best place for her at the moment. They obviously don't know about it, or they'd have shown up while we were there.'

A brief spell of uncertainty crossed Sean's mind, but Clive's judgement had always been sound and there was no reason to believe that it wouldn't be now. 'Okay, I'll call her and let her know what's happening.'

Two hours later, a Mercedes SUV rounded a large pile of logs that they'd hidden behind. Pete was driving and Steve was in the passenger seat. 'Where are Dorsch's guys?' Clive asked.

'Not very far away, I would guess,' Pete said.

'What do you mean?' Sean asked.

'When we told them Dorsch was dead, they took us to a building on the eastern side. Before they gave us this car, they started packing an arsenal of gear into two Range Rovers and were joined by six other mercenaries before they sped off. I'm guessing they were on their way to the Nazi meeting,' Pete said.

'Holy shit!' Clive said.

'With the amount of gear they were carrying. I doubt that town will be on the map tomorrow,' Steve added.

'I hope they've got a rocket launcher. Wagner's in a helicopter,' Sean said.

'I didn't see one, but who knows. I'm starting to feel like we're back in Afghan,' Pete said.

'You know we're still no closer to knowing who the *Führer* is, or getting any solid proof of Faustein's involvement,' Sean said.

'We found two documents in her room safe. I've got photos of them on my camera, but they're in German,' Pete replied.

'Send them to me. I'll forward them to Liz. She can try to translate them before we get there,' Sean said.

'What do you think Dorsch meant when he said *"it can't be..."*?' Sean asked, explaining the context to Pete and Steve.

All four fell silent for a while thinking, until Clive spoke. 'It has to be somebody he knew, which limits it to somebody well-known, or somebody he knew personally.'

'Yes, but who? I guess the surprise he showed rules out Dorfman, after we'd discussed her,' Sean commented.

After cleaning up his wounds and changing clothes, Sean slept for the remainder of the seven-hour drive to Brussels. When they arrived, Liz and Praew were waiting for them in the hallway. 'Thank god! I was terrified for you.' Liz said, hugging Sean.

The conversation soon turned to the investigation. 'Did you get anywhere with the documents I sent through?' Sean asked Liz.

'Yes, the first one is what we suspected: a treaty change proposal to shift the voting structure to simple majority for treaty variations and new treaties, although it also subtly shifts the power to approve them away from the European Council to the European Parliament.'

'Thus giving the Parliament complete control over Europe: a federal state run by its elected members. It's that simple: EU federation in one document,' Sean said.

'Yep, with Anna Faustein at the helm,' Clive added.

'It's the second one that scares me more. It's another treaty change and seems to be a series of measures, this time not discreetly hidden.'

'Yes?' Sean said, trying to move her along.

'Remember, I used an online translator, so some nuances may be missed.'

'Okay, please,' Sean said impatiently.

'Well, it seems to lay out penalties for any member state, whether currently suspended or not, if at any time they leave, or threaten to leave, the EU.'

Sean frowned. 'What are they, these penalties? Does it say?'

'Yes. They are,' Liz read from a piece of paper. '1) The automatic cessation of all but vital trade with the country. 2) Where trade is considered vital and it is approved by the EU Parliament, it will carry an automatic duty of 40%.'

'Holy shit!' Sean exclaimed.

'Wait, it gets worse. 3) The automatic expulsion of all workers from the member state in question, from all other EU territories. 4) The removal of any automatic visa system. It specifies that visas for citizens of the leaving member state, that wish to visit an EU member's territory, will be granted at EU level, and will only be granted in special circumstances. And finally, the blocking of EU airspace and waterways for the use of any flight or ship coming or going from the relevant member state.'

Everybody in the room fell silent, absorbing the implications of the legislation.

'So any state that leaves will be completely economically and physically isolated? Hitler's blockade tactics to starve Britain into submission,' Clive said.

'It's worse than that. It says that any state which *threatens* to leave, which of course the UK just has, courtesy of our friendly pervert Halliday,' Liz summarised.

'Surely that won't get through?' Clive said, the colour draining from his face.

'If the first treaty change gets through the Council — and she must know that she has the numbers — then this one will automatically be transferred to the Parliament,' Liz said.

'Where it'll sail through based on the direction of her thumb. It's exactly what they want. A Europe controlled by them, that nobody can ever leave,' Sean added.

'It'll start another war,' Clive said quietly.

'Against the massed ranks of the EU states; twenty-seven countries against one? I doubt it,' Sean countered.

'Then how do we stop it?' Clive asked.

Putting his hands on his face, Sean blew out a huge gasp of air. 'I can't believe I'm about to say this, but we publish it tonight, before the treaty change goes to Council on Monday.'

'Why don't you want to do that?' Clive queried.

'Because, for the second time in one year, I'm about to give away a story worth millions... for nothing... by just sending it out on a news wire.'

'Very commendable of you.' Clive smiled.

Shaking his head at Clive's attempt at humour, Sean stood to walk to the toilet. When he reached the door of the dining room, one of Dorsch's men pushed him back in. Then the two others drew their weapons, pointing them at the small group.

'Empty everything from your pockets and sit at the chairs,' Dorsch's man, who'd previously pretended not to speak any English, said.

'That's how Anna knew it was us,' Clive said. 'I knew there was something not quite right about it.'

'Shut up!' the leader of the three mercenaries said, pushing Clive into the chair.

One by one, the leader tied the hands of each of the six people: Clive, Pete and Steve first, then Sean, Liz and Praew, while his comrades guarded the room with their weapons ready. When he'd completed the restraints, he looked up. 'Just because *Dorsch* was a gay Jew pig traitor, it doesn't mean that *we* aren't loyal to the Fatherland.' He clicked his heels together and performed the Nazi salute. '*Sieg heil,*' he said in unison with the other two mercenaries.

The Treaty of Lisbon allows any member state to withdraw from the Union for its own constitutional needs under Article 50.

The terms of the withdrawal then need to be agreed by a qualified majority of the European Council, and later, the European Parliament.

European hardliners in the Parliament believe that any country that leaves, and thus weakens the Union, should receive very unfavourable settlement terms.

More extreme federalists believe that states trying to negotiate a better deal by *threatening to leave* should also be penalised in some way.

Chapter Fifty-Four

Saturday, 13th February. Brussels, Belgium.

The pain from his leg injury was getting to a point where Sean was struggling to bear it. He could see that the clean dressings that he'd applied in the car were now soaked in fresh blood and the area around the wound was starting to swell up, tightening the bandage and cutting circulation from his leg. The cuts on his arms and hands from the glass in the Range Rover were also hurting, but he couldn't see them to see if they were bleeding, as his arms were tied behind the backrest of the dining chair.

Opposite him, Clive scanned the room, with the other four prisoners either side of the dining table; all with their hands tied. Standing by the door, the leader of the three mercenaries kept watch. The others watched TV in the adjoining room. Before the tape had been applied to their mouths, Liz had spoken a few words in Thai to Praew and she seemed to settle down. Two hours later they changed guards and the leader left.

Throughout the night, the guards changed every two hours, while the others slept. But nobody around the table slept at all; it was impossible in the uncomfortable position. Sean was so tired, he thought he'd started to hallucinate.

When the light came up in the morning, nothing had changed. They were force-fed some dry bread and water by the guards, before they switched back to the same two-on, two-off routine.

It was 1:15 p.m. on the wall clock when Sean heard tyres on the gravel driveway outside. It sounded like there were multiple vehicles — at least three — followed by a series of opening and closing doors.

A few short moments later, Anna walked into the room, followed by Wagner. She was dressed in tight black leather trousers, knee-length high-heeled boots and an expensive black fur coat, making her look more like a film star than a politician. Equally well-dressed, Wagner wore a designer black suit, with a long black overcoat.

As the guards stood back, Anna strutted around the table to Sean and leaned forward in front of him, grabbing his cheeks with one hand and pulling them tightly. 'So cute; such a waste.' She looked up at Liz, disdain written on her face. 'A blonde Aryan boy like you, clever and brave, why would you waste your time with this yellow bitch?'

Refusing to be baited, Liz stared ahead, ignoring the comments.

'Did you tell her how you salivated over my naked body in my apartment? I bet you didn't. Did you tell her how hard your cock was? How much you wanted me?' Anna reached down and grabbed Sean's crotch, making the point. Then she stood upright and pulled the tape from Sean's mouth.

Before Sean could speak she kissed him forcefully on the mouth. 'One last kiss from an Aryan princess, but it won't be enough to save you, I'm afraid.'

'You're a psychopath,' Sean said.

'And you and your friends are spies,' Anna said.

'Spies? Are you completely mad?' Sean questioned.

Suddenly, Wagner stepped forward and struck Sean across the face with a pair of leather gloves. 'Silence! The *Führer* has seen the evidence and has declared that you are all enemy spies. As such, you are not entitled to protection under the Geneva Convention and you are to be executed by a firing squad of the Fourth Reich.' Wagner clicked his heels together. '*Sieg heil.*' he said, with the others, including Anna, following suit quickly.

The ridiculousness of the words and act was drowned out by the sheer terror that it generated. Sean knew that Wagner wasn't an actor playing a part. He genuinely believed that he was part of the resurgence of the German Reich, and that they were still at war with Britain.

'Your *Führer* died in 1945,' Sean said.

'Is that so? Did you claim his body?' Wagner said.

'No, but … ' Sean started to speak, but was interrupted.

'Then I suggest you listen to somebody who has seen the *Führer* since this invented death in Berlin. *Vizekanzler?*' he introduced Anna.

'It's true, Sean, my grandfather, the Gross Führer and Chancellor of the Third Reich, Adolf Hitler, died in 1984 in Brazil. I know. I went to his funeral. It was a beautiful day and he was buried in full uniform in a garden filled with Edelweiss.'

Struggling to think, Sean reminded himself of the point he'd made to Liz: that it wasn't important if *he* didn't believe the story; what was important was that *they* did. 'And he's communicating to you from the grave now, telling you that we're spies?' Sean pushed his luck a little.

Wagner's fist struck hard into the side of his face. 'Insolent dog,' he said.

From his experiences in difficult situations, Sean knew that opportunity came from tension and that it could lead to confusion. He shook his head to relieve the pain. 'Well, you said it was the *Führer* who condemned us to death, so either he didn't die in 1984, or you're a medium. Which is it?' Sean deliberately tried to provoke Wagner.

It worked. Wagner kicked the bleeding bandages on his leg, sending a jolt of pain searing through his body. But Sean didn't even flinch, gritting his teeth hard.

'You make light of things you could never understand. Just like the British,' Wagner said, pulling his leg back.

'Just like the Germans to have no sense of humour as well,' Sean replied.

This time no blow came. 'I'm sure you won't find it so funny when a German bullet explodes in your heart in the morning.'

Undaunted, Sean carried on in an attempt to create an opening, just something that would create that window of opportunity. 'Why the morning? It's a bit theatrical, isn't it? I think you've been watching too many reruns of war movies.'

'For that, I'll make sure you're the last to die. You'll watch everybody else die first, including your Asian whores.' Wagner leant forward and struck Sean firmly on the cheek, turning his head to one side.

Before Sean centred his head again he spat some blood onto the floor that had accumulated in his mouth. He noticed that the guards had all joined them in the room and were laughing as Wagner beat Sean. Their positions were relaxed, with their weapons by their sides. *If I could just free my hands, I'm sure I could get a weapon.* He carefully wriggled his hands in the ties, trying to slide one out without it being noticed.

In order to continue the distraction, he carried on goading

Wagner. 'So where is this *Führer* then? Having his moustache trimmed?'

Wagner smiled. 'You are a very funny man, Mr McManus, but if I told you the truth you wouldn't be joking,' Wagner looked at Anna for some kind of confirmation and received a confirmatory shrug in return.

'The *Führer* is in a secret location. The world isn't ready for him yet, but you will be the first non-Nazi party member to see him, because he wants to pull the trigger himself for your execution.'

Sean smirked. 'The world isn't ready for him yet? What? Have you resurrected Hitler from the dead?'

'In a way, yes,' Anna interrupted.

A puzzled expression suddenly crossed Sean's face.

'You British are pathetic. You waste the greatest technology in modern times to make a sheep. We Germans are more ambitious than that. There are already enough sheep in the world. We used the same technology to make a person, and not just any person, but a perfect replica of the greatest man to ever live,' Wagner said triumphantly.

'You're not serious?' Sean said, with his mouth aghast.

'You'll see for yourself tomorrow,' Anna butted in. 'Now forgive us. We need to leave. I won't be there to see your death tomorrow. I have to conquer Europe for the Fourth Reich. But I'm sure the *Führer* will make it quick. He's an excellent marksman. Sweet dreams,' she said, blowing Sean a kiss.

As they went to leave, the leader and another guard escorted Anna and Wagner out of the house, while one guard stayed behind to cover the room. Taking the opportunity, Sean struggled against the ties again, but it was no use; they were just too tight.

When the leader returned, he quickly taped up Sean's mouth again, slapping him on the cheek as he did it.

Chapter Fifty-Five

Monday, 15th February. Brussels, Belgium.

The previous evening had been much the same as the first evening, except all of the group collapsed onto the table exhausted, sleeping with their backs arched and their heads on the table. All except Sean, that is; a combination of the excruciating pain from his leg and the complex thoughts running through his mind kept him awake.

It was now 7:30 a.m. and the guards were packing up to leave. The leader was barking orders in German, as the two other guards carried out boxes of equipment. When the leader's phone rang, he went into the adjoining room to answer it, leaving the group alone for the first time in two days. Sean's mind was a haze of tiredness and pain, as he fought frantically again with his ties.

Just then, Praew jumped from her seat and pulled a knife from the side table. Moving silently, she freed first Steve, then Pete. Sean thought he was hallucinating again when Steve jumped from his seat and in four paces disarmed and knocked the leader out. Pete quickly helped Praew untie the others, then put his hand to his lips, as he and Steve lay in wait for the other two guards.

The speed of their actions was incredible, as the two unsuspecting guards fell to the floor. Then Clive assisted Pete and Steve in tying and gagging the three mercenaries, before he joined Sean and the others at the table.

'You're so clever. How did you do that?' Sean said to Praew.

'I did it when we were first captured. Then Mum told me to wait for the right time,' Praew said grinning.

The Thai words Liz had said to Praew before they were gagged. Once again, he was amazed by Praew's strength and resilience.

'We need to stop that vote in the Parliament,' Clive said.

'How?' Sean shrugged.

'Release the story. That should create enough of a stink to scare a few politicians off,' Clive suggested.

'It's too late,' Sean said, looking at the clock. 'It'd never get released in time to stop the vote.'

'We need to get this right. It's not the Parliament: it's a treaty change. The Parliament has no say until the first change is passed. We need to stop it in the European Council,' Liz said.

'Yes, Liz is right,' Sean agreed. Then he suddenly realised what was happening. 'That's why the second treaty is written differently: she doesn't intend to show it to anybody until the first one gets through the heads of state. Then she'll present it to Parliament using the newly granted powers,' he said.

'Finally,' Liz said in frustration. 'I was beginning to think you weren't listening.'

'She must know that the first one will get through the remaining heads of state; she's probably lobbied them. But the second one may spook them, so that's why she's leaving it for the

Parliament, where she knows it will go through,' Sean continued.

'Yes, that's what I was saying. When the first treaty is passed, there's no longer any need for the heads of state or unanimity; the Parliament takes over and a simple majority wins,' Liz said.

'You have to admit, it's brilliant in its method,' Sean said.

'Yes, but how do we stop them?' Clive interrupted.

'The only chance we've got to stop this is to get at least one head of state to vote down the first treaty amendment. If that gets through, then the EU becomes an instant federation that nobody can leave,' Sean said.

'Controlled by a Nazi who believes that she's Hitler's granddaughter, and that Hitler himself has been cloned back to life,' Liz added, as she searched for a computer. She hit a few keys. 'Look, there's a special summit of the European Council today; that'll be to agree the treaty change. It's here at the Justus Lipsius Building, opposite the Berlaymont, at 9 a.m.'

After searching through drawers, Clive quickly passed back the phones he'd located, that had been taken by the guards. 'How are we going to get anywhere near a head of state? These guys have serious protection, you know,' he said.

'Not just that. What are we going to say if we get to them? We have to assume they know what's in the first treaty change and that's what they're here to vote on. Will sighting the second one be enough to scare them?' Liz questioned.

'I don't know, but we have to try,' Sean said, turning his phone on. He then sent a text message with a short note. *Need your help, call. Urgent, re: the attached.*

'Could you get me a few paper copies of the document?' Sean asked Liz.

Liz immediately went to the printer and started scanning the copy of the second document.

Two minutes later, Sean's phone rang. When he looked at the screen, it read '*PM*'.

'I'm assuming this is you, McManus,' Halliday's unmistakable voice said.

'Yes. Did you read the document?'

'I did, but I don't fully understand. What is it?'

Quickly explaining the situation to Halliday, Sean asked, 'How do I get hold of the heads of state?'

'You don't, but I will if it's not too late. If they start at nine, they'll be on the way by now and their security won't let you near. I hope they're taking calls. I'll call you back when I've spoken to the ones I have numbers for.' Halliday hung up quickly.

'Was that who I think it was?' Liz said.

'Yes. He's going to try to get hold of them,' Sean replied.

'What if he can't?' Liz questioned.

'I don't know. Why don't you go to the public gallery at the Parliament and keep an eye on Anna. I'll go to the Justus Lipsius. You take Clive. I'll take Pete, Steve and Praew. We can't stay here in case anybody else comes,' Sean suggested.

'Okay. I've made ten copies. Stay in touch,' Liz said.

'No weapons, guys,' Clive said to the team. 'We'll get arrested for the wrong thing.'

Chapter Fifty-Six

Monday, 15th February. Brussels, Belgium.

Grabbing their coats, they ran out of the building and climbed into the van that the mercenaries had left in the drive. When Sean saw the two bench seats and handcuff rails down the side he shivered; how close they had been to being transported to their death. The front section of the van was piled high with steel boxes, which contained the military equipment Dorsch's men had loaded, leaving just enough room for them to squeeze in.

When they got clear of the house, the traffic on the road towards the EU quarter from Woluwe St Pierre was moving extremely slowly and Steve was banging on the horn, trying to force his way through.

It was 8:30 a.m. and they still had over a kilometre to go. 'We're going to have to run,' Sean said.

Pulling over sharply, Steve stopped the van and jumped out with the rest of the team. They scrambled up to the footpath that ran along the park and into the EU quarter and then picked up a steady pace. Every step sent an excruciating bolt of pain through

Sean's calf, but he gritted his teeth and carried on, clutching the sheets of A4 paper in his hand.

It wasn't long before Praew began to tire of the fast pace, but Pete swiftly picked her up and carried her on his back, still managing to keep up with the group.

When they arrived outside the Justus Lipsius Building at 8:44 a.m., Liz quickly pecked Sean on the lips and wished him good luck, before she and Clive continued running towards the Parliament building.

In front of Sean a mass of photographers were surrounding the entrance to the building, with a metal crowd barrier and armed police protecting the cars that were arriving. 'Shit!' he said. 'We won't get near them without getting shot.'

Just then the phone vibrated in his pocket. It was Halliday.

'Yes?' Sean said.

'I'm sorry, nobody's taking my calls. I've tried everybody I have numbers for.'

'You know what that means?' Sean said.

'Yes,' the quiet voice came back.

'Is there any other way?' Sean asked.

'It's too late. They'll all be in the room by now. Once they close the doors, they can't be interrupted for anything.'

'Bollocks!' Sean said and hung up.

As he put the phone back into his pocket, a black Mercedes S Class pulled up by the barricade. Sean instantly recognised the national flag of Malta, as the police made way for the car to stop, pushing the journalists back.

When the crowd was clear, two people climbed out of the car: a woman in a black pinstriped suit and a middle-aged man, with greying hair and olive skin. 'Fernardu Dalmas, the Maltese Prime Minister,' Sean said, jostling forward.

Facilitating his push, Pete and Steve started pulling people out of the way. The Prime Minister and his aide walked towards the entrance, ignoring the throng of cameras.

When he arrived at the railing, flanked by Pete and Steve, who were holding angry journalists back, Sean shouted and waved the bill in the air. 'Mr Dalmas, I have a very important thing for you to read before you go in there,' Sean said.

Without stopping, Dalmas looked at him briefly, but then looked away.

In desperation, Sean instinctively lunged forward and rolled over the crowd barrier onto the pavement, waving the documents in the air. Dalmas suddenly turned to face him, but within seconds, two policemen were standing over him, pointing pistols and shouting at him in French, and Dalmas turned away, walking quickly towards the door.

A feeling of despondency took over Sean as he lay still on the ground with his arms in the air, watching Dalmas walk away. Then, out of the corner of his eye, he saw Dalmas turn around to greet somebody. A small girl had slipped through the barrier in the commotion and the intruder quickly passed Dalmas two sheets of white A4 paper. Sean watched in awe as Praew curtseyed, then ran back to the barrier undetected.

When Sean was unceremoniously dragged to his feet, he watched Dalmas strutting into the Parliament building holding the two sheets of paper, but his heart sank when he handed the papers to his aide, without even glancing at them and then walked away from her, escorted to the meeting by a delegation of bureaucrats.

Making his humble apologies to the police and trying to make a joke of it, Sean showed them the papers, saying that he meant no harm. They didn't appear to see the funny side, but they still just pushed him back through a gap in the barrier and into the crowd, letting him go.

'We've blown it. He was our last chance,' Sean said, as Steve walked around to get him. 'I don't know about you, but I think I'll go and live in Korea with Liz. It's not going to be great to be English in the coming years.'

When Praew arrived at his side, he stroked her hair and kissed her head. 'Thanks, you did really well,' he said.

Feeling completely dejected, Sean guided the group of four people away from the crowded entrance to the Justus Lipsius Building and started to walk in the direction of the European Parliament.

'We could still try to stop that Nazi bitch, even if we can't stop the legislation,' Pete said.

'How? She'll be untouchable by midday,' Sean replied, barely mustering the energy to speak.

'Not if we can tell people she's a Nazi,' Pete continued.

'But we've got nothing to prove it. We'll never get it published, and if we just put it on the Internet it'll be dismissed as conspiracy theory nonsense.' Sean shrugged. He really didn't feel like talking and the four of them continued to walk in the direction of the Parliament in silence.

'Wait!' Steve said, putting out his hand to stop Sean. 'We need to go back to the house. The German, Dorsch, he was a gadget freak yeah, and unbelievably paranoid. I've never seen so much spy gear. I'll bet he had cameras in the house, keeping an eye on us.'

At first, Sean wanted to just ignore him and move on, but Steve had a point. 'You could be right, but it won't be in the house. His guys cleared everything out. It'll be in one of those boxes in the van we abandoned on the way here.'

The reality quickly hitting home, all four people immediately flipped around and started to run in the opposite direction, back towards the van.

Chapter Fifty-Seven

Monday, 15th February. Brussels, Belgium.

Both Liz and Clive entered the Parliament building sweating and out of breath, which caught the attention of the security guards. But after some quick talking by Liz, where she convinced them that they just didn't want to miss the chance to get in before the start of the special plenary session, they were allowed in and escorted with a small group of other observers to the viewing gallery.

Unlike the debating chamber in Strasbourg, this chamber was more sumptuous, with wood panelling and comfortable leather seating. The house was already full, just managing to accommodate the smaller group of MEP's since the suspensions.

Searching around, Liz quickly located Anna; she was busy moving from group to group, shaking hands, shoring up her final numbers. Unlike the psychopathic Nazi Liz had observed on Sunday, Anna was now the confident politician, dressed conservatively in a dark suit, and walking with the swagger of somebody who knew she had the confidence of the house and the numbers to get her way.

'Within the hour, she could be the most powerful woman in the world,' Liz said, with hate etched across her face.

'Not if I can help it,' Clive said, his eyes not leaving Anna for a second.

A few short words from the speaker and the house was quickly called into order. The MEPs hastily took their seats, and both Liz and Clive slipped on their headsets to listen to the translations.

The first few minutes were taken up with formalities, letting MEPs know that this was an extraordinary meeting of the Parliament, convened by the Commission President, at the request of Frau Faustein.

Accepting the heavy applause, Anna stood at the mention of her name and pulled the desk mic forward. She started to speak calmly, in German, her voice carrying the air of authority that would be expected from the political leader of a huge federation of nations.

Judging by the start point of the speech, which was the formation of the Council of Europe in 1949, Liz realised this wasn't going to be a quick affair. Obviously Anna wanted to take time to gloat in her moment; to savour every minute of her final ascension to power.

When, after thirty minutes, she'd only got as far ahead as the signing of the Benelux treaty in 1958, Clive was clearly starting to become agitated, shaking his head.

It was a further thirty minutes before Anna mentioned the reason for today's meeting: the passing of a historic treaty amendment; one which would set Europe free from tyranny for ever, and finally make Europe one nation, answerable to its people.

'Very soon now, the reporter from the European Council is going to enter this chamber to announce that the treaty amendment has been passed unanimously by the heads of state of every one of the current member countries of this EU.' Anna said, to thunderous applause from the gathered MEPs and the Commission and Council observers.

'When this is announced, I intend to propose a further amendment to protect the people of Europe from the shame of nationalism,' she said.

Liz's stomach curdled as the noise level in the chamber redoubled. 'Surely they know that they're only going to be able to do this because of the dubious suspensions of a few states? A fucking technicality,' she said to Clive. 'How could they be so corrupt?'

'Look at them. They're consumed with an uncontrollable lust for power. This is everything they've ever wanted, they don't care how they get it,' Clive replied.

As Anna started to speak again and the cacophony died down, Liz stood up and plucked up her courage. 'Have you told them that you think you're Hitler's granddaughter and that you're the second-in-command in a Nazi organisation called the Fourth Reich?' she shouted at the top of her voice.

The activity in the chamber suddenly stopped as all heads turned towards Liz. When Anna turned around and saw Liz, shock seemed to cross her face, but then she tried to make pretence of laughing it off. It didn't fool Liz. She could see the anger in her gestures.

Before Liz could speak again, she was grabbed by two uniformed security guards and asked to leave, before being frog-marched from the gallery, followed closely by Clive.

'Leave her alone,' Clive protested. 'She's allowed to state her case. I thought Europe was a democracy?'

The guards just ignored him and held onto Liz until they'd

reached the exit doors, where they pushed her outside and, in broken English, told her not to come back.

'Sorry, I couldn't help myself. She's such a manipulative bitch,' Liz said.

'If you hadn't said something, I was going to.' Clive laughed, walking Liz over to a bench in Parc Leopold, close to the Parliament entrance.

Chapter Fifty-Eight

Monday, 15th February. Brussels, Belgium.

Sean was amazed that the van was still there and hadn't been towed away by the police, when he saw the no-parking sign next to the abandoned vehicle.

When they reached it, Steve pulled the keys from his pocket and jumped into the driver's seat, while the others climbed into the rear. Sean felt two bumps as they mounted the kerb and turned around. 'Hold on,' Steve shouted through the small grill that separated the cabin from the van area.

Ten seconds later they swerved sharp left and two further bumps confirmed that they were back on the road. This time they were moving, heading away from traffic, until Steve pulled the van over into a quiet side street.

When he joined them in the rear of the van, Sean, Praew and Pete were rifling through the various boxes of military hardware.

'It's a good job we got to this van before the police found it,' Pete said, pulling ammunition out of a metal case. 'Look at this lot. The anti-terrorist guys would have put the whole of Brussels into lockdown.'

'Here,' Praew called as she opened up a case that held four military style impact-resistant laptops.

'Do these things work the same way as normal computers?' Sean asked Pete.

'Yes, they're the same thing basically, just a bit tougher.'

Grabbing one computer each, they opened the screens. 'Password protected,' Praew said first, as the others all saw the same thing.

'Anything obvious you can think of about Dorsch?' Sean asked.

'No, he was both smarter and more paranoid than that,' Pete said.

'Damn!' Sean put the computer to one side in frustration.

'It may be ultra-violet,' Steve said. We used to use it for codes when we had a few machines.' He pulled a key fob from his pocket with a small torch attached and shone it on the bottom of the computer. 'Nothing,' he said.

Next to him, Praew was examining the inside of the stainless steel case that her computer was housed in. Then she pulled at the foam padding to reveal the inside of the casing. Steve quickly scanned the area with his ultra-violet torch.

A series of nine numbers and letters lit up.

Reading from the case, Praew quickly typed the series into the screen, but the password was rejected.

'Try it backwards,' Pete suggested. 'That's what I used to do.'

Quickly reversing the numbers, Praew hit enter. Suddenly the screen lit up and began to run its log-on sequence. Then the same process was repeated for the three other machines.

'What are we looking for?' Praew asked.

'Recent video files. Anything that shows the room where we were held captive,' Sean said.

For the next few minutes all four people were sitting with their faces fixated by the screens, clicking the mouse to change the files. Then Pete stopped. 'This is the room,' he said, as they all looked at the screen. The clip showed Dorsch sitting at the table alone, working on some electronic equipment. It was the confirmation they needed that he had been watching them.

'I hope those goose-stepping morons didn't pull it out when they captured us,' Sean said.

Clicking on files, Steve was now busy scanning contents. 'Bingo!' he said a few moments later. The video they saw running on the screen showed Anna and Wagner walking into the room.

'Any sound?' Sean asked.

Steve hit a key and suddenly they could hear Anna's voice as clear as day.

'Brilliant! You're a genius,' Sean said as he kissed Praew on the head and Steve closed the laptop.

'What now?' Pete asked.

'I need to get somewhere where I can upload this and get it out,' Sean said.

'Would an Internet café do?' Pete asked.

'Yes, but a hotel would be better. At least we'd have some privacy. We can go back to the Sofitel; it's really close.'

A couple of seconds after Steve climbed back into the driver's seat, the van shot forward and five minutes later, they were pulling over at the far end of Place Jourdan, well away from the hotel. 'If somebody accidentally sees what's in here, we don't want them to find us too easily,' Steve said.

When they reached the hotel doors, Steve went into the lobby with Praew, while Sean and Pete waited outside. The sight of the blood dried onto Sean's leg and the cuts on his arms would almost certainly put the receptionist off giving them a room.

Five minutes later, Praew came out on her own. 'We're in, Steve's going to bring you in through the car park. It's just around the corner,' she said, before she ran back through the revolving door.

As Sean rounded the corner of Place Jourdan, the shining towers of the Parliament building came into view across Parc Leopold. He instantly thought of Liz. *Is she there watching Anna Faustein being crowned the Queen of Europe?* Liz had immediately picked up that there was something wrong with Anna's story and with Anna herself, but Sean had chosen to ignore it and chased the story. *I'll never ignore Liz's instincts again.* He pulled his phone out and sent a text:

We're at the Sofitel when you get out. We failed, sorry!

The final recognition that he'd failed made Sean shiver, even though they had some evidence that would be enough to get Anna Faustein removed from the Parliament, and probably to ensure that it wasn't overrun by Nazis, Sean knew that they'd failed in the real task, which was to stop the treaty change passing the Council, and prevent the final loss of UK sovereignty to Europe.

His mind drifted to the Allied war veterans who'd fought to maintain sovereignty for their countries. What would they think, when so many of their friends and family had died for the right to run their own country? How would they react when they saw that everything they fought for had been just given away by incompetent and power hungry politicians, to a group of people that wanted power at any cost? How would they feel when they woke up tomorrow to be told that Hitler's dream of one Europe had been fulfilled... without a bullet being fired?

Chapter Fifty-Nine

Monday, 15th February. Brussels, Belgium.

The vibration in her pocket snapped Liz out of her daze. Since they'd sat on the bench, neither her, nor Clive had spoken. They just huddled together in the cold, staring up at the huge glass tower of the Parliament building.

Okay, We'll be there soon. We got thrown out! I made a bit of a scene! she responded to Sean's message.

'Sean and the others are at the Sofitel. They didn't get anywhere with the heads of state. It's over,' Liz said to Clive.

'Okay, we should go. Faustein and Wagner will be after us now that they know we're still alive and who knows when Koryalov might show up again.'

Feeling shattered, Liz pushed herself up slowly from the cold bench. Her body was sore and she was tired beyond a point that she'd ever been before. All she wanted to do now was have a hot shower, curl up in bed with Sean and try to forget that the whole thing ever happened.

'Hold on,' Clive said, grabbing her arm, then pulling her behind a column. 'Look at that,' he said.

A gaggle of journalists were following the short figure of Anna Faustein, as she marched across the courtyard in the direction of the road.

'It must be over,' Liz said.

'Let's follow her, and see where she's going,' Clive suggested.

'Really? I'm not sure I have the energy,' Liz said.

'You'll be okay once you're moving,' Clive said giving her a fatherly hug.

They let Anna pass before they stepped out and joined the rear of the group of journalists. 'She looks angry. I thought she'd be floating on air,' Liz said.

When Anna reached the end of the concourse, she turned right towards the Berlaymont and Justus Lipsius Buildings.

'She's going to claim her crown,' Clive said.

'God help us all,' Liz added.

As the growing group of journalists followed behind, trying to keep up with Anna, Liz caught sight of a familiar face. 'Nathan!' she said, grabbing his arm.

'Channing,' he said laughing. 'Nice speech in there. Funny, I didn't have you down as a whacko. You must have been spending too much time with McManus.'

Liz had forgotten what a pompous prick Shaw could be and she bit her lip. 'What's going on?' she said, pointing towards Anna.

'You tell me. She spent the whole morning boring everyone to death, building up to the big moment when the great white fairy would arrive and transform her from the Wicked Witch of the West into Snow White, and then ten minutes ago, her aide walked in, said a few words to her and she stormed out. All a bit dramatic really.'

'So the vote didn't happen?' Liz asked.

'Not yet.'

The group sped along the footpath, past yet another monolithic EU building that wasn't yet finished, and then came alongside the Justus Lipsius Building. Outside the main door, there was a large group of journalists and TV cameramen jostling for position. Anna marched straight towards them.

'What's happening?' Liz asked.

'I don't know, but I think there're going to be fisticuffs. I do hope so.' Shaw jousted with his hands childishly.

With complete disregard for anybody, Shaw pushed through the journalists roughly, creating a space for Liz and Clive to follow. When they got near the front, the figure of a short middle-aged man, with grey hair, olive skin and a thoughtful face came into view. He was making a speech to the gathered journalists.

'So why did you block the treaty change, Mr Prime Minister?' a journalist shouted in English.

'It's Fernando Dalmas, the Maltese Prime Minister,' Shaw said.

'I didn't block the bill. I simply asked for more time to consider it,' Dalmas replied quickly.

'What changed your mind when all the others voted for it?'

'Strangely enough it was a young girl,' the Prime Minster said and then paused for effect. 'This young lady took a great risk to pass me some information before I went into the meeting this morning, and wherever she is, *whoever* she is, I'd like to thank her on behalf of the Maltese people.'

'What was the information?'

'It was rubbish; just anti-European propaganda,' Anna said, stepping though the police cordon.

'Oh, this is getting interesting,' Shaw smirked.

Not put off by Anna, Dalmas held his ground as she marched

towards him. 'That's your opinion, Frau Faustein, and as always, I'm respectful of the opinion of others. But as I said, I would like time to investigate the information myself.' Dalmas nodded and thanked the gathered press, before turning around and walking back into the Justus Lipsius Building.

Before Anna turned to face the journalists, she smiled, trying to fake indifference, but it was impossible to hide the rage burning inside her. 'This highlights the problem with the EU as it stands. One man, who represents a population of less than a twentieth of that of Berlin alone, can stop something which the other 99.9% of the population want.'

Before she could carry on, Liz stepped forward staring straight at her from less than five metres away. 'Kidnapped anybody lately, Anna?' Liz shouted.

The comment snapped Anna out of her speech and she stared at Liz, suddenly lost for words. Then turned to her left, quickly pushing her way back through the police cordon, as the cameras turned to face Liz.

Ignoring the sudden attention, Liz followed, forcing her way through the journalists.

'Channing, wait! What's going on?' Shaw shouted after her.

Clear of the main group of journalists, Liz ignored him and kept Anna in her sights. She had no idea what she was planning, but she stayed ten paces behind, as Anna walked quickly back towards the Parliament building.

A string of journalists trailed behind them and Liz turned, looking for Clive, but didn't see him. Still focussed on Anna, she kept going, trying to think of a plan. When they walked past the Metro entrance, she pulled out her phone and dialled Sean's number.

'Liz, where are you? I was worried when you didn't show.' Hearing Sean's voice suddenly made her feel better.

'Did Praew pass the documents to the Maltese Prime Minister?' Liz asked.

'Yes, but he didn't read it.'

'He did and he voted it down,' Liz said.

'What? Do you mean it didn't go through? What about the Parliament?'

'Didn't even get there. No point, I guess.'

'Where are you now?'

'Following Faustein. She went to the Justus Lipsius to give the Maltese guy a piece of her mind, but he just fobbed her off. Then I confronted her.'

'What did she do?'

'Just ran. I'm following her now.'

'Leave her. We've got video of her and Wagner at the house. It's enough to send them to prison.'

'No way. I'm not letting her sneak off and get on a plane back to Brazil.'

'Is Clive with you?'

Liz looked around. 'I can't see him. I'm sure he's here somewhere though. It's madness. There are journalists everywhere. I saw Nathan Shaw.'

'Liz, don't follow Anna alone; it's too dangerous. What if Wagner turns up?'

'There are at least ten TV cameras pointing at me right now, I doubt I'm in much danger,' Liz said, as Anna reached the corner of the Parliament buildings. 'I can't let her go inside. There must be a hundred ways out of there.'

'I can see you on TV. I don't know what they're saying, it's a Belgian channel. What are you doing? DON'T!' Liz heard Sean shouting as she surged forward to stop Anna from entering the Willie Brandt Building.

Unsure of what she was doing, Liz's only thought was that she had to stop Anna getting away, and she knew that once she entered the Parliament building she'd be gone, never to be seen again. Her head was a blur of reality and illusion as she ran forwards to tackle Anna.

A strange flash of light from a parked car, a loud crack, then a piercing pain in her stomach, sent Liz tumbling to the ground. She clutched at her stomach as blood started oozing out through her fingers, then her vision blacked out.

Chapter Sixty

Monday, 15th February. Brussels, Belgium.

'LIZ!' Sean shouted, jumping to his feet. He sprinted to the door of the hotel room and located the stairs, gritting his teeth hard against the pain in his calf as he jumped three stairs at a time, with Praew behind him and Pete and Steve following on.

When he reached the front door, he almost knocked it off its hinges as he barged through and turned right towards Parc Leopold. Ignoring the traffic he dodged between cars and ran into the park. He couldn't feel the pain in his leg anymore, adrenalin was pumping through his system and all he could think of was Liz.

By his side and keeping pace with him, Steve charged past the lake, while Pete made sure Praew was okay and kept pace with her behind. As they ran up the hill on the opposite side of the lake to Place Jourdan, the three glass towers came into view above the tree tops and Sean knew that Liz was only a few hundred metres away. He needed to get to her; to save her.

The gate to the park was wide open and he sprinted through

at full speed, turning left for the main entrance to the Parliament, then running through the tunnel towards the entrance to the Willie Brandt Building.

When he exited the tunnel he could see a large crowd gathered on the other side of the concourse; the place that he'd seen Liz fall. He sprinted with every ounce of energy that he had, pulling journalists out of the way.

When he finally got through the hordes of cameras, there was a large oval space in the middle. Liz was lying with her arms by her side and Clive was kneeling above her, with his hands on her stomach. Sean waited for a second, watching, then Liz's chest rose… she was still breathing. He dived to the floor beside Clive.

'What can I do?' he said.

'Nothing now. We just need to keep pressure on the wound until the ambulance gets here,' Clive replied.

Looking past Liz, Sean glanced towards the door, where two people were kneeling over another body, obscuring his view. He pulled a puzzled expression to Clive.

'It's Faustein. She's dead as far as I can tell. The bullet was meant for her. It passed through her and into Liz. Luckily, she slowed it up a bit so there's no exit wound.'

As Sean was trying to descramble his mind and work out what was happening, a clearing opened up in the crowd and two uniformed paramedics ran in with a stretcher. They quickly applied a pressure dressing to the wound and pulled Liz onto the stretcher.

When Sean was leaving with Liz, he looked across at Anna. Just before the other team of paramedics lifted her onto a stretcher, they covered her head with a blanket. Clive was right: she was dead.

The ten-minute journey to the hospital was agonising as Sean watched the paramedics attaching a drip into Liz's arm. At one stage he thought she woke up, but it was just the jolting of the ambulance, as it bounced over a bump at high speed.

A soon as they reached the hospital Liz was whisked straight into surgery and Sean was told to wait outside. A few minutes later, it was no real surprise when the Belgian police arrived to ask Sean some questions.

While he was being interviewed, Clive, Praew, Steve and Pete ran into the waiting area, out of breath and sweating.

'She's in surgery,' Sean shouted to them.

When he saw that Praew was crying uncontrollably, tears streaming down her face and her nose running onto her coat, Sean held up his hand to the Belgian policeman and asked for a minute. He ran over to Praew and pulled her into his chest, squeezing her. 'She'll be okay,' he said, gently rocking from one foot to the other. 'She'll be okay.'

'Did they say anything?' Clive asked.

'No, there wasn't time,' Sean said.

It was two hours before the door to the operating theatre finally opened and a surgeon dressed in scrubs walked out. Sean could see that his hair was soaked in sweat and he jumped up and ran over.

'Are you a relative?' the surgeon asked.

'I'm her fiancé,' Sean said, suddenly petrified by the question.

The surgeon bowed his head slightly, clearly searching for the right words. 'I'm sorry, my English is not perfect,' he said. 'Your fiancée is in a critical condition. She died twice on the operating table, but we managed to bring her back.'

Sean's head was spinning and his vision was suddenly blurring, he didn't know what to say.

'Will she live?' Clive said.

'If she makes it through the night, I think there is a strong possibility that she'll live. But you need to prepare yourself,' the surgeon said.

'For what?' Sean asked, still trying to control his palpitations.

'I don't know if there will be any brain damage from the few moments that she was dead.'

'Brain damage?' The words hit Sean like a sledgehammer and he buckled over, shaking.

'You need to be prepared for this. But first we need to make sure she lives through the night, which is not certain by any means,' the surgeon said.

'Can I stay with her?' Sean said.

'Yes, of course. She'll be transferred to an intensive care ward and you can be there the whole time.'

The small private intensive care room was cramped, with Sean, Praew, Clive, Steve and Pete all crammed into it, while the door was guarded by a uniformed police officer.

On the bed, Liz was breathing with the aid of a respirator, a drip fed vital fluids into her arm and her eyes were closed. Sean stared at the monitor showing her heartbeat; that and the slow rising and falling of her chest were the only signs that she was alive.

'It's my fault,' he said.

'No it's not, Dad,' Praew encouraged him.

'It is. She never wanted to restart this investigation. I should've listened to her.'

'Sean, wallowing in self-pity isn't going to do anybody any good,' Clive said firmly.

Somewhere in his mind Clive's words registered and snapped him back to reality. He realised that he had to be strong for

Praew's sake, and for now, he had to believe that Liz would pull through; he couldn't think anything else. 'Who do you think shot her?' Sean asked, swearing to himself that he'd kill them.

'I've been thinking about that. I think it had to be Wagner. Faustein had failed and she could finger him,' Clive said.

It confirmed what he'd been thinking as well. He could get his revenge on Wagner when he passed the video to the police. Wagner would be charged with kidnapping, and with further investigation, probably the murder of Allsop, Phil and Dorsch. It wasn't a huge leap to add Anna Faustein to that list. When he looked at Liz again he thought *If she is added to that list, I won't be going to the police.*

'We have video evidence of Wagner and Faustein's involvement in our kidnapping, and them telling us that we'll be executed,' Sean said, realizing that he hadn't told Clive.

'How?' Clive suddenly turned his stare away from Liz.

'Dorsch was spying on us, as well as the rest of humanity,' Pete said.

'Where is it?' Clive asked.

Suddenly the room went quiet and Pete jumped to his feet. 'It's at the hotel. I'll go,' he said opening the door and running out.

Seventeen minutes later, Clive's phone rang. Sean watched as Clive took the call nodding. 'Get a cab to the house in Wulowe, then call the police to come and get the three Nazis we tied up. They may testify,' Clive said quickly, then hung up.

'Your hotel room's been broken into and the computers are gone,' Clive said, relaying Pete's message.

'Shit! How did they know?' Sean said.

'Maybe tracking devices in the van, or the computers themselves. Dorsch had traitors in his group. They'd have known about them if they were there.'

'The three at the house?' Sean suggested.

'Probably. That's why I've sent Pete.'

A further twenty minutes passed before Clive's phone rang again. 'Okay, I'll see you back here soon,' he said.

'The house has been cleaned up. No sign of the three Nazis,' Clive said, after hanging up.

Feeling his life slipping out of control, Sean looked at Liz. She was breathing through a tube, fighting for her life. It didn't matter that they had no evidence against Wagner. If Liz died, he'd get his revenge anyway.

Chapter Sixty-One

Tuesday, 16th February. Brussels, Belgium.

It was 4:30 a.m. when Liz opened her eyes. First it was just a flicker and Praew went to get the nurse. By the time she'd returned, Liz was awake, taking in the sights of the room. Her hand suddenly tightened onto Sean's, where he'd been holding it since he arrived, some twelve hours earlier.

A tube in her mouth was preventing her from speaking, but following a few checks by the doctor, she was taken off the life-support system and was now breathing on her own.

'I love you so much,' Sean said, his eyes never leaving hers.

'That's good, because it'd hurt if my feelings weren't reciprocated,' Liz said quietly, a smile breaking out on her face.

The doctor put his head into his hands and blew a sigh of relief. 'Thank god, no brain damage,' he said, smiling at Liz.

When Liz fell asleep about half an hour later, Sean turned to Clive. 'What are we going to do about Wagner?'

'I'm going to pass the information on 4R18 to MI6. We've got nothing we can use against Wagner now. It'd just be our word against his, and with no evidence, he'll walk,' Clive said.

'So we just let him go after he shot Liz, murdered Allsop, Phil and Faustein?' Sean showed surprise at Clive's comments.

'I didn't say that, but I think it's a matter for the police now. There's nothing we can do.'

Unsatisfied, Sean brooded for a little while. He knew the emotions he felt were nothing more than the desire for revenge; something which Clive would always counsel him against as a starting point. But he hated to see somebody just walk away, especially somebody who had nearly killed Liz.

'Are you going to write about any of this?' Clive asked.

'Yes, the bits that I can. It should put paid to Grossi and I think I owe it to Blom to put the record straight about him. It's a good story and I think it'll sell well,' Sean answered.

'Halliday?'

'No, much as I'd like to include him, I agreed not to and I have other plans for him anyway.'

'What about Koryalov?' Clive asked.

'Yep, I've already written a piece on him in my head, using Dorsch's evidence. It should be enough to get the UK authorities to freeze his assets, which of course are actually Volkov's ill-gotten gains. Then I think he'll disappear without a trace. If he loses £8billion of Volkov's money, we'll be the least of his worries.'

'Where's the info?' Clive asked.

A sudden bolt of panic shot through Sean, when he realised it was on his computer in the hotel room. 'At the hotel,' he said. 'But it's backed up in the cloud,' he relaxed again quickly.

'Another good story,' Clive said.

'Yes, it'll more than pay the costs of the last few weeks and oddly, we'd never have got to the truth about Koryalov if the Allsop investigation hadn't led us to Dorsch,' Sean agreed.

At 9 a.m. Liz was awake again and seemed even more responsive to conversation. She was quizzing Praew about school subjects and claimed that she wasn't even in any pain. They were interrupted shortly after she woke by the detective who'd interviewed Sean the previous day. When he asked Sean to step out of the room, Sean declined, saying that he had nothing to hide from the people in the room. The detective nodded and stepped inside.

'Mr McManus, yesterday you suggested that Ulrich Wagner may be responsible for the shooting?'

'Yes,' Sean said.

'We found Mr Wagner this morning in the back of his limousine. It was parked in a quiet layby near the town of Düren, just over the border in Germany. He had a single bullet hole in his forehead, as did his driver. They were executed some time yesterday afternoon.'

'It doesn't rule him out,' Sean said defensively.

'No, it doesn't, but it does suggest that there's more to this and the timing would have allowed the same killer to both make the shot in Brussels, then kill the two people in Düren.'

Signalling to Sean, Clive quickly agreed with the logic of the detective.

'Is there anybody else you can think of that could have done this?' the detective asked.

'Grossi?' Clive suggested.

'The President?'

'Yes,' Sean said.

'Why?'

'No reason. Just a hunch,' Clive said quickly before anybody else could speak.

The detective frowned at Clive. 'Some hunch. Mr Grossi was

found dead in his Frankfurt hotel room this morning, so why don't you tell me what you know?'

'We've told you everything we know,' Clive said.

'I doubt that,' the policeman said. 'Who else was involved in this conspiracy? And who would want Faustein, Wagner and Grossi dead?' he asked, moving his glare from person to person.

Nobody spoke as the people in the room exchanged glances, none willing to comment about what they were all thinking.

The detective didn't thank them and left the small hospital room shaking his head angrily. 'If I find out that you're withholding evidence, you won't like the consequences.' His parting words echoed around the room.

Once he'd gone, Clive, Liz and Sean all exchanged looks again before Sean spoke. 'No, it can't be. That's just crazy.'

'Wagner, Grossi and Faustein were probably the only three people who would know his real identity,' Clive said.

'Whose real identity?' Sean questioned.

None of them spoke, all too unwilling to admit that it might even be a possibility.

'Is it that unfeasible?' Clive said, shrugging his shoulders.

Before anybody could answer, Sean's phone rang. He looked at the screen and answered it immediately. 'Prime Minister,' he said.

'Mr McManus. I'm calling to make sure that your fiancée, Miss Channing, is okay and to ask you if there's anything you need?' Halliday's voice was loud and triumphant, unlike earlier when he'd seemed broken.

'She's awake. Why don't you ask her yourself?' Sean said clicking onto speakerphone.

'Miss Channing, I'm glad to hear that you're still with us.'

'Thank you,' Liz replied, pulling a face and mouthing the word '*pervert*'.

'No, thank you. The British people owe you, Mr McManus and Mr Miller, a debt of gratitude, the size of which they'll never understand.'

'What about Praew?' Liz said quickly.

'Are you referring to the young lady who I've just witnessed on video, slipping through a police cordon to pass old Dalmas some sheets of paper? The young lady that Dalmas acknowledged as changing his mind when he spoke following the summit?'

'I am,' Liz said defensively.

'The same young lady that's responsible for the global "Shame your Bullies" movement?'

'The same one, yes,'

'Well, I was saving some special comments for her.'

A sudden surge of panic rose in Sean's body.

'I believe that her brave actions and quick thinking quite possibly saved a whole nation from subservience to an out-of-control European machine,' Halliday said.

As Sean breathed a sigh of relief, Praew beamed with delight, holding on to Liz's hand.

Halliday continued. 'I nominated young Praew for the George Cross twenty minutes ago,' he said.

The room fell silent as they took in the news.

'Prime Minister, while I'm sure Praew really appreciates the offer, there is a more important thing to her and us… ' Sean said tentatively.

A brief chuckle came over the phone. 'Mr McManus, how could anything be more important than a George Cross? It's the highest honour for bravery a civilian can be awarded,' Halliday's pompous voice echoed through the small room.

'Well … ' Sean started again.

'Sean — I hope you don't mind if I call you that — obviously you don't know much about the George Cross?'

Sean screwed up his face and looked at Liz, who shook her head. When he looked up, Clive was grinning from ear to ear. 'No, I don't, but Clive seems to,' he replied.

'Mr Miller, would you like to explain?' Halliday said.

'Delighted to, Prime Minister,' Clive said, turning to Praew. 'The George Cross can only be awarded to Commonwealth Subjects. I think the Prime Minister may have some news for you, Praew,' he said, wiping a tear from his eye.

'What? How?' Sean said leaping up from the bed.

'Just over an hour ago I had a meeting with my Home Secretary. I didn't want to be embarrassed by offering the George Cross to somebody that was ineligible. So I automatically upgraded the young lady's residence application to a citizenship application. I'm also pleased to tell you that it was approved by no less than the Home Secretary and the Prime Minister as soon as it was upgraded. Congratulations Praew, you're not only the United Kingdom's youngest ever recipient of its highest honour for bravery… you're its newest citizen.'

The dingy hotel room in the red-light district of Frankfurt was a far cry from the riches he'd experienced in the past years as a guest at Ulrich Wagner's house, but it was perfect for his purposes. The receptionist hadn't even thought it strange when he didn't remove his motorbike helmet at the check-in desk.

He opened the silver case and touched the stock of the disassembled marksman's rifle. He would throw it into the river later, along with the computer from the hotel in Brussels. But first he had to clean them of any trace of DNA and wipe the hard drive of the computer.

Standing in front of the mirror, he carefully shaved the small square moustache from his upper lip, ensuring that the hairs were all washed down the basin. Then he pulled the new hair clippers from his bag and began to shave his head; starting at the long parted fringe. When completed, he scrupulously collected every hair and placed them in a paper bag. They too would be thrown into the river.

Only an hour after he checked in, he walked through the reception area and out onto the street, unrecognisable. Then, following a brief detour to the river, he entered the main train station and boarded the first intercity train out of Frankfurt.